Twelve Lessons

By Kate Spencer

Published by Katherine Spencer Publishing

COPYRIGHT © KATE SPENCER 2012

ISBN 978-0-9934416-5-3
Paperback

Third Edition: 2015

A CPI Catalogue for this title is available from the British Library.

Printed by Lightning Source, Milton Keynes, UK

For my sister, Emma.

The bravest little soul in the world.

Praise for Twelve Lessons

"It is a fabulous read, a real page turner and you just cannot predict what is going to happen next – all the attributes of a great novel and one which many well-seasoned authors still struggle to achieve, let alone a first-timer! I'd recommend this book to every woman, whether she wants pure entertainment or a path to follow to transform her life."

~ Tina Bettison (Author)

"There are many teary moments along the way and others that make you feel genuinely glad for Steph, but there are also moments when I had to put the book down and think about my own life. This book has come along at a perfect time, when people don't know what to do with their lives, or perhaps have been swept along a route that they never truly wanted. Kate Spencer has created an insightful masterpiece here."

~ chicklitclub.com

"I guarantee this book will make you laugh, cry, gasp for breath at times, shock you, but most of all leave a warm fuzzy feeling in your heart and restore your faith in the ability to have hope, have faith and ultimately in the healing power of love. A really beautiful story, truly uplifting."

~ Nicola Cook (Author, A New You)

Reader Reviews

"I LOVED this book and read it within 3 days, then 4 days later after having it on my mind, I started to re-read it and am currently enjoying it all over again. It made me laugh out loud, it made me teary eyed, it gave me goosebumps and made me shout out loud with joy. It wasn't like reading a book, it was like spending time with your best friend."

"I've laughed, cried, raged, wondered and reflected. What a fabulous book. You can't help but recognise yourself in some facets of Stephanie's life and it certainly makes you wonder how much you would benefit from following in her footsteps. Amazing work!"

"Fabulous read, hard to put down, thoroughly recommend it, just my kind of book - exciting, modern, look forward to some late nights as you won't be able to stop reading it!"

Chapter 1

It felt like an ordinary Thursday really, even though 2012 was only two days away.

This week was the no man's land between Christmas and New Year. The week of turkey sandwiches, *The Wizard of Oz* and half-price sales. Most people wanted to get the tree down and reclaim their front room, while they switched their focus to a nicotine patch or a half-arsed diet. I can honestly say, looking back at that morning, I had no idea that particular week was going to be as significant in the life of Stephanie Slater. There was no clue at 8:25am that the universe was about to turn the snow globe of my life upside down and shake it furiously. Everything I knew was about to crash into the pit of oblivion, leaving me to catch any fleeting bits of reality as they rained down in a blurry mosaic. But for now, ignorance was bliss, with a side order of Christmas Blues thrown in.

Jay snored lightly and I tiptoed around the bed. I would sneak in later and wake him when I got back, spooned into his back. Maybe he'd roll into me and we'd connect again, fully. I knew the feelings were still there for him too, they had to be. I couldn't allow myself to contemplate anything else. Two coffees and a GHD moment later, I was nearly ready to hit the road. The car had been running for a while now, sod the environment. I wasn't going to stand out there and freeze to death with a plastic scraper and a woolly tea cosy hat. I sipped coffee and watched the windscreen demist from the warmth of my front room.

1

I was a girl-next-door type and made the best of what I
had been given. I had good skin thanks to the whole
cleanse, tone and moisturise habit I had adopted early on,
when acne and hormones had set in and Grolsch bottle
tops were still on my loafers. My eyes were green and I
had a scattering of freckles over my nose and cheeks, and
my light brown shoulder length locks were transformed
once every six weeks to 'hot honey'. I just wished that I
could shed a few pounds; I hoped that this was not an
early onset of middle-aged spread. The way I was going
this would creep up to the dreaded outsize section soon.
Elastic waistband territory might be just around the corner.
Maybe I should look for some exercise DVDs in the sales
and jump round with *Davina* twice a week. I breathed in
and zipped up my ironically 'slim fit' black trousers and
pulled over a baggy black top, multitude of sins etc. With
my high-heeled boots and a retro scarf, a swish of
hairspray and a generous squirt of Calvin Klein's latest
creation I was ready to face my public.

People think being a sales person is glamorous; you
have to look the part but believe me it stops there.
Massive targets, long days on the road and conferences
with drunken colleagues trying to get to know you better
were the reality of the job. The perks were good though, a
nice car, mobile phone and laptop and to be fair the money
wasn't bad. End of month bonus payments were generous
when your sales were good, and mine always were. God
knows I needed the money, final demands form 'Mr
Barclaycard' were a good motivator. Things used to be far
easier. I naïvely didn't realise what a financial hole a
wedding and a house move would make in the same year.

Just months after Miss Binks became Mrs Slater, what had
started out as easy repayments on the wedding loan began
to creep up in line with the Bank of England base rate, as
did our credit card APRs.

My obsession with doing better than the Joneses had
made things even worse. I had to make sure that everyone
in my life saw how well we were both doing. My ego
couldn't bear anything else, no matter what the cost. It
wasn't until later I realised that my filling the canyon in
my life called 'self-worth' with more stuff, was not going
to get anyone to like me more. And this was especially
true for how I felt about myself.

The first summer in the new house cried out for patio
heaters, an oversized gas barbeque and a joiner to fit the
sustainable decking that was imported. Then there was the
fire pit, garden lighting and cast iron table and chairs. A
couple of the neighbours were green with envy, especially
the ones next door; they had the best view from their spare
bedroom window. I invited them over with the rest of the
curtain-twitchers to 'christen the barbeque' once the word
was out. I know they say you can't buy friends but it
seemed like they were all happy to get to know the
newbies as they drank our Pinot Grigio and ate our rib eye
steaks.

As summer faded into autumn I planned an extravagant
Halloween party. Helium balloons, life-sized cut outs of
witches and vampires as well as compulsory fancy dress
were all on the list. I carved out two large pumpkins and
they were placed on the gateposts, and I made goody bags
for people to take away with them. No expense was
spared. I wouldn't want anyone to think that we couldn't

afford it, even though the thought of November's Amex bill made me feel nauseous.

I insisted on 'doing' Christmas that year and ended up with a house full of relatives from both sides. There were fourteen in total and, by the time I had finished my preparations, the house looked like something from an interior design magazine. There were vases of fresh holly wrapped in tartan ribbons in each room, a hand carved nativity scene on the hearth and mistletoe hanging beautifully in the hallway. The two trees that I had chosen from a forest shop nearby were adorned with the most expensive and elegant decorations. They all hung from white silk ribbons. The silver snowflakes, glass baubles and faceted crystals all caught the glint of the tiny white lights as they glowed on and off in the background.

Yes indeed, I knew how to spend money on looking the part. But no matter how much I spent or what I had, I could never fill the gaping hole I had inside me that felt 'not good enough'. I kept up the act at all costs—and cost me it did!

Snow fell lightly against the backdrop of a grey December sky and the windscreen wipers swished quietly. I day dreamed my way through my appointments, some with gritted teeth. One in particular involved hitching up my skirt and pushing up my cleavage more than I would have liked, but I got the sale and this January's bonus was in the bag.

I sat in the car with the radio on and finished off my paperwork. My phone bleeped and I opened the message envelope from Jay, and any hope of a lunchtime romp faded:

Might have to stay out tonight, sorry difficult client wants to see me first thing.

He was an account manager too. He worked for a wine company who were very tight in the free samples department since the credit crunch. His job regularly took him away from home these days. He had to manage more accounts than before since Glen, the old timer, had been cut loose. When you are home alone the nights are long. Some of the places he went to were rural and there was no mobile signal. I missed him terribly, not just when he was away, but when he was home too. It felt now like the version of him that I had fallen in love with had faded into someone different, and distant. Our relationship felt like a colour TV that had been converted back to black and white. The disconnection made my heart ache.

Once things were back on an even keel we'd be fine, and there wasn't much that you couldn't fix with a Brazilian and some chocolate body paint in my experience, usually. I sighed and thought of the long night ahead, then sent my friend Lizzie a quick text to see if she was free later on, I hadn't seen her for ages and I didn't fancy a night of Christmas re-runs on the television like this time last year.

Sorry, I am at a girly night in with wine and fortune-teller later on.

I called Jay and left a breezy voicemail, I didn't want him to see through the glaringly unattractive cracks in my feelings. I hung up and the familiar loneliness washed over me. I would much rather have some company tonight, so I took a chance and sent a text back to Lizzie.

Maybe I could come along?

Two minutes of text tag later I had the address and knew I needed to be there for 6:30pm. It wasn't my thing but who knows, I might be pleasantly surprised.

I made my way home somewhat deflated, knowing that Jay would either be gone or packing to go. When I saw the car in the drive and the bedroom curtains still closed I felt a glimmer of hope that he was still in bed. Maybe I could persuade him to stay after all. I carefully turned the key in the lock as quietly as I could. I slinked out of my jacket and dumped my bag and boots in the hallway. I crept up the stairs. The bedroom door was slightly ajar. I fluffed up my hair and swallowed my fear of rejection. *He loves you, you know he does,* I said in my head as I hovered for a second or two. That's when I heard Jay speaking in a hushed voice.

"I'll see what I can do, although it sounds like that will be up to you, not me." I stopped and listened, holding my breath. There was something in his tone that was familiar, it was an inflection that was kept in reserve for those intimate conversations that you have between couples. I knew this because he used to talk to me like this - pillow talk. Our exchanges recently seemed so much more 'married' than what I was hearing now.

"Me, too," I heard him say before he hung up.

Please God let this not be the start of another easily impressed nineteen-year-old slapper. Project 'new start' had cost me emotionally and financially and there was no way my sanity or self-respect could take another knock like that. I wanted to show the whole world we were on track and in love, and that his little indiscretion meant nothing, even though it had lasted a couple of months. He had come back to me and that was all that mattered. And as far as I knew, no one around here had any idea about our past, and I'd like it to stay that way.

Several thoughts ran through my mind at once, adrenalin raced through my veins and my breath quickened. I tried to convince myself that I was overreacting but my gut feeling was telling me different. Stacey was a fling and didn't mean anything, he had said that with absolute conviction when he came back home. She threw herself at him when he was vulnerable. We had been arguing and he was desperate, afraid he had lost me and she offered him comfort and a DD chest to cry in. We had been over this so many times I didn't dare to raise it again, he had lost patience with my feelings of insecurity and said he couldn't be my emotional crutch. Get over it or separate basically, so on with my poker face.

My stomach was flipping over with butterflies; I breathed out and then in again and padded down the stairs backwards. I opened the front door and closed it again, then coughed and rattled the bunch of keys down on to the hall table. His response sounded controlled and guarded, maybe I was picking this all up wrong because of the distance I felt between us.

"Oh you're back earlier than I thought. Had a good morning?"

I loved him so much, to my very bones and core of who I was. I would keep on trying to get things back on track no matter what, but the emotional tightrope that I was walking had no safety net to catch shattered feelings or broken hearts.

"Well, you know, just work stuff," I responded coolly.

He simply hated the whole desperation thing, it was a massive turn off he said and made him want to run a mile. Whenever I had told him that I wanted more affection and that I needed to feel loved he withdrew from me even more and told me to "get a grip" of myself. I found it near impossible at times to act all nonchalant and easy going about our relationship when inside I was fractured, wanting him to touch me or say those three words.

If ever I did weaken emotionally in front of him I'd get, "Come on, you know I love you. I married you for God's sake," in an irritated tone. No more hearts and flowers here. Apparently I shouldn't need them, but I craved anything at all that would show that he loved me. I knew that my desperation to get closer was driving him away, the irony tore at my heart but I couldn't stop.

Variations of this conversation included clingy, bunny boiler and screwed up. He had convinced me to get over myself or I would push him away for good. He was such a good catch and someone like me should be grateful and work hard at keeping him happy.

He spoke again, "Did you get my text? Early appointment in the morning," and waited for my response.

"Oh right. I hope they appreciate all of this extra effort." I tried to sound as normal as possible. "I'm out myself actually, with Lizzie, some fortune-teller thing."

He mustn't have listened to his voicemail yet. I entered the bedroom and took off my scarf. Jay was climbing out of bed with his back to me. He was tall and quite stocky, he had dark brown hair which had started to thin and he had taken to having his head shaved. There was still a hint of his colouring in the stubble on his chin. He walked past me to the en-suite, I wanted to reach out and touch him but his body language said no.

He seemed a bit distracted, but I guess you would be if you had to do a quick turn around and start packing for an overnighter, or if you had been on the phone in secret to someone you shouldn't have. The days were gone when he would have ravished me there and then, sod the packing. Gone for now that is, but not forever, I was going to lose some weight and become irresistible again, and then he would be phoning me throughout the day with his come to bed voice.

"I'll have a quick shower," he said, following it up with obligatory small talk. "Did you get any sales today then?"

"Yeah not bad, made target so that's good. At least I can rely on Pervert Pete to create some volume in exchange for an eyeful, he saved the day for me again this month." I had to speak above the sound of the running water.

"Yeah, it's all part of the job." His words sloshed in and out of my ears and he was laughing at the same time. "What we have to do, it's a good job people don't know."

"I know, we could write a book!" I said with considerable effort to sound calm. Making regular sentences when you have a head full of questions buzzing around is not easy.

"Or make a movie!"

"X-rated confessions of a salesman!" he laughed and it felt good. The connection was back, even if it was brief and more likened to best friends rather than lovers. As long as there was something, I knew I could rekindle this eventually. I could fan a faint plume of smoke into a roaring fire of passion, somehow. I hung up my work

9

clothes with the intention of spending the afternoon in
pyjamas. Sitting on the edge of the bed in my underwear, I
smoothed body milk across my thighs and arms, my
grateful skin soaking up the moisture.

I could still hear him chatting, "I'd lose my best clients
if it all came out."

I could hear him drying off and running the hot tap. He
rubbed the heel of his hand over the steamy mirror to
make a porthole that he could use for shaving. Tap, tap,
tap of the razor and I took this as a cue to start brushing
my hair, chatting and shaving didn't work. I could feel
emotion at the back of my throat and tears started to prick
my eyes as my thoughts re ran another betrayal scenario.
Pull yourself together, I said to myself, and part of me
wanted him to go now so that I could cry privately.

I drew my hair back into a pony tail and started to
smooth the rich body cream onto my neck and shoulders,
when I felt his hand touch my back from out of nowhere. I
gasped and sat back up again, turning towards him and he
cupped my face in his hands. He pulled the tie from my
hair and it fell again in dark soft waves against my pale
skin.

My heart started to race as he leant in to kiss me softly,
his fingers glided over my cheek and he tucked a stray
lock of hair behind my ear. I kissed him back gently at
first and then greedily as he stood over me with a towel
wrapped around his hips. I could see a bulge appearing at
his groin. I made to stand up but his hand pressed me
down onto the bed again, the other hand was at my back,
unfastening my bra.

Gratitude and lust were flooding through me in equal measure, he wanted me and that's all I needed, my heart felt like it was going to burst. I had to stop making up nonsense in my head. I knew he still loved me and that things would be alright between us, I just wanted to feel him inside me now and feel his weight on top of me as we really made love for the first time in months.

He ran his hand over my breasts and I gasped as his touch was feather light in the main and then rougher on my nipples, my skin responded and I was now covered in goose bumps. I wanted more of those beautiful kisses, my lips and hips ached for him now and I wanted to look into his eyes and connect fully, to read him and to drink him in visually. I made again to stand up.

"I love you," I sighed as I reached for him and again he pressed firmly on my shoulder with his right hand whilst he parted his towel with the left. I fell to my knees and my heart sank as he panted out the words,

"Open wide baby." He cupped my chin with his hands and I obediently parted my lips and took him deep into my mouth.

Maybe I'd let him have his way just for a minute; and then we could draw back the sheets and feel our bodies entwined, skin on skin and feel our hearts beating in synch with love and passion. This was simply the warm-up. The main event was going to unfold any moment.

I tried twice to get to my feet again and both times he held me in position until the thrusting and groaning became faster along with his breath. It ended quickly and I tried to retain some air of dignity as I discreetly reached for a tissue. I stayed on my knees and threw my arms around his waist, my cheek flat against his stomach.

"I love you," I said, the sheer emotion of the event made my voice crack and tears spilled down my face.

BLEEP BLEEP.

A moment-shattering text message blared from his discarded jacket.

"I love you too," he said in a distracted tone, stroking my hair in a half-patting kind of way.

He leaned away from me and I let my arms give way now, suddenly embarrassed that I was crouched on the bedroom floor wearing nothing but a pair of black lacy knickers and my wedding ring. I felt horribly exposed and crossed my arms over my breasts, grabbing the damp towel nearby and covering myself up. I shivered. He read the text and then replaced his phone in his jacket pocket; he walked back over to me and kissed my forehead.

"Sorry I'll have to pack, the meeting is definitely on."

He slipped on some underwear and started to look through his side of the wardrobe.

"Where's my black shirt?" he asked absently as I turned my back to him and wriggled back in to my bra.

"Erm, I think it's in the ironing pile – sorry I haven't had time." I felt apologetic, even though I had a demanding job as well.

"I guess I'll have to do it then," he said in a neutral tone.

He waited for a split second for me to jump in and say "no, I'll iron it, no problem," as I usually would. I couldn't this time, I just wanted a moment to pull myself together. I avoided eye contact, as seeing me crying would have opened up the whole 'desperate' can of worms. I started looking through drawers for something to wear. Who knows I might find something to fix my mangled heart.

I pulled on some jeans and a dark purple jumper dress and started on my make-up -foundation first, my hands were a bit shaky for the mascara. I was angry and embarrassed. I wanted to get our sex life back on track, so why did I feel like this? Maybe it was the start of things changing and him being interested in me again, even so I felt like I wanted to hide away and pull myself together. It's just that blokes were selfish and they think with their balls. I should be grateful, it's a good start.

I would plan something romantic he couldn't resist for the weekend. But that text message was bugging me, I was sure it was his personal phone that he had used and not his company mobile. Why would colleagues or clients have that number? I was paranoid I told myself, and if I didn't snap out of it I would spoil a good thing and it would all be my fault.

I waited until I could hear him in the utility room, dragging the ironing board out of the long, skinny gap between the fridge freezer and the wall, then I moved quickly over to the jacket. Still scolding myself, I pressed the right keys to unlock the key pad and was asked for a pin number. I tried his date of birth, pin for his credit card and combination of the two but after eight attempts felt embarrassed and frustrated.

It's nothing, I kept telling myself, *I have to move on and stop contaminating everything by being so insecure.*

I finished up with the same black boots I had worn for work and made my way downstairs.

13

I hardly tasted the wine as I gulped down a glass in the kitchen. I went to kiss him and he kissed me back. He knew exactly which buttons to press. I wanted to stay and prolong the moment but knew that I felt emotionally fragile and that he had me by the heartstrings. I didn't want to ruin it for myself by coming over all needy. I grabbed my keys.

"Have a good one," he called after me. "Say hi to Lizzie for me"

"I will. Hope the meeting is ok tomorrow. I'll see you for the party tomorrow night." I closed the door and *bleep bleeped* the car open. The drive was only about fifteen minutes and it would give me time to decompress a bit and get a grip.

I turned on the radio.

"I want your loving and I want your revenge, you and me could have a bad romance," Lady Gaga sang out the paradox of my life to me as I drove up the street.

Chapter 2

Like many things in life, this seemed like a good idea at the time. And as I sat and shuffled the cards in front of 'Psychic Sue' (as it said on her card - she looked more like a Brenda to me), I felt a combination of scepticism and trepidation. The cards were bigger than playing cards and well-worn, some were a bit dog-eared and didn't slip back into the pack easily.

"Take your time; you will know when to stop." Her voice was nothing unusual and wouldn't be out of place on the supermarket checkout or behind a bar. The glimpse that I had when she came through the door and was bustled upstairs was of someone ordinary that quite frankly could have done with watching a bit more *Gok Wan*. He can do wonders for pear-shapes.

I wished she would lighten up a bit; I only came for a laugh and a catch up with Lizzie. Quite honestly I could find other things to spend twenty quid on right now. I finished shuffling and handed her the pack, she wore a wedding ring and slightly chipped nail varnish in a light pink colour that matched her scarf. The lighting was dim due to a small bedside lamp that had been left on and the curtains were drawn, to create ambience I supposed.

I noticed that Sue had her eyes closed and was taking a deep breath, no doubt to connect with the 'other side'. I smiled to myself, whatever.

Then her eyes opened and she laid out twelve cards in front of me, face down.

"Before I start to read the cards for you I want to let you know that what you are going to hear today will be life changing for you."

This technique probably worked a treat on most of the numpties she saw round here. In the 'spirit' of playing along I said nothing and nodded.

"Well, my love, your guides tell me that you are a bit of a non-believer!" She smiled at me in a knowing sort of way, or patronising actually. "You are going to have some big changes coming your way really soon," her eyelids flickered open, closed, open. She paused and then with a sigh she said, "You won't feel ready for this but it's something you have to go through, and it will ultimately be the making of you." Random bollocks time then.

I thought she looked like about 45. She had shortish brown hair with some highlights pulled through, tucked behind her ears and a little make-up. She was a cardigan person.

"They say also that you'll come back and see me again in the near future for more clarity."

She actually said this with a straight face. *More like another twenty quid you mean. Very clever—put the fear of god in them and get them to come back.*

Her voice took on a more serious tone and she smiled slightly before continuing.

"This year is going to be like no other for you, you are going to be fast tracked through lessons that you never thought existed. There are twelve cards here as there are twelve lessons for you. Each lesson will build upon the next and within a full calendar year your life will be transformed." She paused and looked at me for some acknowledgement before she continued.

"Ok," I said, and tried to pick some of the bits out of the monologue that made any sense to me. Lessons? That sounded a bit scary, good job it's all bull.

The cards had been arranged in two lines, six in each, and I guessed that these represented the months of the year. This was confirmed as the first card was turned over and Sue started to speak again. The first card showed the image of flames leaping into the shape of a bird and the word *Phoenix* scrolled across the bottom. The sky was overcast and there was a fork of lightning striking the earth. Perhaps a little unnerving if you believe in this kind of thing. I waited for her to speak.

"Ah yes," she nodded and it seemed like everything had morphed into slow motion.

"All good I hope?" I blurted out in a tone that was inappropriately cheery.

"Well now, that depends on your point of view." she said, and I could tell that she was choosing her words very deliberately and was trying to be considered in what she was about to say. I could feel goosebumps rising on my arms and wondered if the heating was on.

"Don't get me wrong, love; it's ultimately a very good outlook for you in your life as a whole."

Thank God for that.

"But you are going to have to go through some challenges and obstacles initially that will seem like the end of the world to you at the time," she continued, trying to be tactful and not spook me too much, and quite frankly failed on that score.

So get ready for the shit to hit the fan then, brace, brace, brace.

I feel there is a significant date coming up for you in a few months, a birthday and I get the number thirty." she said.

OK that could still be random, I was thirty later in the year but that didn't mean she was anything. She was still just a woman with a pack of cards and my twenty quid.

"And that there is going to be a sudden change in your circumstances," she paused, more goosebumps. *What circumstances?* Jesus this woman was scaring me a bit now.

"I know you must be wondering what circumstances I am referring to…" she said, drawing another breath and closing her eyes again, eyelids fluttering.

No shit, mind reading as well as psychic reading.

"*All* of your circumstances are going to change." She opened her eyes and I couldn't help the corners of my mouth smiling slightly as the sarcastic part of me commented slyly in my mind, *yeah here it comes the standard garbage – it's all going to change for the better, have faith, etc, etc.* A nervous laugh escaped from me, which she ignored. "Your guides say that you won't believe what I am saying to you right now, but that it will become clear later," Sue spoke again and I began to relax more and tune into the laughing and chatter that was going on downstairs. I was now resigned to the fact that this was a complete load. Creepy, but still a complete load. The woman was an oddball and she was making me feel uncomfortable because of her blatant act. All that I was

going to find out was the standard and very general guff
that was churned out by these people time after time.

"They say you need more evidence to believe in what
they are telling you. They speak of your life at the moment
and say that you are living an illusion." As she spoke these
words she looked at me for a reaction. *Illusion? Sorry I
think there is only one of us here under an* illusion *Sue,
and it's about to come to an end.*

"No I think you have got me wrong," I started, fiddling
down the side of my chair and zipping up my bag ready to
go. What an out and out cheek, who did she think she was
speaking to?

"I mean maybe the connection isn't there with me or
something, and I'm sure it happens but we should maybe
leave it and I can go and get the next one in?" The
question was made into more of a statement as I stood up
to go.

"Your whole life, as you know it, is a façade. An illusion
that you share with others in order to make yourself feel
better. Everything about you is fake and shallow and you
are covering up a whole load of cracks in your finances,
relationships and work, in order to fool others into
thinking you are ok. But the only one that you are not ok
with is yourself." She spoke in a tone that was caring, the
way that you deliver bad news with compassion, like a
death or getting the sack. "Your relationship is shallow
and you don't have the intimacy and emotional connection
that you crave, he is charming and handsome but a cad, he
uses you and leaves you to pick up the emotional pieces."
She drew a breath. "I can see him standing over you in

what looks like a towel and you crying on your hands and knees in front of him."

Although I wanted to run a million miles away now, through complete embarrassment, I realised that she was reading my life like an open book - and she was bang on so far.

"Your friends who know you will see the real you, but most of the world sees this artificial representation of who you think you should be. You have been stripped of all of your confidence and self-worth in this marriage, which by the way is on the rocks. He has cheated on you before and he will again and you just keep taking him back. You love him so deeply, but you don't love yourself." She looked up at me for a moment and I blinked back tears.

"Your real self is desperate to get out, but your own fear is keeping you trapped in the illusion and you are the only one that can save yourself. But this will be shattered any day now, and you are going to have to pick up the pieces."

Sue stopped talking and had a sip of water from a glass that I hadn't noticed when I came in. She realised that I was shell shocked and, as she made to turn over the next card, I heard myself saying "No! I can't take any more of this rubbish it's not true."

Tears pricked my eyes again and one spilt onto my fiery cheeks as I choked on my words.

"You can't know all of this, how do you know, you don't know anything about me!" I had to make a conscious effort to keep my voice low so that they didn't hear me downstairs.

"I don't know how I know, sweetheart, it just comes through," Sue replied, looking calm and sympathetic. I guessed that she had probably had several meltdowns to deal with in her time. She gestured to me to sit back down again and continue, but the moment was lost for me now. I felt that my life was being stripped completely naked in public and I couldn't take any more for one night. There were many other skeletons that were hidden so deeply, and I did not want them dragged out of the cupboard by her. I only came to make up the numbers because Sylvia Ashton couldn't make it and Lizzie said she wouldn't come if less than five punters turned up. It was lucky that I had called Lizzie then, I was nothing more than a token last-resorter and I could do without being scared shitless.

"Thanks, but I don't want to go on," I said as I sniffed and thought about my mascara.

"The next twelve months will either make or break you." She tried to reach out and touch my hand but I pulled it back. "And you will come and see me again, soon." As Sue spoke, every fibre in my body resisted telling her to piss off. She handed me the *Psychic Sue* card and, just to pacify her and get out of there, I shoved it in my jacket pocket. There was no way on earth I wanted to see her again, ever.

"Fine, whatever you say," my sarcastic-self started to kick in again as I regained some composure and turned towards the door.

"One more thing," Sue's voice rang out and cut through my irritation as my hand was on the handle of the door. "Your guides say that this unravelling of your life has already started."

"Thanks a bunch," I said as I closed the door on her ordinary face.

Chapter 3

I took a breath and shouted down the stairs, "OK I'm done, send the next one up!" as I retreated into the bathroom. I closed the door with my back and leaned against it, letting out a big sigh and then a sob. There were footsteps coming up the stairs and I heard the bedroom door open, then close and muffled pleasantries being exchanged.

How could anyone have known the truth of my life when I spent so long giving the world a completely different version? I felt sickly, probably a combination of no food and shock. Of course it could all be coincidence - but then again, no. I know I was trying to kid myself, she had been right and I knew it.

My life was an illusion, a façade, a fake and so was I.

I looked in the mirror at myself and couldn't see anything genuine. My hair was highlighted, my tan was sprayed on and my eyebrows were plucked into oblivion. My forehead was Botoxed into next week and my foundation was YSL's way of knocking 5 years off. Contact lenses gave me bright green eyes for the evening which complimented my laser white teeth and push up cleavage - thanks to the chicken fillets and underwire.

My earrings looked stunning just as the eBay Powerseller had promised. 'Only you will know they are not real diamonds.' I knew alright as they were itching like mad and my lobes were taking on a slight green tinge.

I ran the cold tap and splashed some water on my face, dabbed at the mascara motorway on my cheeks with some wet tissue and started to rake in my handbag for concealer.

I knew I only had a couple of minutes to pull myself
together and get downstairs before the whole barrage of
questions came about what Psychic Sue had said.
Breathing deeply and flushing the toilet, I finished off
with a dab of powder on my nose and cheeks and a swish
of bronzer. There, good as new.

I opened the door and made my way downstairs towards
the banter and giggling.

"Well? What did she say? Did your Gran come though?"
Lizzie was the first to ask. I guess I paused a little too long
when I answered, "Yes, it was fine, great I mean, she
picked up on loads," because Lizzie felt my artificial
enthusiasm.

"Are you ok?" she said, and put her hand on my arm.

That's when the floodgates opened and there was no
disguising the fact that I was upset. Lizzie put her arms
around me and I heaved a couple of sobs into her jumper.
The others had stopped talking and were looking a bit
uncomfortable when I surfaced looking all snot-faced.

"What the hell did she say to you?" Lizzie said, asking
the question on everyone's lips.

I thought quickly and took a breath, speaking through a
half smile, "It was my Gran, she came through and said
she's so proud of me and what I have made of my life."

Half a glass of wine later and sympathetic looks all
round told me that all was well again - for now anyway.

The girly chat continued and I found it easy to be my
(fake) self again and join in the conversation as, one by
one, the others went upstairs to see how their lives could
be unstitched and ruined within approximately half an
hour. As the evening wore on, and to steady my nerves, I

had another three glasses of wine. After all I had brought
the bottle and it was my favourite, as well as the best part
of a pot of humus and various chopped up veg. Bloody
rabbit food if you ask me, I could always pick something
up on the way home anyway, I'd phone Jay on the way
home and see if he had eaten. Then I remembered that he
wouldn't be there and felt sad again.

I scanned the room as I stifled a yawn and saw that we
were currently three, and I could hear Lizzie on her
mobile in the kitchen. Although I had small talked with
India and Jane throughout the evening, they weren't
people I found particularly interesting. I'd really just made
conversation to be polite and they seemed to want to talk
between themselves anyway about other fortune-tellers
they had seen and how good they were. Not my bag,
especially after tonight.

I knew that Louise was in there now and, although I
didn't want to break up the party, I really was flagging
now due to lack of food intake. I stood up to make my
excuses - nice to meet you, (kissy kissy), must do this
again, not on a school night - I made my way in towards
the back door. It had occurred to me that if I could get out
soon then I wouldn't have to see Septic Sue again.

Lizzie was standing with her back to me and speaking in
a hushed tone when I bustled in, she blushed pink and told
the caller that she would ring back.

"Oh are you off so soon?" she said, and tried to cover up
the mutual embarrassment.

"Yes, sorry if I intruded, was that Mr Right on the
phone?" I was deliberately light hearted, I knew that she
was seeing someone but it was shrouded in secrecy. You

24

could have cut the atmosphere with a knife. I didn't know why she was so jumpy, it wasn't like they were having phone sex or anything.

"Yes, well maybe not Mr Right, but Mr Right Now anyway," she clammed up whenever she talked about him. Strange but I guess she was hurt so badly by the last one that she wanted to make sure before she introduced him to anyone.

"Don't forget your present, I know we normally don't do gifts but I saw it and thought of you." Lizzie went into the utility room and came back with a gift bag that contained a rectangular shaped wrapped gift and a card. "Hope you have a good one, New Year that is." she said.

I hugged her and she kind of hugged me back, probably desperate to ring lover boy back again, and I turned and left by the back door. As I raked in the depths of my bag for the car keys I heard her whisper, "Yes, come over later I'll text you when I leave here. Love you too."

I smiled to myself. Lizzie deserved to be happy after what she had been though. This new guy must be really something if he'd made it to three months. Since her divorce four years ago, Lizzie had become something of an ice maiden. She walked away with most of the assets, as you would expect on two fronts. Firstly it was her career that had accrued them, so fair's fair. Secondly she was a successful divorce lawyer. Snowballs chance in hell for Dan the man really. It wasn't until after the Decree Absolute and several bottles of bubbly later one night, that we were all completely shocked to witness her unravelling.

The groomed, witty and controlled career woman we were all used to leaning on in our times of need, suddenly hit the wall and confessed all. The thick Toni & Guy fringe started to tremble and then came the sobbing and wailing, with the short punchy, "-but –I–loved–him–so–mu–u-u-u-ch," followed by "how–did–I-not–know-ow-ow!"

They had met in a whirlwind and married within six months. All of her friends, me included, advised her against this initially but we soon changed our story when we met him. He was jaw-droppingly gorgeous, apparently wealthy and definitely charming. He towered over Lizzie and he could sweep her up in his arms in a romantic embrace and kiss her passionately as we all looked on and seethed with jealousy. This was new for Lizzie who usually would shy away from any public display of affection, but being with Dan had unleashed her inner Goddess. But this divine vision of masculine brawn and beauty changed all of that and to top it off he was Italian and he had 'the voice'. It made you go weak at the knees and gooey inside.

He also had Michelangelo, the best Italian restaurant in town, and they had met here one evening after Lizzie had called in for a takeaway pizza to take home as she had been working late. The pizza never got home as it happened, although she did eventually in a taxi, loved up and full of Chianti. Dan had worked his charm and magic on her and from that first night she was smitten. The deal was done quickly and they were Mr & Mrs Giovanni by the time his strange behaviour and cash flow anomalies came to light. Lizzie asked about this and she was told not to worry, but her instinct said otherwise and she started to dig a bit. It didn't take long before she had uncovered his very expensive drug habit.

You can't take it away from Lizzie, she had tried all she could to honour 'for better and worse' at this point and did all she could to help him out of it. Then it got a lot worse really.

She came home early from work one afternoon and found the bedroom curtains drawn and his car in the driveway. Not unusual for someone who can work very late nights to have a power nap in the afternoon. She crept in and up the stairs, hoping to surprise by climbing in next to him for an afternoon romp. She surprised him alright. He was lying on the bed in full makeup with the gardener standing over him in some kind of pouch and nipple tassel combo with a dildo in his right hand.

It turns out that Dan was also Danielle when the fancy took him, and it also turned out that the fancy took Colin the gardener on a Thursday at about two o'clock. Lizzie didn't believe his pleas and excuses about it being a one-off and feeling bi-curious, never trust a man that can apply eyeliner better than you. So the proceedings began and not many weeks into the divorce the police had a tipoff that the restaurant was being used as a drug den and bolt-hole for prostitution. The large and stylish apartment upstairs that was being 'rented to friends' was raided and the whole place shut down. Four years on I hoped that she had recovered from this awful episode and that she could really start to enjoy being in the moment with someone again, she deserved it.

I got in to the driver's seat and turned the key. Cold air blasted on my feet. I turned off the heating until it had a chance to warm up and with a little shiver I turned on the wipers - cold and drizzle, maybe I would get food delivered after all. I backed out onto the main road easily and decided that no one would see in the dark if I rang for food en route. They normally took about half an hour to deliver and I could be in my PJs by then.

The phone rang out about six times then a blue light flashed behind me. No sirens but I knew immediately that it meant 'pull over'. My heart started to race and my stomach tightened as I dropped the phone into the driver's side pocket and indicated left. I stopped a few yards down the road; I hadn't even got up to third gear, so I knew I wasn't speeding - thank God.

The officer came to the driver's window, which I rolled down.

"Good evening, madam," the officer looked about 25 and, as he spoke, I saw that he was getting the full benefit of what chicken fillets and Ann Summers can do as a double act. I smiled at him and turned the charm up a notch, even though my palms were sweaty and I was very slightly shaking. I gripped the steering wheel a bit tighter and responded: "Hello, Officer, is everything alright?"

I knew that the car was in order; it was only 18 months old and had been serviced and maintained by the company from day one.

"You haven't got your lights on, can I ask where you have been this evening?" he said.

"Oh just a friend's house for the evening, I am on my way home now, I just live down the road." Stop rambling,

I told myself, whilst I tried to slow down my breathing as he clearly hadn't pulled me for using the phone.

A long pause followed as he stepped back and looked at the tyres and around the back of the car, I kept telling myself it was ok, there was nothing to find just relax and he will let you drive off any second. Footsteps approached the window again, and his face was suddenly level with mine.

"Have you been drinking this evening?" he asked me, and no sooner were the words out of his mouth as a burly colleague with middle-aged spread appeared behind him.

Fear crept over me like fog, making me shiver more as I spoke, "Erm, yes well just two glasses of wine, that's ok isn't it?"

"We'd best get you breathalysed just to be sure, please step out of the vehicle," Fat Boy said in a no-nonsense tone.

I stood on the pavement, praying that there would be no one coming passed that recognised either me or the car in that moment. Humiliation and fear made me want to vomit and cringe simultaneously, and for the second time that night I felt tears welling up in my eyes and spill over my cheeks. Maybe if I could vomit it would get rid of the last glass of wine, three isn't that many, well four if you count the large one before I left home. I tried to hold it together as I felt the full effect of the cold, rain, humiliation and fear hit me with full force and the combination knocked my legs from beneath me.

A few moments passed and I realised that I was wrapped in a blanket and travelling in the back of the squad car now (no lights) overhearing some mumblings from the

front about me having far too much and doing the test at
the station. I closed my eyes and started to wish and hope
that this was all an awful mistake and that somehow when
I did the test it would be clear. The strip lights glared in
the station and I blinked back the tears as they read me my
rights. Even before the breathalyser lit up like a Christmas
tree, I knew I was over the limit. It was marginal, but it
was there and I had nowhere to hide. How could I have
possibly been so stupid? I had never been a chancer where
drinking and driving were concerned, not like some I
knew. I was furious with myself for allowing my
emotional pain to fuel such a stupid decision, and knew
that I deserved everything I got from here on in.

Full of self-pity, I was bundled into a cell for the night
that I wouldn't have kept a dog in. I curled into the foetal
position and sobbed into the rough and scratchy blanket
that they had given me. These were tears of humiliation
and self-reproach, I felt so ashamed I even refused the
phone call I was offered. I didn't want anyone to know I
was here, I wanted to disappear. I stayed like this all night,
trying to drown out all of the alien noises around me with
my own crying. I was granted bail and driven home in a
squad car. I must have thanked God 50 times that most
people in the street had full-time jobs and wouldn't be
home.

Chapter 4

I sneaked into the house, it was now about lunchtime. Might it be later? Everything about me felt wrecked including my body clock. I closed the door and burst into tears. What was I going to tell everyone? The police had said that there would be a trial in due course but until such a time I was unable to drive. The gravity of what had happened hit me like a punch in the face and all sorts of scenarios started to flash through my mind: *What about my parents? My job? If I had no wage then how could I possibly juggle all of the money around?* I felt sick and ran up the stairs to wretch in the toilet bowl. Although I heaved and heaved nothing came up, which was not surprising as I hadn't eaten now since last night's rabbit food and precious little before then.

I composed myself a little and made my way to the bathroom, turned on the tap and hugged my knees up to my chest as the water ran hot and deep. After half an hour I dried myself off and crawled into some jersey cotton comfy pyjamas and then between the white sheets. I closed my eyes and prayed for all of this to go away, I needed a miracle and I needed one fast.

I woke with a start when I heard the key in the lock. I could hear Jay speaking on the phone and realised quickly that he didn't know I was home.

"I know, it's amazing for me too. I think about you all of the time and I just don't know what to tell her."

The light went on in the hallway and I stayed perfectly still. I could hear the tinny voice of a woman on the other end of the line as well as my own heart beating loudly in my ears. I couldn't make out words but I could guess from his response that Jay was in love or lust or both. I felt like someone had ripped my life apart in one fell swoop, I didn't know if I should make a noise and then let him make his excuses or lie still and be emotionally crucified over and over again.

It was that tone again, the 'couples' tone that I had heard the night before.

"I know, I'm the same - you know I do!"

I could hear a faraway voice responding to him, but couldn't make out the words.

"OK, yes I'll call you, don't I always?"

Laughter.

Then, "OK goodbye - for now that is. No, she has no idea."

No idea about what? Part of me wanted to rant and scream at him for being unfaithful again and having another bit on the side, but the rational part, the part on task to save things and make it all ok talked me round. I told myself it was nothing and that I was overreacting again, I had a habit of doing it and I had to get a grip of myself. Maybe he was speaking to someone to organise a lovely surprise for me and that's what I had no idea about. It could be something for New Year's Eve that he had arranged, an extravagant gift or weekend in a spa.

The straws that I was grasping at dangled like shards of cold icicle glass, cutting me time after time. They pierced through the fragile armour that guarded my breaking heart. Emotion bled from me in silent sobs into the pillow and I felt alone and desperate. I closed my eyes and pulled the duvet over my face, not knowing what to do.

My life felt like it was being unpicked by the seams and my sanity was hanging in shreds all around me. I heard footsteps coming up the stairs and kept still as he opened the door and the light from the landing flooded the room. He gasped with surprise to see my lying there, I made out to be sound asleep and he closed the door.

A couple of hours later, and relatively composed, I emerged. I said that I'd had the worst migraine and that I had taken some really heavy duty pain killers that had completely wiped me out. I couldn't remember anything since getting in and I hoped it was ok that there was nothing for tea. No I didn't want anything, still feeling really rough, just a cup of tea to take back to bed. I didn't know why I was teary, probably PMT.

Jay was overly nice and fidgety around me, he tried a couple of probing questions to see what I had heard and I gave nothing away. I just had to keep it together tonight.

I cried into the pillow for what seemed like the whole night, listening to the muffled sound of the TV on downstairs and the occasional *bleep, bleep* text alert. I must have fallen asleep eventually as the next thing I knew Jay was sliding into bed. I opened my eyes a fraction, 3:32am, the early hours of New Year's Eve. I felt another sob in my throat, and I choked it back as his bare arm touched mine, a combination of both love and hate welled up inside me, like an emotional volcano erupting with both fire and ice. He was soon breathing deeply and I waited until 3:40am until I tiptoed out of bed and into the bathroom.

The light blinded me temporarily, and as my eyes adjusted I could see my red, blotchy, puffy face staring

back at me. I looked like I'd done the last fortnight in
Guantanamo Bay, and actually the last twenty-four hours
couldn't have been much worse than that really. I took a
deep breath and thought about my plight. But what on
earth was I going to do?

I had been completely freaked out by some Spooky Sue
that knew my life inside out and put the shits up me for
twenty quid, and I am probably going to lose my job and
get a drink driving record. And by the way your husband
is knobbing someone else. It didn't sound particularly
good or rational.

I made my way quietly downstairs and poured a glass of
wine - not like I'd be driving anywhere. "Happy New
Year, Stephanie," I said out loud with irony as I toasted
thin air and gulped down the white wine that had been left
out on the bench and was now warm.

My eyes caught the shiny silver of the gift bag on the
table from Lizzie and I wondered if it was a cookery book.
Maybe I could open it now and see what I could rustle up
for breakfast, 'why you going waffles' or maybe 'om –
lette him go' with a side order of 'your life is toast.' I
opened the corner and sure enough there were pages, but
the corner of the cover was very plain for a cookery book.
The plain indigo leather bound book that emerged from
the wrapping was embellished with the word 'Journal'. I
actually laughed out loud. A proper LOL.

What the hell would I want to write about my life for? I
couldn't think of anything less suitable or more ironic.
There was nothing about this moment that I wanted to
commit to paper. If anything I was hoping that I would
wake up anytime soon and the nightmare would end. I

opened the front page and saw Lizzie's familiar
handwriting 'Merry Christmas and Happy 2012, love
Lizzie x'

I turned the pages briefly and the smell of the leather
cover wafted into my nostrils as the pads of my fingers
felt the textured paper, probably recycled. The pages were
edged with silver gilding. Every so often at the top of the
right hand page there was a line of swirly writing. These
were what you would probably call 'inspirational quotes'
if you were in a good place and 'a load of shite' if you
weren't.

When I flicked back the pages and looked at the first
quote I laughed and laughed.

*"No matter how far you have gone on a wrong road –
turn back"* - Turkish Proverb

The road that I had been on for the last few years was
taking me towards divorce, bankruptcy, alcoholism and a
driving ban. Turn back? Back where? I couldn't see any
way back at all, there were no slip roads or signposts on
this road that showed me another way. I reached for the
pot of pens beside the phone and clicked one.

"My life is a shit cart, the end." - Real Life Proverb

As I underlined the words I felt compelled to expand on
what exactly I was dragging in the cart up the one way hill
of my life called 'Tits Up'. The tone soon changed from
sarcasm to self-defeat.

*Happy New Year you washed up silly cow. You have
made a complete mess of things. You are a fat failure
with no money, no prospects, a failing marriage and
probably unemployed imminently. No wonder your
husband is probably going to leave you for someone*

*better and your life is going down the toilet. You never
deserved to be happy anyway, you have been fooling
yourself all of this time, you stupid, silly cow.*

I closed the book and shoved it in the draw on top of all
of the credit card bills and a couple of old charity bags. I
had more warm wine and sat flicking over the television
channels, cried again and then closed my eyes.

I awoke to a pale wintry light shining through the gap in
the curtains and onto my face, I shivered and realised that
the heating hadn't been on long. I also realised why I was
on the sofa and not in bed, flashbacks of the past 48 hours
came back in a blur. I had no idea what I was going to do
next, Jay would be up in a few hours and I knew I couldn't
face him.

It only took me ten minutes to sneak upstairs and pull on
some clothes, teeth brushed, hair bobbled up out of my
face and out. I wound my oversized scarf around twice
and pulled on a pair of black leather gloves. The chill in
the air was bracing to say the least. It felt really strange
walking towards the street, I didn't have any idea where I
was going, I just needed to go. It was slippery underfoot
and the early morning sunshine made the frost sparkle like
diamonds on the pavement. My breath came in white puffs
in the freezing December morning.

I turned right and some of the world was starting to
wake up. The occasional car passed by and also a dog
walker. I felt my mobile in my pocket and thought that I
really should contact work and make something up about
a sickness bug just in case. I emailed my manager, Brian,
who was one of the good guys, old school and covered

your back where he could as long as you got the sales in.
That would at least buy me a few more days. I'd seen
something on the news about a winter vomiting thing
sweeping the country so I was confident it was plausible.

I headed away from the cul-de-sac and onto the main
road into the estate, not knowing where I would end up
but pulling my scarf around me tighter to protect my face
from the chilly air. I stopped and pulled off one glove to
apply a slick of Vaseline to my lips and underneath my
nose, which was red raw from all of the tissues I had
snotted into last night.

A few moments later, and across the street, a bus pulled
in with *Town Centre Shuttle* in LED lights above the
driver. I can't say I thought about it, I just walked briskly
over and jumped on. I bought a return ticket and took a
seat beside the window, three rows behind the driver.
There weren't many passengers apart from me, which
suited me fine, I certainly didn't want to chat to a bus
person. I had no idea if I'd make it to the town centre or
get off in three stops time, I just knew that I was on the
bus for now and I needed to start pulling myself together.

As the cars and buildings passed me through the
window, I started thinking about my life and what a
shambles it was. That fortune-teller had been right. Maybe
I would go back and see her sometime and let her finish
off what she was saying. She had said something about
things getting better and right now I couldn't wait for that
day. I thought about Jay on the phone again and who he
could have been speaking to, I didn't realise I had been
crying until I felt a gentle nudge.

Some woman had sat next to me and was holding out a hanky.

"Bad day?"

Nosey bloody parker. If I hadn't been trapped next to the window I would have changed seats.

"Something like that." I mumbled.

"We all have them you know, chin up love."

The bus slowed down to a stop and thankfully she started to gather together carrier bags and stand up. The bags had a charity shop smell when they moved and sure enough when she lifted them up they were from Oxfam. This is why I was not a bus person, they might not smell of piss anymore but you got some weirdoes. She was probably on the dole and on her way to Farm Foods next to buy a load of oven chips to cook in her fryer whilst she smoked a roll up fag at the back door and did a scratch card.

"Thanks."

I was deliberately dismissive.

Jog on, Mrs Scrote.

Luckily she got off a couple of stops later at some old building in the town and I was left alone with my thoughts again. I watched her put her bags down and dig in the pocket of her sheepskin coat— probably from Oxfam too—and pull out a bunch of keys. The bus started to move as she went through the door, she looked up at me and smiled again. I turned my head away.

The City Centre was looking busy already, it was still before 9am when I found myself getting off the bus and getting my bearings. I usually started this journey from the multi-storey car park, not a concrete concourse. I wanted to lose myself in the crowd where no one would know that I didn't usually look this bad.

It was freezing and I drifted in and out of shops to warm up. I pushed the happenings of the last forty eight hours out of my mind as best I could and started raking through sale rails. I didn't know what to do with myself, there seemed so many options and they all seemed to come down to going back and getting on with it or confronting Jay and risking it all. I overheard someone talking about their plans for the evening and remembered it was New Year's Eve. I looked up and saw myself in a full length mirror and hardly recognised my reflection. There was no way I could go anywhere looking as dreadful as this and we'd been invited to that stupid party later on as well. Maybe I could pull myself together in a last ditch attempt to fix things before my whole life went down the pan.

I knew that I shouldn't be spending anymore. I was at the top of a very slippery financial slope just now. But desperate times call for desperate measures. My life was all about making sure that people thought I had the best and looked the best (even though I didn't feel the best) and tonight felt like the finale.

In truth I was a money juggler. My repertoire consisted of drawing money off one credit card in order to cover a minimum repayment on the others, and also making sure that there was enough in the bank account for household bills. I rarely went over the £2500 overdraft limit that I had, but was never in credit for long. I had to admit that this was really stressful, but the stress would fade into insignificance compared to the excruciating embarrassment if anyone found out the truth.

I also had to make sure that the payments continued on the loan that I had taken out for the wedding, which had left me with the biggest financial hangover imaginable.

It was my craving for a public display of commitment and loyalty that had carried me on the crest of a wave; a wave that had rapidly swept more and more cash into its wake like a financial tsunami. I felt like the centre of attention, even during the planning stage, and the feeling gave me a legal high like a drug I couldn't withdraw from. Everyone was so interested in me and my wedding plans and for those moments I really felt like someone important. People wanted to know about the dress, the flowers, the cake and the venue. All blew sunshine up my backside so professionally; all pandered to me and stroked my ego in exchange for their extortionate fees. I convinced myself that sometimes having your head in the sand and your arse in the air might work out ok in the end. If you had posh knickers on that is.

For richer, for poorer seemed to happen so quickly though. All we had now was two gold rings, a photo album and the bill. I had recently had to make some compromises in the spirit of saving money. I still did the weekly shop at *M&S*, I just made sure that the reduced items were hidden at the bottom of the trolley and that the Chablis was visible as I meandered up and down the aisles. Nails usually weren't a problem as I had quite a steady hand and a French manicure kit from *Avon*. My twice monthly salon visits had stopped a few months ago when my debit card was refused. I made up some story about a new card and not activating it yet and I paid with *American Express*. They laughed along with my story but there was a part of me that suspected they knew the truth, and I couldn't bring myself to go back. That embarrassing incident had saved me about £30 a month anyway, which was a drop in the vortex, but a start.

Any onlooker would think that I had really embraced the idea of a capsule wardrobe with a few key pieces and accessories. No one knew that the designer labels that I boasted about were actually now from *eBay,* and that the capsule concept was not my idea of de-cluttering but down to financial necessity as well as stress-induced weight gain. The capsule would become a miniscule if I crept up another size, but several large glasses of wine and a chicken tikka masala at least twice a week kept the pounds creeping on steadily, comfort eating my way into more debt.

Jay didn't seem stressed about money, he didn't know how bad it was and that was fine with me. He loved a bit of lifestyle as much as I did and he hopefully didn't notice that I was scrimping on myself in order to keep him in spray tans and golf fees. Although I was trying to keep it together, an undercurrent of stress had been welling up between us. Initially I thought that there was nothing specific, there was just a general tension between us and I put that down to money, or lack of it on my side.

And now of course in the light of what I had overhead, I had to face the fact that he might have been seeing someone else. No, I had it wrong, he promised me faithfully that he would never do that again. I had to pull myself together and stop being so paranoid. Maybe I should make an appointment at the doctors next week and see if they can give me something.

41

I tried to convince myself that when I got back he would have a logical explanation for me and tell me to stop being so insecure and uptight, he loved me and it was all a big mistake.

I picked up a gorgeous handbag in *Debenhams* and a scarf in *Primark*. I shoved the *Primark* bag into the *Debenhams* just in case I saw anyone that I knew.

A new start, that's what I needed, a new year and a new life. As every woman knows there is one fail safe way to create a whole new you. So with my best foot forward I scanned the high street for a hairdresser. I had to wait for half an hour in the salon, but snuggling into a corner with *Hello!* magazine and a large cup of coffee was no hardship. I scanned through the latest scandal of the footballers' wives and other celebrities, a Swedish royal wedding and the horoscopes before I read the classifieds.

That's when I saw the advert in bold type with a red border around it, asking all of the questions that spelled out my story. *Did I have mounting debts? Did I have cash flow problems? Did I own my own home? Yes, yes, yes!* Releasing equity from your home and extending the term of your mortgage was so easy and was only a click away! This would wipe away all of those horrid letters and money juggling, along with the degrading *M&S* sneaky shopper routine.

By the time Gemma was ready for me I'd been inspired by Amanda Holden's latest photographs, and two and a half hours later I emerged looking like a modern day Marilyn Monroe. I just caught *Estee Lauder* before they closed and the girl behind the counter spent 20 minutes on making over my face to complement my new soft golden waves.

I caught the bus just as the snow started to fall, and I pep talked myself all the way back home to stop overreacting and to wait until I heard his side of the story. It could be something completely innocent, I was always jumping the gun and being jealous. I had bookmarked the re-mortgage company's website in my phone and by the time my stop came around I had filled in the online application and submitted it.

I worked out on the online calculator that, based on our current salaries, we could borrow another £20,000, which would more than cover what we owed and would leave enough left over for a fantastic fortnight in The Maldives. I could forge Jay's signature really well, and it wasn't really lying, it was to save our marriage.

For better, for worse. I'll have better thanks.

According to the website the forms would arrive within a few days. I could complete them and post back by return. It was only a case of waiting now, once your valuation was done you could draw the funds down within a week. I couldn't wait to see Jay's expression when I waved the acceptance letter at him like a magic wand. Or maybe I should surprise him with the airline tickets instead.

He wasn't home when I got back but there was a note on the kitchen bench saying he had gone to the supermarket to get some wine for tonight. Yet more evidence that I was overreacting and whatever I thought I had heard had probably not been right.

So New Year's Eve was officially on. I took a deep
breath and made my way upstairs to get changed.

Jay wasn't home when I got back. I ran a bath and
carefully tucked my hair into a shower cap, wallowing in
bubbles for half an hour whilst thinking of what to wear
tonight. I was going to go for subtly sexy, something black
that showed a bit of cleavage. I had a gorgeous knee
length dress that would be just perfect. I'd wear some hold
up stockings and make sure that Jay got a flash of them
when I sat down. I knew that I could get things back on
track.

I was dressed when he got back, I heard the bottles
clanking as he came in through the door.

"Wow," he said when he saw me. "You look good."

Thank God he liked it. I swished my hair from one side
to the other.

"You like it? I am so glad. I was worried getting such a
radical change."

"Yeah, it really suits you," he said, looking at me again
and opening a bottle of wine.

He passed me a glass and I leaned in for a kiss. Maybe it
was my imagination, but he seemed to pull away too
quickly. His words and his body language were
incongruent and the familiar feeling of desperation crept
over me. *Stop it you silly cow,* I said in my mind. *He's just
tired.*

"Did your meeting go ok yesterday?" I tried to break the
ice a bit as I sat on one of the high stools around the
breakfast bar and made sure my stocking tops were
peeking from under my dress.

He answered without looking. "Oh, yeah, fine thanks. Just a difficult client wanting to negotiate next year's price lists before he goes away for a couple of months." He glugged his wine and put the empty glass on the bench top. "What time's this thing tonight?"

"Any time after seven, but we should go later or the kids will still be up."

"OK then, I'll just get changed," he replied and went upstairs.

Chapter 5

The party was at the bottom of the cul-de-sac; neighbours who couldn't get a babysitter. They had decided to put on 'a bit of a spread.' It seemed like most of the other people in the street were going to Clare and Andrew's, so we'd accepted the invitation just before Christmas.

I'd almost finished the bottle of wine by the time Jay came downstairs. I stood up to get the coats.

"I don't feel so good Steph, I think I'll have a couple of hours sleep and then come down for the fireworks if that's ok?"

I felt my heart sink through my *Jimmy Choos*. He looked tired I supposed, and although I wanted to say "No actually that is not ok," I reminded myself about not sounding desperate and instead I agreed that a couple of hours rest would do him good.

"There's something I was meaning to ask you," he said as I buttoned up my coat.

"What?"

"Where's your car?"

"Oh, that." I felt panic rising in my tone and made every effort I could not to let it show. "I left it at that fortune-teller thing so I could have a few drinks and got a taxi home. I said I'd pick it up next week sometime."

"OK, just wondered."

Phew! I picked up the bottle of champagne for the party and swiftly turned to leave the house.

"See you shortly," I said as I walked away, praying that he didn't suspect anything.

Clare looked a bit harassed and mumsy in her jeans and t-shirt as she ushered me in.

"Wow, Steph, your hair is amazing. A whole new you!"

I twirled around so that she could see the back as well. "Do you think it's ok?" I said with mock modesty.

"It's really great, it suits you."

Claire then excused herself to get changed and I was left in the hallway momentarily. I took off my coat and headed for the kitchen to put the bubbly in the fridge for midnight.

All eyes were on me when I walked into the front room and I felt compelled to be friendly and interesting, instead of just being me. It's always strange joining a mid-point conversation; you don't understand the context or background of what is being said. Maybe the pre-party bottle of wine I had glugged also influenced my assessment. I heard the word *'Rolex'* and my need for approval and enthusiasm to be involved bypassed my brain as I started spurting out phrases like "I wouldn't wear anything else," and "Timeless elegance, worth every penny". The conversation stopped and I looked around at awkward expressions and fidgeting. There was a stifled snigger.

Clare came bustling downstairs, transformed and fully made up in a flattering v-neck dress. She must have found her magic knickers then.

"I think you know everyone, Steph, well apart from Gregg. He's my cousin but he lives in Switzerland now, and works for Rolex." She smiled and let the bombshell drop silently as she walked past me into the kitchen "I'll

get you some wine." I was now holding the hand grenade
of embarrassment with the pin pulled out.

I knew in that moment as Gregg gave me a wide smile;
that his bullshit detector was clearly in full working order.
I cringed and hoped he'd be kind.

Gregg cleared his throat and said, "We were just saying
that there are people out there who need expensive things
in order to feel good about themselves."

There was a sharp intake of breath from behind him and
someone stood up and excused themselves for a cigarette.
I scanned the room and suddenly felt like a rabbit in
headlights. They weren't talking about me were they? I
just like nice things that's all. Why shouldn't I have them?
I work hard. So what if nice things made me feel better? It
had nothing to do with anyone, and certainly not anyone
in this room. Clare appeared from the kitchen and put a
large glass of white wine in my hand and I smiled a
nervous thank you. I sensed that Gregg was waiting for
my response to his loaded statement.

"I completely agree, and there are also others that work
hard and appreciate nice things." I tried not to be
defensive.

Gregg smiled and his eyes fell on my left wrist. "You are
obviously a woman of excellent taste."

I suddenly felt very hot and panicky, I could feel my
heart rate increase and I wanted the laminate flooring to
open up and swallow me, stilettos first. He was going to
ask to see it, I knew he was. The watch I was wearing was
an excellent copy—or so the shop owner in Turkey had
told me last year. Although it was discreetly designed with
a chrome strap and wrapped neatly round my arm, it now

felt like a tonne weight burning the letters *f-a-k-e* into my skin.

"Oh, erm, yes." I thought on my feet and planted a quick escape route into the conversation "It was a gift, I didn't buy it."

At least now I had something tenuous to build a story around if I had to.

"A very generous gift I'd say, if that's the watch I think it is." He was baiting me and someone else stood up and left the room muttering something about a top up. The tension was obvious and uncomfortable.

I could feel the alcohol and embarrassment causing me to turn a fiery red. I had drained my wine glass already and either wanted a lot more or wanted to go.

"Yes, I am a lucky girl." I forced myself to smile and, before he had the chance to go on, I raised my empty glass and said, "I need a top-up too."

I made my way into the kitchen, which thankfully was empty and cooler. The patio doors were open and there was laughter and chatting coming from the back garden. The smokers and a couple of nons were huddled round a fire pit that was flaming out heat. I opened the fridge door and the cool air stroked my face like a balm. I looked for the *Bollinger* I had brought for midnight.

I wanted to be alone. I grabbed my coat from the cloakroom and tucked the bottle of champagne inside. They could sod off if they thought they were getting that now. I walked past the living room door and felt compelled to pause for a second and then I heard it.

"Of course it's a fake, just like her. She's all fur coat and no knickers!" then laughter.

I shut my eyes and cringed. Is that what they thought of me? That it was all a front and that I was a fake? They had no idea about me, they didn't know who I really was. After all of the kindness I had shown them, the hospitality and the waiting on them hand and foot. All of the posh canapés and *Hotel Chocolat* creations they had troughed at my expense, which were a whole lot better than anything they picked up at *Asda* every week. I'd seen them unloading their shopping from the boots of their sensible cars, and none of them were used to fine dining. I had given them all a chance to get away from their own mundane BOGOF pie and chips lives for a moment, to see how the other half live and to appreciate a bit of luxury. If anything they should be grateful to me. My life was perfect and something for them to aspire to. At least it had been, in the social screenings that they had been invited to.

I felt like bursting into the room and telling them exactly what I thought of their pitiful lives, but my feet were rooted to the spot. I couldn't move until I had heard the rest of the story.

"Wait, wait, you are all being so unfair." *Thanks June, at least my next door neighbour was showing some loyalty. I did take a parcel in for her last week.* "She's got issues and she tries to hide her insecurities by having lots of stuff. She isn't a bad person, she just thinks that people won't like her for who she really is." There was a pregnant pause followed by a couple of mutterings about "insecure" and "he had an affair you know", then the killer "We should feel sorry for her really."

The irony of them feeling sorry for me would have made me laugh if I had not been so furious. I'd heard more than enough and I turned to open the front door. With tears of anger and indignation I slammed it behind me and made my way home, livid with both myself and the world at large.

I walked through the hall and straight upstairs. I wanted a long hot shower to wash away the makeup and embarrassment. I could cuddle up to Jay in bed.

I turned the water on and as it started to run I quietly opened the airing cupboard for a towel. The bedroom door was still closed and there were no lights on. *I should let him sleep a bit longer,* I thought.

The pile of fluffy white Egyptian cotton bath sheets and face cloths looked about half the usual height. I took the one on the top and made my way back to the bathroom, I looked behind the door. His bathrobe had gone. I opened the bedroom door carefully, expecting to see him sprawled out and snoring. But the bed was made.

I ran to the wardrobe and threw open the doors. There were empty hangers clanging on the rail and a crumpled up dry cleaning receipt in the corner. I ran to the study and his laptop had gone along with books from the book shelf and a signed watercolour of a spider's web in a forest that we had bought on a whim at an exhibition.

I opened the bedroom curtains and looked out on to the empty driveway I had just stumbled across. I hadn't even noticed that his car wasn't there.

The story continued throughout the house and with my sobs ringing out, reality dawned on me. He had moved out of here and straight into somewhere else. The note was on

the kitchen windowsill and had been written on the back
of a letter that was addressed to us both.

*Steph, I'm sorry but things have changed between us
and I have not been happy for a long time. I think we need
some space to see how we feel about each other and to
find ourselves again. I will be in touch with you to sort
things out.*

I swallowed and clutched the letter to my heart, my eyes
closed and the tears ran freely. So this was it. The
beginning of the end.

After I don't know how long, I made my way up to the
shower and stood as my tears were drowned by the hot
water and they disappeared down the plug hole, along
with any hope I had left of saving things. Loneliness
descended over me like a black veil. The house felt
strange; a representation of the life I was building—The
Marital Home.

The décor and picture frames seemed completely
irrelevant now I knew that the metaphorical foundations
were crumbling beneath me. I had no hope of
underpinning them really and I knew it. I sat on the bed in
a towel and cried more. Then I reached for my mobile and
rang Jay. Voicemail. I didn't leave a message but, as soon
as his voice had finished, I hung up and I rang back. I
don't know how many times I did this, or why. It was
torture and ecstasy at the same time to hear his voice, like
injecting a drug that you know will only screw you up.
But I couldn't help it, I missed him with my whole heart. I
allowed the desperation to rush over me freely, it had been
lingering on the edge of my life for so long now and the
dam was bursting.

I scrolled through my address book to L and found Lizzie. The phone rang out three times and then voicemail. I couldn't believe that she had dumped my call in my hour of need. I had a rational moment and realised that she wouldn't know it was my hour of need, she was probably busy with her new man.

I sent her a text instead. Surely she would ring back when she knew what had happened.

Then I finished best part of the bubbly myself and I was in bed by the time the fireworks started to bang and fizzle outside, alternating between being sick in a bucket and crying into my pillow.

Chapter 6

I had started out the New Year with a thumping headache and vomit in my hair. I turned over and found that I had slept alone and the memory of Jay's note came back to me in a flash. I caught my tears in my throat and staggered to the bathroom mirror, squinting at my reflection. I looked as bad as I felt, or maybe worse. I brushed my teeth, tied up my matted hair and made my way downstairs. The near empty champagne bottle and television remote were on the coffee table, along with the cardboard core from a loo roll. The little white balls of tissue were all screwed up in a pile in the bin, full of tears, snot and self-pity.

Last night's party memories emerged in vivid detail into my conscious mind and I put my head in my hands. I was now a laughing stock that my neighbours took pity on, and I had been royally dumped on New Year's Eve. I dragged my self-reproach along with a pint of water and two paracetamol back up the stairs, went back to bed and wished the world away.

The next ten days were spent in a weird kind of waking coma. Nothing felt real except the pain. I found myself constantly raking over memories to connect with Jay again, even though it was unbearable to relive being with him. When the pain got too bad I drank wine, it didn't matter if it was day or night anymore my body clock was objecting to being kept to a routine.

I regularly compromised my dignity by sending pleading text messages and voicemails, I got into the habit of checking for missed calls at least every half an hour just in case he'd called me.

Jerry Springer became my new BFF and I even started seeing fragments of myself in his guests as they whined about boyfriends that had left them, hit them or worse. I felt empathy for them, and in my more lucid moments I knew that this was a very disturbing place to be.

I kept the curtains closed, with no cars on the drive the neighbours might think we were away somewhere. When I was hungry I ate what I had in the cupboard or what I grabbed from the corner shop late at night when I went for more wine. My skin reacted to the lack of daylight and sleep, and the overload of alcohol and crisps. I was spotty and pale.

It was now nearly two weeks since I had seen Lizzie and all I'd had were three text messages from her, one was the obligatory New Year round robin message and the others were just general. When my mobile rang and I saw her number, I hesitated to answer. This was day eleven and I was ok generally and getting through so far, but when some kind person said "are you alright love?" I couldn't keep up the brave face. It had happened twice so far, once with the postman and once in the corner shop. I knew I looked a bit rough and they were just being kind, but this was like picking at the edge of a scab and lifting it up to expose the raw, bloody mess that was going on in my life.

I took a breath and answered.

"Hiya Steph, sorry it's taken me so long to call you, I got lumbered with a big case last week and I have had no time for anything…"

Good job I had time for you when 'Titmarsh' was playing with your husband's tits.

"Are you ok?"

I couldn't really remember what I had said in the
messages that I had written, other than things were bad
and he had gone.

"Well, you know… as well as can be expected when life
has kicked you in the teeth."

Tears well up.

"Oh you sound awful… if there is anything I can do,"
uncomfortable pause which I broke with a sniff, "you
know, just let me know."

"I could come over maybe and bring some wine? We
could have a sleepover and slag off men with a Chinese," I
said, trying to pick myself up. I craved some company,
more than anything else right now, and I needed to spill
my guts and cry into my chardonnay with someone other
than just myself.

"Well, yes, that would be great - it might be better for
me to come to you if that's ok." I guessed she didn't want
me to stay over now lover boy was on the scene. Fine by
me.

"Of course it is, anytime, in fact that would work better
anyway now I have no car…" There you go, bombshell
dropped.

"No car?"

"Well, it was never mine anyway I guess but…"

"Have you been sacked?"

"Not exactly." Tears and shame choked my words back.
"I got caught drink-driving after the fortune-teller night."

"Oh my God, Steph! You really are in the shit aren't
you?"

The conversation after that was brief, Lizzie sounded
distracted and said she couldn't commit to when she could

come over but she would text me. People's lives went on even when mine had caved. She said she couldn't represent me as she had too big a workload at the moment and really if the police had the evidence from being breathalysed it would be quite cut and dried anyway. Small potatoes for her I supposed. She could recommend someone she knew from another firm who was very good and that she would text the number. She was a newly quite newly qualified, but was establishing a good track record and she wasn't expensive. Lizzie had met her at a conference a couple of months ago.

Since I had fessed up once already, I felt like now might be a good time to phone Brian my manager and tell him about the driving incident. He knew me well enough to be sympathetic and agreed that it could happen to anyone, a little bit of poor judgement and a whole helping of bad luck. Wrong time, wrong place syndrome if you like. He also said that he was obligated to pass on the details to head office and that I would be on gardening leave until things were concluded. He would arrange collection of my company car until we knew 'what was what'.

I knew this wasn't good, there had been cut backs and pay offs already and the company had used the credit crunch as a reason to sort out who they wanted and who they didn't. The people who had been let go were those that were suspected of fiddling expenses, known skivers and the like. Anyone really that was not towing the company line and bringing the sales in. Although my sales were always good I knew there was no way I could keep my job if I couldn't drive, and that over the last week I had become a liability. It was probably a good idea to start looking for something else sooner rather than later.

BLEEP BLEEP

Fully expecting it to be Lizzie with the number she had promised. I opened the message envelope without preparing myself.

Jay mobile – hi hope you are ok, just wanted you to know that I have had time to think and maybe we could meet up and discuss.

Thank God! My breath caught in my throat and my heart started thudding, butterflies danced in my belly and the Halleluiah Chorus rang in my ears.

An end to all of this misery. He still wanted me!

I replied quickly, well as quickly as you can when you are excited and you have sausage fingers and predictive text. Arrangements were made to meet tomorrow evening. I asked him if he wanted to come over and he said no it would be better to meet somewhere else. He must want to make it like a date! I was so excited I didn't know how I would get through the next thirty-one hours and seventeen minutes.

I hugged my knees up to my chest and let the tears fall again, this time of relief and gratitude. Things were going to be alright after all.

I ran upstairs and started to try on clothes, pleasantly surprised that I had lost a few pounds due to the stress and wine diet I'd been on for one week and four days.

I ran a bath and started shaving, buffing and plucking. By the time I was finished I'd be irresistible.

I hunted out an old copy of *Men Are From Mars* and reminded myself about his cave and his elastic band, had more wine and went to bed to dream of our reunion sex.

I woke to the sound of cars in the street.

People going to work—I wondered when I would be working again. I checked my phone and there was an email from Lizzie's office entitled Hannah Stanton. I saved the numbers in my phone and looked at the time. Too early to ring yet, I'd wait until ten-ish or maybe after morning television had told me what I simply must have this season to avoid looking like a high street pleb, or maybe even after *Jerry* had told me who the daddy was.

Or, I could stop procrastinating.

9:10 am and I dialled the number just imagining what Ms Stanton would think of my tits-up life.

"Sprocket and Spinks, good morning"

Move over 'Chuckle Brothers' here come Sprocket and Spinks, they're cheap and cheerful and you always get a really good LOL.

"Hello there," I said in my telephone voice, "I was wondering if I could speak to Hannah Stanton please."

Twin set and pearls replied, "Please hold the line and I will see if Ms Stanton is available. Who should I say is calling?"

"She doesn't know me, I am a friend of a friend, she has been recommended."

Pause.

I could feel suspicion grow on the other end of the phone. I wasn't going to say I was a drink-driver needing her help, thanks. Especially not to someone who sounded like they were from a generation that could feed eight

people with a pound of mince and knock up a sponge
pudding with the one egg a week. The 'never did us any
harm' brigade.

"Well then, just hold the line please."

Greensleeves.

After the second chorus, the call connected and I heard a
muffled throat clearing, then "Hello Hannah speaking, can
I help?"

"Oh, erm yes. I am a friend of Lizzie Brooks. She met
you at a conference recently and she thinks you can help
me."

"Lizzie, ah yes I know who you mean. She's a bit of a
high flyer isn't she?" she laughed.

"You could say that," I agreed and continued canvassing
her for 'Team Steph'. "It's just that she couldn't help me
and she said that you might be able to. I've got some stuff
going on at the moment that I need some representation
and advice with."

"And she picked me? Wow, from all of the people that
she knows she sent you to me? That's made my day." She
sounded really made up that Lizzie had thought of her so
highly, and I felt in that moment whether she liked me or
not she was going to make sure that I got the best possible
outcome here. I was becoming a door opener for her with
Lizzie and her far more prestigious firm. As they say, it's
not what you know but who you know and as long as I
could get through this, I didn't care whose name I had to
drop.

I gave Hannah a brief overview over the phone and a
preliminary meeting was arranged for that afternoon. She
was optimistic about the driving charge and said that she

would be able to comment further after we met in person. 3pm was agreed and she would email directions.

I really hoped that this was the start of me getting out of the mire.

I decided to take a shower and clean the house from top to bottom, including clean sheets. All of the empty wine bottles made their way to the wheelie bin. Jay didn't need to know I had gone to pieces, that wouldn't be very attractive and anyway it was temporary. It was probably just stress and he needed space and time to clear his head. I would be super supportive and lovely to him and before long we'd be back on track, I wouldn't burden him with the car thing or the job thing tonight. I had better wait until the time was right and he was back home. Anyway, there was nothing to tell. And I wouldn't be insecure and allow myself to make things up that were not there. No more contamination from me. He'd explain that what I had overheard him say on the phone was nonsense and that I'd got it all wrong, and we'd even laugh about it.

The morning was passing quite quickly as I pottered around in my joggers dusting, sweeping and mopping. The sheets were dancing on the line in a slight breeze, it was sunny but frosty. Virginal white—tonight we'd be between them again and I'd make sure it was like the first time—well maybe the second as that was better if I remember.

I heard the mail drop from the letterbox and picked it up, junk mail, junk mail, free paper, final demand and letter to us both.

Mr & Mrs, I'll take that as a sign thanks!

I sat on the bottom stair and noticed the post mark, halfway through January already.

I opened the letter and scanned it. The letterhead was from the Equity Release people and 'Regarding Your Advance' was the subject of the letter. Perfect timing! I could book the holiday with a deposit today and tell him about it tonight. Things were turning out for the best, I just knew it.

I read on, paused and went back to the beginning of the letter. There must have been a mistake. They were refusing the drawing down of funds due to the mortgage account being in arrears. Arrears? There had to be a mistake or a processing error or something, that couldn't be right, Jay paid that on the first of every month and I paid the rest of the bills.

I picked up the phone and rang the customer services team frantically on their premium rate number.

Full name, date of birth and mother's maiden name later, I was through to Megan who would be glad to help me.

Her slight Irish accent would probably have been melodic in different circumstances, as she explained to me very nicely that they had written to me several times in the last three months regarding the missed payments on the mortgage account. I put her onto hands free and started to rifle through the draw crammed full of unopened letters and charity bags.

My descent from the moral high ground was rapid. The unopened envelopes confirmed the story so far, I ripped open a couple and it appeared that we owed in the region of £2,400 without interest. I was transferred to the legal department and a nice bloke called Carl listened to me whine for five minutes about how I couldn't believe it and that there must be a mistake. One of the standard responses he heard day in day out I supposed.

Payment plans were not an option now, due to our lack of contact as from the end of last month, I had to either pay in full or face repossession and a county court judgment. I'll have a side order of bankruptcy and a smattering of nervous breakdown please. Apart from the marriage-saving shagathon I had planned in The Maldives slipping away, there was also the embarrassment of losing the house. How would I ever live that down? There was no way I could raise the money, I was maxed out completely. I guessed Jay was too, as the mortgage payment was meant to be coming out of his account every month like we had agreed.

When I did my financial juggle at the beginning of the month I always presumed that the one payment that he was responsible for would be made. I started to cry now with temper and ended the phone call, the details of which would be put in writing and sent out first class.

Why hadn't he told me? Looking at the stack of letters crammed into the draw it was quite possible that he had no idea. Amongst the bills there were bank statements and council tax reminders, neither of us had any idea what the whole picture looked like. I was at the top of a slippery slope with wheels on my arse.

And really I was no better than him. I had hidden all of the escalating credit card bills. Maybe he was just trying to protect me because he loved me, oh the irony! I told myself that this was the case and took some deep breaths. I could still claw this back, I knew I could.

This was never going to get any better until I had the guts to face what was going on. I might not be able to save my credit rating but I had to try and keep the house, especially if I wanted to make our marriage work, and I did above anything else.

For richer and poorer.

I bundled up the letters into a carrier bag and put it beside the front door. I had passed a citizens advice place on the bus the other day and I needed advice more than ever. If I left a bit earlier this afternoon I could call in and see if they could help me before I met Hannah.

By 1pm I was heading for the bus again with my financial time-bomb in a carrier bag.

Three quarters of the way into the journey, the charity bag lady got on and I looked away. She had a whole lot of tomatoes this time, what the hell was she going to do with all of those? She caught me staring at the bag and read my mind.

"Soup," she said and smiled. Her face lit up with that smile and I felt embarrassed. Maybe there was more to her than I first thought, maybe I had been judging her and not known the first thing about her. She stood up as the bus slowed down and made her way to the front. She turned and smiled again.

"Take care you," and she was gone. She made her way up the steps to the same old building.

The Citizens Advice Bureau was only one stop away.

They were really nice, but the message was loud and clear, I needed to get my stuff in order. I felt such chaos in my life that I didn't know where to start. I had shed a few tears in front of Brett—it must happen a lot as he had

some hankies on his desk. He had encouraged me to pull
out anything relating to the mortgage and pending
repossession so that he could try and help with the most
urgent matter first. He asked me to phone and tell them
that he was my advocate so that he could speak on my
behalf. They said that I would have to pay off the arrears
within the next fourteen days in order to keep the house
and avoid repossession. This seemed out of the realms of
possibility for me with all of the other monthly payments.
Brett wrote down all of the details anyway. I knew now
that I would have to speak to Jay about this and once we
were sorted in a week or so we might be able to catch up.
Not tonight though, perhaps in the morning after our
reunion. He might be able to draw the full amount off a
credit card or even apply for a new one with a fast cash
advance that could save us. He might even have saved the
money and it could be sitting somewhere ready to pay the
mortgage anyway.

I kept the photocopied notes and the reference number,
Brett kept a copy too. There was then talk of making
agreements with credit card people and stopping interest
accruing, which sounded encouraging. I made an
appointment to come back once I had my paperwork in
order. Brett said that I could stay for the afternoon and use
their shredder and hole punch but I declined. I did
however ask if I could leave the bag under his desk whilst
I met with Hannah. I wanted my first impression to be a
bit less 'bag lady'.

Hannah's office was only a short walk away, just off the
main street. My feet followed a short stretch of cobbles

that I would not have liked to navigate in high heels and I buzzed the door.

"Steph Slater here for Hannah Stanton."

Buzz

"Push the door."

Reception was small with five of what looked like someone's dining room chairs and a two-seater black sofa with chrome feet. A cheese plant and water cooler completed the look and 'twinset and pearls' sat in the corner, peering at me from behind half-moon shaped glasses on a cord. She shoved a pad across the desk along with a biro and said, "Sign in," in her haughty taught tone. As I was filling in my details she picked up the phone and told Hannah I had arrived. "Just have a seat, she knows you are here."

I opted for the sofa and picked up a copy of *Reader's Digest* to flick through. By the time Hannah smiled hello, I had learned how to make my own compost, invest in premium bonds and I could say 'toilet' in five languages.

Hannah was not what I had imagined, although I guess my impression of female solicitors was based solely on Lizzie and people I'd seen milling around her office at times. She was shorter than me, looked like a modern, funked up Tinkerbell, in a combination of designer labels and charity shop chic.

"Hi, Stephanie!" She shook my hand and I noticed an unusual silver ring, lots of thin wires had been combined into a rope that wound around a chunky, clear crystal. She followed my gaze, "It's from Bali."

"Oh right, it's lovely."

"Do you want a cup of something before we get started?" Hannah asked. "Tea, coffee, water?"

"I'd love coffee please," I replied.

"No problem. Joyce, we'll have two coffees please in goldfish bowl one." Twinset and pearls gave a "humph" under her breath and Hannah showed me into a small meeting room with a huge glass window overlooking reception. She slid the card to 'occupied' and closed the cream opaque blinds.

"That's better, now Miss Marple will have to find something else to look at." I liked her already.

Hannah took notes as I told her my story, shed more tears and generally spilled my guts. She was both understanding and intuitive and her questions drew the information from me that she needed without making me feel more embarrassed. When we had finished she scanned over the pages of notes and underlined a couple of things.

"OK. So we need a plan," Hannah broke a momentary silence.

"So you can help me?" I asked.

"Of course I can," she replied. "I never get anyone I can't help in some way. I attract people, the right people at the right time, and people just find me when they need to."

A strange feeling of déjà vu poured over me and I looked at her and blinked.

"You ok?" she asked.

"Yes, fine. Just having a weird flashback or something, it does feel like I was meant to find you." I said.

"Well you know there are really no coincidences. I'm just learning about it all myself, apparently there is a universal law of attraction that draws people and things together. It's amazing stuff. There is so much out there that we can't explain, I just love all that. I've got loads of books about it if you want to borrow any, I've got some here actually." I think I had just found Hannah's specialist subject and she had switched from serious to animated. Well, second specialist subject I hoped.

She reached into the worn brown leather, oversized satchel she'd carried into the meeting room and pulled out two books. One had a picture of the earth on the front and a golden key, and the other was a book I had heard of vaguely called *The Secret*. Hannah handed me both and said that they would help me with the outcome of both the relationship challenges and the drink driving case.

I didn't see how that was possible, but my options were running out and I had a feeling that next time I saw her she'd ask what I thought. I thanked her and stood up to make my exit and as I moved towards the door Hannah threw her arms around me.

"I am a hugger! Can't help it, sorry!" She laughed as I stood like a telegraph pole. "You'll get used to me, I'm like *Marmite* that's all."

"I like *Marmite*," I said as I relaxed and hugged her back. Can you become friends with your lawyer? Why ever not?

Chapter 7

The taxi came at 7pm. I fiddled with my earrings and put on more lip gloss in the back seat. To say I had butterflies was an understatement, my stomach was doing somersaults and I was a bit tipsy into the bargain. I wondered if he would be there when I arrived or if I would have to wait. Or maybe he wouldn't show up at all and I would have to fake a mobile phone conversation about a crisis coming up to avoid being crucified with embarrassment. You never know I might even pick up someone else if that happened. I looked alright tonight in long, indigo, kick flare jeans, high-heeled shoes and a black bustier top. I had styled my hair into loose curls and my make-up was subtle but sexy. I was wearing Jay's favourite perfume, nice underwear and my wedding ring.

Here we go. Heart in mouth I paid the driver and made for the entrance to *The Dragon's Den*. Thai fusion food and a fantastic bar that overlooked the river, with optional karaoke after 8pm on the top floor.

Where was he? I scanned the place and checked my watch, 7:22pm, he had said half past.

I ordered a large glass of white wine and as I was reaching for my purse I saw him arrive. He looked around, then his eyes rested on me and I tried to read his expression. Relief was the main emotion that I picked up and after that he was really hard to work out. He insisted on paying for my drink and ordered his own. He suggested that we make our way to the sofas that were opposite the bar where it was easier to talk.

Conversation was forced, as if he was skirting around the issue. How can you not small-talk with someone who has shared your bed for years? We drank more and more and after about an hour I decided that it was now or never. I casually unwrapped the black pashmina that was hiding my figure and leant forward to have a long slurp of my drink. I made sure that he got an eyeful of the breasts that he had a handful of a couple of weeks ago. He adjusted his position in his seat and uncrossed his legs.

"Do you want another drink?" he asked.

"Yes thanks, same again." My head was swimming a bit now but it's not like I had to go to work tomorrow.

He came back to the sofa with the drinks. We had avoided this for long enough now, he was obviously embarrassed that he had needed time out and he wanted me to make the first move for him to come home. OK, I'd frame it up and then he could have the glory.

I took his hand in mine and, in the least pissed voice that I could muster up, I asked him straight.

"So what exactly is it that you want?"

"I don't know, Steph, I really don't know." His voice said one thing and his eyes another, they were undressing me as we sat there. I knew he still loved me deep down. "I want to be with you sometimes and at other times I don't. It's confusing. I think I need more time."

"You are just confused," I said. "You have been under so much pressure at work and you needed some time out, I get that. But I want to support you - please come home." He looked away. "Jay?" He wouldn't make eye contact with me. "Jay? What's wrong? You know we are good for each other, please come home, this is just a blip." Uh oh, sounding desperate alert. I reached out and touched his face to turn it to mine and he pulled away. "Please," I said weakly. "I thought this was about you coming back."

"It's not," he looked at me this time. "I'm sorry Steph, this is about us getting a divorce."

Oh my God!

"I can't keep pretending anymore, it's just not working for me, I feel trapped. The last thing I want is to feel like this for the next God knows how many years and look back over my life with regrets. I don't want to hurt you, but I have to get out of this marriage, it was a mistake."

He was half-shouting, but not in anger, the music was quite loud. I could hear *Ting Tings* singing *'Shut Up and Let Me Go'*.

A mistake alright.

The big mistake that I had made was to continue in the illusion that I could fix this marriage and save us. He didn't want me and he had never loved me like I loved him, this was becoming abundantly clear now. I felt like a fool - a cheap, tarted-up fool who had been used and discarded time after time. A doormat covered in *Chanel* with her tits hanging out and mascara running down her face.

"Why?" I shouted through my tears. "I have done everything for you, why? I deserve to know."

He looked away again.

"Jay!" I screeched at him though gritted teeth "Why?"

I reached out and grabbed his face and turned it towards me and he pulled my hand away.

"I've met someone else," he said and cast his eyes downwards.

And there it was. The ultimate betrayal and humiliation that I had been fearing and anticipating all along. He was leaving me for someone else.

There was no point now in going into the details of the house repossession that was pending, or my imminent career change to dole waller. I had lost everything in that one short sentence and I just wanted to go. There was nothing worse he could do to me now, and nothing else he could take from me. I was hitting the bottom and I wanted to do it alone thanks.

Someone on the karaoke started belting out *Enough is Enough,* and I quite agreed.

I stood up and the room was spinning, he steadied me by holding my elbow and I moved away from him. High heels, wine and trauma were not a great combination when it came to staying upright.

I managed to make it to the toilets and there was a queue. I noticed that there was a disabled loo and I tried the door. I didn't vomit, but it took me a good few minutes to compose myself. I tried to call for a taxi but there was no signal in there. I guess I would have to walk outside and cross the road to the taxi rank on the other side of the street. I didn't know and didn't care if Jay had left or not. I just needed to get home. A million questions were flying through my mind. *Why someone else? Why now? Where had he been staying? How long had he been planning this for? Was it someone I knew? Why was I not good enough?*

I wrapped my pashmina around me tightly and with my hand on the door and my focus on survival I pushed it open.

"There you are, I was worried," and before I knew it he was in there with me.

"I, I, I can't take this in Jay, really, please, just let me go home now and we can talk another time."

"I can't leave you like this," he said, coming closer.

He put his arms around me and I sank into him sobbing and trembling. He held me tight and I breathed in his familiar scent. I put my head on his chest, heard his heartbeat and I couldn't take anymore. I stood for what seemed like a long time with him stroking my hair and saying, "It's alright, I'm here," over and over.

What did that mean? He was leaving me after all. Maybe he was being supportive and kind in my hour of need, or maybe this was more mind games? I was totally confused. Whatever the reason I was grateful. I was crumbling and needed someone in this moment.

Perhaps he'd seen the way I had reacted and it made him reconsider. He did love me after all and he had followed me into the toilet to tell me it was all a misunderstanding or a mid-life crisis and he was coming home with me now, for keeps. No one need know about all of this.

He reached behind him and locked the door. I snuggled further into him and breathed him in again. I started telling him through exhausted sobs that I loved him and that I would do anything to fix it—anything. Maybe we could call a taxi and go home to the white sheets and champagne that I had on ice. I was sure that I could still pull myself together and pull off a bedroom performance.

More hair stroking and he kept speaking in a low voice, "It's ok, come on now, you'll get through it."

It was then that it went dark.

He was closer to the light switch than I was and when the light went off I felt momentarily disorientated. "It's ok, just relax."

He wanted that moment as much as I did—the connection of us both in the dark—holding each other and surrendering to the love that we still shared. I was fractured but so grateful to have his arms around me as I stood snivelling and trembling in my heels.

It was then that I heard the sound familiar of a zip and his arm moved from around me to over me. He cupped my chin with one hand and kissed my forehead and then started to push my shoulders down. It took me a moment to register what was happening and I pulled away from him and shook my head in disbelief, which he couldn't see in the darkness.

"Jay, I can't... I can't do it like this..." I objected, as he thrust his erection into my hand and moaned in my ear. He pulled my hair to one side and started to kiss my neck and I melted into more tears and longing for him.

"Not here Jay, please, I'm all ready for you at home if this is what you want...really we can be together at home...please..."

He kissed my mouth roughly and, as I started to kiss back, I could feel his lips curve into a smile, taunting me in some way or another, maybe being playful,. He wanted to come back home as much as me—I knew it. I grabbed him harder and he groaned again.

"Let's go home, Jay, and start again. Please, we can fix this, I know we can." It was far too late to worry about sounding desperate.

The music was loud and my head was swimming with
emotion and alcohol, but in that moment the sound that
came from his lips could have been mistaken for a snigger.
He pushed my shoulders down firmly and this time I
didn't have the strength to resist.

"Come on, Steph, you know you want to. I'll let you do
it one more time and see how I feel when you're done."
My knees hit the hard tiled floor and the smell of
disinfectant and urine filled my nostrils. My stomach
lurched at the sheer indignity of what he expected.

"After all, you are still my wife, for now that is."

The sound of his heavy breathing mixed with the music,
which had changed to soft rock.

*'Wake me up inside, wake me up inside, Call my name
and save me from the dark.'*

Something inside me snapped in that moment, and that
final insult became the catalyst that I had needed all of this
time to see that he didn't care about me one bit. Making
love in my clean sheets and making a go of our marriage
were obviously not on the agenda here. One last quick
blow job in the bogs was all I seemed to be worth. He was
a liar and he had stolen my dignity one time too many. I
felt sick and stone cold sober.

"Hold on," I said and I took his manhood in one hand, as
tears of anger and humiliation dripped off my chin. "It's
tricky in the dark."

*'Bring me to life, I have been living a lie, there's nothing
inside.'*

I pulled his jeans and boxers down to the floor with the
other hand and started to grip rhythmically. Bastard. I
couldn't turn off the love that I felt—it was still there

somewhere—but it was being eclipsed by the fury and hatred that was welling up inside of me now. He didn't notice in those few seconds that I was moving around him in a circle and crouching now, not kneeling. I kept gripping and he kept moaning, his legs splayed apart and his arms out to each side, bracing himself for his release.

"Suck it, Steph," he panted. "Suck me off."

He brought his right hand round to the back of my head and held himself with his left, ready to force himself into my face.

"Go on, Steph, you know you want to…" I turned my head sideways and felt his hot skin on my wet cheek.

'Save me from the nothing I've become.'

I felt for the door handle in the dark and once I'd found it I slowly started to stand up and he pushed me down again.

"Be a good wife, Steph, and we'll see where we go from there…come on, you want it, you know you do…"

God knows how I found my feet or my inner strength, but I did.

"No I fucking don't!" I shouted through tears as I lurched to my feet. I opened the door wide, flicked the switch on the wall and pulled the disabled emergency cord at the same time. Lights, camera, action. I turned on my heel and walked away, out onto the street, but not before I caught a quick glimpse. I could see a room full of people staring, pointing and laughing at him as he tried to cover up his cock along with his embarrassment. For better, for worse you bastard, I hope you feel a whole lot worse.

'Bring me to Life.'

Chapter 8

In the days that followed I wondered how on earth I had
allowed myself to go along with this charade of a
marriage for so long. I kept playing over and over again
nights when he had stayed away, weekends he'd been
golfing and days he couldn't meet me for lunch. Were
these all stolen moments with a mistress I had no idea
about? I tortured myself about what she looked like, how
good in bed she was, how old or young? Within the thick
fog of pain and heartache there were thunderous bursts of
anger and fury, but no matter what I couldn't switch off
the love. Or for that matter the loneliness. I had never
thought that feelings could be so changeable within the
same day, hour or even minute. I was now an emotional
chameleon.

There was so much time for reflection. I was starting to
face facts that I had gone along with so much in order to
keep the peace, make him happy and keep him with me.
Little pieces of me had been sacrificed one at a time, and I
had hardly noticed until now. Now I felt I was running on
empty.

This was not altogether a bad place to be, at least there
was a bit more certainty. I wasn't wasting time or energy
wondering and wishing that he would come back and
we'd be all *Brangelina* and loved up.

I was proud of myself for facing reality at last, but as I
lived in and looked around the home I had once loved, the
cues of togetherness were driving me mad. I had removed
all of the obvious reminders, wedding photos and the like,
but it seemed like nearly everything whispered a memory

of the two of us. Regardless of how the house was taken
out of my life, I knew now that my time here was limited,
if I wanted to stay sane.

I had been fighting the urge to go back and see Psychic
Sue again, but the day came soon enough when I felt
compelled to hear the rest of what she had started.
Everything had been right so far and I wanted to know
what else she saw coming for me and when things were
going to change for the better.

I looked in the pocket of the jacket I had been wearing
the night I had first met her, and sure enough there was
her business card with all of her details. I was going to
phone ahead but, after a split second's consideration, I
realised that I had nothing to do anyway so I may as well
just turn up.

I found the address with and after consulting the online
bus timetable I was on Green Lane by 9:30am. I tried the
buzzer for 38a and there was no answer. My stomach
rumbled as the smell of coffee wafted towards me. I saw
that there was a café two doors up and I was getting cold.
Half a latte later, Sue's familiar face was passing the
window, carrying a pint of milk, obviously expecting to be
here all day then—at least she was optimistic.

In a rush to get to her I burnt my mouth on the second
half of the coffee, and made my way to meet and greet my
destiny once again. This time I might even stay and get the
really gory details.

"Hello again lovely!" Sue was in the street, raking
through her handbag for the right set of keys.

The snow started again lightly.

"Hi Sue," I said in a tone that showed far more humility than the last time I had spoken to her.

"There they are!" she said, as the key turned in the lock. Behind the door was a flight of stairs covered by a worn brown carpet and some kind of hanging crystal thing from the ceiling catching the light. Feng bloody Shui no doubt.

"Would it be ok to come and see you again?" I asked in a small voice. "I'd like to hear what the rest of the message was please."

For a second Sue had the opportunity to make me squirm, and God knows I would have done so if I'd been in her shoes. Instead she looked on me kindly and said, "Of course you can, come on up."

There was a tiny waiting room with a stack of magazines about fate and destiny, and leaflets from people that did massage, reiki, numerology and the like.. Sue gestured to me to have a seat here and she went through a glass door into another room. The glass was bevelled for privacy I suppose.

I heard a *click, click, whoosh* sound and the smell of council house gas fire filled the space. I heard water and then the kettle rumbling into action.

"Do you want a cuppa?" Sue shouted above the water boiling.

"Erm, yes please I'll have anything." Anything to warm me up that is, I was freezing.

"OK, come on through," Sue's voice sounded commanding and calm now, she must be in the zone.

The room was small with one window onto the back lane and some old curtain nets hanging up. There were a couple of posters on the walls of angels and some thank you cards blue-tacked up in between. There was a table and two chairs, the gas fire on the wall and a chest of drawers.

I huddled my cup of tea and breathed in the hot, sweet steam as Sue produced the cards. My fingers were so cold I wondered if I'd be able to shuffle them again, or if they'd drop all over the floor. I was so nervous to take them from her, she must have sensed this as she reassured me.

"I know you are feeling nervous, but you have done the right thing in coming here. Your guides say that the process has started and that you need some help and direction now." She handed me the deck.

"I need more than help Sue, I need a miracle." As I thought of the destruction and chaos that had ensued in my world since our last meeting I wanted to cry my heart out again. There were no more tears though, things had actually gone beyond the point where I could shed any more.

I shuffled the cards as best I could with my eyes closed this time, my actions were mirroring my emotions again, but this was a complete contrast to the way I had felt the first time. "Please, please help me," I kept repeating in my head.

Sue took a deep breath and her eyelids fluttered. Sue drew five cards from the deck and placed them face down in front of me.

"Why are there only five?" I asked.

"Because your guides want you to know that they are going to share with you the first six lessons now and then the next six in six months' time." Sue explained. "They say it will be easier for you this way, otherwise you will be fixated on what is happening ahead and not get on with what is happening now."

"Oh, right. But there are only five?" I questioned.

"Yes, you are having the first lesson right now," Sue looked me in the eye and smiled. "You have come back, so that means that you are open now to things you were once closed to. Remember *The Phoenix?*" She smiled and I found myself smiling back and nodding reluctantly in agreement.

"That was your first card and its message is all about the burning and transmutation of your past that no longer serves you and then rising from the ashes of this with new wisdom and perspective. It's about going through the short term chaos and pain to emerge from it stronger and with the faith that you can build again and be stronger than before. The Phoenix is a mythical bird that helps you to be open to possibilities that you never considered before. It helps to open you to new ways of thinking and feeling and therefore new ways of creating," she said.

"Your guides are saying that there is something really important that you have to do along the way, you have to write down each of these lessons in turn. They say that you have a book already that you can use. They say that the reasons will become clear and that you have to start with lesson one when you get home."

My mind took me back to the journal and I remembered that I had already begun to fill the pages with self-pitying scrawl, I could always tear that page out and start again.

"And you have to leave in what you have already written," Sue said.

I nodded again, you can't argue with that.

"In fact you had better write down the lessons that are coming through for you now." She gave me an appointment card and a biro and wrote the numbers 1 – 6 down one side. "When you get home you can write the lesson along with the relevant month down on a calendar or in a diary so you know what is coming up and what you need to complete."

I wrote next to the number one – embrace radical change and acceptance of new things, be open to possibility.

Sue took a deep breath and her eyelids fluttered again. She opened them fully and turned the first card.

"*Shadow self,*" Sue spoke slowly as the eyes on the card stared into mine and my stomach flipped.

"This card is all about you looking at the parts of yourself that are creating sabotage and holding you back."

I took in a sharp breath and sighed it out slowly through puffed cheeks.

Could I not have had 'love thy neighbour' or 'thou shalt not steal' as lesson two?

I thought of my life for a moment and what might be holding me back.

Images started to stream through my mind of all of the times I'd elevated myself above other people and all of the stupid things I'd bought in an effort to look the part.

Handbags and glad-rags.

Then a shameful, sickly feeling washed over me along with the memory of being breathalysed and spending a night in a cell, comparable only to getting home on New

Year's Eve and your husband has left you for someone else.

Thankfully Sue's voice butted in on the onslaught from my own subconscious.

"Your guides are saying that the most important thing here is that you take responsibility of your life from here on in, don't allow this part of you to play out anymore. You need to start loving yourself again and stop beating yourself up."

I sighed and a tear rolled down my cheek, what happened to no more crying? Sue reached over the table and put her hands over mine and my tears plopped onto brown formica.

"This is probably the hardest one love," she said softly.

"Great," I sniffed. "Looks like I am in at the deep end then."

Sue handed me a tissue and I trumpeted into it.

"That's why it's come up first, once this one is done the rest will be easier. Without this you couldn't progress through the rest of the lessons anyway, they are in a sequence." Sue patted my hand in a 'chin up' context and continued speaking about the card.

"You need to get to a place within yourself that you can accept that what you are thinking, feeling and doing is creating what is going on around you. This understanding and realisation alone will change your life even if you don't continue through the rest of the lessons your guides are bringing to you."

"I might have read something about this," I said quietly, casting my mind back to the books that Hannah had given me. "Is this the stuff about your energy and vibration and attracting things to you?"

"Yes! Yes it is!" Sue sat up a little straighter and looked at me as if I had just called 'house'. "That's what it's all about and if you can understand and apply that then you'll be great."

Sue reached out and turned the next card.

"*Attraction*," she said and paused.

I wrote the word next to the number three and put March in brackets next to it.

"This lesson is going to be about you digging deep into your own reserves of strength and faith and accepting that you are attracting what you are. It's the next level in personal responsibility and means that you will have to get real about your thoughts and feelings."

I paused with the pen and looked at Sue for guidance.

"I attract what I am," she prompted me and continued to explain as I wrote this down in tiny squashed up letters that would hardly fit on the line.

"You see, there are lots of people who think that they are attracting what they are becoming, especially people who are on their spiritual journey. But the truth of the matter is that if there is an experience in your life right now, then it has found a frequency within you that is the same and matched it."

"OK," I said. "So everything that is happening now is a result of what I am sending out?"

"Yes."

"And the same with the past?"

"Yes."

It felt like Sue had started to turn cogs in my mind that had not been used for years—if ever. This was a whole new way of looking at my life and meant that there was no way I could shirk the responsibility anymore.

April's card was turned and I saw a picture of a girl trapped in a web.

"*The Web*. See how she is stuck and cannot move?"

I was relaxing a little now, and things were making more sense.

"This shows that she is unwilling to move forward and let go of what does not serve her anymore. This might be old beliefs or attachments, or actual physical items that you do not need anymore that are clogging up your life and symbolically and literally keeping you stuck."

Sue looked at me for confirmation and I thought of the carrier bag stuffed with letters and bills, as well as the clutter in the loft and the kitchen cupboards, not to mention the garage.

"I think I get what that means," I said, and wrote April – let go of what does not serve you.

Sue nodded in approval and continued on with the next card.

"*Universal Magic*" Sue smiled and sat back in her seat. "This is something of a turning point I feel, things are going to start to go your way."

"Thank God for that!" I replied in a half sarcastic tone, rolling my eyes and smiling to myself.

Sue laughed and explained that this card showed a man standing with a wand pointing up to heaven in one hand and the other pointing to the earth, showing that he has mastered the power of the universe to bring forth what he wants and needs in his life.

"This card says that you are going to be good at bringing in what you want at this time, presuming that you have completed all of the lessons before this one..." She made a mock stern school teacher face, then laughed when I did. "You will complete them all by the way, so if and when it gets tough just know that you were always meant to get through this."

The next card was then turned and I saw the words *Cause & Effect.*

"This card means that you have had an awakening and there is a new way of looking at things for you now. There is an energy here of healing deep wounds and putting them behind you in order to move on, and a definite feeling of karma being resolved for you—I feel this is the essence of this card for June."

"What do you mean by karma being repaid?" I asked.

"This will become clearer at the time and all of the right information will come to you when you need it. As with all of these lessons you will have the tools to hand in the moment that you need them. It's up to you to see them and know their value," she answered.

"Oh God, what if I miss the signs?" I asked, unfastening my scarf now as the room was getting warmer.

"They will keep coming around until you do see them," Sue assured me. "But the quicker you see them and learn the lesson within the designated month, the faster you will have the life you want. Your guides are saying that this will have to be completed within the next year and the next and so on until you get it all in sequence. It was all agreed before you came here."

"Agreed? I would never have agreed to any of this and what do you mean before I came here? Came where? Here?" I gestured around the small room with my hands and rolled my eyes again.

"Not here, they mean here on earth!" Sue laughed. I shook my head in bewilderment.

"Remember, Lesson One, be open to change and the possibility it brings."

Well this certainly wasn't.

"We all make soul agreements and promises before we come to earth about the lives, experiences and learning that we are going to encounter here when we get into physical bodies. There are loads of books you can read about it if you want to."

"I think I'll just take your word for it at the moment, I have got quite a busy six months ahead of me."

Sue laughed again, I had let my defences down at last. She was one of the few that had seen the real me—the vulnerable and authentic me without my guard up and my armour of designer labels and general bullshit.

So here lies the next six months of my life, I was grateful at this point that we had not done all twelve. There seemed like a lot to take in.

"Is there anything else you want to ask?" Sue put her elbows on the table and her chin in her palms.

"Just how am I meant to get through it?" I answered.

"You just get through it. I know that sounds too easy, but you are the keeper of your own destiny and you will just get through it day by day and month by month. And you will do it first time."

"It just seems so huge, that's all."

"It does right now, but look how fast a year can pass."

Sue was right. A year could pass in a blink, and although I didn't know much yet about how all of this worked, I did know that if I thought I couldn't do it then I couldn't. So I decided to change that quickly to an affirmation about getting through the lessons easily, hoping that the universe would rise up and send me some of that.

I declined a second cup of tea and asked about the bus home.

It turned out that there was one I could take that wouldn't involve a change, although it would take a bit longer that sounded good to me. I wanted time to think.

I left Sue and promised to stay in touch if I needed to, I would be back in the summer for the next 6 lessons. I didn't have any money on me to pay but she said that she knew that before she did the reading, and that I would come back at the end of the twelve lessons and pay what I felt it had been worth. I agreed and made my way onto the street, pulling my scarf around me now as snowflakes danced from the sky.

The feeling of returning to an empty house was not getting any better as the days passed, but today I had something to do as soon as I got back. After hanging up my coat, flicking the heating on and making more tea, I pulled out the journal and turned to the first clean page.

Stephanie's Journal - Lesson 1
Change Brings New Possibilities

I write this at the outset of an amazing and terrifying journey. Everything that I knew to be real and tangible somehow seems to have shifted into the realms of the unreal for me. As much as I don't understand why or how, my life has been turned upside down within a matter of weeks and I now find myself on a path that I cannot return from. I don't think things will ever be the same and I guess ultimately that will be a good thing. I find myself having to admit that my reality was very limited and shallow, and that I did not have an awareness of the bigger picture at all. Hopefully this will change as I go through these lessons and find the real me again, I am staying open to the possibility at least.

"A Journey of a Thousand Miles begins with a Single Step." Lao Tzu

Chapter 9

Snowdrops were scattered amongst the frosty borders in the front garden the day that the divorce petition landed on the mat. I cried at the definition of unreasonable behaviour and Hannah assured me that this meant nothing really, and of course she would represent me. It was quite a standard reason when you really meant 'I can't be arsed to stick at it' or 'I just want out'. I called Lizzie and she confirmed this, then dropped into conversation that Jay was using a colleague from her firm to represent him.

It was bad luck he had simply been off the mark faster than me and managed to bag Mark 'Bulldog' Blackett. He came across as a charming, well-spoken and mature man, but had a reputation of ripping apart the opposition in the courtroom.

This meant that there was no way that Lizzie could represent me, and anyway I couldn't afford her. *MBNA* must be paying for the bulldog.

So I was on the cheap seats with Hannah, whom I am sure would make a lovely appetiser for Mr Blackett.

I dipped into the books that Hannah had lent me and they spoke a lot about intention and vibration. As I read on, it became clearer that this was energy speak and that all it meant was the energy vibe that you put out there into the world would bring back the same to you, as confirmed by Sue.

In other words you get what you give, and this principle is universal.

My gardening leave became quite literal as I fell into the habit of sitting out in the sun, even though the weather was still bitter, it seemed to lift me. I was fortunate that the back of the house was south-facing and sheltered by tall trees around the perimeter, even though it was perishing sometimes, the feeling of warmth on my face was wonderful. My afternoons usually involved reading a little and then reflecting on what I was learning. It was a slow process as this subject was completely new to me. I also started to practise some of the principles of changing what I was putting out there in order to draw different experiences in. Even the guest on last week's *Loose Women* who was rambling on about creating a parking space by asking the angels was starting to seem more credible—only slightly mind.

I started to feel more in control than I had in years and I was eating better and drinking far less wine, which was amazing considering my life was a complete mess really. Upon introspection and with Sue's words ringing in my ears, I had reluctantly admitted to myself that putting junk food and wine into my body was actually something that was sabotaging me and stealing my energy and focus. I had been fooling myself all of this time that this was an act of love and that I was 'treating' myself. Digging a bit deeper helped me to uproot the illusions that I had created to support this behaviour and keep it going. Mr Patel up the road would probably think I was dead, I hadn't been in for a bottle of chardonnay for nearly two weeks.

It turns out that your feelings and thoughts have an effect on your energy vibration as a being, and that this vibration has magnetic properties. It will draw to you what you are focussing on or feeling, and when I really sat and allowed myself to be honest, it was painfully obvious how I had created the life I was living now.

Throughout all of this I lurched between loving Jay and wanting him back and then hating him and wanting him dead. I was emotionally bipolar.

Sue had told me to look at my shadow self, the dark parts of me that were carrying the hurt and pain of my life. She said that by healing and releasing these parts I would be able to eliminate the vibration from my energy and stop attracting painful and hostile experiences. Introspection is not my strong point, I am more of a papering over the cracks sort of person, I had really wished for something easier for lesson two.

At least it was easier to have a go at it when you are not pissed every night.

Self-analysis is always difficult. And having no siblings to speak to made me even less objective about my past and the experiences I'd had early in my life. The experiences that had shaped those magnetic beliefs.

I thought long and hard about my past and what feelings and history I could be carrying around that was affecting me in the present moment. Of course when you start this process you find that you have buried them so deep and covered them with years and years of trivia that these memories are hard to uncover. There was however one particular incident in my past that stood out to me.

I could remember school and being above average but not what you would call clever. There was a brief bullying spell when I was about fourteen when a couple of the girls in the same year group decided to make me a target because they saw that I was wearing something second hand.

My dad had lost his job at the time and my mum was trying to make ends meet. They didn't have the money to be able to buy me the new denim jacket I wanted. My mum saw one for sale in the local charity shop and took it home, washed and ironed it and it was hanging up in my room ready for me coming home one day. I was thrilled and tried it on in front of the mirror, hair up, hair down, with jeans, and over my school uniform. I looked like the other girls, the 'trendies' who always seemed to score a snog with the bad lads around the back of the sports hall.

It wasn't until I got to school the next day that the penny dropped. I did look like the other girls, in fact exactly like Jessica Mason had looked last week just before her mother had dropped half of her wardrobe off at the local *Age Concern* in a bin bag. They had been shopping and there was just so much that the old had to go and make way for the new. Come to think of it she had been wearing a new jacket since Monday.

She recognised one of the buttons that she had changed to customise the jacket and that was the beginning of a very bad day for me. Kids are cruel, and spoilt kids are even worse. They didn't hurt me physically, but the verbal sticks and stones that came my way were painful. I kept it together until home time and as soon as the bell sounded I ran. I ran all of the way down the school drive and home, up the stairs and cried on my bed.

When my mum came into my room I yelled at her to get out and she too stood in tears, not knowing what had happened or what to do.

"You can take that stupid jacket and burn it! I don't want it, and I don't want anything more from you!" I spat my words out in temper and saw her shrink.

She closed the bedroom door and left me alone until supper time when she brought a tray up with a sandwich and a cup of tea. I felt bad for shouting, I knew it wasn't her fault, she had just been in the firing line. The jacket disappeared the following day. I think that this was the first real incident in my life that made me feel 'less than' or not good enough. This feeling stayed with me through High School as I was now labelled a bit of a no hoper by the most popular peer group. Off the cuff comments and sniggering often happened when I walked past. I just had to get on with it though, and kept myself to myself.

There was one person that I was friends with, they were in many ways a male version of me. We had our lunch together most days and skived PE when we could. He was called Damien and he was the only person at that time in my life who really knew me, and liked me for who I was. I felt this way about him too and he was easy company for me.

We saw each other out of school under the guise of project work and then later on revision, but most of the time listened to music, watched television or read magazines.

Damien was taller than me and average looking. His bed head and occasional acne flair had earned him the nickname 'pizza face'. He wore glasses and his parents were both teachers who fully expected him to go to university.

We talked about everything together and when his grades came back, in perfect time to shatter his parent's illusion, we bought strong cider and sat in the woods drinking and making a fire.

The sun went down and the trees were briefly silhouetted against a pink and burnt orange backdrop, then the cold set in and we huddled together in front of the flames.

That's when Damien crept his arm around my shoulder and pulled me closer. Then he kissed me.

It took me completely by surprise, it was the first time I had been kissed properly and his lips felt soft and his chin a bit rough. I kissed him back, his sweet taste of cider along with the smoky forest smell filled my senses and made me feel giddy. My heart was beating faster and I realised in that moment that this is what it felt like when you were in love. Our lips parted and he looked at me sheepishly.

"Sorry, I shouldn't have."

"I'm glad you did." I felt my face flush in the semi-darkness, I leaned back in for more.

That's when I heard a stick snapping behind us and a snigger.

We both turned around, but it was difficult to see in the darkness who was there, but I recognised the voice when I heard Jessica Mason.

"I always knew you were sad Steph, but please! Snogging with the geek? It's bad enough that you let him carry your school bags round like some kind of lap dog."

Three others came out of the shadows, two boys and a girl that I didn't recognise. Both boys looked older than

Jessica and one put his arm around her waist and pulled her close. I guessed that this was the guy she had been talking about at school, the one from out of town and probably his two friends.

"What's up Desperate Damo? Cat got your tongue?"

Damien looked away and got to his feet, he grabbed my hand and started to step backwards away from the fire.

"Don't you want to hang with us Steph? Or would you rather stay with loser boy?" Jessica goaded me.

"We were just going actually," I said.

"Oh come on now, you don't know my new friends. Don't be so rude."

I had no idea what she was playing at, this girl wouldn't even give me the time of day at school and now she wanted me to hang out with them? No way.

Damien sensed my fear and the imminent danger and he pushed me behind him.

"Run," he whispered, "over the tracks."

We moved behind the fire so that the flames created a curtain between us and them, and for a split second they didn't see me turn and run into the darkness. My feet and my adrenaline carried me through branches and bushes onto the old train tracks that were never used now. This was a place that was hard to find in the daylight, and near impossible in forest blackness.

I crouched in the old disused tunnel under the tracks and I heard the echoes of laughing and the cries of pain for some time that night. My own tears flowed at the same time as I tried to be quiet, afraid that I might be next. The demonic laughter and innocent cries haunted me in nightmares on and off for years after the event.

Things were never the same after that.

Damien had changed and I was asked to keep away from him by his parents. I didn't want to cause any more trouble, so I kept my distance for the next couple of months hoping that it would come good. They said that they knew it was nothing to do with me, but he was very fragile.

I walked past one day in the school holidays and saw them packing some stuff in the car, his mum said that they were going away for a while. I asked how Damien was and she was polite but vague.

I made my way home and sulked in my room with sad music and chocolate for the rest of the day. It wasn't until just over a week later that I was passing again and I noticed that the house looked strange. Curtains were half closed and the grass looked a little too long. The bins weren't out, and I knew that there was a reciprocal arrangement with the neighbours to do this for one another when each took holidays.

I lingered for a moment and thought about going to look through the front room window, just then a white van pulled up and a man sat in the front seat checking the address off a clipboard. He climbed out and went to the back door where he pulled out a red, white and blue 'For Sale' board. I'd held onto some hope of seeing Damien again until then, and as he hammered the board into the ground it felt like my heart was being boarded up simultaneously.

That was the moment where part of me shut down.

The incident in the woods and the pain of losing my best friend had haunted me since that time. On reflection that experience was a major influence on who I was, and the thoughts and feelings I carried now. I could see how this had contributed to what I had attracted in my life in bucket loads. Not feeling good enough, being a loser, not fitting in, being loved but then losing, living in fear, having to be seen to have loads of stuff, the list was probably endless. The scary part was that, according to what I had been reading, nothing could change unless I started to unravel my own mess and change these patterns. I'd just keep attracting more and more shit. And God knows I'd had enough of that to last me a lifetime.

I decided that the time had come to let go of these feelings and to heal the past, sending forgiveness back to the parts of me that were still stuck in this drama. I closed my eyes and visualised myself going back in time and connecting with that younger version of myself. In my mind I projected thoughts telepathically to myself and spoke words of comfort, understanding and forgiveness. I reassured myself that things were going to turn out for the best and that it was time to let go and allow this to heal. I felt some resistance, but when I allowed the scenes and memories to flow very strong emotions enveloped me. I relived the scenes of me crouching in the woods and hearing Damien crying for help and then later seeing the board go up outside the house to announce the sale. I cried it all out then and there, years later in my front room. I poured out the grief and anguish, the feelings of being helpless and bereft.

When I opened my eyes and came back to the room, I felt exhausted and a bit shaky. Once I had regained my balance, I made my way into the kitchen for tea and toast and I gradually felt like all the scattered parts of me came back in to my body.

　After a second cup of tea I picked up my journal and turned to the next fresh page.

Stephanie's Journal - Lesson 2
Self-Sabotage

These are the parts of you that lie so deep within your soul, you may not know that they exist anymore. They are thoughts, experiences and events that you have covered over so that you don't have to process them or accept them as a part of you. Even though you cannot see these parts, they all carry an energy vibration and an influence on how you think, feel and behave. They work as attractors in your life and bring things and people to you that match them. So no matter what you are harbouring in your core, you cannot hide from their energy. In order to be free you need to release them with grace and love.

"It is not the mountain we conquer, but ourselves."
Sir Edmund Hillary

Chapter 10

I had an appointment with Hannah for 10:30am, I hoped she would be able to help me understand how energy worked in a more practical way, she had been learning for longer than me. She said that I was correct in my understanding, but that actually drawing what you wanted to you and not attracting what you don't want is where the practise starts. She talked about alignment and allowing— things I had read about but didn't understand yet.

Apparently you needed to get your energy into alignment with what you wanted and then release any resistance to it coming into your life. In other words 'allow'. It sounded easy but, based on what I had allowed in the past, I guessed that I could do with some practice.

We talked about divorce proceedings and she said that it would be quite straightforward. There were no assets really to split. No assets perhaps, but plenty of debt. It felt strange being so matter of fact about the way my marriage had ended. I could be practical when it came down to the paperwork, but it still hurt like nothing on earth when I thought of him with someone else.

Most of the debts we had taken on as a couple were stacked in my name, and really this was hard lines. Even though I could prove the money had been spent on him and myself in roughly equal measure it was a case of my name, my problem. Hannah said that she could try to create an argument that he should take on half of it, but it really would come down to being a goodwill gesture if he did. And from the tone of the Bulldog's correspondence to date, they seemed to be in short supply.

I knew the likelihood was that I was only going to get one more monthly salary before the pin was pulled on my career, and there was no way that I could do anything other than keep juggling.

I hadn't made any progress with the house and it looked like I had to be out imminently. It had been valued and there was no money in it really, the 10% deposit we had put down had now been swallowed up by the credit crunch and we were effectively in negative equity.

Hannah spoke to me about my options, which were not great. I could go bankrupt; this would be the easiest option and allow the repossession to go through. This may mean that Jay would go bankrupt also, depending on what else he owned in terms of assets and what he owed out in terms of debts. Or I could fight through the courts to allocate half of the credit card debt to Jay and I could try to come to an arrangement with the bank whereby I could pay the mortgage arrears off over a longer term and possibly keep the house. This would depend on me keeping my job of course, which was looking unlikely, and Jay signing over the mortgage to me and the bank approving all of this based on my salary and astronomical outgoings. I either needed a miracle or a reality check.

Bankrupt and homeless was looking likely. I cried and Hannah handed me tissues.

"You could look at this another way, you know," she said softly from across the desk. "By letting all of your old stuff go you will be making room for new and positive things to come into your life. I know it's hard, but perhaps this is part of the plan."

I knew she meant well, but that night I called Lizzie and left her a message. I wanted a second opinion. She called me back half an hour later and said that from her standpoint it was pointless fighting for anything. The bulldog would have a strong case for me keeping the debt in my name and I would stack up loads more costs if it went to court. The net result would be the same and I would be bankrupt anyway. Just get it over with, no point in pulling a band aid off slowly.

Time to face facts, my marriage was a band aid. A totally ineffective band aid that had done nothing to protect or heal the gaping raw wounded feelings that were now spurting everywhere.

She sounded a bit flat, she said she was just tired and had to go. Thanks friend!

Hannah said that the paperwork would take about a few weeks to draw up and she would start some tentative negotiations about how to divide the joint debts accrued. I tried to control my thoughts and feelings in the spirit of drawing good things to me, but it was hard and felt fake. My spiritual self was feeling a bit pissed off, if that's allowed.

The time was coming when I would have to tell my parents about what was going on. I kept dodging phone calls and sounding breezy when they did catch me— hopefully they did not suspect anything. I'd rather delay this until absolutely necessary. I could do without the "told you so" routine.

It was the last week of March when Hannah called me to say that negotiations were not great and that we needed to meet up. I made my way back into town on the bus again, feeling a bit low but trying to remain positive about the future once this was all done. I had learned about the power of positive affirmations and I was trying to use them to change my focus and ultimately change the course of my life.

I am happy and healthy, I have all I need. I was repeating in my head.

I could have done without anyone making small talk with me at this point, I just wanted to keep affirming and hold it together. When carrier bag lady got on the bus, I accidently made eye contact and thought *don't sit next to me*. It was as if she was magnetised to me with another charity shop bag, this time with some stuffed toys and what looked like tea towels.

"How are you, love?" she asked me.

Her well-meaning and kind voice was the catalyst for the floodgates to open and I was cross with myself for crying again in public. There was something about her that made me feel compelled to tell her my story, I felt like I knew her in some way but equally I had the anonymity of speaking to a stranger. Whatever the reason, she was easy to talk to and once I had started I saw no point in holding any of it back.

What was wrong with me? Pouring my heart out to some random person who showed the slightest bit of interest? It didn't occur to me at this point that I had really only given Hannah the full story, my so called friend Lizzie was in a complete lockdown, and I was lying to my parents through my teeth. I had been plastering over holes in my emotional dam for too long now, and the capacity was all at once too great to hold back anymore.

Of course she had another clean hanky to offer me and as I sniffed and snotted into it she listened and made comforting comments.

"I'm sorry for dumping all of this on you," I said. "It's been bottled up for such a long time and I just…"

"Oh don't you worry, it's my job to put people back together."

"Your job?" I looked at her again and felt ashamed with myself. I had presumed that the charity shop bags and travelling on the bus through the daytime meant that she was on the dole.

"Yes my job. I run a refuge in town for women who are down on their luck. You have to wear lots of different hats in my job—cook, cleaner, babysitter and of course friend and counsellor."

I was surprised and intrigued, and let her continue.

"I started the project about ten years ago now and it has grown and grown, from little acorns and all that! And now we have six self-contained units and they are always full. It's heart-breaking if I have to send someone away but, as my husband says, I can't save everyone."

I looked at the bag she was holding on her lap. "Is that for the refuge?"

"Yes, we had a woman arrive last night with two little ones and they had to leave quickly so couldn't bring any toys. All they need is a bit of a clean-up and they'll be fine."

"That's really kind of you," I said, feeling humbled.

"It's just what I am here to do," she replied. "I'm Josie"

"I'm Stephanie, well Steph."

"Well Steph, you are welcome anytime at Prospect House. We have an open door policy and plenty of tea and hugs." She stood to get off as the bus slowed down and I felt a bit sad that she was going so soon. "I mean that," she said, as she waved before stepping out onto the street.

And in that moment I felt that she did.

I signed all of the papers that Hannah had prepared for me and she suggested we went for lunch afterwards. She wanted to know how I was getting on with the books. Strange to think that I had found a friend in my divorce lawyer. I told her about the lady on the bus, synchronicity she called it.

"I bet she has a message for you," she said excitedly. "You saw her three times and that just cannot be a coincidence. You have to follow it up and go and see her!"

I said I would, but truly I didn't know when as I still had so much to sort out in my life before I went off making loads of new friends.

"Anyway, have you thought anymore about what you do want to happen next in your life? You have to know what you want in order to manifest it." Hannah took a slurp of her diet coke and continued. "You know how this works, we are magnetic and we attract what we focus on, but you have to know what you want in order to do that. Otherwise you just get a jumble of random bits and bobs that come into your life and screw it up!"

"That's the problem Hannah, I am so focussed on just getting through the jungle at the moment, I haven't got a clue what I want when I get out of the other side. I am really struggling with it. When I try to think about what I want, I just have no clarity at all."

Hannah could see my frustration. "To start with, the more you keep saying that you are struggling and you have no clarity, the more you will struggle and have no clarity…"

I laughed at the obvious irony here.

"Ok, I see that. But how do you start the process of knowing what you want when you don't know what you want?"

"You stop saying you don't know what you want!" She laughed with me now and continued; "You start affirming that you have clarity and insight into what you want to create. Make up something that works for you about moving forward and your perfect life blue print revealing itself or something. I don't know, it's got to be personal to you and feel right, but one thing is for sure – the more you keep telling yourself you are stuck and don't know what to do, the longer you will be stuck not knowing what to do!"

She was right, I hadn't given any thought to what I wanted to create for my future. So far I was just focussing on getting through each day as best I could. And I knew that if I didn't change my focus I'd be getting more of the same.

"Remember Steph, you attract what you are." And in that moment I remembered the lesson.

We finished up lunch and hugged each other genuinely.

"Life is a boomerang Steph. What you send out there comes back to you," Hannah shouted over her shoulder as we parted.

I reflected on this on the journey home and started to think of some affirmations that I could use to help me. I needed to align with the right energy to help me create a vision of my future. Before long I was repeating alternate statements silently to myself.

My life is filled with love, beauty and joy and I can see it clearly.

I easily connect with possibilities in order to create them.

I thought about Josie and the way that I had initially judged her as being not good enough to sit next to me on the bus. I sighed and my cheeks coloured slightly with shame. This was another part of me I had to let go of and stop sabotaging myself. My own arrogance could have stopped me from having the conversation with her about the refuge and her work. She was a modern day Mother Teresa by all accounts and all I had seen was a bus person with charity bags. Something told me that she would mean something in my life, she had already taught me to let go of judgement and arrogance.

By the time I got home I was feeling much better. Once I felt relaxed, I asked from my heart for help and guidance and suddenly a kind of knowing flooded through me and my heart opened. I stayed in this space for a while, observing the detail of the life that I wanted. Before I left it I got a strong feeling that I needed to write it all down.

Stephanie's Journal - Lesson 3
You Attract What You Are

I am learning that all I think and all I feel combine to create a magnetic field around me. This magnetic field draws things, experiences and people into my life, but the amazing thing is that they match my feelings and thoughts. So what I think is what I create in my life. I need to have the strength to take responsibility for what I have created so far and, moving forward, I can't blame the big bad world anymore!

"Be the heroine of your life, not the victim."
Nora Ephron

I thought for a moment and tapped the pen on my teeth, what was it that I truly wanted right now? I allowed my feelings to flow again, this time in the present tense so that I could truly align with what I wanted. I remembered something in one of the books I had read, saying that in order to attract what you want you have to see it like it's happening right now, not in the future. Otherwise it will always stay in the future. I closed my eyes and saw what I wanted, then wrote down the detail.

I live in peace and happiness, and inner peace. I love myself and my life. I am in a safe and comfortable room that to others might be basic, but to me has all that I need. It is uncluttered, clear and light. I am contributing to other people and helping them and this gives me great satisfaction and purpose. And I am in love and loved in a way that I never have felt before, it is genuine and heartfelt. I love myself and I love my life, it is now full of prospects I never thought possible.

That night I slept peacefully for the first time in a long while, and I dreamed of the room that I had written about. Someone had left flowers in there for me, and they stood in a clear square cut vase on the windowsill. Big blooms of lilac, and when I woke I was sure for a moment I could smell their sweet, heady scent.

Chapter 11

What you feel is what you get.

Now I had committed all of my hopes and desires to paper, they felt more possible, although the responsibility was a bit scary. I woke early and walked to the corner shop for a roll of bin bags, if I was going to let go of the past it was going to be literally as well as emotionally. The world was starting to feel like a different place to me, it was subtle and I was not sure I'd be able to explain it to anyone.

I was experiencing a weird kind of déjà vu sometimes, like I knew what was going to happen just a split second before it did. And I felt sometimes like I was not alone. When there was no one else around, I could feel a type of presence with me. It also felt like coincidences were happening all around me—strange serendipitous events and occurrences that had no rhyme or reason—and certainly no explanation.

As I walked back from the shop in the bright sun, my mind turned to the drama of the drink-driving episode. I just wanted it over, I knew it was going to be some kind of ban and probably a fine that I couldn't pay. The uncertainty made me feel unsettled and I needed to start getting closure on all of the open ended catastrophes in my life. Failed marriages and stuff like that.

I breathed in the air deeply and said in my mind; *I am moving on in my life, all is resolved for me, my path is clear.* I repeated this over and over as I walked towards home. I took a detour through the park and sat a while. I watched a mother and child in their own world for a moment and tried to stay present as the sun warmed my face and arms. *I am moving on in my life, all is resolved for me, my path is clear.*

The child's ball bounced in my direction and the mother walked over.

"What a beautiful day, the sky is so clear isn't it?"

"Not a cloud in the sky," I agreed, and that's the way I felt.

I stood up to leave and a council worker was unloading some gardening equipment from the back of a yellow truck. He was about to start working with a strimmer, cutting back some of the overgrown plants that spilled from the borders. He'd probably weed by hand when he'd cut back the thick of them. Daffodils and tulips sprouted up from planters, some were open and facing the sun, some were still buds.

"Lovely day," he smiled. "Not often you see such a clear blue sky."

I smiled back at him and inwardly too. It was working.

"Just making sure that the path is clear," he spoke as I walked past. If I had needed further confirmation, there it was.

I opened the front door and the postman had been. Junk, final demand and a letter about my court hearing next week. I called Hannah. She kept me calm and said that it would all be fine. She was sure I would get a minimum penalty and was making the case to support this and holding that intention. If we both kept believing there would be a positive outcome we could influence the situation. In the past I would have mocked this kind of thinking, but it seemed like more and more evidence was coming my way to show that this was in fact true. Hannah pointed out that intention was really important and I was not a person who would deliberately go out and drink drive on a regular basis, I was generally responsible and I had made one bad decision. It wasn't right but it wasn't the end of the world, and I had learned from it. I agreed whole-heartedly that there should be some payback for this and we were going to take it on the chin. It was important not to go into victim mode here and to have the faith that whatever was coming my way was fair and would help me to take responsibility for what had happened.

Just a few days of anguish then, just enough time to have a nervous breakdown. I heard my own voice in my head.

I observed these thoughts and then stopped myself. *What you think is what you get Steph, if you want anguish you'll get it so just keep telling yourself that.* I remembered a quote from somewhere or other that if you changed your thoughts you could change your life, so I decided to shift my focus.

I felt like I was another person watching myself in the movie of my life. Once I started to notice the thoughts and feelings that I was streaming through my mind and body in every moment, it was amazing at how many times a day I caught myself in doom and gloom thinking. And now I knew that each thought would trigger a frequency that would bring that experience to me. I was practising all of the time to stay in the present and not get into the drama that had been my old life.

All is well with the court case, it's all turning out for the best became my mantra. I even wrote it down and stuck it

up on the fridge door with a magnet. I grabbed the first
one and I had to laugh when it said 'Don't give up' with a
complimenting cute kitten illustration.

As the court case was now in the hands of the universe,
and Hannah, I decided could do something positive in
order to make progress towards moving day. I had chosen
to call it this rather than the repossession day—these two
words made me feel like a failure. And that was something
I did not want to attract into my life, so instead moving
day and moving on day were the feelings of choice.

I had exchanged a couple of brief text messages with
Jay. I wanted to limit contact as much as possible during
the withdrawal period. I had told him about the house and
he didn't seem surprised or bothered, and had a 'get rid'
attitude. He said he wanted to move on in his life. As
crushing as this was emotionally, I knew that it was right
and his attitude was helping me to keep going. In my
weaker moments I took myself back to the toilet in the
nightclub and reminded myself that I was worth far more
than he ever realised.

I started the marathon clear out, I knew that I would
have to leave soon—God knows where to. One thing was
for sure, with no car and limited funds I needed to travel
light.

Armed with my roll of bin bags I started with the loft.
Two hours later, thirsty and covered in dust and cobwebs,
I climbed back down the ladder to survey the scene. The
loft was empty, but there were boxes, bags and piles of
stuff all over the landing and spare bedroom. I hardly
knew where to start.

"I find it easy to clear out what I no longer need," I said over and over. I went downstairs for the radio from the kitchen and made a cuppa before returning to rake through my life in bin bags.

The radio playlist made me laugh as I said my affirmations out loud with meaning and the following songs filled my ears—*Go Your Own Way* by *Fleetwood Mac* and *Toxic* by *Brittany Spears*.

I allocated the master bedroom to things I wanted to keep, the study to charity and the bathroom to junk. I decided that I wasn't going to give myself the time to dither, so I would pick something up and put it in the appropriate place. I'd be done in no time.

I hadn't realised though that the first bag would be my wedding dress. I pulled it out of the bag and fluffed it up. It cast tiny rainbows on the walls thanks to the hundreds of *Swarovski* crystals on the bodice. The lace detail on the train was stunning and I remembered holding it in my hand as we danced for the first time as Mr & Mrs I didn't cry, but I could have, and it took me a moment to stand up and allocate it, but it didn't seem to fit anywhere. I didn't want to keep it, or give it away, or throw it out, it had cost a fortune.

I sighed and closed my eyes. What on earth could I do that would feel right? As I started to consider the options, *New Jerusalem* by *Carly Simon* started on the radio and I paused. An inspired idea flashed through my mind, an idea that would help me in more ways than one.

eBay!

I could list all of the stuff I didn't need and couldn't take with me and make some money at the same time! I was a genius.

The rest of the day was spent clicking a digital camera and organising things into new piles, categories that suit *eBay's* listing framework such as *household, women's clothes, accessories* and *miscellaneous*. It would take me a couple of days to list everything, but that didn't matter it was a good distraction and I needed the money.

The first item I listed was the wedding dress, I took several photos from different angles and wrote a show-stopping description. I had looked at other listings and it seemed that the average price for a wedding dress was going to be about £200. Many listings showed pictures of blushing brides and stories of people emigrating or clearing out because they had started a family. I could hardly write a love story about this dress— *'Cursed Wedding Dress for sale, guaranteed to bring you bad luck and end your relationship within months, don't let it get away—this dress is a real spoiler!'* I laughed out loud and finished the listing for real.

'Fabulous designer wedding dress by Lynn Harvey, size 14–16, only worn once and has been dry cleaned beautifully. Size 6 ivory satin shoes and matching veil available by separate negotiation. Cost £2,100 when new, willing to take whatever the universe feels is right for me for this item.'

I clicked the complete button and started the auction at 99p, whilst affirming "I am receiving what is right for me right now." Before *eBay* allowed me to go live, I was asked if I wanted to donate a percentage of the sale price to charity. I stopped and paused, now this was interesting. I felt torn between my own crisis and needing the money badly, and my new way of thinking. I knew that if I could give something away it would be with the energy that I had more than enough, which was creating a conflict right now as I felt poor and far from wanting to give away the little that I had. However if I could get into this energy of having more than enough, then this is what I would attract. So by giving it away and being in a good place about doing this, I would be opening myself up to receive more. This felt fine in theory but wobbly in practice and it took me a few minutes and a cuppa to decide what to do here.

"It's time to walk your talk Steph," I said out loud and the decision was made.

Within two more clicks I had agreed to donate 50 percent of proceeds to charity.

eBay then asked me which charity I wanted to support and gave me the option of searching by category or postcode. I typed in the first letters of my postcode and the charities within the area were listed. One stood out to me straight away—*Women in Crisis*. If I could help someone else like me or in a worse position, that would be worth getting rid of my wedding dress for. It was then I noticed the full profile of the charity and recognised that it was based at Prospect House! So I could help Josie into the bargain. Perfect.

I finalised the listing and went on to complete the rest of the clothes and some household items. The rest would have to wait for tomorrow as I was tired and hungry. Just before I shut down my computer I checked my *eBay*. I was shocked to see that the wedding dress already had bids and was up to £37 with eight people watching it! I also had an email from an interested party asking if I would take an offer privately outside of *eBay*. I replied that I would consider it, and were they interested in the shoes and veil as well.

Yes they were and would I accept £200 for the lot, they could collect. I didn't quite know what to do so I went back to my *eBay* and the dress was up to £59. What was going on? I didn't want to be hasty so I didn't reply to the email enquiry, but by the time I'd had poached eggs on toast I had another email from someone else offering £250.

This was crazy. I *googled* 'Lynn Harvey Wedding Dress' and I was astonished at the results that came back. It turned out that this was a real life rags to riches story. One month after my wedding, Lynn had been commissioned to make a dress for the one of the younger Royals that I hadn't heard of but Her Royal Horsiness had done her the favour of her career. She now had a waiting list and was working by taking commissions only. You couldn't get hold of one of her creations for the next two years!

I felt giddy!

I decided to let the auction run and politely responded to the other enquirers that I was worried about breaking *eBay*'s rules and getting bad feedback. I stayed up really late and by the time 1am came around the dress was up to £812 with 27 people watching. I went to bed and tried to sleep but got up again at just after 2am to check again. Who would have thought it could be so exciting? The different time zones around the world meant that there was always someone up bidding and I was delighted to see that I now had someone in Australia offering me £1100!

I couldn't believe that this was happening, but I realised I needed to believe it in order to stay in that energy and keep attracting more and more. I started to tell myself that the dress was selling for the most possible profit. I kept affirming this and eventually felt tired enough to sleep.

When I woke up I couldn't wait to check my computer. The current bid was £1742! I scanned my other items and I had 99p bids on a couple of t-shirts and a coffee machine but nothing else. I photographed the sofas, washing machine, tumble dryer and kitchen table. I was in a place where I was ready to let go and move on, I knew I couldn't receive what I needed until I could release what I didn't. Curtains and cushions came next along with bedding and the ironing board. Even though the items hadn't gone yet, the intention of letting go made me feel really good.

I was all '*eBay*ed' out and decided that staring at the screen would eventually give me a headache and not influence the outcome. I pulled on my trainers and walked out into the sun. I bought drink at the corner shop and went back to the park, which was now empty. I sat on one of the swings, it had been flung over the cross bar during the night and the chains were shorter so my legs dangled. I leaned back and stretched out my legs. I moved slightly. I was soon flying high, giggling to myself and letting the wind blow through my hair. I couldn't remember the last time I felt so free and I knew that all good things would be coming to me.

I stopped at the chip shop on the way home and bought a bag of chips with salt and vinegar. They were raising money for a local school and I put a pound in the box while I was waiting. I gave the man behind the counter a ten pound note and he gave me my change as he was chatting to someone on the phone about napkins and wooden forks. He gave me £18.50 change.

A moral dilemma moment crept up on me. The old me (also the skint me) wanted to say "thanks" and walk away. However the new me (also the wise me) knew that this energy would send out signals of scarcity. He was on the phone for another minute or so and I waited patiently, arguing with myself that this was the right thing to do.

When he looked at me and said, "Yes love?" I told him the truth. He looked at me completely dumbfounded. It turned out that he was actually the owner of the shop and he did a shift at each one of his seven shops once in a while to 'keep his hand in' and so that the employees did not think he was up himself. He had been in the business for 18 years and he had never had anyone be honest in these circumstances.

I felt a bit embarrassed, it was only a tenner and really it was no big deal.

But to him it was a big deal and he thanked me profusely and told me to keep the money. I hardly knew what to say! I knew that it was important to receive and not create resistance when good things came your way and that this was a representation of how far I had come. I smiled and thanked him, then thanked the universe as well.

Those chips were the best I'd ever had.

The wedding dress was nearly at £2000, but there was still one day left and with nearly 30 people watching now there could be a last minute bidding war.

Hannah called me to see that I was prepared for my court hearing. She coached me for a couple of minutes on my defence and commented that I was in a good place. This was my cue to tell her all about the day I'd had and how my affirmations were helping me hugely to attract what I wanted.

"It's amazing how fast this works," I said in an animated voice.

"I know," she replied. "Truly amazing. You had better be careful what you wish for, lady, you are obviously in the zone!"

We made the final arrangements to meet up next week, half an hour before the court hearing. I also told her I would send a text when I knew what the final figure was on the wedding dress.

I did some more clearing out and sorting before bed, all with the intention of letting the old go to make room for the positive, new exciting life I was creating.

I could hardly contain myself as I watched the last half an hour of the live auction. The price on the wedding dress had been going up steadily all morning by a few pounds here and a few pounds there, but this was the big one now—serious '*eBay*ers' left their bid until the last minute or even the last thirty seconds in a kind of gazumping frenzy. I felt like a Cullen in an abattoir, I was bursting with excitement!

Ping, you have email.

I screamed and jumped up and down in the kitchen in front of my laptop, who would have ever thought that the dress would realise £6789! I called Hannah straight away and whooped down the phone to her, she could not believe it either.

"You have to celebrate!" she said.

"You know what, I think I might."

I knew I had some money in my purse, my profit from the chip shop. I went to the corner shop again, where I was becoming a regular since no car meant the big shop was off for now. I bought a bottle of cheap cava, brown paper and a roll of sticky tape and I still had a tenner left. I started walking home in a great mood. Ready to start packaging up my life and posting it around the world.

The wedding dress was being collected, they would email to make arrangements.

Three doors down from the corner shop was a sandwich board on the pavement, announcing that the hair salon had a trainee in post and was looking for 'models' for a cut and restyle for ten pounds. I glanced over to the window and saw two girls chatting with cups of tea. My hair reflected back to me through the window, I looked a lot less Marilyn and a lot more Myra now the roots had grown in.

It wasn't exactly *Toni & Guy* but it was cheap and it was time to let go of the old, and a half done, grown out, brassy barnet was certainly old. I had no idea what I wanted when I walked in and they both looked me up and down. My corner shop carrier bags and roots at least an inch long made it pretty obvious that I had come in for the 'special offer'. I had to stifle a giggle when I put the bags down and the wine bottle clanked on the floor. They exchanged glances that meant 'drinker'.

"Hi there, I was wondering if you could fit me in for the restyle for ten pounds please?"

The oldest girl quickly clicked into professional mode and opened the diary. It was painfully obvious that there were no appointments booked in all day, but she shuffled and turned pages for a moment before coming back to today's date.

"Actually, Shania can fit you in now if you have time."
Man I feel like a woman.

They took my coat and offered me a coffee, sat me in the chair for a 'consultation', which really meant Shania taking my bobble out and finger-combing my shredded wheat hair over my shoulders to expose even more hideous roots and try not to look at me with disdain. Her hair was in a trendy geometric bob, layered and flicked to perfection.

"What type of thing do you want today then?" she asked, in a tone that was meant to manage my expectations. A combination of my lack of maintenance and her lack of skill might end up in a scare cut, we both knew it.

I really wasn't sure so she tottered off on shoes that were back-breakingly high and totally unsuitable for the tiled floor and came back armed with a stack of magazines.

I flicked through pictures of celebrities and catwalk models, long, short and mid-length.

Shania tried to be helpful with the odd comment about colouring and framing my face etc, continuing to fuss about and fan my grown out fringe over to one side. This was quickly dismissed as it made me look like I had arrived with a carer.

I turned the page and then I saw it.

"That's it," I said with conviction and Shania did a double take.

"Well it's drastic," she said, "but it would really suit you if you want a complete change."

"I do, that is exactly what I want, a complete change."

About an hour later and after much snipping and drying I emerged looking like a different person. All around my feet were long strands of bleach blonde hair that would be swept up and put out with the rest of the rubbish at the end of the day.

I was back to my natural colour, a deep brown, cut really short and funky, which felt like me again. I now had nothing to hide behind.

I made my way home feeling like a weight had been lifted and that several layers of bullshit had dissolved as well.

The rest of the 48 items that I had sold all needed to be packaged and posted. I put the radio on to help the time pass and opened my cava with a celebratory 'pop'.

Three parcels in and I really wanted someone to share my victory with, so I rang Lizzie on her mobile. It went straight to voicemail again and I wondered if she was ok. I wrapped parcels four, five and six and couldn't settle, so I rang her office.

"Tucker and Blacketts, can I help you?" I had met the receptionist, Stacey, once at a Christmas Party. I think it was the one after the Dan incident and Lizzie didn't want to go on her own.

"Hi Stacey, it's Lizzie's friend, Steph. We met ages ago at a Christmas party. I think I gave you my spare pair of tights in the loos."

Short pause whilst she placed me. "Hi, Steph! Yes I remember—Natural Bamboo what a life saver! How are you?"

"I'm good thanks, I was just trying to get Lizzie. I've tried her mobile loads of times and I just keep getting voicemail. I just wanted to know she was ok."

"She's not here Steph. She's gone on holiday with the bloke she's been seeing, it was a last minute thing. I think they've been having some problems between you and me. I haven't met him but I have overhead her speaking on the phone a couple of times and I think he might be married."

"Oh, no." Poor, poor, lovely Lizzie.

Not again. No wonder she couldn't take on my problems as well. It sounded like she had her own going on.

"Mm, I know. She should be back in about two weeks but they have said that if she needs to extend it just to ring. I can leave a note on her desk to say you called."

It was so out of character for Lizzie to just take off like that, especially for a fortnight when she was apparently up to her neck in it at work. My intuition was telling me that something was wrong. I was concerned about her to say the least. And to not have her Blackberry on was bizarre. She was glued to it any other time.

"Thanks Stacey, I'll ring in a couple of weeks then."

"OK Steph, take care."

"You too." I hung up feeling uneasy.

I went back to my parcelling and packaging, idly thinking how great it would be if we could use sticky tape

to mend our lives back together again when things went
wrong.

I had time to do one post office run before they closed,
and I might have to do two more in the morning. It was
really hard without a car but I managed with two big
carrier bags and a backpack. Luckily I had given up on
being worried about what the neighbours might think…
finally!

Stephanie's Journal - Lesson 4
Release What Does Not Serve You

Cluttering any aspect of your life up with old stuff stops
the flow of new, positive energy coming your way.
When you hang on to the old this is usually through
fear, and this fear can take many different forms. It can
be a fear of moving on, a fear or not having enough in
the future, or even a fear of being successful sometimes.
This keeps you stuck.

Old and stuck energy can take the form of actual
physical things like clutter, junk or old clothes, or it can
be more subtle such as thoughts, patterns and
behaviours. Whatever it is in your life, we need to let go
of the old to make room for the new.

Ask yourself 'does this serve me right now?' and if the
answer is no, find a way to let go.

"Change is the essence of life. Be willing to surrender
what you are for what you could become."
Mahatma Gandhi

Chapter 12

The day of the court case crept up on me and I suddenly felt scared and unprepared. I had done a pretty good job of staying in the present and not worrying and fretting about today—until today that is. I wondered now if the distraction had been worth it or if I should have given more time and thought to what I was going to say. In reality I was going to tell the truth and give an account of events as I saw them, so really I suppose there was nothing to prepare.

Although the weather was quite warm now, I dressed in a black suit. I probably looked like I was going to a funeral. It was a permanent goodbye of sorts—goodbye to my career in sales. There was little chance I would ever be offered another position with a driving ban on my record. But I had created this myself and needed to get on with it.

The court building was intimidating. They scanned me with one of those metal sticks they have at airports. The kind that shrieks at your belt buckle or knee replacement and makes everyone stare at you whilst you feel like you are in the 'accused spotlight'. Then you have to find out where you need to be and get there. There are different floors and rooms. This sounds easy but when you feel like your arse is going to explode with nerves, and you have to find a toilet quickly en route, believe me it's not. Especially when there is a queue in the toilet and you have to wait, and then when it's (eventually) your turn you know that the other queuing people are standing just inches away from your farting and purging. I opted to stay in there a few minutes, post flush, hoping that the smell would clear a bit and the queue would have gone down and I might be able to come out without people knowing I was 'The One'.

Public dumping has always been a traumatic thing for me. I'd rather be uncomfortable all day at work and wait until I got home to my own throne or drive bloody miles out of my way to nip back for a daytime poo. There's another pattern I need to get over then, whilst I'm on letting go of all of my shit, maybe I should try and make that more literal. I managed a chuckle at how silly I was, hiding in the loos, and I slid the lock along and opened the door.

There were a couple of distasteful looks and a child visibly gagging (whose mum was saying "stop being silly, we all have to go") as I walked to the wash basin with a cloud of stink following me.

"Sorry, I've got IBS," I lied, as my face turned bright red and started to wash my hands.

I am washing my hands of all of the shit in my life, I laughed to myself. *It's all going down the plug hole.*

Where have you been?" said Hannah when I joined her in the communal holding area "You just disappeared when we got through the doors."

I told her and we both stifled our laughter as we waited for me to be called.

A six month ban and a fine, as well as points on my licence were incurred. Hannah said I got off lightly, if the judge had wanted to make an example of me then it could have been worse. I'd been dished out what was fair and in line with a stupid and irresponsible decision, but not hauled over the coals. I could pay the fine thanks to me

recent *eBay* endeavours but my career was headed down
the pan, along with what I had left in the ladies.

Hannah tried to jolly me along. "Come on, it could have
been so much worse, really you got off lightly."

"I know, I know. I just feel like I have let myself down,"
I said. The whole embarrassing incident rehashed had not
done wonders for my feel good factor. I knew there had to
be a payback for what I had done, like all things in life
and I needed to take responsibility for what I was creating,
but that doesn't mean it didn't make me feel like a moron.

Hannah drove me home and I promised that I would
snap out of it soon, and she said I was allowed one day off
being Pollyanna, but that she'd ring in later on.

I knew I would have contact Brian and let him know the
outcome. I opted for an email instead of phoning. He
replied within the hour from his blackberry saying that he
was sorry but that due to the zero tolerance company
policy and the fact that there was a clause in the fleet
insurance that would not cover me, the company would
have to let me go. I knew this would be the case, but to
see it in front of me was really hard. He also wrote that
because of my exceptional performance whilst I had been
with the company he had managed to persuade them to
give me a bonus in my final month's salary, even though I
hadn't been out on the road these last weeks generating
sales, my territory had come in on target and the bonus
was rightfully mine.

I felt really touched by his generosity and kindness. I
was grateful there were people in my life who were trying
to help me, and that I was in a place to receive.

Six months wasn't that long anyway, when I looked
back at how fast the last few weeks had gone I couldn't
believe how much had happened in a short time. It was
now nearly August.

I thought I'd cheer myself up by looking at my account
balance, all of my *eBay* listings had finished now. In total
I had made £7996, that meant that after fees there was
£3678 for me and the same for Prospect House.

I hadn't felt so proud of myself in years. I so wanted to
tell Josie about it, but there was also a part of me that
wanted to retain a dignified air of silence. I didn't want to
end up being egotistical about giving to charity, I'd seen
that before and thought it really bad taste. I was hardly
The Secret Millionaire.

It was a week of endings for me, and hopefully
beginnings too. The buyer that was collecting the larger
items like the washer, sofas and dining room suite was
coming the day after tomorrow. She had sent a text asking
if mid-morning was ok, she couldn't give an exact time as
they were travelling up the country and it would depend
on traffic. So that would be goodbye to my furniture and
shortly after that it would be goodbye to my house, and
my credit score.

I still didn't know where I would end up. I kept holding
the vision of a peaceful and happy life in a clear and
loving environment. The more often I allowed myself to
relax into the visualisation, the more detail came forward
for me, and I was continuing to dream about the place too.
I had started to keep a piece of paper next to the bed and I
noted down the changes I noticed each time I went to 'my
room'. There was a small, clear faceted crystal hanging on

a clear filament at the window that caught and fragmented the sunlight into rainbows around the room. The bedding was white, but there was a thick, cream, bobbly woollen blanket that was used as a throw across the bottom of the bed. There was a watercolour on the wall that looked part abstract, but not, like a human and angel combined with blurred edges and what looked like wings unfolding in beautiful pastel colours. There was a small purple glass candle holder next to the lilac on the windowsill, although I did think that this was a detail that I had imagined as I had found exactly this item when I was clearing out the loft. It didn't make it to my *eBay* pile as it reminded me of the last family holiday I'd had with my parents, years ago now and before I met Jay. I did know for sure that the place I kept seeing in my mind's eye was certainly not my parent's house, which was very much my plan B. I definitely would not like to go back 'home' labelled one of life's failures. I knew my parents would be supportive about my circumstances, and perhaps quite pleased as they never did like Jay, but I was holding out hope that the right place for me was on the way. I could only put up with so much of the 'poor you' routine with tea and sympathy now. In truth I knew I was creating it all anyway by what I was putting out there.

There were a few things that had not sold on *eBay*, which I parcelled up in a charity bag that I was to leave out on the step for the morning. As I tied a knot in the top I noticed that it said 'No Shoes, No Bric-a-Brac, No Books' on the side. I couldn't believe how fussy they were when people were prepared to give things away for free!

And there was nothing wrong with the two pairs of trainers, table lamp, handbag and tea towels in there.

That's it! I thought. I knew who would want the tea towels and the whole lot probably. My first visit to Prospect House was overdue.

Chapter 13

I hoped Josie would be there when I arrived, otherwise I
might feel a bit silly. It was typical that she didn't find me
on the bus like any other day! I got off at the same stop I
had seen her get off at, and walked the few short steps to
the old building I'd seen her enter. There was a small
plaque on the wall that was tarnished and looked really
old. 'Prospect House' it said, and there was a buzzer
underneath with a number pad for people that knew the
entry code.

I buzzed and waited.

"Hello?"

"Oh yeah, Hi…I'm here to see Josie please."

"Who is it?"

"It's Steph. Steph from the bus."

Long pause, then a buzzing noise which I thought meant
'come in' so I pushed the door.

There was a little entrance hall inside with a letter rack
on one side and numbers one to six, a couple of seats and
a coffee table with some fresh flowers in a vase. The floor
was stripped floor boards and the décor was neutral, with
bright and cheery abstract prints framed tastefully on one
wall. There was a coat rack with a couple of jackets and a
black hoody strewn over it, and a door with a small sign
saying 'WC'. I heard footsteps and another door marked
'Private' opened and Josie's familiar face appeared.

"Steph, it's lovely to see you!" Before I could say hello
back, her arms were around me and hugging me tight. She
noticed the bag I had with me. "Clearing out?"

"Yes, and I thought...well if you didn't mind...that I would give them to...well donate them to you and you could find good homes..."

"We never refuse anything here! Thank you so much for thinking of us, whatever we can't use or pass on 'in house' if you know what I mean, gets sold to raise funds."

"That sounds great." I turned to go as she picked up the bag.

"Don't you want the tour?" Josie asked. "If you've got things to do then another time, but you know, since you're here..."

I didn't really have anywhere to go and I would be really glad of the company, it would be a good distraction for me to be able to chat and find out about someone else for a change.

Josie started with the ground floor, which consisted of the office, communal kitchen, front room, quiet room, playroom, toilet and way to the outside. At the back of the building there was a beautiful decked area with plants and trees in pots, wooden garden furniture and a sand pit. I also noticed there was a bench near the high perimeter wall and a sign that said 'Smoking Area'. It was a sun trap, a bit like my back garden. My senses filled with familiar sounds of buzzing bees, warm sun and heady scents. I couldn't put my finger on it but a sense of déjà vu was coming my way again, and I knew that this was meant to be happening right now. Maybe it was the smell of the lilac blossoms that kept me drifting back to my dream of the place I was wishing for.

Each floor had two self-contained units, making six in total.

Most were being used but there was one on the top floor
that had just become vacant yesterday. As we walked up
there, I noticed the whole feel of the place was one of
support and encouragement. Although all of the units were
in use, it wasn't noisy, but there was sound on one floor
that I knew was chatting and laughing, and on the next
floor I heard someone singing along to music from the
radio. What the place lacked in grandeur it certainly made
up for in spirit. I looked past the flaking paint and shabby
curtains and instead opened my heart to the intention that
vibrated through this building. There was a pulse running
through it of life and love, and anyone passing through
here would be given the time, space and dignity to find
themselves again and reclaim their own inner beauty and
self-realisations.

A door opened and a care worn face appeared on the
landing.

"Hi Josie," she spoke and, as she smiled, her mouth
looked slightly crooked on one side. "I'm going down to
the shops, do we need anything?"

"Hi Sarah, you could get some tea bags if you don't
mind. Just get the money from the petty cash tin please.
How's things?" Josie enquired.

"I'm getting there thanks," Sarah replied with
enthusiasm. She looked at me. "Are you new?"

"Oh, erm, no, I'm just looking round." I floundered a
bit. I wasn't really sure why I was here myself, apart from
dropping the bag off and that had been done.

Josie rescued me. "Sarah has been with us for a few
weeks now, and she is making great progress."

This was Sarah's cue to tell me more.

"This place saved me. I can never, ever repay you Josie, you really saved me." I saw tears sparkle in her eyes.

"You saved yourself, Sarah, it's been our privilege to support you through that," Josie elegantly corrected her and hugged her at the same time.

Sarah told me a bit of her story and the abuse she had suffered for years before she had finally decided that she could no longer live that way. She spoke of the trigger moment that had changed her life—the event that had finally made her see sense and leave. That moment seemed almost insignificant compared to the endless control, criticisms and beatings that she had endured, but it was the final straw.

Her husband had come in drunk one night and the cat had followed him and was weaving in and out of his legs hoping to be fed. Her cat. The cat she'd had for eighteen years who was nearly blind and a bit skinny these days. Sarah had heard him come in and warily made her way downstairs, as was the routine to make him a sandwich. She just wanted to get it over with and get back to bed as fast as possible, in case he was in a bad mood and she copped for it again. She had her back turned and her head in the fridge looking for the cooked ham when she heard the dull thud of his boot and the agonising cry of the cat as she was propelled across the room and her head collided with the plinth that ran under the sink unit.

"Stupid bloody thing," he had muttered, as he staggered into the front room and passed out in the armchair.

The cat was warm, limp and dead when Sarah picked her up. She cuddled her in close and spoke softly to her about how very, very sorry she was and that she had always loved her. Her tears fell steadily as she wrapped the grey and white fluffy body in some clean tea towels. She went upstairs, listening nervously for a break in his snoring, which thankfully never came and found a pillow case to put the cat into.

Sarah then quickly pulled out a suitcase from under the spare bed and started to fill it with the essentials. Amongst her clothes were her toothbrush, a few other toiletries, some photos of her son who had emigrated to Australia years ago with his gay partner (this is when she had been hospitalised and her face was scarred from the kicking), as well as the pass book for their joint savings account.

She had zipped up her coat and tucked the pillowcase under her arm, then carefully, using her key in the lock to ensure no unnecessary noise, she pulled the front door shut behind her. Sarah told me that she had then posted the key back through the letter box and before it hit the mat she was running down the street.

And that was just a few weeks ago. Josie had buried the cat in a large planter in the back garden and bought a special rose bush in memory of the much loved pet.

"I just sit there sometimes and reflect. The beautiful smell of the flowers seems to bring back the happier memories from my life, way before Dave was depressed and changed into a bully," Sarah said.

"It's magical here, you know. It's like everything falls into place once you arrive," she concluded and zipped up her coat—the one she left in I presumed.

Josie smiled as Sarah's footsteps made their way down the stairs.

"She's right you know, it is a magical place. The right people always turn up at the right time here, I can't really explain it, it just happens." She shrugged. "Like the way a sun catcher in a window can split the light into rainbows, allowing you to see the individual colours that were hidden in the light. This place unveils the beauty in everyone that comes here. It's always been there but they just haven't seen it for themselves yet."

I agreed. I felt a bit strange that people kept referring to aspects of my dream, but I guess that is the way the law of attraction works—you draw to you what you have been focussing on.

We carried on up one more flight of stairs and there were two doors on this level. As Josie turned the keys over in her hand, all on a large metal loop, she explained that these two rooms were a bit bigger but to be careful of the angle of the roof and the head height. These two rooms were nicknamed 'peace' and 'serenity' by everyone as they were away from the general everyday comings and goings of the place. I smiled to myself, the universe was definitely matching what I was sending out.

Josie opened the door to the top floor room so that I could see one of the units. As she turned the key in the lock time seemed to stand still and her voice trailed away. I knew what was going to be behind the door as it opened, and the vision that I had been holding for my perfect space unfolded in front of me. I walked into the room and didn't know what to say as I looked at the clean white bed linen, with the fluffy blanket on top. The chest of drawers, reading lamp and laundry basket - all as I had imagined. There was a pastel water colour painting on the wall, a bit abstract but it looked like a girl with wings. The smell of lilac filled the room as the sun shone on the blossom that had been picked from the garden and placed in a vase. Rainbows danced on the walls from the sun catcher at the window.

I literally caught my breath and looked again and again around the room. I couldn't believe that this was the place I had been dreaming of. There was a skylight as well as the dormer window that overlooked the busy street. The room was just so light and airy. The en-suite shower room was perfect and the small kitchenette included microwave, fridge and a kettle. I walked around in a daze and Josie broke the spell by asking; "Are you ok, Steph? What do you think?"

"You are not going to believe this," I replied. "You will think I have lost the plot."

"Try me," said Josie, with a twinkle in her eye, and she looked younger for a second.

"I have seen this place before." My tone said I was telling the truth and my face said that I was bracing myself for her rejection.

"I don't remember you ever coming here, I'm so sorry if I didn't recognise you…" Josie started to apologise.

"No, you don't understand. I've seen it before, I've never been here, but I have seen it in detail in a dream I keep having. It's exactly the same. You must think I'm crazy." I felt excited and bewildered at the same time, and I became aware that I was talking quickly and becoming more animated.

"Even the sun catcher and the lilac, the picture and the fluffy blanket—I saw all of this before I saw it, if you get what I mean."

I was rapidly joining the dots in my mind as I stood there. I just knew that this room, this place was where I needed to be, but how could I say that? It's for someone in crisis with nowhere else to go and I would be a fraud if I took it. I had my plan B and now a plan C since Hannah told me I could sleep on her sofa for a while.

"Well, Steph, I don't believe in co-incidences. Ever since I managed to get out of a marriage that was failing in so many ways and created this place, I have always had faith that the right people come here at the right time. Maybe it's the right time for you to be here?"

I turned around to take in all of the detail again and she continued to speak. "I had an inkling when we first met, but once I heard your full story I just knew that there was something I could do to help you and that you could help me." She hugged me again. "I mean three times on the bus?" and now she laughed and held me at arm's length, "That has to be a sign!"

We laughed together and it felt really good.

"But I would be taking the room from someone who really needs it," I objected.

"According to what you have told me, you do really need it," said Josie.

"Actually I do," I said and smiled at her in gratitude.

We drank cups of tea and chatted about things—my life, her life and Prospect House. It turned out there was plenty I could do to contribute to both the project and the other people here in exchange for the room for a while, and that made me feel good. There was a real culture here of people drawing on their skills and talents and swapping with each other, or using them to raise funds for the project. There was a resident at the moment who was a hairdresser and she traded with people regularly, as did the lady who used to work in an alterations department of a men's clothing store if anyone needed repairs. Someone was always pottering in the garden or the kitchen, or occupying children if need be.

Josie told me that the project had been under threat for a couple of years now due to a possible redevelopment of the site and, although these plans had been dormant for some time, there was a renewed interest in them recently and talk that this project would have to relocate. She seemed positive and upbeat that there would be some resolution to the pending crisis, but I could feel an undercurrent of concern.

Maybe this was something I could help with, I knew for sure I could help with fundraising after my recent *eBay* extravaganza and maybe Hannah could help with any legal advice. Josie hadn't mentioned the *eBay* donation and I thought better of it, but I did feel more comfortable about taking her hospitality when I knew I had in some way paid it forward.

We talked some more and then loosely made plans for me to come back in a few days' time - this time as a resident and not just a visitor.

Stephanie's Journal - Lesson 5
You are a Creator

Today I have had unequivocal confirmation that the laws of attraction work. I know now that when you are prepared to release your old stuff and align with what you want, that you can use your energy and intention to create what you want. You are the director of your life and when you are prepared to integrate this belief into your life and live it, amazing things can happen.

If you want to change or create something in your life, it is no good being a victim and blaming the whole world, the buck stops with you and you have to make the change within you that you want to see around you.

Change your energy to draw to you what you want. This is real life magic!

"Every thought leads to either love or fear."
A Course in Miracles

Chapter 14

I made my way to the bus stop and passed *The Citizens Advice Bureau*. I remembered the carrier bag full of financial nonsense that I had shoved to the back of the wardrobe, promising myself that I would get round to sorting it out after my visit there. I had made so many excuses not to look in this envelope nest so far, and none of them stood up now. I had to take some parcels to the post office, but even two runs would take less than an hour. I didn't want to drag all of this unsorted fear-based energy and chaos into my new life. There was nothing for it, I just had to get over myself and start sorting it out.

As soon as I got home I started to gather up parcels in the two large bags and reloaded the backpack for the '*eBay* run' as I now called it for my own amusement. I was up and down in 20 minutes and only had to take one bag and the backpack on the final trip. I bought a sandwich to eat on the way back so that I didn't procrastinate even more by faffing round making something.

I settled in the front room with a hole punch, cardboard dividers, a lever arch file, a biro and a bin bag. I turned the radio on and it was Abba Hour—*Money, Money, Money*—of course, what else!

Once I got going, the process was easier and faster than I thought it would be. There was some junk mail in there and a copy of the free paper, which went straight in the bin bag and there were marketing letters from credit card people wanting you to open up with them and consider a balance transfer. Once I had whittled the pile down to what was actually relevant, I was surprised to see that what I was left with was only about a quarter of what I had started with. Phase one complete.

Phase two was sorting into piles of what was what. This was quite easy as I just focussed on the logo and letterhead and not content of each letter. Shortly I had eight piles in front of me, seven for each category / lender and one for miscellaneous. Phase two complete.

I then set about sorting through each pile and realised that I was keeping so much of the same information it was silly. I didn't need every single credit card statement that I had ever received in my life, I only needed the most recent and up to date ones to see how awful the situation was. I scrapped the back statements apart from the last three months for each credit card and I started to write on the buff coloured tabs of the dividers.

I added up roughly all of the total amounts owed and then did a separate calculation for minimum monthly payments. It wasn't a pretty picture. Not including the loan there was £14,320 in credit card debt that was going to cost £698 per month just to stand still. The loan repayment pushed this up to £1048.

There was no way I could possibly make all of these payments now that I had no job. It looked like I was going to have to go bankrupt after all. I caught myself thinking this way and, as fake as it felt, I changed the dialogue in my head. *I am financially solvent, money is coming to me easily,* became my mantra for the next five minutes as I closed my eyes and said it over and over. I opened my laptop to start a spread sheet. If getting organised was the key then it starts here. Once I had logged everything, maybe I could speak to someone about a consolidation load or something—they were always advertising on the television.

My attention wandered and I idly typed 'Debt' into the search bar.

Loads of adverts popped up from debt management companies, and I scrolled down two pages looking for any information I could. I realised my search was too wide and I started to type into the search box—*joint debt, allocation and divorce.* Before I pressed 'go', a one liner caught my eye at the bottom of page two that my initial search had thrown up, *Karmic Debt.* I clicked the link and the article opened up.

Karma is about cause and effect. In basic terms whatever intentions you put out into the world will come back to you at some time as a lesson. This return of energy or exchange may not be from the same person or situation, but the essence will be the same. This could happen at any time in your current life or your next incarnation.

I thought about that for a moment.

The intention and energy that you put out there, in other words what you did to other people, would in some way be returned to you. Is that what had triggered all of the recent pandemonium in my own life? I remembered that Sue had spoken of an agreement, a catalyst for change, and that this was meant to happen on my birthday. But what was the essence of what I was learning?

I scrolled down.

In order to overcome karma, you must repay a karmic debt to someone, this does not have to be the same person, but it often is. Or you can learn from the experience when it is returned to you and change the energy you send out in future.

There were pictures of happy people sitting at the top of mountains doing yoga at the bottom of the web page— probably vegans.

I sighed and my mind started to search for whatever it was I had done in my past that had caused such an upheaval in my life now. I knew there were things that I could have done better, but I didn't feel like I had been a bad person. I wondered what the cause had been of each of the lessons that was coming my way. Maybe I would never know, especially if it was in a past life (if you believe in them). However, I did know I didn't want anything but good karma from now on and I was going to look for every opportunity I could to send out good vibes, so that's what I could expect to come back.

I was running out of energy and motivation to complete the paperwork I had set about sorting with such enthusiasm, so I quickly finished writing the tabs on the dividers and started to fill the lever arch file. The spread sheet could wait. I knew that if I didn't do it now then I never would and I'd be forever trailing around a carrier bag full of mail. Shredding felt satisfying, but there was so much to do that I decided I would take all of the rubbish out into the back garden and burn it instead. I have always loved watching fire, and there is something so ceremonial and final about burning things.

I cremated all of the envelopes, old statements, free paper and circulars and the smoke drifted up in plumes high above the house into the bright blue summer sky.

That felt so much better, if only it wasn't for the file indoors bulging with debts accrued. I wished in that moment I could burn every last trace away and erase it from history. If only I could take myself back to a time when I didn't know about overdrafts or charge cards, it felt like a type of karmic payback alright—if you are an arse with a credit card you get crippled with debt. Cause and effect, you cause the problem, you get stuck with the outcome.

My mobile rang from indoors and I walked in and picked it up. A number I didn't know flashed up and I had that couple of seconds of *should I answer or not?*

I pressed the green button and the voice sounded like I was hearing it twice, once down the phone and once from the hallway.

"Hi there, yes I bought the furniture from *eBay*. I'm at the door."

I laughed and walked down the hallway.

"Hi, ladyluck27! Sorry, I was in the back garden and I didn't hear you knocking," I said.

The woman looked a bit puzzled and I stepped back to look at my reflection in the mirror. There were three little flakes of gossamer thin white paper in my hair and some soot on my nose.

"I look a mess! I've been burning all the old paperwork ready to move." I invited her in and asked if she'd like a quick cuppa before she started to load up the van. I presumed someone else would be pulling up in a minute or two to give her a hand, the child in the front seat engrossed in their *Nintendo DS* certainly wasn't big enough to help with much more than scatter cushions.

146

"That would be great, if you don't mind. I have something I need to tell you though, I'm really sorry." She looked like she was about to burst into tears.

"That's ok, what's up?" I needed the money for the furniture and I did not have the luxury of time on my side, so please, please don't mess up, ladyluck27.

"I was supposed to be getting the keys for the new house this afternoon and the estate agents rang me about half an hour ago and said that it's fallen through." She looked devastated, and my face softened. I might be going through some challenging times at the moment but I didn't have a child to consider. That must be really hard.

"Oh no, what are you going to do?" I reached up into the cupboard for emergency chocolate biscuits and clicked on the kettle. She looked like she needed caffeine and sugar.

"I don't know really. Our old house has new people moving in today so I can't go back there, and anyway I need to be here, my new job starts in a few days' time. I'm sure something will come up for us but it took me so long to find this one so I just don't know." 'Lady Luck' now had an ironic ring.

"It's not something I want to rush into because you have to sign an agreement for six months so we'll be stuck there for at least that long." She dunked her biscuit into her tea and sighed.

"How did it all fall through? Is there no way back?" I asked. "Does the agent not have a responsibility to find you something else?" I tried to make sense of it.

"No, sadly not. I don't know why we can't have it anymore, she just said there had been a change in circumstances and that it wasn't available now. All our

references were fine, it's just one of those things. The
house was near here actually, Brook Burn Road. I need
somewhere in a cul-de-sac you see, although Max is nine
he's autistic and I need to know he's safe." As she spoke I
started to get distracted by the very slightly crooked front
tooth. It reminded me of someone and I couldn't think
who. "I hope he settles up here, he got really badly bullied
at his last school, it was awful."

I nodded in the right places as she went on to say that
the school Max would be attending was a mainstream
school, St Bede's, and it was only a short walk from here.

She drained her cup and dug deep in her jacket pocket,
pulling out neatly folded bank notes.

"This is for the furniture," she said handing it over. "If I
can get sorted quickly I'll come back and get it. If not then
I'll just have to lose the money. Either way you sold it to
me in good faith and I want to honour that."

I gratefully took the money and thanked her for being so
honest. "I'll do whatever I can to help you," I assured her.
"Just keep me posted."

"That's so kind of you. Moving is so stressful, but I
guess you know that too. Are you going far?" she asked.

"In a few days' time actually, so I hope you get sorted
before then." I wasn't going to tell her the place would
likely be boarded up with the furniture inside if she didn't
get a wriggle on.

"Me, too. Are you selling to someone nice?" she asked.

"Well, not really," I said, squirming in my slippers. "It's
kind of a business arrangement."

"Oh sorry, I didn't mean to pry. I didn't realise it was an
investment property. If your new tenants let you down,

please get in touch!" She was hardly two steps up the driveway when the light bulb went on for me. That might just be the answer to all of my prayers.

"Actually, if you give me a couple of hours I might be able to help you," I said in a bit of a fluster, my mind was racing ahead.

"Really?" She looked hopeful for the first time since she had walked in.

"Really." I sure hoped so, if I could save her ass, I'd be saving mine too.

I called the *Citizens Advice Bureau* and spoke to Brett in a garbled, excited manner, spilling ideas and information all over the place. He pulled out my file and still had the details of my mortgage lender as well as the reference number that said he could act as my advocate. Once I had repeated the story again, Brett said that he'd call them on my behalf and ring me back.

I fiddled and fidgeted around for all of five minutes and my mobile rang.

"Hi Steph, it's Brett."

"Hiya, what did they say?"

"Well it's certainly possible, even at this very late stage to call off the repossession, as long as you can clear the arrears in full, which are now over three thousand pounds. They would then need you to start to make the monthly payments regularly, in full and on time." Brett's tone indicated that this was now a closed chapter, no money plus no income equals no more house.

"OK, that sounds good. What about Jay? Did you ask about that?" I waited impatiently, pacing the hallway.

"Well I did Steph, but I don't know how it's going to help you. They said that if he was prepared to transfer the mortgage to you then you would be completely responsible for the whole debt, and then if the house was repossessed that you would be the only one that would be affected. In real terms you'd be letting him off the hook, it's probably not my place to say, we are meant to be impartial but it just seems wrong to me." He spoke professionally but with a sympathetic undercurrent.

"I know Brett, thank you so much for all you are doing to help me. I'll update you in a couple of days."

I clicked into my *PayPal* account, now the last bits and bobs had been paid for and *eBay* had taken their fees I was left with four thousand two hundred and fifty seven pounds. I had another three hundred in my back pocket from the sale of the furniture, and my last ever salary should have hit the bank around now, with bonus.

Rightfully I should be doing the monthly juggling act and making the payments from credit and store cards, loans and household bills. But this month I had a different plan. I transferred the funds to my current account and called Hannah.

Initially she thought I was losing the plot altogether, but once the penny dropped she saw the genius in my thinking. Transfer the credit card debt and loan to Jay, which totalled around thirty thousand, and get him to transfer the mortgage to me, which was around six times that amount. Make up some cock and bull story that I couldn't leave the house that was filled with so many memories and that I'd rather take on the massive debt and try to find a way of keeping it, somehow, against the odds

and all that. This made me out to be so reasonable that
Hannah was confident in threatening even The Bulldog to
a showdown in front of the Judge if they didn't go for it.

She also said that the court would really frown on the
fact that Jay had allowed the mortgage to fall into arrears
and risk our home, but that we could say I would be
prepared to find a way of clearing this as well if I could
have the title deed and mortgage amended.

It was almost close of business and Hannah wanted to
try and get The Bulldog on the phone and run the deal past
him. So I had another agonising wait. I thought about
ringing Lizzie, but that wouldn't be fair as he was her
colleague after all.

I flicked through the channels on the television and
slurped a *Pot Noodle*. *Relocation, Relocation, Flog It*, or
Deal or No Deal —I had to laugh.

The phone rang and I nearly jumped out of my skin and
noodles escaped all over the laminate floor and burnt my
foot. I had to quickly peel my 'chicken chow sock' off and
pray that my voicemail didn't kick in.

"Hi!" I barked as I answered.

"It's me!" Hannah's voice, sounding quite cheery, I had
everything clenched in that moment. "Well, do you want
to know what he said?"

"Of course I want to know! Come on spill—no don't
spill!" I was getting a bit hysterical. Surely she wouldn't
sound this happy if it had been a big sod off. "I mean yes,
tell me, but I've had a spill...no I'm fine just tell me for
God's sake!"

"He said that you sounded like a misguided idiot and
he'd be glad to do it. He is going to draw the papers up as

soon as he can before you change your silly little mind."
Hannah laughed. "I've printed off a tenancy agreement for
you. You had better ring Lady Luck. Her luck is in, and so
is yours!"

So I did, and things began to fall into place beautifully.

My *PayPal* funds cleared in my bank account three days
later and I was able to send what was owed to clear the
mortgage arrears. The transfer was completed later that
day by fax, and the land registry had been informed that
the house was now mine—well sort of. I had extended the
loan by four years and this had reduced the monthly
repayments to six hundred and fifty pounds, and they had
fixed this for three years. I had already established from
Lady Luck in the kitchen on day one that she was going to
be paying six hundred and ninety five for the initial house
rental, so I knew that I would have a little left over for any
repairs or maintenance.

I finished packing my own things into two suitcases and
one medium-sized cardboard box and hovered around
while I waited for my Lucky Lady to arrive. I wanted to
pass the house on with the best possible energy I could,
reading all about karma had made me more aware of what
I was giving out and what I wanted to get back. I'd bought
a bottle of wine and a 'New Home' card, which I'd put on
the kitchen table and there was a vase of flowers in the
front room. I'd put the money for the furniture into a
holding account as the deposit and today I would get the
first month's rent in advance once the tenancy agreement
was signed.

I flicked the duster over the windowsills and coffee table and I stood back to take in the scene. I smiled to myself, this was karma.

Jay - who had left me for someone else, deliberately loaded up debts in my name, missed our mortgage payments, stole my self-worth and generally treated me appallingly - was now having to pay off the wedding loan and credit cards that he willingly transferred to himself.

Whilst I—the one who had given love, affection, understanding, forgiveness and my whole self to our marriage—was now being justly rewarded by the return of all that good karma, which was actually pulling on to the drive in the same white van.

"Hiya, come on in!" I waved the duster out of the front door.

Lady Luck was beaming as she took Max by the hand and brought him in.

"You didn't need to clean you silly girl! You have done more than enough for us."

"It's fine, I wouldn't want you to be anywhere that was less than perfect." I put the kettle on and Max explored upstairs and chose his bedroom.

"We are so grateful for this, you'll never know what you have done for us. If I can ever repay you or help you in any way please just let me know." Lady Luck had her hair tied up today and there was something familiar about her that I couldn't put my finger on. It was in her voice and some of her mannerisms, a feeling that I'd met her before or at least someone like her anyway.

"You are helping me too, and there is nothing to repay. I'm glad you and Max can get settled here and its perfect timing for me to move on." I put the tenancy agreement on the kitchen bench along with a biro. "My solicitor says this is a standard short term agreement and that after the first six months, if both parties are happy to continue, we can just roll it on from there, if that's ok with you?"

"Absolutely," she said, picking up the pen and filling in her details. I watched from the corner of my eye feeling strangely compelled. Even her handwriting was triggering some kind of déjà vu.

She signed her name with a flourish, and I countersigned. It felt fraudulent to be writing my married name under the circumstances, but in the eyes of the law it's who I was.

"Ah, Jessica Simmons, I had wondered what your real name was 'Lady Luck'!"

"Yes, but not Simmons for long. Part of this relocation and new start is because I'm getting divorced. I'm going to be going back to Jessica Mason before long." She smiled and the slightly crooked tooth seemed ridiculously obvious to me now.

"Jessica Mason?" I must have sounded surprised as she paused and looked at me quizzically.

"Yes, that's right." She waited for my response.

"Jessica Mason from Blackwell High School?" I could have added 'Jessica Mason that tormented the life out of me because of a second-hand jacket,' or 'Jessica Mason who's gang beat the living daylights out of my best friend and made him move away'. But in truth, I saw before me 'Jessica Mason that was trying to get her life together'. Someone from a broken marriage that was trying to raise her vulnerable son on her own and protect him from the

154

school bullies—the image of her former self. I also saw someone that was going to be paying off my mortgage for me month by month, someone who had been cruel to me in the past because I'd not had much money. Now that's a karmic debt repaid.

"Yes that's me. I'm ashamed to say I wasn't very nice to know back then. I didn't like myself very much and I used to be a bit of a bully sometimes." She cast her eyes down to the floor and I sensed her embarrassment. "I've had loads of counselling about it and I'm a lot better now than I was. I've forgiven my dad for the affairs and making my mum's life such a misery, then showering us with extravagant gifts when he was caught out. It all made for a very confusing upbringing."

"I'm sure it did." Any residual anger melted into compassion in that moment and I changed the way that I saw the school bully from all those years ago. I felt sorry for her now and I could see she was playing out a response to what was going on behind those big, posh, closed doors.

I took a breath and reached for her hand. "But this is your new start," I found myself saying. "Your chance to wipe the slate clean and begin again in your new life. It sounds to me like you've paid your dues and now it's time to look forward and not back."

She looked at me and blinked back tears. "Yes you're right, I know you are. And you have helped me so much, thank you." She paused for a moment. "Did I know you at school?"

"Not really, I was a bit shy." I decided to let her off the hook then and there, no point in dragging round old hurts in order to get one over on people. I didn't want that intention returning to me. I'd had enough insight into how karma worked for one day. I gave her one copy of the agreement and I kept the other. She handed me a cheque for this month's rent and the bond. She would set a direct debit up with the bank through the week and pay that way in future. I called a taxi and the driver carried my two cases whilst I took the box. It's odd seeing someone wave you away from your own house but, as I waved back, I knew this was an end and a beginning in one, and in about half an hour I'd be unpacking in my new place. The place I had been dreaming of for weeks now.

Stephanie's Journal - Lesson 6
The Law of Karma

There is a universal force of cause and effect called karma, based on the age-old principle that whatever you give out in life comes back to you. It may not come back in the same form, but the essence of what you have thought, said or done will be returned at some point. This might not even be in this lifetime but, good or bad, what you give out you get back. This is motivation to live your life differently if ever there was.

"There are the waves and there is the wind, seen and unseen forces. Everyone has these same elements in their lives, the seen and the unseen, karma and free will." Kuan Yin

Chapter 15

The taxi pulled into a loading bay and, as the driver stood my cases on the pavement, I counted out the fare, plus a tip. This was the first time I had looked at the building properly from street level since when I had passed on the bus, I had been looking down on the five large stone steps and the wrought iron handrails painted black. I hadn't noticed above the door there was a keystone that announced the year 1892 or that there was a half-moon-shaped window below this to let light into the hallway.

I took a breath and let it out slowly, as if I was composing myself for a really big step, when in fact I was as excited as I was anxious.

I took my box up the steps and put it just underneath the buzzer and then, one at a time, brought up the two cases. I buzzed and waited.

"Who is it please?" Josie's voice was familiar with a professional gloss over the top. This was probably a version of her telephone voice.

"Hi Josie, it's Steph." I spoke into the meshed microphone.

"Come on in!" She sounded so pleased to see me, and as I pushed the door I could hear her footsteps in the hallway. She took one of the cases and I managed the other in one hand and the box on my hip.

"Welcome to Prospect House, Steph, I hope your time here brings you exactly what you need." She hugged me genuinely and put a key in my hand. The key was on a small fob that was made of smooth wood, oval and varnished with the word 'Peace' written in beautiful calligraphy on both sides. There was nothing identifying where this key belonged, it was explained to me later that if it was lost, stolen or ,in one case, pick pocketed from a resident by an ex that was stalking them, then there was no identification of where they might be staying.

"I guess you'll want to get your things upstairs, I'll give you a hand." She took one case and I took the other and the box, as I followed her. I could hear some muffled sounds of television, conversation and also the faint smell of incense.

Three flights of stairs, and a lot of huffing and puffing later, I stood outside my new front door. "I'll put the kettle on, come down when you are ready and we'll go through the house rules." Josie left me to put the key in the lock and open up my new life myself.

Everything was as I had remembered; apart from the lilac in the vase was slightly wilted. I allowed the door to close behind me and I looked out of the window and on to the street. Traffic was coming and going and there were people walking up and down, going about their daily lives. There was a café opposite called 'Baps', a takeaway pizza place that was closed, a pawn shop, an electrical spares and repairs and a shop that sold everything for a pound. I preferred this outlook to the garden, I could see more of life and its variety from up here.

I walked around the space, feeling at home and surprised that I felt this way, given what had gone on in my life recently. There was a feeling of belonging, that I knew wouldn't last forever but I did have certainty that I was in exactly the right place at the right time, and that was something I had not felt for ages. I opened the cardboard

box and took out some books to put on the shelf on the
wall near the painting. I plugged in my radio alarm clock
and set the time, and set my *iPod* docking station on top of
the drawers. The small purple glass tea light holder was
put in its rightful place on the windowsill, and my vision
was complete.

I decided to leave my unpacking for later and made my
way downstairs to find Josie.

A tray was ready with a teapot all pom-pommed up in a
knitted cosy, cups and saucers, milk jug and some custard
creams. Josie handed me a skinny folder entitled *Prospect
House – Rules and Behavioural Standards.* She asked me
to flick through and read the code of conduct, health and
safety guidelines and fire drill. Then I had to sign and date
a form to say that I had read and understood everything
and Josie countersigned. There were two copies, one for
me and one to keep on file.

The whole ethos of this place was built around respect
and love for others, regard for other people's feelings,
contribution and positivity. It was a supportive and caring
environment that would tolerate no one pulling anyone
else down, or making anyone feel uncomfortable. There
was a zero tolerance approach to this, and anyone that was
felt to be violating this would be given a warning in the
first instance and if things didn't improve they would have
to leave. The police would be involved if necessary. Josie
said this was just something that they had to put into the
agreement, and in all the years of being open it had only
happened once.

"I so appreciate this Josie, I shouldn't need to be here too long, taking up a space that someone else might need," I said.

"You can stay as long as you need to Steph, that's a given. We don't rush people off the premises as soon as they start getting it together, but we do encourage independence and personal growth. You will know when the time is right for you to go. There are people that come here who need a bit more of an obvious approach when they are ready to get back out into the world, but you won't be one of them!" she laughed.

"OK I just think there must be people out here that need this more than me. I feel a bit guilty if I'm honest, but really grateful as well." After all I did have Mum and Dad's to go back to.

"There may well be others that need the room Steph, but I have a feeling that I need you here." I looked inquisitively at Josie as she continued; "The thing is that you are a very clever girl. You are confident and capable. I need some help and I think that you'll be perfect for the job."

Josie poured more tea for us both and I sat up straight in the chair. I wondered how she saw me fitting in. She had obviously given this some thought.

"I know your story," she stirred sugar into her cup and the spoon 'ting-tinged' against the bone china, "now it's time you knew mine."

Josie went on to tell me that the building we were sitting was in dire need of funds being raised for both the day-to-day running and also for any relocation that may be forced if the redevelopment plans went ahead. It turned out that she was completely overstretched in terms of her time and energy and she had little time or know-how to devote to generating donations or funding.

"In terms of heating, lighting, water rates and the other month-on-month expenses we need to have at least £1200 per month. That's before wages or other expenses, and at the moment we aren't bringing in nearly enough. I know we are a registered charity, but it still has to be run as a business. I'm all about helping people get back on their feet and, to be honest Steph, I really struggle with the business side of it and that's where I hope you can help." She sighed and looked at me hopefully.

This was something I could get really excited about. My background in sales had made me savvy in profit and loss, cold calling, marketing and much more. And now I knew how I could use my intention to multiply these results many times.

"I would love to help you with that!" I was genuinely enthusiastic. Something I would love doing and I would feel that I could justify having the space upstairs—not that I needed to but I had read so much now about fair exchange and I knew that there had to be some intention of this in order to stay in the flow and keep good things coming my way.

My head started buzzing with loads of ideas, corporate sponsorship, the local press, bag packing in supermarkets and much more. I started chattering and thinking out loud and Josie threw her hands up in the air.

"Wait, wait, enough already!" she laughed again. "I knew you'd be able to help, but all of this is over my head, that's why you are the best girl for the job. And you can

start whenever you want to. Just use my office if you want
to, the photocopier, fax and computer are totally at your
disposal. I'll get the accounts for you to see tomorrow so
you can get the whole picture. I just know that I bumped
into you three times on that bus for a reason."

"Me, too," I said. "It must have been meant to be."

I jotted down the access key on the wireless broadband
hub so that I could connect my laptop and phone to the
network and drained my second cup of tea.

"I'll go and hook up now so that I can get started first
thing in the morning," I said, and made my way upstairs
as Josie gathered the cups back onto the tray.

My heart felt like it was singing. I was full of positive
energy and, for once in a long while, I felt like I had some
direction again. I was worthy of being here and I could
help someone with a worthwhile cause, helping all of the
people that this project supported. I felt important again,
part of a team, valued and cared about. I turned the key in
the lock and once again shook my head in disbelief that
this scene was an exact replica of the dreams and visions I
had been experiencing just weeks before. The way that
energy worked was truly amazing—and so fast too. If I
could bring this to me then I could bring anything, I just
knew it. I was buzzing with excitement as I lifted the first
suitcase onto the bed and started raking through clothes
and toiletries, looking for the beach towel I'd wrapped my
laptop in. It must be in the second one. I opened this one
onto the floor and two handbags, one pair of shoes and a
swimming costume later, the pink and purple, fluffy,
flower design peeked out at me.

I unwrapped it carefully and opened it up. 'Low Battery' flashed back at me and I dug deeper in the clothes nest for the charger. I found a plug near the window and dragged the chest of drawers a little closer to it so as not to overstretch the cable. Perfect, a temporary desk, all I needed was to bring a chair up from downstairs and I was off.

As I stood back to admire my handiwork, there was a gust of wind that caught the plain, white, voile panels that hung at the window. The window had been left open slightly and the breeze lifted up the fine, sheer fabric the way you would have your bed turned down in a posh hotel. This gave me just enough of a view out of the window to see a familiar figure sitting across the road at the café, tipping a sachet of sugar into a tall cup of cappuccino. There were three chrome tables outside on the wide pavement where you could eat and people watch at the same time.

Lizzie looked glamorous, as usual, in a black, knee-length, pencil skirt, heels and oversized sunglasses. I'd so missed my friend these past weeks. Yes I had met new people, but there was something about being able to really pour your heart out to someone who knew you inside out and all of your hang ups.

Someone who had held your head when you were being sick down the loo after too much cheap wine, and someone who had picked you up when you felt like the whole world was against you. We had both been there for each other through thick and thin, and I meant that literally after the three month *Weight Watchers* holiday diet two years ago.

I knocked on the window and waved like the village idiot.

"Lizzie, Lizzie, up here!"

The traffic noise drowned out my voice and frantic banging, I remembered guiltily that I had neighbours now and they were probably thinking it was ironic that I had been put in a room called 'peace'.

I reached for my phone and called up Lizzie's number. I saw her reach into her bag and pull out her Blackberry. Then the strangest thing happened, she actually paused and looked at the number. This lasted about four rings and then voicemail cut in as she dumped the call. She stirred the sugar in and stared down the street.

In that moment I felt like I was spying on her. I let go of the voile and it flapped gently in the wind again. I felt both self-conscious and embarrassed. Why didn't she want to hear from me? I back tracked on our last conversation to see if there was anything there that would have offended or upset her and I couldn't think of anything. I could still see her, but I knew she couldn't see me. I didn't leave a message after the tone, there was no way I'd have known what to say, I was completely bewildered.

I stood and watched her a moment longer and thought about going out of the front door and just 'turning up' at the same place, making it look like a complete co-incidence, just to see how she would react if we were face to face. I shook my head in disbelief and felt like I was going to burst into tears. She was the only thing I had left from my old life, the only thing worth keeping really, or so I had thought.

Just then someone walked over and pulled out the chair opposite to sit down. I blinked, and then blinked again. I really couldn't believe what I was seeing. Jay was scanning the menu card and trying to catch the attention of the waitress. He looked her legs up and down as she walked away scribbling on a little note pad. I could feel my heart racing and my breathing became more rapid. I started to tell myself to calm down and stop overreacting. He looked every bit as handsome as I remembered and, even though he had treated me badly, I still craved him, his touch and his love. I hadn't managed to block this feeling out altogether since we split, but it had been diluted a little everyday as I fought my way back up the rock face of my life, usually with the prevailing wind blowing a bloody hooligan. It had been an awful few months and now, just when I was feeling alright—like things were coming together, there he was, like a bad penny. And I missed him in that moment more than I ever had. Memories of good times merged and magnified the effect as I stood staring at him.

They were probably just going through divorce stuff or something. After all, he was a client of her firm. Dotting the Is and crossing the Ts, as well as holding hands now - wait a minute - what was going on? Jay then leaned right into her space, speaking as she looked down at the table. His stance quickly became overbearing and Lizzie seemed to shrink back into her seat as she pulled back her hands and dropped them into her lap. He threw his head back in an exasperated manner and folded his arms. He turned away from her and shook his head. She still didn't lift her gaze. I could see him speaking to her again, one syllable words shot from his mouth and across the table and Lizzie seemed to flinch with each verbal bullet. I knew what an out and out bastard he could be and from where I stood it looked like he was being just that to her.

I didn't know why or what I was going to say but, before I knew it, I turned on my heel and I made for the stairs. I heard the door to my room swing shut behind me as I bounded down two steps at a time. Josie wasn't in the office now, I could hear what sounded like washing up and the radio on in the background. I passed a young woman in the hallway with a carrier bag and a duffle coat. I smiled a quick hello and stepped out onto the street.

There was a yellow bus parked on the other side of the street, I could see through the windows but only because they were standing up and leaving. Cars rushed past me, then a transit van, a motorbike, a taxi, more cars and then the bus pulled away. I saw Jay in the distance walking away quickly and Lizzie blowing her nose and trying to keep up. She had no chance in those heels.

Let it go, Steph. Whatever it was, it wasn't about you.

But I couldn't imagine why he would be so angry with her? Maybe he felt stitched up about me keeping the house and him getting all of the credit card debt? But surely that was something to rant at The Bulldog about and not Lizzie.

I walked back to the steps and sat on the bottom one, watching people walk by and thinking that their lives were all completely different, strangers I would never know anything about. It felt odd to me now that the two people in the world I was closest to a few months ago, now felt like total strangers to me.

166

A tall, willowy girl with dark hair and a lost property box wardrobe smiled at me as she made her way past and up to the front door. I guessed I'd meet them all in due course. I stood up and made my way back in. I turned my attention again to fundraising to try and distract myself from all of the chatter in my head about what I had seen.

I hadn't noticed the time passing until my stomach started to growl at me. I'd filled the first eight pages of my notebook with ideas and resources and I was already starting to feel a workable plan coming together. I looked at the clock, it was nearly seven and I was suddenly starving. The smell of garlic and spices drifted up through the window, and I started thinking about the pizza place two doors down.

The house was alive with conversation downstairs. I could hear the television on in the front room and the unmistakeable sound of *Dot Cotton* putting someone straight on a thing or two along with obligatory bible quotes. There was the sound of dishes clanking and clinking coming from the kitchen and also laughing, like a hysterical shriek, the kind of laugh that made you want to laugh as it was so extreme. I felt a bit shy about introducing myself tonight. I'd rather remain relatively anonymous until tomorrow. All I felt was tired and hungry.

I ordered my pizza and instead of waiting on the wooden bench inside underneath the menu, I walked a few metres down the road to the paper shop and bought milk, tea bags and cereal for the morning.

I collected the pizza and snuck back upstairs. I ate it straight from the box and opened my free can of pop to glug down as I watched some re-runs on my laptop. Tonight would be the first night in this new place, I had no doubt I would sleep soundly. I was emotionally mangled after the day's events and physically worn out. This morning seemed an age away.

I found my toothbrush and toothpaste in case one and pulled on pyjamas from case two. I shut the window but left the curtains open. I wanted to see the first rays of sun catch the crystal and make the tiny rainbows spin around the room. I closed my eyes and sank into the mattress, wondering how many people had been saved from themselves in this room—saved from the life they were running from. I hardly had time to speculate as sleep crept over me and I was soon snoring lightly, surrounded by peace, literally.

Chapter 16

When I woke the following day I felt like I had not moved all night, I stretched and opened my eyes to see multi-coloured sparkles cascading all around the walls. It was early, but I'd had eight hours sleep so the clock time made no real difference. I did make a mental note to be quiet for the people below me. As far as I could tell I didn't have a next door neighbour at the moment. Either that or they were able to move around without a sound.

The shower was hot and I washed my hair. I didn't bother blow drying, I just combed it through. I started to review my notes from the following day and saw that there were lots of phone calls I needed to make. I continued making lists of fundraising ideas. My tea went cold but it didn't bother me. It was good to be absorbed in something other than the drama of my own life.

The radio announced that it was now nine o'clock on July 6th and I stretched and picked up my note pad to go downstairs. Then a niggle in the back of my mind prompted me to look at my diary. There was one word written against 9am on 6th July, and that word was Sue. I had completely forgotten that way back in January I had agreed to go back and have another reading to find out the next six lessons.

I was late! Panic!

The good thing was that I wasn't a bus ride away now and, ten minutes later, out of breath and flustered, I had made it to Green Lane. Sue heard me coming up the stairs and shouted; "Hi Steph," from the little room that I had been in only six months ago.

"Wow, your hair looks amazing!" Sue said, as I rambled an apology for being late.

"Oh thanks, it was time to let the old go and be myself at last." I declined a cup of tea but was glad that I had brought a bottle of water with me after my pavement power walk.

We chatted briefly about the changes that had happened in my life and Sue interjected here and there. Once I'd brought her up to the present moment she passed me the well-worn cards again and I took a deep breath.

"Just the same as last time, shuffle as long as you need to and focus on what is right for you coming through," Sue said with a smile.

I closed my eyes and started to say in my mind that all of the right things were going to come through in this reading for me, everything I needed to know right now. I laid the deck face down on the table and Sue dealt six cards in front of me.

"So let's see what is coming up," she said as she turned the first card.

"*The Law of Reflection,*" she said and started to do the eyelid fluttering thing again. "Your guides say that this is a time of growth and introspection. They say that you have done so well on all of the other lessons and passed with flying colours…and that now you need to reflect on your own progress and start to see that others will reflect back to you who you truly are now."

"I don't get it, sorry," I shrugged my shoulders.

"It means that they want you to become aware of another of the Universal Laws and apply it in your life. There is a 'Law of Reflection' that is active all of the time, and it means that everyone we interact with is reflecting back a part of us." Sue looked at me for confirmation that I was following.

"So if someone is greedy, it means I'm greedy? Or if someone is lazy, it means I am lazy?" I questioned.

"It's sometimes that obvious, but often far more subtle than that. It works with aspects of ourselves, not just our whole selves."

"So you mean that there may be a tendency to have the characteristics that you see in others, but it could be to a more or lesser degree?"

"Yes that's right. And once you start to see yourself in others you will know what you need to work on to make progress yourself." Sue turned the next card, for August.

"*Forgiveness and Compassion*, for yourself and others. There is going to be a situation occurring that you will find really challenging, and your guides are asking you to remember that everyone involved is doing their level best. Even when you feel terribly wronged, you must remember that."

"What do you mean?" I asked.

"There are people in your life that will appear to do you a disservice, to hurt you and to wrong you. From a spiritual perspective they are giving you a gift. The gift of learning and growing, you will have the opportunity to show them compassion and forgiveness for what they have done."

"And are you going to be really busy in September!" She continued as she turned the card and I saw an image of the sun beaming down on a beautiful day. The word '*Acceptance*' was highlighted. "Things are really going to be coming together for you, and there will be a lot of hard work but also great rewards and satisfaction." Sue tapped the image in the middle of the card with her finger. "You really are going to come into your own here and see the benefits of all of the lessons so far. This is a great time for you."

I smiled. At last it looked like things were turning out well. I relaxed back into the chair and let Sue continue.

"There is however a lesson that comes with this card for you, and your guides are saying that you will need to take note of everything you have learned this year so far. They say there is a possibility that when you are evolving and things are looking good for you then you can start trying to fix other people." She looked at me with her head tilted to one side.

"Fix them?"

"Yes, there are people awakening to their path every day here on earth, but we are all at different stages and some will not awaken in this lifetime at all. They will stay stuck in their illness, their drama, their poverty and their victim thinking. You now have an insight of how they could change and create a different experience for themselves don't you?"

"Yes"

"The lesson that you are going to learn is that you need to honour them for where they are, and not judge them or try to rescue them. Simply put, it's not your stuff."

"So you mean don't help them?"

"That's the point. You can help people of course, and sign post them, make suggestions and the like, but you have to know that it is their responsibility to help themselves and get on board with creating their own life. It's about accepting yourself and accepting others as they are right now."

"Ah, I see. Well at least I think I do."

"Don't get too hung up on it now, you will have opportunities to practise throughout the month."

Sue turned the next card which was *Serendipity* with a haunting image of an illuminated full moon.

"This card is about intuition and serendipity, following your gut instinct, and becoming aware of signs and signals from the universe. It's a calling to you to tap into the matrix of possibility and start to join up the dots on all of the so called co-incidences and serendipity that life shows you every day. If you see things three times or more, that have the same theme or message, then you can be assured that the message is for you."

"Like what sort of thing?" I asked.

"Like if you see something on television about the benefits of being a vegetarian and then you overhear a conversation about vegetarian cooking and then you went to the supermarket and the vegetarian meals were all half price. That would be a message that your body wants a break from meat and that you should go veggie for a while."

"Right, I get it." Come to think of it, I had never met a fat veggie—maybe I should give it a go.

Sue smiled widely as she turned the next card, which was called *Two Hearts*.

"And look at what we have coming in for you here. Looks like you aren't going to be feeling the chill in

November! You are going to be cuddled up with someone special and falling in love!"

This came as a bit of a shock. It's not that I hadn't considered the possibility of meeting someone. It's not that I don't want to ultimately, but just that whenever I think of being close to someone else I could only think of Jay.

"This will be completely different to anything you have ever known, although there will be a strange kind of familiarity, which I can't put my finger on...you'll know when it happens. The lesson here will be that you have to believe that you are good enough to experience love like this. Your first instinct will be to create some kind of resistance as you will feel like you don't deserve something so beautiful and genuine in your life, but you need to let that old part of you go now and know that you are more than deserving." Sue reached out her hand and touched mine. I had hardly noticed that my eyes had dropped and that there were tears on my cheeks.

"These are old wounds and they need to be healed. The man that is coming into your life will have wounds of his own and you will help each other to make sense of this and to move on. This is part of the exchange that you are destined to have together."

"Will he think I am good enough?" I sniffed, and managed to look up and meet Sue's gaze.

"Of course he will, because by the time you meet him you will know you are good enough, and that you always have been."

I nodded and smiled weakly. With all I knew now, I could see that I would only attract someone who loved me when I finally got to a place where I could love myself. Jay had been a perfect match to the feelings of worthlessness and insecurities I had bundled up inside of me all those months ago. By working on how I felt about myself I knew that I could be happy with someone else.

The final card stood between me and my destiny now, and Sue turned it with a flick of her wrist.

"*The Flow*—I thought so!" She smiled again, and shook her head slightly.

"You have no idea yet how much your life is going to change! This card is all about wealth, success, happiness and everything good. You are going to find that December opens up a whole new level of you getting what you want in your life, it's like you can't put a foot wrong."

I wiped away the tears and sat up straight.

"The lesson here is that you need to stay in the flow of giving and receiving, and that you can use your good fortune to help others. It's about letting go of resistance and allowing all of the goodness into your life that you have been asking for. This will be very easy for you and will be more of a completion than a lesson. I can't say more than that as I am being told that there will be a surprise that your guides do not want to spoil. They say to stay aligned with being happy, being in the flow and being in love—the groundwork is already in place for this and it is all going to come to fruition for you at the end of the year."

I looked expectantly, but there was no more.

I had noted the name of each month down along with the name of the card and the lesson beside it.

I would have to fight the urge to sneak online and look for their definitions. Although that would probably end up like the time I looked in the medical encyclopaedia and diagnosed myself with an infestation of candida, when actually my itchy bum was due to a change in soap powder. It's a shame that I hadn't thought about that before I had been interrogated at the counter in boots on a busy Saturday morning, whilst squirming in my pants. And it was a cotton-lined gusset thank you, handsome young male assistant, and no, I didn't have threadworms in my stools.

I hugged Sue and promised to come back at the end of the year to update her. She held me at arm's length and wished me luck before I made my way to the stairs and back out on to the street towards the bus stop.

Chapter 17

Josie wasn't in the office, but the door was open and the computer was on so I guessed she wasn't far away. I picked up a biro and started to underline the places I wanted to ring and jotted down a couple of notes about what I was going to say. She appeared in the door looking like a child on Christmas morning.

"Steph! I am so glad you're back! Wait until you see this!" She was talking fast and started to 'click', 'click' the mouse on the computer screen. "Look!" she pointed to the figure on the screen "It's as if someone is looking out for us!" My eyes scrolled down to the bottom of the screen where all of the charitable donations from that month had accumulated. Josie threw her arms around me and she sniffed back tears. "I can't believe it Steph, I set this up ages ago and I have only ever made a couple of pounds here and there, and look! £3678!"

Events were unfolding at such a whirlwind pace for me. I hadn't given any thought at all to the donation I had made from the sale of what was, in essence, my old life. I hugged her back and swallowed a lump of pride in my throat. I was fighting back the tears myself. Maybe now was the time to come clean and tell her that it had been me, I'd have all of the glory and be on a pedestal for the whole time I stayed, no matter what else I managed to bring in.

Then a strange thing happened, a flashback to the New Year's Eve party with the fake *Rolex*. How eager I had been to get involved and show everyone how much I had and how important I was—but for what? For pride, and to make myself feel better, like I mattered. The pain and embarrassment of squirming on the spot came back to me in that moment—the fear of being exposed as a liar and a shallow, silly girl who thought she couldn't have friends unless she impressed them with the high life that was all a façade anyway. I made the decision then not to tell Josie and to remain dignified and proud of what I had done privately. My ego no longer needed a round of applause.

After the initial excitement, Josie had to go and meet with the landlord to discuss the redevelopment plans and I got stuck into making calls and emailing people that I thought could help with generating support and, more importantly, money for Prospect House. I dropped Lizzie a one line email to check in and see how she was doing. I wondered if she had seen Jay again and sighed.

Although the office door was closed, I could hear the comings and goings of a regular day here and voices that were new to me. Part of me was glad to be hiding away in the office, but I knew I couldn't stay here forever. For one thing, I was desperate for the toilet. I opened the door slowly and did a quick scout around the hallway. No one was around so I strode across the floor to the small cloakroom. My plan almost worked perfectly, apart from when I tried the handle it was occupied.

"I'm nearly done!" I heard a Scottish accent holler at me from behind the locked door.

"OK," I replied and felt like I had to wait now for her to finish. Flushing noises, then what sounded like nose blowing and then hand-washing. The sound of the lock turning was the final announcement that Sheila Henley was in fact done. She opened the door and looked me up

and down, not in a condescending way, but in a curious
way with a hint of suspicion. She looked as hard as nails, I
could only imagine, looking at her ears and her nose, what
else she might have pierced under her clothes. Her
knuckles bore the remnants of *love* and *hate* gone really
bad, faded letters probably done with a compass and an
ink cartridge when she was fifteen years old, skiving
maths. Some letters were in lower case and some capitals,
either way they were a mess. One gold tooth blinked at me
when she smiled, and the smile softened her whole face.
In that moment she morphed from battle-axe to beautiful,
and I noticed that she had scars on her face as well as
laughter lines and crow's feet. I knew that those lines and
scars would be part of a story that would carve Sheila out
to be one of life's survivors, a fighter who had been
hardened by more than just the school of hard knocks. My
instincts told me that life had kicked the living shit out of
her.

"Hi there," she said and told me her name. "Are you
new?"

"Yes I am." I felt a bit awkward as I genuinely did want
to make friends here but I was bursting for the loo.

"Oh God, don't mind me. I'll get out your way! You
don't want a bloody audience!" She moved out of the way
and laughed loudly. "I'll put the kettle on if you fancy a
brew."

"Thanks," I shouted from behind the closed door, feeling
a bit nervous like the new girl at school on her first day.

I walked to the door labelled 'Kitchen' and peeped
inside. There was Sheila standing by the kettle and
someone peeling vegetables beside the sink.

"Tea or coffee?" Sheila spoke just a little bit too loudly. I supposed it was over the noise of the kettle boiling and the radio was on in the background.

"Tea thanks, with milk. That would be great. I'm Stephanie by the way, well I get Steph."

"Well, Steph, what brings you here?" asked Sheila, and the other woman cocked her ears in my direction.

"Well, I guess my life just went a bit tits up and I needed a place to be for a while." I decided to leave out the bits about tarot cards and life lessons. "I'm helping Josie with some stuff as well." Sheila passed me my mug of tea and put a few biscuits on a plate.

"Want a brew Jude?" She asked 'twinset and pearls' beside the sink.

"I'll make my own thanks, I can't bide it when you put the milk in the mug with the tea bag, Sheila, you really should just make a proper pot!" Her tone was mock school teacher, but underneath that I detected a pet hate—people who couldn't get the basics right.

"Please yourself Lady Muck". Sheila rolled her eyes and sniggered at her. "I'm afraid we're all out of *Earl Grey.*"

Jude laughed now and I could see that this kind of banter obviously went on between the two of them most of the time. Just then the kitchen door flew open and a slip of a girl entered, dressed in indigo skinny fit jeans and a jade green sari. She started to unload a carrier bag on the bench containing tea, coffee, sugar and milk as well as two packets of digestives.

"Hi, newbie!" she smiled at me, her eyes were a similar green to her sari and her features dark and Indian. "I'm Asha."

Sheila nodded at each of us in turn. "Asha, Steph. Steph, Asha."

"Hi" I said and she smiled at me again.

"Are you making a pot Jude? You are a saviour. I've trekked up and down that bloody street, I'm knackered now." Asha sat in one of the kitchen chairs and looked even shorter. I briefly studied her face and thought she must be about nineteen or twenty. "Sheila you're going to have to cut Jamal's hair. People are going to start slinging wooden balls to try and win him if it gets much longer. Poor little bugger's got that from his father's side. Bloody *Velcro* head when it's short as well, but what can you do? He's cursed with the 'Ahmed Barnet' and there's nowt I can do for him." She laughed and snaffled some of the biscuits.

"OK, ok I'll get the clippers in a minute, just let me finish this." Sheila slurped another mouthful of tea.

"No rush right now, he's gone over in his buggy, he's just in the hallway," Asha said.

"You're not going to let her near him with clippers are you?" Jude started to poke fun. "Sheila bloody scissor hands? Did you not see what she did to me?" Jude pulled a tuft of short cropped greyish hair from near her left ear.

"Christ, Jude, you said you wanted a new image!" Sheila turned the volume up.

"A new start you said, something totally different. If we're being honest you were like *Barry* bloody *Gibb* in a frock when you showed up here! I did you a favour getting rid of that silly bloody *Penelope Keith* meets *Pan's People* do. In case you hadn't noticed it's not 1976 anymore. So keep your legwarmers in your suitcase and drag your arse into 2011!" Sheila laughed raucously and Asha nearly choked on her tea.

"Cheeky, cheeky buggers." Jude shook her head. "At least I know how to make tea properly."

She snooted her nose up into the air and laughed too.

"You don't mind Jude, this is a lovely brew. Not like some I could mention. It's obvious you took your duties as a housewife very seriously." Asha tinged her tone with sarcasm. "Until you put your notice in that is."

"Notice? That would have been nice. You don't get much time when you're traded in. I wonder how she's enjoying the reality of living with him. I hope it's everything she thought it wasn't going to be. God bless her. He'll expect a casserole in the oven, a line of washing out and a hand up the u-bend before 9am. Maybe she puts her hand up his bloody u-bend and that's why I'm out on my ear."

They all laughed together and the conversation turned to men in general. Snippets of opinions and fragments of their history were revealed, all underpinned by the darkest humour that united them together. I contributed to the conversation, happy to share more of my life in exchange for their stories.

Asha was here to escape an arranged marriage gone wrong. It had been to a cousin and was intended to heal a rift between two sides of the family. The rift soon became more like the Grand Canyon when things began to spiral between them, and in the end there was a threat of physical violence so she fled with her son.

Sheila had been in a yo-yo relationship for years now, full of promises, debt, alcohol and the odd good hiding. She couldn't break the cycle of going back, getting involved for long enough to see his true colours (again), and then escaping. She had spent many a night in a refuge and a handful on the street, she just couldn't see a way of making it work without him.

"You coming for supper tonight?" Sheila asked.

"I don't really know how it all works yet." I said.

"We all chip in a fiver a couple of times a week and someone cooks."

"It's shepherd's pie tonight followed by fruit crumble," Jude said.

"I'd love to," I said.

"I'll pass on that if you don't mind," Asha butted in.

"You don't have to get in a halal huff miss, I've made you the veggie option." Jude sounded all school teacher.

"OK, thanks Jude." Asha gave her a hug and put her mug in the sink.

"It's about 6pm Steph, and if you want to eat in your room its fine. Some people just come down and collect a plateful if they've got kids or if they don't want to socialise. It's up to you." Jude started rubbing margarine into flour.

"OK, I'll see you then, thanks for the tea and biscuits." That was my cue to leave them to it and return to the office.

Josie came back deflated and looking worried, a complete contrast to the way she had left. It turned out that the landlord of the building really had no choice but to sell. It was something called a 'Compulsory Purchase Order' as the whole block was going to be ripped down to make room for a new supermarket. I could see from Josie's face that her heart would be ripped out along with the fixtures and fittings.

"I just don't see a way out of this Steph, I can't afford to fight it and the way that he was talking there's no point anyway. We've had it good for so long now, I've practically had the place for nothing and the rent we pay is far less than what could have been realised. Supporting a project like this has been David's way of giving back. We once helped his sister and he pledged from that day on we could have this building for as long as we needed it and at a minimal rental." Josie sighed and put her head in her hands to wrack her brains for a solution.

"I just don't know what we can do. I believe in miracles and God knows we need one now."

I left Josie on the phone to the landlord again, and went to my room to call Hannah.

"Hi, stranger! You settling in with the waifs and strays?" she sounded happy.

"Yes thanks, its fine here, I'm just getting used to everyone."

We chatted about the people I'd met and how she was thinking about booking a holiday. I waited for a gap in the conversation and asked her what she knew about property law.

"Not much really, but I know someone who does and he's shit hot. You don't need a lawyer, Steph. You need someone who specialises in leases and agreements, rates, that sort of stuff. I'll send you his number—in fact no, I'll drop it in, I want to see your new place."

"Great, see you after work, I'm not going anywhere. I'm right on the top floor."

"I know, you have only told me a million times! You manifested the penthouse suite, clever girl!"

I showered before dinner and, as I stood in the steaming water, emotion flooded over me quite by surprise. I remembered the night I had been to see Sue for the first time, and the whole bedroom interlude with Jay before I'd left. I didn't know if I was crying for myself or crying for him, but in that moment I felt so lonely. Talking about our situations in the kitchen had raked up more for me than I had realised and, although I knew he would never be what I really needed, in that moment I wanted Jay near me more than ever.

By the time I was dressed and my hair was dried I was feeling better. My failed marriage was still a backdrop to the main event of my life but I could grin and bear it once more. The show must go on.

I passed someone on the stairs I hadn't met yet. She smiled and squeezed past with a large plateful of dinner and a plastic dish full of mashed potato with a *Teletubbies* spoon stuck in.

Jude was dishing up in the kitchen and Sheila and Asha were hovering around.

"Should have waitress service for a fiver you know." Sheila held out her plate.

"I'll give you short rations mind!" Jude responded.

We all made our way into the front room where there was a small fold away dining table that had been set with six places, complete with checked table cloth and a small vase of flowers as a centre piece.

I sat with Sheila and Asha, waiting for the others. Both of them picked up their cutlery and started straight away.

"We don't stand on ceremony here," Sheila said, so I followed suit and started eating.

The food was delicious, real country kitchen, homemade and hearty. I wondered what Jude's husband would be eating tonight.

Jude came to the table and so did someone I didn't recognise. She was quiet and sat with her eyes on her food for the most part, laughing in the right places but not really joining in. The door buzzer went halfway through and Sheila answered it. I recognised Hannah's voice and stood up to hug her.

"This is Hannah everyone, she's my friend and…erm my fantastic divorce lawyer too." Hannah laughed and so did I.

"That smells so good," Hannah said, as Jude excused herself and came back with another plateful.

"Come on, dig in, there's plenty to go round," she said and slipped the plate under Hannah's nose.

"Are you sure?" said Hannah, who was clearly starving but didn't want to take someone else's share.

"Yes I'm sure," said Jude. "And when we are finished I can pick your brains."

"You've got a deal." said Hannah in between mouthfuls.

I helped Sheila with the dishes while Jude told Hannah her life story and asked about settlements. Hannah took notes and said that she would gladly represent her and raise a divorce petition against her husband.

Once Hannah could escape, we made our way upstairs and I noticed light shining from under the door next to mine. I guess I had a neighbour.

I opened my door and walked in ahead of Hannah, switching on the lamp and turning around to see her reaction.

"Wow, Steph, its perfect, just as you described." She walked over to the window and pulled back the voiles to get a good look at the street below, then turned and smiled. "It's gorgeous, really Steph I am so happy for you."

"Well its home for now," I said and filled up the kettle, pleased with her response.

"Coffee or tea?"

I made two teas and I perched on the bed as Hannah sat on the chair next to the window.

"So what do you think of the others?" I asked.

"Well they're certainly different!" Hannah replied. "I mean you've got every walk of life in here, Steph, you certainly won't be bored! Sheila is a one off, Asha cracked me up and it looks like Jude is my next divorce client. Not a bad nights work all in all."

"I know what you mean, they are all so different aren't they? Yet we are all here—here in the same boat— paddling along on the river of survival." I laughed at my own mockingly melodramatic tone.

"It's like I see bits of me in each of them, you know, like elements or fragments of my life now or my life before.

It's hard to explain but it's like they are all me in some way."

Hannah looked thoughtful.

"You're right you know, in more ways than you think…you've just reminded me of something." She put her mug down on the window sill and dug deep into her battered, brown satchel bag. She pulled out a book and started to thumb through it, leaning towards the lamp so as not to cast a shadow on the pages.

"There we are," she said and pressed the pages open to make a clear crease at the start of chapter eight. The title read 'The Law of Reflection'. Hannah scanned the first few lines with her index finger and muttered under her breath for a moment and then became more coherent and quoted from the text.

"The universal law of reflection states that when we recognise traits or characteristics in others, either likeable or not, that these traits and characteristics are being drawn to us in order to reflect and amplify our own awareness of our strengths and shortcomings."

"Of course!" I interrupted her. "That's it!" I made my way to the wardrobe and started to look through my jacket pockets. My fingers felt paper and I pulled out a bus ticket, then tried the other side. Bingo. I unfolded the piece of paper and read out loud, "Introspection and the Law of Reflection."

Hannah looked vacant, and I realised that I hadn't told her that I'd been back to see Sue.

I started talking and filling in gaps, as she scanned the remaining lessons.

"So that must be it." I eventually stopped for breath.

"I think it means that people in our lives show up and behave in certain ways that reflect back to us who we are, so that we can work on our stuff. Like if someone is lazy, then there must be part of you that is lazy and if someone is kind then you are kind etc."

She shrugged her shoulders in a questioning kind of way.

"But why would that happen?" I asked.

"I think..." she went back to the book and scanned another paragraph, nodding. "I think it's all about the quantum thing again, the law of attraction you know. Like attracts like, and if you are giving of a signal or emotion in your vibration or energy then the universe will find a match for it and send you that person or experience. Apparently it's a fantastic way to be able to see what you should be working on and looking inside yourself at any given time." She read on, and I lay back on the bed and thought about that.

What were the main things I was seeing around me in the people that I knew? Sheila was a person with low self-worth, who kept going back and being treated badly. Yes I could certainly relate to that from my past and, judging on what Hannah had said, I must still have a bit of that hanging round. Asha fled when things weren't right. She hit her threshold in a split second and scooped up her child and left. I remembered that moment in the toilets on my hands and knees when I reached my own snapping point. And Jude had been traded in—no medals for joining the dots on that one. And there was Hannah, confident and self-assured and on her journey to being empowered and living her truth. This was a reflection of the part of me that was growing and healing the rest of my life.

"We have to learn to step back and really look at what we are being shown. Instead of judging others and their behaviour, we need to look at the parts of us which has brought this in. This is the way we can find out what we have to work on and to clear out of our energy. And, according to this book, once we have made progress on something we'll stop attracting it in." Hannah spoke the wise words that she held in her lap.

"I'd never have thought of it that way," I said. "But now I can't stop thinking of all of the people I have known and what they may have been showing me."

"God I know, I have hung out with some weirdoes!" laughed Hannah.

"Me too, I wonder what that says about us?" I laughed too, and the world felt good.

"Should we sneak out for a drink?" Hannah said in a stage whisper, once she caught her breath. "Do you have a curfew?"

"Course not!" I laughed. "That sounds like a great idea."

I pulled on my coat and we made our way down the stairs into the night.

Stephanie's Journal - Lesson 7
The Law of Reflection

What we see in other people are reflections of parts of ourselves. These reflections are attracted to us as they match something in our energy. This is an opportunity to grow and embrace the people that are reflecting to us as masters and teachers. They are literally showing us the way to our own growth and enlightenment if we can suspend our judgement and ego and see this in them. The ones that push our buttons most are our greatest teachers.

"The good we find in others, is in you too. The faults you find in others are your faults as well. After all to recognise something you must know it." Unknown

Chapter 18

The following day started early. The night had been hot
and heavy and I had slept with the window open. The
sound of rain and the rumbling of thunder woke me at
about 5am and the world outside was starting to come
alive again. Buses pulled in to the kerb and one or two
people were walking around with umbrellas. I closed the
window and snuggled back into my bed, drifting into the
in between place that existed when you were neither
asleep nor awake. My thoughts turned to Jay and how sad
it felt to sleep alone now.

Sleep crept up on me and my subconscious mind threw
up images of Jay and I together, some good times and
some bad. They all merged into one experience and one
moment when he stood before me with a full length mirror
in his hands and spoke in his familiar voice,

"Look at your own reflection Steph. Go on take a long,
hard look."

Snapshots of my life flashed before me, anything and
everything I wasn't proud of, and each picture stayed just
long enough for me to register that feeling of dread,
embarrassment and pain before it changed to the next one.
Each one compounded the agony I felt about my life in
that moment, as if I was briefly reliving it. Tears poured
down my face and, in my mind's eye, I saw myself falling
to my knees and pounding the mirror until it cracked and
the shards fell around me like daggers.

I looked up as Jay towered over me laughing, and
pointing at me as blood ran freely from my wrists as I
realised that I had taken some of the glass and cut myself.

His face contorted into a grimace and seemed to age before me as I screamed for help and he turned his back.

I woke with another scream caught in my throat and my pillow wet from crying. I sat up and let the tears continue. No matter what he had done and how he had treated me, I felt so lonely, and even though I tried to forgive and move on, the facts were that his were the last arms around me.

It took me a while to compose myself, as well as two cups of tea and a hot shower. I put on some make-up to hide my puffy eyes and made my way downstairs. I used the office phone and contacted the property man that Hannah had recommended. He was in a meeting but his secretary would pass on the details. I could hear chatting and the sound of cups clinking in the kitchen, but I didn't feel like company. I quickly weighed up my options - go back to my room and hide for a while or go out for the morning and stop moping. I went back upstairs and found a lightweight raincoat just in case there was another downpour and stuffed my phone and purse into the pocket.

I made my way down the stairs and the sound of laughter and smell of coffee drifted into the hallway. Josie came in the front door with a carrier bag of supplies.

"Hi Josie, just going out for an hour or so. If a guy called Pete Simmons rings, it's about making an appointment to come and see you about the Compulsory Purchase of the building. Hannah says he is really good and if anyone can help he can," I said over my shoulder whilst holding the door open.

"Thanks Steph, that's great. Are you ok?" she said.

"Just having a wobbly day I guess." I blinked away tears.

"We all have them, love." Josie smiled sympathetically and I let the door close behind me.

I walked along the street not knowing where I would end up. It was mid-morning now and the sun was shining. I slowed my pace and looked in shop windows as I passed by, seeing but not seeing what they had in store. Before long I was passing the *Citizen's Advice Bureau* and their logo jogged a memory of something I had doodled on a note pad a day or two ago—*housing benefit*. I went in and took my seat in reception until I could see Brett saying goodbye to a mousy-looking woman with jam-jar glasses.

I made my way over and we exchanged pleasantries, then I started to mine for information. I wanted to know if any of the occupants of Prospect House could claim housing benefit while they stayed there and, if so, could Prospect House keep this as rent? Brett listened and mulled it over, then he put in a call to a colleague at the benefits agency. He repeated what I had said and then there were lots of "yes I see" and "ok I'll find out" followed by a "maybe you should". When he hung the phone up he said that it would depend on eligibility for each person and this is based on how much they have in the bank, why they are at Prospect House, income or not, and a general overview of their circumstances. Although this sounded like a minefield, he assured me that there would be people that were eligible and that there could be a way to use this to generate income.

Melanie had suggested that she come out and speak to us as a group and see if anyone could claim this or any other benefits. She could also bring someone from the council's landlords scheme to talk about short term tenancy agreements and payment of rent where appropriate. I had no idea how much people were granted for housing benefit, but it certainly seemed worth exploring.

Brett gave me a compliments slip with Melanie's details so that I could phone for the appointment. I folded it and slipped it in my purse before I left. My stomach growled as I walked back out onto the high street and I realised it was after lunch time. I started to make my way back to the eatery opposite 'home'. There were storm clouds rolling over the tops of the buildings and the temperature was dropping. I stopped a few steps away from Prospect House and pressed for the little green man. I squinted towards the blackboard that they usually had outside with the lunchtime special chalked on, but something else caught my eye. An immaculately dressed Lizzie, in a fitted white trouser suit with her hair all piled up stylishly, counting out money and leaving it on a saucer in the middle of the bistro style table. *BLEEP BLEEP BLEE.P*

I didn't know whether to cross or not and an angry driver tooted at me and waved his hand shouting: "Get over!" His tone broke the spell and I made a dash for it, just as the heavens opened and big, fat raindrops blotted the road and pavement with dark spots. I could see Lizzie gathering up her bag and an A4 black leather-bound folder she had been leafing through. She was struggling with opening an umbrella at the same time. I was only a few steps away now as the folder opened and pieces of paper started to dance and float, then stick to the wet ground.

The waiter rushed to help and adeptly opened the umbrella as Lizzie scrambled to grab client notes and contracts. I reached down to pick up the one nearest to me and she looked up, making eye contact for the first time in months.

"Oh, Steph!" She quickly took the soggy document from my hand. My mascara was probably running down my face the same way that the ink was running down the page. "Hi, what a surprise!" She stuffed the last two letterheaded sheets in the folder and held the file tight across her chest. "How's things with you?" She sounded awkward and insincere.

"Fine," I replied. The rain was pouring from the heavens and I edged further under the flimsy canopy.

"What about you?" I asked as Lizzie squirmed.

"Well, you know, the usual, busy, busy, busy!" She was slowly stepping away in her trademark heels and I shook my head in disbelief.

"What's wrong?" I said "What's going on with you? Why are you avoiding me?"

She forced a laugh and replied, "I'm not avoiding you silly, just busy! Let's do something really soon. I'll call you OK?" As she turned, her expression gave her away. Why would she be feeling regret and sadness when she looked at me?

I started to backtrack things I could have said or done that would have upset her, trying to pinpoint the moment when things changed as I watched her tip tap through the puddles. Just before she rounded the corner I saw something drop onto the pavement, a slip of paper or business card maybe. I had lost so much these past months, and although I was finding myself and rebuilding my life, there was no way that I was going to lose my best friend without a fight. We'd been through so much together and I was sure there was nothing that we couldn't talk out, and anyway, I couldn't for the life of me think what I could have done.

I ran and picked up the saturated scrap with the intention of following her back to the office and handing it over in person. Surely out of the rain and in her office with the door closed her defences would come down we could sort this out.

"I just want the truth," I said. "I just want the truth."

I turned over the paper in my hand. The other side was black and shiny. There was a small image on the paper. It stood out over the background that looked a bit like snow you get when the television is not tuned in properly, but darker. I blinked rain out of my eyes and looked again. It was the image of a baby. I was holding a scan photograph and it had Lizzie's name printed across the top. I looked at today's date and realised that this scan must have been done this morning.

Things started to make sense to me now and, as my feet pounded after Lizzie, I thought about how much of a shock this must have been to her. She had never wanted to have children, this must be what had fuelled the problems in her relationship. Maybe she had relented and agreed to have the baby for him? So many questions but one focus. I wanted to help my friend.

I reached reception breathless and soaking, and I took a moment in the downstairs toilet to use the hand drier inverted to blast my hair dry. It was now more bird's nest than bird's nest soup at least. I dragged my fingers through it and tucked the strands behind my ears. I wet a paper towel and dabbed away the traces of makeup from under my eyes, then stood back from the mirror. At least no one here would recognise me since last time anyone saw me was at the Christmas Party when I was dolled up to the nines.

This however did not hold me in good stead when the receptionist looked me up and down and looked vacant until I said, "You know...Steph...the tights...remember?"

"Oh Yes! Sorry. Natural Bamboo!"

She obviously had no idea of the distance that Lizzie had put between her and the world as she buzzed me in through the first door and said; "I'll just ring and tell her you are coming up, she's got no clients this afternoon. Just go up."

"Thanks," I said, and made my way to the lift.

"I am supporting and helping my friend." I kept repeating to myself with my intention firmly focussed on just that.

Floor seven and the lift doors pinged open.

I took a breath and smoothed out the crumpled, wet picture on my sleeve, carefully so as not to tear it. I walked towards Lizzie's office and saw her through the glass panelling with her back to me, talking in hushed tones on her mobile. The door was ajar and I couldn't make out any words but I could hear her sobbing. Hormones on top of everything else, I had heard other friends say that being pregnant was akin to PMT in the early stages—sore boobs, feeling teary and tired. I wondered if I'd ever get to experience it.

I waited a couple of seconds until Lizzie hung up and I tapped on the door and braced myself at the same time.

"Yes?" she said without turning round, and I let myself in.

"Hey, you," I spoke quietly. "You dropped something"
I handed the scan photo over carefully.

"Yes I did. My pants when I shouldn't have," she said, without looking at me.

"Is that why you've been avoiding me?" I asked.

"I guess so, Steph, I am so sorry." Lizzie began crying again and asked me to close the door and also the blinds, even though there was no one in the open plan waiting area for this floor.

"It's fine, honestly, it's fine. I should have known that you were going through big stuff but I was too wrapped up in my own drama to be a good friend. It's me that should be saying sorry." I hugged her tight and we both cried together before the moment was broken by a text message on her phone.

Her mood changed immediately and she started to reach for her handbag and keys.

"Come on, let's go somewhere we can really talk, away from the prying eyes." There was an undercurrent of urgency in her voice.

"Can I just grab a quick drink of water please?" I had run all of the way.

"Oh yes, fine." Lizzie ushered me out and turned the key in the lock as I walked over to the water cooler and dispensed a plastic cup. A couple of suits walked past me down the hallway, talking about fees as I gulped and more footsteps came as I refilled.

It took me a few moments to place Jay's voice as it was so out of context. I stepped back and hovered behind the water cooler, acutely aware of the 'drowned rat look' I was sporting this season. I had at least hoped. When I did bump into him again, I'd be about three stone lighter with full makeup on my face and *Karen Millen* covering a toned backside. The opposite to how I looked right now.

She ushered him into her office and he slammed the door. I could hear their raised voices as I stood frozen beside the large bottle of spring water, neck down in the chiller.

He was talking to Lizzie and, although she didn't look in my direction, I could feel her radiating embarrassment and awareness of my presence. I could see them through the tilted blinds.

"Well?" he barked at her.

"Well, what?" She was more subdued and kept her voice low.

My heart was pounding in my chest and I tried to control my breathing. It felt so wrong spying on them like this, but I was rooted to the spot.

"Let's see it then. The picture," Jay demanded and, in that moment, I realised he knew. But why would he know that Lizzie was pregnant? And as soon as the question started to form in my mind, he answered it for me. It was his child. "So you are pregnant then." He snatched the wet, flimsy evidence from Lizzie and it tore into two. He pieced them together in a fashion and snorted. I saw her shrink in stature and cringe like a dog being kicked as he screwed up the sodden image and threw it at her.

"When are you going in then?" he spat in her face.

Lizzie started to cry and shuffle towards the door. She stepped into the main corridor.

"I don't know yet, I need to see…"

"See what?" Jay walked in front of her and blocked her route. "You are going to get rid aren't you?" He put out his hand to stroke her face. "Then we can get back to normal." His hand fell to her breast and she pushed it away.

"This has never been normal Jay. It's sick. Now let me go."

Lizzie tried to push past him but he wasn't finished. He grabbed her wrist and pulled her back into the seating area like it was an arena.

"I need you." His fake charm oozed through gritted teeth. "You know I do. Come on let's be reasonable, just get rid and we can move on together."

"You need my money," Lizzie said. "And you aren't having any more."

"You bitch!" Jay looked her up and down and stood back a step, turning up the volume.

"Please Jay, no, not here…"

"Ladies and Gentlemen, come and have a look at what we have here…" If she was going to walk away from him he was going to ruin her career in the same day.

One of the partners came out of her office and asked Lizzie if everything was alright. She shook her head and the partner made straight for her desk to ring security.

"Come on, don't be shy. Have a look at your high flyer in all of her glory." Jay continued to rant and I saw Lizzie trembling now. Every time she side-stepped to get away, he matched her. There was no escaping the humiliation now.

"Just leave it Jay, not here, please…"

"She's nothing but a slut. Someone who rolled over and spread her legs for a married man. And now to top it all off she's pregnant, the stupid bitch." Blinds were twitching and footsteps were coming along the corridor.

Lizzie looked around like a startled animal, caught in headlights a split second before the impact that finishes them off.

"Don't believe him, it's not true, we broke up and he's having a meltdown…" If she was looking in my direction I couldn't see, my eyes were tightly shut and I was trying to control my breathing.

"Well I don't believe it's mine anyway. Christ knows who you have been putting it about with. If you can sleep with their best friend's husband you can't have any standards at all. I bet I am just one of many you fucking slag."

I felt like I was going to pass out or vomit, my heart raced and I was holding back sobs that were beginning to choke me. I wanted to disappear into thin air and rewind time back to the street, to a time and place where I would never have had to witness this awful showdown.

"Right that's enough." Two security guards lunged at Jay and pinned him to the wall, as Lizzie saw her chance to run. She bolted for the staircase that was in the corner just past the lift. I cowered and tried to make sense of what I had just seen and heard.

Lizzie had been the tinny voice on the phone and probably the overnight stay the night I was in the police station. I remembered her sweet talking on her mobile the night of the fortune-teller, and how edgy she had seemed and desperate to hide who she was talking to. My supposed friend could do this to me, all of the questions about how long it had been going on and where they had met to have sex started to run through my head. My fury hit boiling point when I remembered all of the times that Jay had called me desperate and needy, telling me that I was imagining things and that I should stop being insecure. The pin on his phone, the overnight stays were all adding up now.

It would be easy to say to myself that she had been the reason he'd left and why my marriage had broken apart, but in my heart I knew if it hadn't been her it would have been someone else. And there probably had been others along the way. I knew Lizzie well enough to know that she must have been manipulated and desperate to get involved with Jay. She was my friend, at least she had been, and although there was part of me that hated her in this moment, I pitied her as well. She was so protective of her reputation at work that to humiliate her in front of her colleagues was the ultimate embarrassment, and he had known that. He could have easily saved this argument for a private confrontation but that was not his style, he liked to be in control and belittle people. The moment before Lizzie turned and fled down the stairs I had seen a flash of myself in her eyes, the self I thought I had left behind months ago, but judging by the reaction in my gut I hadn't left my past behind completely. I had asked to see the truth and there it was in devastating clarity. The lift doors were closing on Jay with the two security guards and he looked in my direction and for a moment I thought he recognised me, as a high pitched scream rang out from the stairwell.

Adrenaline took over and I ran across the reception and through the door marked 'exit'. I could see Lizzie lying at the bottom of the stairs in a heap, whimpering and trembling with her eyes closed. It seemed like an age for me to get to her.

I took her hand and spoke as calmly as I could. "Lizzie it's me, you're going to be ok." I took her hand and started to cry with her. "He's a bastard Lizzie, I know that and so do you and we'll get through this, me and you, we've got to."

"Oh God, Steph, I am so sorry, I never meant to…" she spoke in quiet breathy words and her face winced in pain with each one.

"I know, I know. Look we just need to get some help. Where's your phone?"

"It's in my bag."

I looked and saw that the strap was caught around her ankle, which was now swelling badly, and supposed that this had caused her to fall—especially on those heels. I took it out and unlocked the key pad with shaky hands and couldn't believe there was no signal. I stood up and changed position, watching for those three little bars to light up, hoping and praying that they would.

Lizzie sobbed again and murmured something about pain, and I crouched down next to her again. That is when I saw the blood spreading all over her white trousers and I couldn't stop myself from vomiting in the corner and screaming for help.

Chapter 19

The ambulance seemed to take forever, and by the time they lifted Lizzie onto the stretcher she was unconscious. They gave her oxygen and, as the sirens blared, I held her hand and cried for myself, for her and for the baby she was losing. No matter what had transpired between her and Jay as my marriage had limped around its last lap, this was far more important.

She was rushed into theatre on arrival and, an hour and a half later, taken on to a ward in a private bay. I didn't have contact details for her parents and I didn't know if she would have wanted them to know anyway, so I was deliberately vague when asked for details.

I sat looking at her until I felt myself nodding off. Her face was as pale as the sheets on the bed and she had some sort of clip on her finger that was reading her pulse. There was a cannula in the back of her hand but no drip, and she had been catheterised. Her left ankle was bandaged. The nurse came in twice with tea for me and, when she collected the second empty cup and filled in Lizzie's chart, she suggested I go home for the night.

"She's not likely to be with it until the morning love, you'd do better getting some rest yourself and coming back then."

"But what will you tell her when she wakes up and asks about the baby?"

"We'll have to tell her the truth, love. That she is no longer pregnant."

I nodded and leant over and kissed Lizzie's forehead. She didn't stir.

I made my way down the long corridors to the lift and then into the car park, past smokers corner. People were milling around in various emotional states, some carrying helium 'it's a girl' balloons and wearing ear to ear smiles, and others linking arms and speaking in quiet voices and sighing. There was a pizza delivery boy carrying a large flat box with a can of coke on the top, a dog tied to the railings and someone on a mobile. Different experiences of the same human condition.

And then there was me. Bedraggled, hungry and knackered. It was early evening now and I had no idea where the day had gone. My head was pounding and I felt like at any moment I could burst into tears. My clothes had dried into a crumpled mess and I would have won the first prize on bad hair day. I couldn't face waiting for the bus so I called a taxi and waited on the wall near the drop off bay. I looked like I needed to go to a bloody shelter so the driver probably wasn't surprised in the least when I gave him the address. He probably thought poor cow's been on the run all day. I felt like it.

I hoped there would be no one around, but wasn't so lucky.

Sheila was the first one to see me and, after that, there was no escape.

"Bloody hell, what happened to you?" Her Scottish accent echoed around the hallway and, before I could answer. Jude and Josie were on the scene too.

"I erm... I don't know where to start really..." And the words stammered out as I cried into my hands and just stood there.

I felt arms around me as I was guided to the front room by Josie and a blanket was thrown around my shoulders as I started to tremble. I don't know if what I said made any sense at all, it was all a bit jumbled up and I had to keep breaking off to blow my nose and sob into more tissues.

I was sick in the waste paper bin when I recounted seeing Lizzie lying at the bottom of the stairs and the blood pooling around her thighs, and I cried hard for the baby that I had wanted with Jay.

Once the whole story was out I felt relieved but exhausted, and Jude asked me if I had eaten. A cup of tea with sugar and a sandwich were soon rustled up for me. I ate slowly at first and then ravenously, pressing my finger onto the crumbs on the plate and licking them off. Jude brought some biscuits and my headache started to subside a little.

"Well it seems like you have been through one hell of a day Steph." Josie held my hand the same way I had held Lizzie's less than an hour ago.

"That's an understatement," Sheila added. "Jesus Christ." She shook her head.

"You must be totally shell-shocked, Steph, is there anything that we can do to help you?" Jude asked.

"No, really, you have been great. Thank you," I said. "I don't know how I feel, it's a weird combination of opposite emotions right now and I can't separate them in this brain fog." I rubbed my temples and pulled the blanket round closer. "Maybe I just need to go to bed."

"OK, love, you know where we are if you need us," Josie said and the others nodded in agreement.

I made my way upstairs slowly. I felt like life had kicked the stuffing out of me again, just when things were starting to get better. As I lay in bed it felt like the world was closing in on me. My world, the one that I had left behind and the one that I was creating, were all really a combination of inevitable hurt and pain. I couldn't believe in that moment that any amount of positive thinking would drag me out of this pit of despair.

Memories of Jay and I were stuck on replay in my mind, interjected with moments of clarity that I had been too blind to see in the moment. My conscious mind was joining the dots on all of the occasions, conversations and evidence that pointed towards him seeing Lizzie when I was at home, waiting for things to get better in our marriage. And although there was more certainty after hours of analysis, there was no relief from the emotional torture.

The night continued to pass slowly and the little sleep I had offered no reprieve from the revelations of the day. I woke before dawn in a cold sweat, from a nightmare of Lizzie bleeding to death in my arms.

I sat with a mug of tea, looking out of the window as the light slowly changed to daytime. I was all cried out now and I wanted to make some kind of sense of the feelings that were ripping through my heart in every moment. I tried to work out who I felt angrier with, Jay or Lizzie. I closed my eyes and allowed an image of them to form one at a time and I checked my emotions. With Lizzie I felt betrayal and sadness, but also pity and love. It felt like having a monumental argument with a family member who had stabbed you in the back. I knew that I was hurt in the moment, but things would move on and heal in time. I tried not to allow myself to create images of them together, but inevitably they came and, as tears rolled down my face, flashes of their naked skin etched themselves into my mind. I knew that if it hadn't been her it would have been someone else. She was a victim in this too and, just like me, had put herself in the firing line.

With Jay I felt fury and devastation in equal measure. He was my drug of choice, life-wrecking and addictive. I knew rationally that I was going to be so much better off without him. There was however a part of me that craved one more chance of a connection so much that I would have walked bare foot over razor wire to have him love me. Love me in the way I had wanted and needed for so long. A true, deep, heartfelt love that grew stronger as you grew older and would bind you together on all levels and get you through anything.

It was time to admit to myself that no matter how much I had put into the relationship with him, there was no way I was ever going to experience this. I had given everything I had to him, naively and willingly.

It was only now, in the aftermath, that I realised the real version of him was the one I had seen in Lizzie's office. Deliberately humiliating and crushing someone until they literally had to run away from him. He was a coward and a bastard, and he would never be the man I wanted. But like a leaky tap I couldn't switch off the feeling of desperation and longing for him. They kept dripping into my emotions like Chinese water torture for my soul.

What he had done to Lizzie he had also done to me in smaller doses over the years. My self-worth and dignity had slowly ebbed away, as I started to believe that I really was overweight or embarrassing or insecure. Whatever knife he felt like twisting in that moment. But much of it was so subtle, like looking me up and down disdainfully and shaking his head before a Christmas Party once and saying: "Well if you are happy wearing that then that's fine...no really you look fine."

Comments like this fuelled me to drink more than I should have, sometimes half a bottle of wine before we left in order to get through it with my brave face on. Not feeling good about yourself exposes various hot buttons that people seem to press unwittingly. This means that instead of seeing things the way they are, there is an insecurity filter that makes you feel like you have to defend, justify and generally big yourself up when people pass comment. These comments can be about anything by the way and, in my experience, the whole dynamic escalates when alcohol is involved. It's like lighting a verbal torch paper.

So there were several occasions I had 'spoiled' and was disgracefully sent home in a taxi on my own. Sometimes he came back that night and sometimes he didn't. The aftermath always lasted for weeks when I would try to fix things, buy things and generally be totally subservient in order to make it up to him, even though he had been the catalyst before and during the event.

It was also a favourite of his to wait until I was wound up like a spring before he started an intimate conversation with a beautiful woman. He would make sure there was a suggestion that he could have her if he wanted to, and there would be long gazes and brushing against each other. He would make sure the entire show would be in full view for me, usually whilst I sat with someone boring from accounts that I couldn't escape from.

Last Christmas it has been Simone, a graduate that had joined the marketing team with long, dark hair, eyelashes to match and a knock out figure. When I excused myself to go to the ladies and deliberately walked past them, he leant in close and whispered something to her before pulling back and saying, "Hi Steph, you don't look too steady. I wouldn't have any more wine." Then he looked back at his companion and laughed. "You should have seen her last year!"

I knew there was no point in even trying to challenge him. It would all be turned around on me again, being suspicious and needing to get a grip of myself. My former self was gradually and invisibly eroded, like emotional sandpaper - a fine grade that will gently lift the top layer away and expose the next. He just kept rubbing and rubbing in one direction as the person that I had been was slowly turned into dust and I was left exposed, defensive and feeling worthless. Filling up my life with more and more stuff and showing the world that really I was good enough, then varnishing over this with a big fancy wedding and a new house. But varnish can crack.

I snapped back to reality as rainbows began to dance on the walls as the sun shone through the window. I sighed. They had caught me unexpectedly as had my moment of realisation. A contrast to the darkness of my thoughts and feelings and a reminder sent at that perfect moment to look for the good.

In truth, Jay had been my greatest teacher.

With distance on our relationship came insight, and that
slowly started to ignite gratitude. I was on a journey to
reclaim myself and heal my life and, just as the rainbows
had contrasted with my thoughts, Jay had given me the
contrast in our marriage that I needed. Introspection was
now allowing me to see the part of the victim that I had
played and perpetuated. The patterns, beliefs and
behaviours that had created the platform for this toxicity
were in me too, not just him.

We had directed each other and created a premiere that
we lived out between us. A romantic drama filled with all
of the essentials, lust, love, money and betrayal. Both of
us had embraced our role fully and brought to it the
experiences we had lived beforehand. I interjected some
victim archetypes, courtesy of the school bullies, and a
great big dollop of 'silly cow'. Jay brought a whole lot of
arrogance and a complete lack of commitment thanks to
his training in the family home, where he had also learned
to have lower morals than a horny dog.

We played full out, scene after scene of our lives
together in a torturous love affair that ended inevitably. I
sighed again. As a member of the audience rather than the
lead role, I felt sadness for us both. I could see that in
essence we were both doing the best we could have done
in the circumstances, warts and all. I drank, he shagged
about and it all went tits up. In reality there was no point
in hanging on to any of it. I needed to take the gift of the
learning and let it go. Forgive even, and let it go once and
for all.

I could hear other people moving around now. I was
going to see Lizzie in hospital so made a move to get
dressed.

The sister on the ward recognised me from yesterday
and I was allowed to slip under the radar, apparently
visiting was strictly 2pm 'til 4pm. Lizzie looked washed
out still but was awake, sitting up and watching *Richard &
Judy*.

"Hi you," I said as I pulled round a plastic chair.

Lizzie sighed and looked away, her eyes brimming with
tears.

"Steph, I can't believe you've come to see me." She
dabbed her eyes with the sleeve of her hospital gown. "I
owe you so much."

"I'm your friend, Lizzie, and we'll get through this." I
took her hand and started crying silently myself.

"Some friend I am," she replied. "You know now why I
was avoiding you. I bailed out on you when you needed a
friend more than ever, because I was so ashamed of what
was going on. I never, ever meant to get involved with
him, and by the time I had, it was too late."

"I know, I know, don't get upset," I tried to reassure,
although the words caught in my throat and they came out
in between sobs.

"Why not? You are upset and it's all my fault. I hate
myself and what I've done."

And there were parts of me that hated what she had done
too, but all of the tears and apologies in the world would
not bring her baby back, or her dignity.

Right then, I had a moment of clarity. I could turn the
screws even more and finish her off emotionally, which

would give me some kind of payback, or I could help her through. I wanted to forgive and move through this so badly. I wanted to learn this lesson and I hoped if she could tell me more about it, then I could forgive both of them, eventually. Forgiveness was certainly the hardest lesson so far and I hoped and prayed that I could complete it.

I poured her a glass of water and passed the tissues.

For the next half an hour we tentatively started to build up the foundations of our friendship again, and I saw in her the parts of me that Jay had mangled months ago, and my anger and indignation melted into pity.

The door opened and the doctors came in for the ward round. I made to get up and leave but Lizzie said, "Please stay."

They were direct and matter of fact, but with a caring undertone that made the delivery softer and less stark. The baby had gone, probably as a result of trauma from her fall. They had conducted a standard procedure to remove everything, limiting any chance of infection and Lizzie could go home later today, as long as she wasn't alone.

"She won't be," I smiled. Sometimes you just have to do the right thing.

Stephanie's Journal - Lesson 8
Forgiveness & Compassion

Forgiveness is a gift you can give yourself. Many people think that by forgiving someone who has wronged you in some way, you are letting them off the hook. This is not the case, you are actually letting yourself off the hook. Forgiveness means that you are able to let go of what has happened along with any judgment, anger and resentment that you are feeling about people or situations, as a loving gift to yourself. Freeing yourself from these negative and destructive emotions that eat you up emotionally and can create illness in your body, is the greatest thing you can do for you. Otherwise these people and situations will always have a hold on you and you will never be free.

Things happen in life that are very, very hurtful and distressing, but in order to find peace within yourself you need to find a way of releasing them and moving on with your life. Forgiveness is an active choice that you can make.

"Forgiveness is the fragrance that the violet sheds on the heel that has crushed it." Mark Twain

Chapter 20

The days were drawing shorter now and the light shone differently through the window. There was still heat in the sun but every day there were more signs that autumn was creeping in. The shops were filled with all things Halloween, and the café opposite had started doing 'soup to go' in a polystyrene cup with a bread bun in a paper bag.

Lizzie had taken a whole month off. Her request was granted graciously and, of course, fully expected. She was recovering well physically, and emotionally she was making progress but still very fragile. This was of course compounded by hormones, the doctor has said that these would take a few weeks to settle down. I tried to make it as easy on her as I could, and I saved my tears for times when I was alone. This was healing me too and, when I let them flow into my pillow, either the heat of anger and rage or the chill of being alone and betrayed left me for a while, sometimes long enough for me to have a full night's sleep.

Dreams enticed me to go beyond the veil of what was real and created illusion. Making love with Jay in these dreams always started out as the perfect combination of the passion and intimacy that I had always craved from him. The feather light touch of his lips on the nape of my neck and smell of his skin on mine were mixed into lucid pictures, part memory and part fantasy that scrolled through my mind's eye as our bodies entwined. These scenes made way for images of me gasping, as waves of pleasure rocked my body with monumental intensity. In that dreamscape moment I felt him inside me, and my body and emotions climaxed together, as did his. And I looked into his eyes, turned his head to face me and cupped his chin in my hands.

"I love you," I spoke softly and urgently to him, and in split second his eyes closed and he pulled away from me.

My cries echoed through the layers of this temporary reality, but no one heard. They tore at my heart as the image grew dark and cold and I saw myself alone now, begging him to come back. That's when the laughter started to ring out, hideous shrieking and howling from the shadows, as I cowered on my knees trying to cover my naked body with my hands and my hair. I always woke in a momentary panic, until my eyes adjusted and I remembered where I was. The tears usually came after my breathing had slowed down, as I hugged my pillow in a foetal position and cried out my pain and loneliness.

Most days I felt a full spectrum of emotions. The girls knew I was feeling down and they jollied me along with funny stories and jokes—a welcome reprieve. I tried to keep a brave face on things but the gravity of what had happened this year seemed to have compounded and drained me of any positivity I had left. It was like them throwing a rope into a dark pit and pulling me up to the light for an hour or so then I would go back to my room and my misery. Maybe this is what it's like when you are a prisoner and you get to go out into the yard for an hour a day like I had seen on the movies, then back to your cell for the rest of the day and night. My own personal *Shawshank Redemption.*

Maybe I was beaten now. This lesson seemed like a
sheer rock face to climb and I felt like I was clinging on
with my finger nails in a force ten gale. I was stuck in this
place - the place of feeling sorry for myself - and unable
to see a way out. Welcome to a town called *Inertia*, you
can visit some of our famous attractions like *The Pits* and
Dead End Street while you are here and don't forget
Round The Bend because you are going to end up there for
sure if you don't pass through quickly.

I had to get a grip, and luckily there was a flicker of
resilience left that prompted me to call Hannah.

"Hi, Steph!"

"Hiya," I sighed down the phone.

"What's up with you?" she asked.

"I think I'm having a breakdown," I said in a monotone
response.

"You don't sound good. I'll come over after work. Hang
in there until then, OK?"

"OK." It felt like I was watching someone else hang up
the call as I curled up again on my bed.

Hannah came upstairs, all bundled up in a scarf, hat and
fingerless gloves with three bottles of wine for a tenner.
She also had emergency chocolate in the striped carrier
bag that clinked and clanged and said that pizza was
coming.

I hardly gave her time to unfasten her coat before I
started blurting out that I couldn't do it anymore, why me,
it's so unfair and any other clichés that were at my
disposal. The victim in me had waited too long to get in
her glad rags and have a good rant at the world and all of
the shit that she had taken all these years. She even went

as far back as the wedding. There was also a side helping of self-righteous crap that she was better than the girls he had shagged on the side and they were nothing more than desperate slappers. Hannah just stood and listened as I paced the floor and told her how it really was, and had been of course. There was liberal use of the F word.

The narration slowed down after about five minutes. Like a car that was running out of petrol. More jerky and disjointed comments spat out, and then finally there was a winding down and a standstill.

Hannah looked expectantly to see if I had finished.

I sighed out the last fumes of anger and disgust with my life, crying instead of shouting now.

Hannah's arms were around me and she rocked me gently as she stroked my hair until the sobs ran dry and there were no more tears. Just two puffy eyes and the snotty right shoulder of her chunky brown jumper.

"It's awful to say, but I feel much better for that," My voice was a little husky.

"It's not awful, Steph, it had to come out - it's how you feel, and that makes it valid." Hannah opened the first bottle and we clinked glasses.

"Here's to a new start now you have let go of all of that crap," she smiled.

"OK, a new start then. But how do I get out of feeling this way?" I took a big gulp of wine.

"You need to work on letting it go and change your focus. You know how this stuff works. The more you focus on how awful it all is, the more awful it all is!"

Hannah laughed and so did I.

"Now what can you focus on that is positive?" she asked.

"I don't know," I admitted. That was the problem.

"What about this place?" Hannah gestured with her hands. "What about the fundraising you were doing and saving the project?"

"I don't know if I can keep going with that."

"Why not, Steph? Life has kicked you in the nuts and you can either roll over and play dead or you can get up and start fighting back. Now what's it going to be?"

Hannah put her hand under my chin and lifted my head to meet her direct gaze.

"Come on Steph. Stop being a victim and get on with it!" Her tone was serious and I knew, in that moment, life was throwing me a turning point. A chance to take one road or another and to choose the life that I wanted. I wasn't going to give up now. I might be down, but not out, and I knew in my core that I had to keep going.

I took a deep breath, puffed up my cheeks and let it out slowly. "You're right," I agreed, "I need to get back up and start looking forwards."

"Exactly," Hannah grinned. "Now there's the Steph we know and love! Welcome back!"

By the time I went to bed, I had promised myself that, no matter what, I would not be a victim any longer. I hoped it would turn out to be a promise I could keep.

The next morning, I awoke around the same time as the high street as I had left one of the windows ajar. I stretched and realised that I had slept all night without a bad dream. This really was a new start. I showered and dressed and made my way straight to my laptop and notepad, finding all of the scraps of information I had gathered about fundraising. There were several ideas that I had on the boil, and they were all at various points of progress. I was determined to distract myself from my own worries.

The next few days passed quickly and, by the end of the following week, I had secured regular donations from businesses that totalled in the region of £1200 per month, food and drink contributions from a local supermarket, maintenance and decorating from the college that had NVQ students needing to practise their skills, and a one-off donation of £500 from Lizzie's firm. I had also started a campaign for people to donate to good causes rather than sending Christmas Cards in the office, which was always a royal pain in the arse anyway.

It looked like some of us were eligible for housing benefit, which could come straight to Prospect House and, although I couldn't use the premises for a fundraiser, I was looking at venues for an Autumn Fayre. The community centre came up trumps and the date that they offered was 29th September, which was my 30th birthday. Each day that passed got a bit better and I found myself wallowing less and less.

Josie was still in talks about the building and it wasn't looking good. I was trying to change her perspective that we should look at saving the project instead of the building. I knew it would be a wrench for her, God knows I knew what that felt like having something you have built up torn away from you. The essence of the project was Josie though, and the safe space that she had created here could be adapted and taken elsewhere if it came down to it. Finding the strength to support someone else was supporting me too. I even tentatively looked into finding other possible venues to buy or rent. Since I had access to the accounts, I could estimate what she could afford. There were some lovely places out there and all I needed to do to help was to keep on finding funds, and that was something I was becoming really good at. I stuck up the details with blue-tack on the walls in my bedroom and started to deliberately align my energy to this project being relocated into the perfect building.

The Autumn Fayre was coming together and, although my thoughts drifted back to my own situation several times a day, I stopped allowing myself to go there as much in my thoughts. Women came and went at Prospect House and their stories were usually much worse than mine. I did what I could to support them and found that this brought me out of my own problems more and more.

When I saw couples holding hands in the street, I thought less of Jay and more of finding someone new that was right for me. I watched couples from my window behind the voile curtain, saw them talking and laughing, touching sometimes. I wanted this again, but in a purer form. I wanted to find my soul mate and, in an effort to draw him to me, I snipped out some pictures from magazines and little red hearts to stick up next to the properties on the wall. Being with someone again was a bit scary, but I knew in my heart the right person was out there for me and that he was looking too.

Josie was coming around to my way of thinking about the project now as the days became shorter and colder, and she even agreed to look at a couple of properties that were available. In between collecting bottles and bits for the tombola and selling raffle tickets up and down the high street, I went along with her to see some places, but they weren't quite right.

I was given the keys for the community centre the day before the fayre, which was great considering there was so much to do. I had to wait until the Fit for Life had finished and a load of oldies that looked like extras from *Cocoon* hobbled out with their yoga mats and water bottles. One old guy stopped and winked at me, he didn't look anything like the picture on my wall with the red hearts. Maybe he had 50 years ago.

Josie and Hannah came over to help and we pulled trestle tables into position and laughed at the bath cubes and the knitted loo roll doll that had been donated for the tombola. Cups and saucers were all laid out in the serving hatch, and the large tea urn was filled with water.

There was a book stall, bric-a-brac, clothes, toys and a table with raffle prizes. The cake stall had been scrapped as we only had a couple of donations and it was agreed that we should slice these and sell them with a cuppa instead. It was after ten o'clock when we stood back and surveyed the scene. I was tired and a bit grubby and I smelt like a jumble sale, but the result was a good one.

Josie locked up and Hannah stuck our '50p entry, kids free' sign on the door ready for the morning.

I hadn't told them it was a big day for me tomorrow in more than one way, in a couple of hours I'd be the big three–oh!!

Chapter 21

I slept well and stretched when the alarm on my phone tinkled me awake at 7:30am. Here it was then, the wrong side of thirty. It felt really strange to not have anyone to share it with, strange but also good to be able to avoid all of the over-the-hill jokes and bad taste cards. Maybe I would come clean later on and buy some takeaway and wine for everyone, but right now I didn't want anything distracting me from the job in hand.

I was showered and dressed in plenty of time and treated myself to a bacon roll at the café. By 9am I was fighting against the wind as I made my way across town to the community centre. It was only a ten minute walk and would blow the cobwebs away. My phone started to vibrate in my pocket and my icy fingers pulled it out to see who was calling.

"Hi Mum!" I turned my back into the wind to hear more clearly and the hood on my jacket flapped over my head. I pulled a bit of fringe out of my mouth.

"Happy birthday to you, happy birthday to you, happy birthday dear Stephanie…happy birthday to you!" She chorused with Dad in the background. I could imagine them standing in their hallway in their sensible three bed semi-detached with garage, axe minster carpet and blown vinyl wallpaper.

I gulped back emotion and stood in a shop doorway to compose myself and be heard.

"Thanks Mum, and you Dad, really, thanks."

"Did you get your present darling?" mum asked.

Oh God, I bet they sent something through the post to the house.

"Erm, I have been staying at Lizzie's this week mum, she's decorating and needed a hand…" I had been playing for time since I moved into Prospect House, sending them the odd text message and phoning once a week to keep in touch, telling them all about how busy I was with work and that things were fine etc. Luckily they lived about an hour's drive away and I was confident that they wouldn't drop in on a whim. Anyway they only really did special occasions on account of them not liking Jay.

"Oh well, it will be a nice surprise for you when you get home. When are you going home dear?"

"Erm, later on, I think. I'm just out to get a few bits and bobs then home again." I could nearly feel my nose growing. I hated lying and cringed.

"I expect he's taking you out somewhere nice tonight then?" Mum's tone changed, she could barely even say Jay's name.

"Yes, yes I hope so. I'm sure he has something planned anyway…"

"Well, what time will you be back then? It's just I can't hear you properly on this mobile phone with my hearing aid, it makes a whistling noise. I'd rather ring you on your house phone when you get back and have a proper catch up."

Oh God.

I thought on my feet. I would ring them from Josie's office phone after the fayre.

"I'll ring you Mum, it's fine. I will definitely be back by about one o'clock." That should give me time to tidy up the community centre.

"OK, one o'clock you say? That's fine. We miss you these days, we know you have your own life but you are still our daughter, Stephanie, and we really miss you. Maybe you could come down here for the weekend soon. You can bring him if you like."

She sounded resigned to the fact that Jay was part of my life whether they liked him or not and, in that moment, I wanted to tell her. I wanted to spill the whole story out, but I knew that this was not the way. She would have so many questions and although there was a part of her that wanted him gone, it would be a shock and I would rather tell them face to face. Next weekend looked good for that.

"OK Mum, thanks. I'll ring you later and we can sort it all out then." I missed them too.

"Love you darling," I could hear dad in the background shouting one more "happy birthday" as I said I loved them too and hung up the phone.

What was I going to tell them? I had no idea, but I knew that I didn't have time to think it all through now. Hannah, Josie and some of the others were coming to help and I had asked them to be there for 9:30am. I was only 2 streets away now and had to get my head back into tombola tickets and toy stalls.

There were leaves dancing around my feet as I turned the key in the door and the bleep, bleep of the burglar alarm pierced the silent building.

"Christmas day" I remembered as I punched in 2512 on the keypad and the noise stopped.

I found the thermostat and notched it up to twenty one degrees, flicked the switch for the water heater and turned on the lights. Although the sun was bright outside it was dull indoors in the main hall until after lunch when it had moved around and could shine through the sky lights.

I was straightening up the table cloths for the bric-a-brac stall when Hannah bustled in and Josie just after. There was someone from the café opposite coming to help for a couple of hours in the kitchen and we had Jude, Sheila and two newbies coming along.

The doors opened at 10am and there was a small queue formed already, a couple of grannies with tea cosy hats, a mother with a child in a buggy and a toddler holding her hand, single man and dog (tied up) and a young vegetarian looking couple dressed in charity shop chic, with piercings and an iPod between them.

They trundled in and the two grannies suddenly morphed from sweet old ladies to sharks in sensible shoes as they quickly found the best items and haggled for the lowest price possible. The one with the limp was miraculously cured and managed a circuit in five minutes flat, and that's with a shopping trolley. They produced carrier bags from their pockets and spoke of this government and their pension, thank goodness for the winter fuel allowance and how would they manage. Once the deal was done and each stall holder in turn had bought hook line and sinker into their hard luck stories, they unrolled their plastic bags for their loot and opened their purses which were bulging.

"Can you change a £20 dear?" granny one winked at granny two.

I had to laugh to myself, but not for long as I had a riot breaking out on the toy stall, two kids and only one magnifying glass. With some mediation and a consolation of a boomerang and a dot to dot book the storm passed and both twins went away happy with a promise to share when they got home.

By the halfway point the tombola was nearly empty apart from some cooking sherry and a packet of Yardley bath salts, and the cake had all gone. Pound coins rattled into the pots I'd put behind each stall, and I did a quick round to collect notes and put them safely in my bum bag. No I wasn't going straight to an eighties night, but I had found it in a bag of donated accessories and nabbed it for the day.

I had taped signs to the lamp posts (above the lost cat Tibby) with an arrow showing people where we were, and this ensured a steady stream right up until noon.

By the time we closed the doors and bagged up what was left over it was nearly one o'clock and Josie took the money back to start counting and Hannah and I set about stacking the tables and sweeping the floor.

"See you back home," Josie shouted over her shoulder, in a half theatrical way. Jude and Sheila quickly put on their jackets and made their excuses about wanting to help count the money and they were off. Strange, but then strange things seemed to happen every day now. The newbies scuttled out and said that they would see me later, seems like I was stuck with the hard work, at least Hannah was here.

The last table was pushed into the long storage cupboard and the dust pan and brush were left on top when my phone rang in my coat pocket. Hannah instinctively pulled it out as it rang off and made to pass it to me.

"Ten missed calls! Wow you're popular today!" She commented as she handed it over.

They were all from my mum's mobile, I checked the clock and it was just after noon. I had promised to call at one o'clock so what was the urgency? Oh God I hoped there hadn't been an emergency, dad had always had high blood pressure, maybe this was the big one.

"You ok?" Hannah asked and her voice jolted me back to reality.

"Yes, yes I'm fine." I looked at her. "No actually I'm not fine that was my mum and I'm scared that there's something wrong, she's never frantic like that to get hold of me..." I could feel that my emotions were about to boil over, and Hannah sensed it too.

"Well just ring her back Steph," she said in a soft voice, her tone was questioning.

"I can't, not yet, not until I have had some time to think about what I'm going to say." Now I felt frantic.

"What do you mean? It's just your mum, what's wrong?"

The phone rang again and I jumped, the Nokia ring tone echoed around the hall and Hannah watched my anxiety grow, as I went to answer then instead dumped the call.

"Steph, what on earth is wrong here?" She was firm now and took my shoulders in her hands.

"I don't know how to tell them…" I started, stammering a little.

"Tell them what?"

"Everything, just everything…."

"What do you mean everything about what?"

"Everything, all of it. They don't know any of it." I bit my bottom lip and the tears came.

Realisation dawned on Hannah's face and her expression turned to disbelief.

"You mean they think that you are still in the house, with Jay?" she asked.

"Yes, and with a job and a car. I haven't said anything to them about it at all, it's killed me at times but I just needed time and space to get my head around what was going on without my mum being judgmental about it all. She is so lovely but she only sees life from her perspective and I just know that she wouldn't approve of what's happened to me…" I pulled out a shred of tissue from my bag and blew my nose.

"Wow. I don't know how you have kept it all a secret for this long Steph, that's impressive." Hannah shook her head.

"I promised I'd call her at one o'clock today and have a catch up, I was going to tell her it all then, when I'd had time to think of what I was going to say. I was going to use Josie's office."

"Sounds like a good idea. Or maybe tomorrow when you have had more time?" Hannah pulled her coat on and scarf.

"No it's got to be today really." I paused and took a deep breath. "It's my thirtieth birthday today."

I looked down at the floor, it certainly didn't feel like a happy birthday right now and I was not relishing what I had in store when I told my mother the events of the last few months and justified keeping it to myself. If only there was a way that the universe could take it out of my hands and she could just find out somehow.

"I know it is Steph," Hannah hugged me.

"You know?"

"Yes silly. I am your lawyer! I have all of your details at the office and I have an anal habit of filling in everyone's birthdays on the calendar when I get a new client. I've got something for you back at home."

She smiled and I felt relieved, at least there was one person that I didn't have to keep lying to.

"Now come on, let's get back I'm starving!"

I checked that the lights were turned off and locked the main hall. I did a toilet check on the way out and noticed that there was one of these awful rectangular hard plastic air fresheners on the window sill, like a box up on its side with slits cut in and a hard red jelly cube wizened up inside. The smell of synthetic rose combined with medicated toilet paper as I pulled a handful of sheets off the roll to blow my nose. Clint Eastwood bog roll – hard as nails and takes no shit, as we all said at school. I splashed some cold water on my face and dabbed on lip gloss before I left the pastel pink walls that were desperately in need of a makeover.

"Come on!" Hannah was getting impatient. "We can talk on the way and get a plan of what you are going to say when you phone home."

We linked arms and made our way back over town and by the time we got back to Prospect House Hannah knew all about the traditional values of my parents, and the difficult times they had been through when my dad was out of work and they fell on hard times. She understood that this had hardened my mother and made her feel defensive now about things being done properly and having nice things. There was many a December when I knew my mother hadn't been able to scrape enough together to buy me gifts and she had joined a "Christmas Club" which meant that she could pay weekly for what I wanted, and paid over the odds of course. She was thrifty and could feed four people with a tin of corned beef, and came from the school of Make Do and Mend.

I didn't know anything about her upbringing so I couldn't share this with Hannah when she asked, but I do know that she felt embarrassed about having less than others and that being hard up for her was as hard on her ego as it was on her pocket.

I put her pickiness down to this. She would never miss an opportunity to pass comment on Mrs So-and-So's lovely new whatever and how much it cost, and poor Mrs So-and-So, who still has the same winter coat this year as she did last year. There was a certain irony in this as she had only been able to afford opinions like this since my father's mother passed away, and with him being an only child he got the lot. They say don't forget your roots, the only roots she seemed to think about now were the ones she had coloured every six weeks. I had just left home when this happened, and it wasn't long after this that they abandoned the two up, two down I'd grown up in and went detached. I guess my mums influence had rubbed off on me more than I'd realised.

A silver saloon flashed past us in the bus lane and the bus driver tooted, for a second it looked like my parent's car and my heart flipped over in my chest.

I laughed at myself, I knew by now that thinking about things made them happen and what did I expect, I'd spent the last 20 minutes talking about my parents, I was drawing examples to me.

I could see Prospect House now from the top of the street and Hannah seemed to be speeding up.

"Come on slow coach!" she laughed.

"What's the hurry?" I panted.

"You'll see!"

And when we got to the bottom of the steps there was no way that I could have missed the bunting on the fence, the balloons and banners and huge homemade poster in the window that shouted out "Happy Birthday Steph".

I looked at Hannah and pointed my finger in a mock scold, complete with school teacher tone.

"You lady are in trouble!"

She laughed and hugged me before we made our way inside to the thunder of party poppers and the squealing of joy as my new friends threw me my thirtieth birthday party, and the music started with Cliff singing me his congratulations.

Once I had taken it all in and composed myself, someone was tapping a glass with a teaspoon and shouting "Speech, speech!"

I cleared my throat as all eyes were on me, and willed myself not to cry.

"I don't know what to say… honestly." my hand fluttered up to my neck and I fanned back the tears. "This year has been the most incredible and scary year of my life and I can't believe that I am still going and getting through it…"

Clapping erupted and then faded.

I looked around at each person in the room, I knew their story and they knew mine.

"And you have all kept me going. Some of you don't even know that you have, but your story, your courage, your kindness...." I looked at Sheila. "Your haircuts..." laughter broke out in pockets and Sheila beamed back at me, "and your casseroles," Jude took a theatrical bow, "have all helped me beyond measure."

I locked eyes with Josie.

"Prospect House is a gift for everyone that comes here and no matter where we take it, the life, soul and essence of it will come along." Josie nodded in my direction.

"Here, here" echoed throughout the room and Josie stepped forwards.

"It seems a good time to do this, Steph. I want to say a few words." She cleared her throat.

"Since you have been with us you have made a monumental difference. You have worked tirelessly to help with this project and you have secured monthly income for us and also one off donations. I have the grand total for today's Autumn Fayre." She reached into her pocket and started to unfold a scrap of paper amongst shouts of, "Come on, get on with it!"

"I want to get it exactly right, so I have written it down... £2312.47."

More party poppers boomed around the room and their stringy nonsense rained down on me as I was hugged and kissed on both cheeks. The music was turned back up and Cliff was singing again, more congratulations and I felt like my heart was going to explode. What a day, and it wasn't over yet. Now the cat was well and truly out of the bag about my birthday I thought Hannah might want to go for some drinks later, make a night of it and celebrate like I should have been all along.

Josie caught my eye and gestured for me to go over for a moment.

"I know it's a bit sudden and that you will want time to think about it Steph, but I've got a proposal for you..."

"Sounds intriguing..." I shouted over *Devil Woman* and wondered if anyone had music from after the seventies.

"I'd like you to think about working here, properly with a salary and all. You are doing such a great job of fundraising I'd love to be able to keep you here for a while longer, and the money that is coming in now can support a part time wage." She looked expectant, even though she had reassured me I could think about it I knew that she wanted to know sooner rather than later.

"Josie I would love to!" I mouthed with a thumbs-up for good measure.

She hugged me and I hugged back tight, I could hardly believe it. A job where I could contribute to others and do something I loved at the same time, it was made for me.

It was then that everything seemed to lapse into slow motion for a moment, and I felt like I was watching a movie scene of myself unfold before me. I was aware that someone had come into the hall way and my intuition was doing overtime making butterflies flutter in my solar plexus. I knew who it was before Jude showed her in and the music went down.

Sensible shoes, country casuals trousers and a classic
taupe mac. Minimal makeup and stud earrings and a face
like a smacked arse.

"Stephanie?" in her best and loudest posh voice.
Everyone stood still and waited.

"Mum!" I walked over to her and hugged her. She did
her 'telegraph pole' where her hands and arms were frozen
to her sides. "Everyone, this is Anne Binks, my mum."

She mustered up something of a smile and necked the
glass of bubbly she was passed, then held the glass out for
a refill.

Chapter 22

"Well you had better start talking young lady, your father and I have had a dreadful shock and we want to know what's going on." She was stern and her face had started to colour up, a combination of anger and alcohol. That's where I get it from. She was speaking out of the side of her mouth. You are the weakest link, goodbye.

"Your father is parking the car, we've been round and round looking for somewhere, God only knows how far out he'll have to go and then walk back, and his bunions…" She held her glass out for a third top-up and I shook my head at Jude, too late, she had started swilling.

"Is there anywhere… you know…" she looked Sheila up and down disdainfully, "private?"

I took her by the arm and turned the music back up on my way out of the room. Her sensible shoes followed me upstairs. I managed to mouth a quick "sorry" over my shoulder.

It turned out that they had been to my house and that "some girl" had opened the door and claimed that she was living there, so they had told her that this was not the case and that she had it all wrong. When she had insisted that this was the case my mum and dad had called the police and reported me as a missing person, telling the nice lady that they had only driven up as a surprise for my birthday and could my father use the toilet please, it's his prostate.

They were going to wait in the car for the police to arrive but she offered them a cup of tea (with sugar for the shock), and showed them the tenancy agreement that I had countersigned. She then told them a bit of the story from her point of view.

That's when my parents had called the police back and explained that I in fact was not missing and I was in some kind of halfway house, perhaps I'd had a breakdown. Yes they would phone back if they didn't find me but actually they had spoken to me just a few hours ago so this didn't exactly constitute a "missing" person, possibly a person who was hiding, but not missing.

Mum went on to tell me the unfolding drama of dad's driving through a busy city centre that he didn't know whilst under stress anyway, one way streets, bus lanes and people honking at them.

"And then to top it all off we find you here!" She threw her arms up in despair at the room I loved and had provided a safe haven for me. I resisted the urge to defend my situation and allowed her to continue her rant, through experience I knew that it was best to let her get it all out.

"It's full of waifs and bloody strays Steph, what on earth are you doing here?"

Rhetorical, she took a short sharp breath and kept going.

"I mean for God's sake what on earth went wrong? I mean you had everything, your beautiful house, Jay... where is Jay? What does he think about all of this?" she was on her feet now pacing up and down.

"Mum," I interrupted.

"And what have you done with your hair Steph? You always looked so smart and beautiful, the homeless lesbian look just doesn't suit you darling."

"Mum!" I spoke louder.

She started to fiddle with my hair and shake her head.

"I suppose it will grow eventually but it's such a shame,
did you have a stupid moment darling? Like when you
used the Domestos wipes in the loo? Remember you burnt
your bits and we had to go to…"

She was clearly feeling the effects of alcohol, little food
and shock combined.

"Mum!" I stood up and took hold of her shoulders,
looking her in the eye. "I need to tell you but I can't when
you won't stop wittering on! Please sit down and I'll make
you a coffee!"

She reluctantly wilted into the chair and I sighed whilst I
filled the kettle and switched it on. I could hear her
disapproving tutting over the sound of the boiling water.
Just then there was a knock on the door that made me
jump, I guessed it was Dad before I saw him. He was
huffing and puffing like a steam train, ruddy faced and
livid.

"Bloody parking is terrible here!" he announced as he
looked past me at my mother. "I've had to walk bloody
miles you know, my feet are killing me!"

Mum gave me the "told you so" look.

"Well come on in and take the weight off Dad. I'll make
you a brew," I said as he hobbled past and sat down.

"Steph was just about to tell me what's going on," Mum
piped up as I passed steaming cups around.

"Thank God someone knows what's going on, it's
beyond me. Did you know there's some bugger in your
house?" Dad took a slurp.

"Of course she knows, she signed the agreement. We
saw it!" Mum put her cup on the windowsill.

"I know what we saw Anne, I'm just bloody saying!" he slurped again.

"Well stop bloody saying and let her bloody say so we bloody know what's going on!" Mum spat her words out.

"Ok, ok, no need for you two to fall out, I'm going to tell you what happened if you both calm down and give me a chance!" I sat on the middle windowsill and faced them both, I took them right back to January and told them all about the driving incident and Jay leaving me. They were both quiet throughout, with the odd "Never in the world!" and "Dear God!" being muttered with plenty of shaking of heads and mouths agape.

I moved on to the divorce, the debts and the house repossession. I wrapped what I was saying in verbal cotton wool as much as possible but it didn't stop the pain and concern radiating from their faces in my direction. The odd "bastard" slipped out and even Jesus Christ came into it too.

It wasn't until now in that exact moment that I realised how much I had survived this year, and what enormity this must have for my folks. Even a small incident in their lives was whipped up into an almighty drama, so who knows how they were going to feel about my life. Good job Mum had had a drink.

I thought I had them onside when I started to talk about moving here and renting out the house, and I told them about the job I'd been offered and the friends I'd made. I spoke about the fundraising I was doing with passion and how we were going to save the project even though the building had to go.

I stopped talking and looked at them both for a reaction.

Mum was sitting shaking her head, looking like she had just been told someone had died.

Dad had his poker face on and was looking straight ahead, no slurping now.

"Well?" I asked in a cagey tone.

Dad sighed and shook his head.

"I don't know what to say pet, really I don't. Why didn't you tell us all of this was going on?" He looked at me and I felt the tears welling up. "And if I ever get my hands on that shit of a husband... I mean I never liked him, I always knew he was trouble. I mean what kind of bloke gets a bloody spray tan? Dale bloody Winton that's who and we all know what he is, maybe he was a shirt-lifter too and that's why he bailed out on you love..."

"I just, I don't know why dad....I didn't know what to say or how to tell you, I thought you'd think I was a massive failure... my life was falling apart and I was trying to get used to it myself, I just couldn't..." my words came out between sobs and he hugged me in tight. There is nothing like a dad's hug no matter how old you are.

"It's ok love, it's ok," he said and stroked my hair. "We'll get through it. You are better off without him and we can sort the rest out, it's ok love."

Mum stood up now and joined in, "Yes love, come on we'll get you sorted."

Dad stepped back and then Mum's arms were round me. I could smell her perfume and I felt like a child again.

"Yes we'll sort you out love, just get your things together and Dad will get the car." Mum patted my back.

"The car?" I looked up and sniffed.

241

"Yes darling, the best place for you is home," Mum said in a tone that was filled with certainty.

"Isn't it?" she looked to Dad for backup.

"Yes love, you need to come home and you can stay for as long as you like, let us put you back together." He passed me a tissue from his pocket.

"I'm fine here, really, it's all coming together now. My job and everything, I want to stay." I objected.

The events of the last months had been delivered into my life one by one and in segments that were just about the right size to cope with. My parents on the other hand had been stuffed full of the whole drama in less than half an hour, no wonder they wanted to rescue me. In their perception I was living each moment all at once in the now time, maybe I should have offered them more of a drip feed.

"You can't stay silly, not here with these people Steph, it's just not for you..." Mum was fiddling with my hair again. "We can get you home and I'll book Michael to come to the house and see what he can do with this..."

"Michael the mincer," Dad's futile attempt at making a joke. "Bloody hell they're taking over"

"Michael is a bloody good hairdresser! Even if he is a homosapien," Mum joined in and their banter made me smile.

"No Mum, I have to stay here. I want to, this is me now." I brushed her hand away from my fringe.

"It's just not you darling, you're fabulous!" Mum said in a tone that meant 'they aren't'. She reached for one of the suitcases I'd brought and opened the wardrobe, taking things off hangers and roughly folding them. "You are coming home Steph, this is no good. You can look for a proper job from home and dad will drive you to the interviews, we will tell people that you were made redundant and that your hair was some kind of sponsored thing for charity...you know they make wigs for people that survived Chernobyl, it's been on The One Show..."

"No Mum, I want to stay!" I started to take the things out of the case and put them back on the hangers.

"Tell her!" Mum snapped in dad's direction. "Tell her this is no good!"

"Your mother's right love, you'd be better off at home. Staying here is, well, it's..." he looked up at the paint work that had seen better days and then in the direction of the kitchen area with my Ikea start up kettle and he shook his head. "It's polishing a turd Steph."

"Dad I like it here, this is me now!"

"But darling..." Mum interrupted.

"No Mum, I love you and I know this has been an awful shock, but no. This is my life and I am eventually getting it together, I can't come back with you I'm sorry." It felt awful watching my mum cry but I knew that I had to stand up for myself and keep going. Dig deep Steph. "It's good Mum, really it's all good. I'm finding myself here and I am happy with my life." I spoke softly but with conviction.

"Oh, Steph." She cried more tears and looked at Dad.

"Come home Stephanie" he said once more.

"I am home." I replied and a moment of silence followed as they exchanged glances and mum shrugged her shoulders.

We chatted some more and I found out about their next
door neighbour's conservatory, and him at number 33 who
had got sick of cutting the grass and let the pikeys lay
block paving, which everyone was going mad about
because it looked such a bloody mess. That's where Dad
had picked up the turd polishing quip then. After his
second coffee dad checked his watch and started getting
twitchy about the parking ticket. This was the cue to hug
more and promise to keep in touch this time, Christmas
arrangements were loosely made and Dad nipped to the
loo before the drive. The hallway was empty but it
sounded like the party was in full swing behind the closed
door of the day room, I could only imagine what was
going on as I heard squeals of laughter mingling with the
chorus from The Rivers of Babylon.

"Go on love, get back to your friends," Mum said
through her final hug and Dad made his way down the
steps carefully on his bunions. They linked arms and
walked down the street into the autumn leaves and traffic
noise, I could see they were talking and guessed it wasn't
about the weather.

When I opened the door and peeked through there were
cheers and whoops of, "Come on Steph! It's your party!"
and before I knew it I was tipsy on cava and remembering
Zion with the best of them.

Stephanie's Journal - Lesson 9
Acceptance

Everyone is doing the best that they can in a given moment. It doesn't seem this way when people are behaving in ways that are not in line with our own expectations, but it is important to remember that they are doing what they think is right in that moment and that they are on their own journey. Other people can provide useful reflections for us to see where we need to grow and change, but it is not up to us to fix anyone else or make them conform so that we feel more comfortable. If you have the opportunity to share wisdom or information, do this in a way that is not patronising or in judgement of someone. And know that it is their choice to take or leave what you have said. Take responsibility for yourself and be a shining example and reflection to others, but give up the need to try and fix anyone. We are all in the right place for us.

"When you judge another, you do not define them, you define yourself." Dr Wayne Dyer

Chapter 23

The days were growing even shorter now, and as I made my way back from the estate agents the moon peeked over the top of the buildings ahead of me. Her light shone like a cosmic spotlight and the city silhouettes looked beautiful and somewhat haunting. It made me feel wistful and I started to wish that I had someone to share it with, and maybe even stop on the street corner for a kiss under the lamp post.

I had a stack of detail sheets under one arm, all buildings that we could relocate to after January when the demolition was scheduled to start. Some were near here, and similar in style and size and some were miles away in the surrounding areas with pretty views and fresh air. They all had one thing in common, the thing that was going to be the perpetual stumbling block, and that was the cost.

I was managing to increase funds slowly but surely, and campaigning hard to get one off donations and monthly commitments too. I had applications in all over the place for grants and lottery fund money. I had also cut out a picture of this week's *Secret Millionaire* and stuck it in the wall for good measure. We only had eight weeks left now, nine at the most and the pressure was building. I was using everything that I could to get the money in and trying to hang on to every last drop of faith that things would be alright. Josie was really worried, she had started to talk about retirement and letting it all go at the end of the year, but I knew that this was bravado and that in truth she lived for Prospect House and the women she could reach out to and help.

I was trying to follow my intuition and manifest the outcome we wanted, but this became increasingly hard as the fear of not succeeding crept in, and my mind wandered through the thought process that maybe this was impossible to save. Staying in the present moment was the key for me a lot of the time, not letting myself get dragged in to the what if's that my ego dangled in front of me and my mind wanted to dissect. That's where the moon came in, noticing the beauty around me and being grateful to be in the moment was helping me to stay in my core and get on with the job in hand.

I arrived back to the smell of something good coming from the kitchen and the sound of the television on low in the day room. I made my way upstairs and looked out of my window at the moon again. There must be a way to find what we need to move. I knew that in my heart that something so good, that could help so many people, had to continue. There simply must be a way, and I had to find it quickly. I stuck the best four properties up on the wall and sat back to take it in. I allowed my eyes to scan over the pictures of the couple in love at the same time and thought about how great it would be if it all came together at once. Maybe I could find a millionaire to fall in love with me and he could help us with the project? I laughed to myself, stranger things have happened but I wasn't going to hold my breath.

The next two weeks were filled with fundraising by canvassing local and national businesses for donations, and filling in forms for every single grant for which I could tenuously link our situation to their criteria. Businesses usually had their preferred charity that they supported and it was impossible to break through this as an objection. Grants on the other hand seemed to exist for nearly everything if you trawled the internet for long enough, but nothing specifically for a half-way house for women in crisis. It seemed projects for every other social group were funded. The homeless, artists, overweight children, homosexuals, the deaf, the blind, ethnic minorities and rescue animals to name but a few. I found myself getting more and more creative with the application forms, weaving stories and examples, exaggerating about the issues that came through the door in order to secure something that would help. If only we had a one legged Asian lesbian challenged by autism and a hearing aid, with a rescue cat and artistic flair.

When I did have any down time I flicked through estate agent websites in the hope that something perfect was just being uploaded, within our price range. I spoke to a few and had learned that I needed to sound confident that our funding was in place in order for them to give you more than the time of day. I convinced myself that it wasn't really lying, it was market research.

I had to maintain the charade when I went out to look at properties, and I started to understand estate agents speak a bit more. "Needs some updating" meant blown vinyl wallpaper, aubergine bathroom suite and rising damp. "Plenty of Character" meant nothing has been done for years but it does have a fire place. "Finished to a High Standard" meant magnolia paint throughout.

Viewing so many places was a useful but time consuming exercise, and meant that I was developing discernment. I took the pictures down from my wall and started to snip out the features that I had liked in each property. Before long I had a collage consisting of six bedrooms, three bathrooms, a country kitchen, front room, garden room, vegetable patch and summer house. I added in pictures of planters filled with colour and hanging baskets, a wind chime on a tree and a bird table.

I spoke to Josie about what I'd seen and tried to keep her spirits up as well as my own, but had to admit that there was nothing in the area that we could afford – yet. I was feeling the pressure as much as her as the days ticked by. It felt like time and hope were trickling through an hour glass and we just couldn't stop it.

"Who said you need to stick to this area?" Josie asked me one day, and it made me stop in my tracks.

"Well I thought... I guess I thought that you would want to stay here I suppose," I answered.

"No, no, no!" Josie shook her head and laughed. "We can go anywhere Steph, there are always people that need a safe place no matter where you are. The right people find us at the right time."

"Right, ok then. I'll cast the net a bit wider then." I had never considered looking any further afield, but this was all of the encouragement I needed to start changing parameters on all of the searches I'd done so far.

I took a deep breath and closed my eyes.

"The perfect place is being drawn to me now to help this project continue," I said out loud with conviction.

After an hour or so of clicking and scrolling I uncovered a small estate agents not far from where my parents lived, that boasted the right solution for my house move. I blinked and thought about putting the kettle on and having a break, but before I stood up I opened their home page and scanned over the first five properties.

I blinked again and shook my head in disbelief. The first place underneath the company name looked almost exactly like the hotch potch of scraps stuck on my bedroom wall, even down to the geraniums in planters on each side of the doorstep.

I quickly clicked through the rest of the images and apart from a few minor details, this place was exactly what I'd been looking for, and I laughed out loud. I felt butterflies stirring in my stomach as I scanned the description of this six bedroomed country residence set within an acre of grounds complete with vegetable patch. Even the name was perfect, The Haven.

I squealed with excitement and ran downstairs with my laptop.

"I've found it Josie, look!" I burst into her office and noticed how tired she looked.

"Steph it's great! Really perfect for us, but how are we going to be able to afford it?" She sighed and shook her head.

"Well it's for sale or rent, and we could just about make the monthly payments with the money we have coming in with regular donations and if we were to take on a mortgage to buy it we could….."

"Wait, wait, wait. We would need a deposit of at least 10 per cent and that would be £40,000 thousand! Not to mention legal fees and stamp duty…" Her voice trailed off as she stood up and took her coat down from the peg on the back of the door.

"I just don't see how we can possibly do it, I know you believe in positive thinking and manifesting and all that but I'm running low on faith at the moment," she smiled weakly.

"I know Josie, I know." And I did know. I knew that this was the place for us and there had to be a way to get us there.

That night I couldn't sleep, opposite emotions kept me awake as I found myself either overwhelmed with excitement or gripped with panic. I knew that this place had to be the one, but the end of the year was galloping towards me at lightning speed and we had no real funding. I looked at the collage again on the wall and smiled as I noticed that there was still a picture of Mr Right up there, if I could find The Haven then maybe I could find him too. Hopefully he'd not be so difficult to acquire.

I rang the agents at 9am.

"Rural Residence, how can I help you?"

"Hi there, I was looking at your website and wondered if I could arrange a viewing please?" I spoke in my telephone voice, although the receptionist seemed to have forgotten hers. The conversation didn't really flow and she seemed distracted as she pencilled me in for later that day, 2 o'clock to be exact.

"Who is it I'll be meeting with?" I asked.

Pause.

"Hello?"

"Well me of course!" she was impatient to say the least.

"And you are?" I asked.

"Chardonnay." Then I heard the dial tone.

I hadn't expected to be able to see it so quickly and I had totally forgotten that I had no car. I had a look at the property details to see if it was within walking distance from a train station. It looked to be about ten minutes from the town centre, that would give me a change to get a feel for the place and be able to direct people in the future when they arrived by rail. I booked my ticket for five past eleven, thinking that I'd have time for a look around and maybe some lunch. I hadn't had an afternoon off in ages. I rang mum and dad and asked if I could stay overnight there, and told them I'd get the train the four more stops into Wilmslow where dad could pick me up.

It was all looking good until the pitter pat of rain drops started against the window pane and the sky turned black. I wrapped up in my raincoat, scarf and hat and made my way out into the storm. My umbrella turned out to be more of a nonsense than anything else, turning itself inside out and nearly dragging me into the oncoming traffic. I pulled my hat down over my ears and stuffed the metal mixed up frame with quick release button and tartan covering into the nearest bin, along with its cover. Was I meant to be going here today? I was meant to be following my intuition after all and things weren't exactly flowing, as I thought this a bus pulled in near the kerb and soaked me from head to foot. When I opened my eyes there were kids looking out of the window pointing and laughing, little shits.

That's it I would have to go back now I was cold and wet and this clearly was not the right place to be going today. I looked back at the kids, one who was sticking his fingers up and the other had his bare arse up against the glass. The moon! I had to laugh, and as I did I noticed that the advertisement on the side of the bus showed a happy elderly couple on a garden seat and the words The Haven Rest Home above them in fancy calligraphy.

"OK then," I said to no one in particular and turned in the direction of the train station.

The train was on time, which gave me time to go to the ladies and also nip into the shop for a magazine. I turned to the back page for my horoscope. It was all about love and taking chances, changes and being happy in the moment. A bit vague and certainly not as entertaining as *Katie Price* and the photographs of her new man on page twelve, this was the real thing now apparently.

The train pulled up and I sat in a window seat, I could now alternate between celebrity style and the beautiful country views as we pulled out of the city.

Before long we arrived at Westfield, a traditional village that had an eclectic array of shops ranging from the traditional tea shops and bakers to the off licence on the corner and a pound shop. The rain had eased off and the sun was trying to peep through the clouds as I walked over cobbles onto the main street. It was only just after twelve so I had plenty of time to get my bearings and have a look around. My stomach growled at me and I realised that I'd had no breakfast, I scanned up and down for eateries and realised I was spoilt for choice. There was a deli that looked popular with poppy knot buns in the window and homemade pies, a traditional looking pub called The Black Swan with "food served all day" written on the blackboard, and a bistro type place with long windows looking straight out onto the street. I just loved people watching and opted for the bistro, I nabbed the seat in the corner where I could see all of the comings and goings whilst half camouflaged behind a neatly tied back floral curtain.

I ordered the soup de jour which turned out to be cream of asparagus with a crusty bun, it tasted divine and I couldn't help mopping up the last drops with the bread. I sat back and observed, people from all walks of life were passing by, some alone, some couples and some with children. I idly wondered if I would ever be walking down a road like this with grey hair and a walking stick linking arms with someone I'd been married to for forty odd years. I'd better hurry up and find him first, he had to be out there somewhere. I kept asking that the perfect person for me would turn up in my life and hanging on to the faith that I had been heard.

A large latte and caramel slice later I was finished at Katie's Kitchen and pulled on my coat. I still had about an hour to kill but I had noticed a closing down sale at a shoe shop on the other side of the street. I paid the bill and left a tip, with the intention of staying in the flow, and made my way to the zebra crossing.

I looked in the window and took a sharp breath in with excitement. There they were, the boots of my dreams! And they were half price! I just had to try them on, I bustled into the shop and tried to look cool for a moment and browse until someone came over and asked if they could help. It was posh in here, there was no denying it, the kind of place I'd shopped in for bags and shoes before my life had started to change. I suddenly felt a pang of guilt, should I really be spending over a hundred pounds on a pair of boots? And then I remembered that I should be letting the past go, I was buying these because I loved them and I needed them, not to impress anyone or to be showy. "It's fine Steph, you are allowed nice things, in fact you deserve them," I said to myself as Barbara smiled at me waiting for instruction.

"Hi, oh sorry I was miles away... yes I'd like to try on the boots you have in the window please, the ones with the fluffy lining," I said.

"What size please madam?" she asked whilst gesturing for me to have a seat.

"Seven and a half please." I unfastened my coat, it was warm in the shop.

"Oh they don't do half sizes I'm afraid." Barbara raised her eyebrows, which were pencilled in a bit on the bold side and she looked surprised instead of questioning.

"Well a seven then please" I said and started to slip off the shoes that I had on which had seen much better days.

Whilst Barbara was in the stock room a man came into the shop and Barbara's colleague tottered over to him and asked if she could help. I could only see him from the back as he was facing the fixture behind me with 'Gents' written in gold calligraphy on a mirror strip above the shoes on display.

He sat down behind me and started to speak to Jean, being a bit presumptuous and using her first name, which I think she liked as it made her tone quite flirty. "Yes, no problem I'll see what we have sir. What size please?"

"Thirteen please, my mother says it's a good job I wasn't a girl with massive paddles like mine!" Jean giggled and made a comment about ladies having dainty

feet as she scuttled off. I looked at hers as she walked past
and she looked about a size four or five.

Barbara came just as I was daydreaming about what the
man behind me looked like, he smelled nice, a
combination of whatever aftershave he had on and the
leather of the shoes was making me a bit giddy. Barbara
passed me the box and the phone rang, he muttered that
she would just be a moment and made her way to the desk
to answer "Harpers Shoes, how can I help?" Her voice
trailed away as I started to unstuff the paper from these
beauties and feel the soft, warm lining that would be soon
keeping my both toasty and stylish. I wriggled into the left
boot and managed to get two thirds of my foot in there,
but that was it. All new boots were like this I told myself
and I took my foot out and pulled my sock off. Barbara
could see what I had done and gave me the stare, flapping
around a couple of American Tan pop socks and still
speaking about someone's fallen arches and could they
help with insoles. I turned away and got a good grip on
either side of the boot and tried again. Still not quite. What
I needed was a good shove, so as Jean came back and
started showing him the loafers in brown and black I went
for it and yanked the boot as hard as I could and pushed
my foot in at the same time. It did feel snug I have to
admit and the zip felt like it had badly chaffed my ankle,
but it was on. I stood up triumphantly as the man behind
me started talking on his mobile about rearranging
appointments and excused himself to take the call outside.
He was pacing up and down outside and talking about
something that looked like it was making him a bit
stressed. He still had his back to me and ran his fingers

through his hair in an exasperated gesture, then put his hand back in his coat pocket, which was three quarter length, dark grey and looked expensive. I thought about how funny it would be to find the man of my dreams here in a show shop, and just as I was planning on what to say when he came back in Barbara bustled over and looked at me over her half-moon spectacles with gold chain, and asked how the boots were. Her tone was edged with slight irritation which I took to be due to the fact I had dared to put a bare foot in a designer boot.

"Oh erm, fine thanks, I mean they are lovely but…" I lowered my voice as Jean flustered about tidying up a display methodically whilst allowing her eyes to flick to the window every now and then to see if her customer was coming back in.

"But?" Barbara asked, getting a bit snippy.

"Well, maybe it's a bit tight that's all. Could I please try a bigger size?" I smiled nicely, come on Barb. She looked down at my other foot that was bare now as well, ready to be snuggled in new boots. Barbara put the pop socks down on the seat next to me.

"We have to use these for health and safety," she said, and then with another quick look at my right foot. "I'll see what I've got in an extra wide fitting." As Jean raised her eyebrows, Barbara made her way back the store room and came back with a size eight. She took the boots out if the box one by one and removed the stuffing as I tried to get the boot off my left foot. I wriggled my toes and pushed down with the ball of my foot whilst trying to lever the heel away from my chunky ankle area. It wouldn't budge at all. Barbara looked concerned and asked me if I'd like a hand, then produced a long black plastic shoe horn.

I laughed nervously and made a comment about using a pop sock after all while I tried to slip the shoe horn down the back and give my left trotter a bit of help in slipping out. There was literally no room at all to get the shoe horn down the back of the boot, and when I pushed it hard I squealed like a baby when it took a thin layer of skin off my heel. Please don't let me bleed into the furry lining.

I was suddenly very glad that Mr Interesting was still pacing up and down on his phone and praying that the conversation would last long enough for me to get out of here, with or without the boots.

"Any luck?" Barbara was definitely snippy now and starting to panic a bit, her cheeks were glowing red as were mine from a combination of exertion and embarrassment.

"No sorry, I erm, I'm so sorry but I think it's stuck." I said in a sheepish tone.

"It can't be stuck, we'll get it off, come on Jean!" Jean put down the duster and the fifty percent off poster and came over to see what she could do. I braced myself against the seat and Barbara pulled. Nothing happened. She pulled again a bit harder and nothing happened.

"Right Jean, keep hold of her!" she shouted. "Remember that time when the vicar tried the wellingtons on with three pairs of socks?"

Jean's arms were now around my waist.

"Yes Barbara, you're going to have to go for it again, give it some welly!"

Barbara took a deep breath and rolled up the sleeves of her navy blue cardigan and a sound that reminded me of the rugby world cup started to resonate in her throat. She grunted and growled like the New Zealand All Blacks warming up for the Haka and she gripped like a bloody vice. The zip was being pressed right into the thin skin on my ankle again but this probably wasn't the time to point it out, but it made me wince. Then she adopted the stance of a tug of war professional. With a low centre of gravity in her A-line skirt, she yanked with all of her might.

I yelped like a piglet and Barbara fell over backwards into the handbags, with her own court shoes in the air above her head and a brief glimpse of what looked like Sloggis. But the important thing was that the boot was in her possession and no longer welded to my left foot, which was now swollen even more and bleeding a bit on the ankle bone. I had the imprint of half a zip on the inside of my calf. Jean let go of me and went to give Barbara a hand up.

"Well done Barbara, you've done it again!" She put Barbara's name badge right whilst Barbara smoothed down her blouse and sorted out the gold chain form her specs. I continued to sit and get my breath back.

Mr Interesting at that point came breezing back in and continued with Jean, I didn't know how much of my ugly sister routine he had witnessed and turned my face away as he apologised and said that he'd take them in black thanks. Jean put them on the counter and asked him how he'd like to pay, when his mobile rang again.

"I'm so sorry, I need to take this call…" he said as he made his way back outside and started pacing again.

I relaxed a little and agreed with Barbara that I'd take the extra wide boots in a seven and that they would be fine, I said that I didn't need to try them on, it was all good thanks. And I was sorry, really, really sorry. She said it was fine but there was a definite undercurrent and I was now just desperate to pay and get out. Barbara didn't even bother with the usual obligatory talk you get about polishes and suede brushes, I think we were both on the same page now. The page entitled Pay and Sod Off.

She put the box on the counter and the phone rang again, in her telephone voice she started to explain their returns policy on children's school shoes, and waved Jean over to put the plain brown box in a Harpers bag and take my payment. There was a revolving door and as I was going one way back onto the street, Mr Interesting was coming in to pick up his shoes. I sighed and thought about how lucky it had been that he hadn't been there to witness my muppetry. I wondered if Barbara and Jean would tell him, I guessed so as they all seemed to be laughing as I walked past and looked in the window.

I had about half an hour to go before my appointment time, and I was starting to need to go to the toilet. I thought about going back into the café that I'd had lunch in but it looked really busy now and there was bound to be a public loo here. I asked a couple that were sitting in a bench looking all loved up and happy if they knew where I could find one, they weren't from round here and didn't have the foggiest idea.

I made the decision to keep going and get to The Haven, I could use the facilities there. The short walk was pleasant but fresh, with the autumn wind tugging at my scarf and the leaves dancing around me. The sun was low and I squinted my eyes as I made my way out of town and along a street lined with houses that were all set right back from the road with long driveways. None of them had numbers, only names on brass polished plates or mailboxes and in one case stone pillars topped with sculptures of horses with their manes flying behind them.

Castledene, Overdene, The Old Vicarage, Orchard Cottage and Ivy House all protected by high hedges and sometimes gates in wrought iron or wood. I kept going, trying to recall from memory of street view how far along the road I had left to go. I was just about to reach into my pocket and have another look on my phone when The Haven came into view. The gates were wrought iron and had been chained together with a padlock, but the chains were wrapped around one gate only now and the padlock dangled uselessly. The driveway was long and lined on both sides with trees, it was gravel and opened out more at the entrance of the house. A discarded for sale sign had been laid up against some shrubs, and now had a greenish film growing over the surface. It had probably blown down in the wind.

The gate squeaked a little as I tentatively pushed it open. I walked towards the house, breathing in deeply the earthy smell and noticing that some trees had lost their leaves altogether as others had turned rich red and gold, and were hanging onto leaves that were flying in the wind. They fluttered all in the same direction and one or two spun down and scattered on the ground. A robin darted in and out of the undergrowth and stopped to peck at berries that hung in big handfuls from an elderflower bush.

The trees soon parted and I stood in front of the house
with its imposing double rectangular bay windows and
massive front door. There was a symmetrical beauty about
the building, and the stone that it was made from looked
old and worn, but strong and traditional. I heard the faint
tinkling of a wind chime in the distance and made my way
around the side.

The back garden was expansive and mainly flat, with a
good sized vegetable plot and greenhouse, potting shed
and compost bins. There was a large lawned area with
some disused rusty croquet hoops just visible above the
long grass, and a bird table. A patio area had a couple of
old benches facing out onto the garden, and there were
trees all around. Some I recognised as sycamore and ash
and there was a large gnarled tree in the bottom corner
that I thought could be almond. Beyond the garden the
trees grew thicker and I remembered in the estate agents
details that there was a wooded area behind this street. I
sat down on one of the benches and closed my eyes, the
sun warm on my face and the wind ruffling my hair. This
was it. I just knew it, every cell in my body was
resonating to the fact that I was home. I opened my eyes
and froze perfectly still, a young deer was eating the grass
just yards in front of me. The sun light illuminated the
dappled pattern on her back and her huge brown eyes
looked up at me as she chewed. And then she was gone
and all I could see for a moment was her tail bobbing up
and down as she disappeared back into the trees.

This place certainly was magical.

Chapter 24

I stood up and walked around the whole perimeter again and then checked my watch, the agent must be running late as it was quarter past now. There was a light drizzle starting and I made my way to the back of the house again to wait on the bench, there was nowhere to sit at the front. I would hear the car pull into the driveway.

I was just taking in more of the garden, when the heavens opened and the rain started to pour from above. I instinctively put the carrier bag with the boots in on top of my head and sidled up as close as I could to the wall of the house, there was a narrow ledge between the first and second floor that deflected some of the rain. So there I stood, getting more or less soaked with a carrier bag over my head pressed up against a cold stone wall waiting for the rain to pass, and the sky became blacker and blacker.

After a few minutes my arm was aching and I was shivering. I should probably just ring Dad to come and collect me and get back to their house for a hot bath and an interrogation about why I looked like a drowned rat.

I sighed with frustration, I had so wanted to go and have a look inside. I turned and scooped my hands around my eyes to cut out the reflections, as I pressed my face into the window pane. All I could see was a big open plan kitchen diner with what looked like an Aga and a massive old pine table, no chairs. There were a couple of chairs made from cane with garish cushions on them and a dust pan and brush all pushed up against one wall. There were no lamp shades, just bare bulbs hanging down.

Now I had moved the bag the rain was running down the back of my neck and my teeth started to chatter. I stood back and looked up at the heavens, it didn't look like this was going to pass any time soon. I don't know what happened next, it just came over me to try the door handle, and as I pressed down and heard an audible click, the door opened and I stepped inside. I pulled it closed behind me and looked in awe at the kitchen as I dripped a sizeable puddle on the floor.

There was so much that I couldn't see from the other side of the window pane, there was the height of the ceilings and the exposed beams, as well as the adjoining garden room. My footsteps echoed on the tiled floor and my heart thundered in my chest as I went from room to room, gasping with excitement that I had found exactly what I'd been wanting, for all of us. I could visualise the kitchen being full of people and love, pans boiling up homemade soup and bread in the Aga, while some people tended the vegetable patch and others read in the garden room. This was a place of healing and hope, a real sanctuary. If ever a building had a heart, this one did.

I went up the beautiful staircase and the first floor opened up into beautiful bright bedrooms, I easily saw past peeling wallpaper and faded curtains, none of that mattered. The bathroom was large with a roll top cast iron bath and a walk in shower, which was dated but it had said on the website that it was in full working order. And the master bedroom was en-suite, in an eighties whisper pink but again this wouldn't matter initially. There was more than enough room in each bedroom to have a small kitchen corner and in at least one other the possibility of another en-suite bathroom.

The toilet in the main bathroom was a high level flush, and I felt instant relief when I had finished but realised that there was only a shred of toilet roll not much bigger than a postage stamp left on the cardboard tube. I started raking through my handbag and found little of use, just when I had resigned myself to pulling my knickers up fast I had a brain wave.

The paper in the boots! I'd only need a little bit! I opened the carrier bag and then the lid on the box which was slightly soggy now, and saw a pair of size thirteen men's black shoes.

"Bollocks!" I said to no one in particular and shook my head.

Thanks Barbara. Now I'd have to go back and see them again and experience even more humiliation. The good thing was that there was loads of tissue paper stuffed in the shoes, which was not entirely unpleasant to use, but looked very odd when I had finished. My multivitamins turned my pee bright neon yellow so it looked a bit like Flash Lemon Multi Surface, and the tissue had "Harpers" printed all over it which was all smudged now and in some places said "Harp" and in others a weird anagram or "arse" with a couple of letters missing. I had to laugh, but needed to flush because the asparagus soup I'd had a couple of hours ago was now making the place smell like a herd of male cats had been marking this as their local hangout for the last decade.

"Phew!" I said out loud wafting and fanning the air in front of my nose and reaching for the chain to pull.

Clang.

"Oh my God!" I exclaimed.

Clang.

"The water must have been turned off! Why am I talking to myself? Get a grip Steph!" I laughed and dabbed hand gel on my palms, rubbing them together as the smell of synthetic aloe vera masked my vile urine for a moment. I dropped the travel sized bottle back in to my bag and made my way downstairs. The rain had eased off and there was a beautiful rainbow visible from the landing, and something that I hadn't noticed caught my eye. A small crystal sun catcher winked in the light and cast smaller rainbows around the room. This was the place for sure.

I would have to get back to Mum and Dad's soon and ring to rearrange another viewing, obviously not telling them that I had been inside today. I followed my own footsteps back to the door and tried the handle. It wouldn't budge. I tried it again, and still it wouldn't budge. I frantically pushed it down as hard as I could and although the handle did move slightly the bolt did not. It seemed that the bolt had become stuck and the mechanism was not going to budge.

"Calm down," I said to myself, although I could feel my heart rate galloping.

I ran to the front door which was secured with some kind of deadlock, and the same was true for the back door in the utility room. I was locked in a house that I had effectively broken into, I was trespassing and I would have to break a window to get out. I thought about phoning the agents and explaining what had happened, that I was sheltering from the rain and desperate for a wee and that it was sort of an accident. Or maybe I could ring my dad and seeing if he could come and get me out.

I reached for my mobile phone and tried the back door handle again while I scrolled through dialled numbers and looked for Dad Mobile. I found it and pressed the green button, it seemed like I waited an age with the soft click, click, click in my ear and then the message on the screen that I had no signal and couldn't connect.

I could feel myself on the verge of tears and I started to feel really cold again, at least if I'd had my boots I could have put them on, what bloody good were a pair of size thirteen black men's shoes? Just then I heard it, the sound of a car engine and wheels on gravel. I was saved. Actually now I was in big trouble. I was not meant to be here, and all at once several scenarios ran through my head, but as the key turned in the dead lock the only one that seemed to make some kind of crazy sense was to hide.

The door of the cloakroom closed quietly as the front door banged open and I tried to slow my breathing down as I shuffled further back. I jumped when I touched something furry, but with the light of my mobile phone screen I saw that it was some kind of old donkey jacket and nothing to be scared of. There was also an old vacuum cleaner in here and a broken rocking horse.

I could hear someone walking round and opening the interior doors, ready for a viewing perhaps, maybe even mine! I could sneak out the front and stand on the step, knock on the door and pretend I had just arrived. Perfect. I just needed to wait until I knew that they were at the other end of the house, but it was tricky to hear when you are shut in a coat cupboard. I waited for the footsteps to sound above my head and I knew that at least whoever it was was now on the first floor. I held my breath and gently pushed the door open a crack, which made a theatrical creak just like the bloody gates and the footsteps stopped.

"Who's there?" A man's voice shouted down the stairs and then there was a pause.

"It's no one you silly bugger, stop getting spooked," he said to himself.

I recovered for a couple of seconds and took another breath, this time I tiptoed two steps out of the cupboard and could see the open front door and the world outside.

"Bloody hell!" I heard from upstairs and a retching sound. Then the sash window in the bathroom was being thrown open and he was coughing and spluttering out of it. "Dirty bastards!" he muttered and, "Phew that stinks!"

I kept on tiptoeing towards the door, and was almost half way there when I heard the footsteps coming my way again. What should I do? If I went for the door I would have to run now and that would make a noise for sure, and if I stayed and hid I might get locked in and have to break myself out later... in a moment of panic I retreated back to the cupboard and pulled the door closed again, telling myself under my breath that I was an idiot and a grade A moron.

Then I heard him on his mobile phone, he must be on a different network to me.

"Yes, hello officer, I'm calling from Rural Residences to report a break-in at one of the properties we are selling..." He was pacing up and down and as he continued I felt that there might have been something familiar about his voice, but I didn't know what.

"I haven't had a proper look around yet but there is some vandalism, toilet vandalism if you know what I mean. No not that but it's bad enough, the water's off and it won't flush away. I'll never sell the bloody place smelling like it does now... yes squatters maybe, I hadn't thought of that."

More pacing.

"Ok I'll wait here until you arrive, officer."

I gritted my teeth and shut my eyes tight, what the hell was I going to do now? It's not like I could step out into the hall now, give him the fright of his life and confess everything.

I heard his voice again, making another call.

"It's me. You won't believe what's happened down here, some dirty sod has broken in probably with a urine infection, stunk the toilet out and buggered off. No she's not here yet, probably another bloody time waster, I should never have agreed to take this instruction... don't let me bullshit you about intuition again!" There was a forced laugh and then a sigh. "It's the icing on the cake quite honestly, you wouldn't believe the day I'm having. I seem to have bought a pair of women's fluffy boots in size 8 extra wide fitting. Some poor chunky girl with freezing cold feet is trailing round a box with my loafers in, Jesus Christ."

He walked away and his voice drifted as I stood there in the pitch dark, joining the dots and realising that this was the Mr Interesting that had been in the shoe shop the same time as me. And even worse than that, he had called the

police and they were coming here! They would surely
search the whole place and I would be arrested for
breaking and entering, I had to make a run for it I had no
choice. This was it, no messing round this time it was now
or never. No matter what I heard I had to keep going, once
that cupboard door was open I was committed and I had to
keep going.

Then I started to hear his voice again, this time in a more
hostile tone and accompanied by the banging open of each
door in turn as he shouted,

"I know you are still here! You dirty bugger! I've seen
your footprints all over the kitchen floor! There's a bloody
puddle there, so you must still be here! The police are
coming so you had better get your story straight!"

Although he was trying to sound angry there was a
wobble in his tone that made him sound a bit less than
scary, just a bit mind you.

I huddled into the donkey jacket with everything
clenched and held my breath. Then it happened. Vodafone
miraculously found me and my coat pocket started to
vibrate and the ring tone shouted out my whereabouts.

I flustered and grabbed my pocket which was
illuminated for a few moments through the inside lining,
and tried to press the red button to dump the call. I could
hear footsteps running towards the cupboard now and the
shaky voice shouting,

"I know you are in there, you moron! Get out of there
you idiot!" and the door flew open.

This all happened rather quickly and while he was
shouting and I was quaking under a coat in a house I had
broken into, my mother was having a one way

conversation in my pocket about her neighbour's daughter doing a course in beauty therapy and wanting to wax me.

I started to sob quietly under the coat. From his point of view he could probably see it shaking, with of course my legs sticking out from underneath it, and the shoe box next to my feet.

My mother's tinny voice kept squawking on about,

"It's your top lip darling, I noticed it when I saw you but I didn't like to say. Darling, it's ok, don't cry I have mine waxed every four weeks and you've never noticed have you?"

I fumbled in my pocket to try and get the phone out and disconnect the most hideously embarrassing conversation I could imagine anyone overhearing, never mind anyone male and half interesting that smelled lovely and bought nice shoes. I could hear him breathing so close to me now as I continued to sob and sniff and the worst possible thing happened. I couldn't see much under the coat and I was trying to be fast, but instead of cutting her off I pressed loud speaker and then I dropped the bloody thing on the floor.

"I know you probably don't want to talk about it darling, because us girls don't but you know you have always been really hairy and she could do your top lip and your downstairs as well for just ten pounds if you fill in the disclaimer. She's got no insurance you see, not yet anyway, but she will once she's qualified. And Mrs Jessop's eyebrow grew back, so all's well that ends well..."

Pause for breath.

"Quite honestly darling now you're single you have to make more of an effort. Any way when you can give me a ring and dad will come and pick you up. Bye darling, kissy, kissy."

The phone went dead, as dead as I wished I was in that moment. I could only imagine what I looked like under that coat. I'd gone into the cupboard bedraggled, wet and shitting myself and now I was covered in snot and fluff from the lining of the coat and unbearably hot.

"You'll have to come out sometime," he laughed and I started to cry harder.

"I won't you know, just leave the door ajar and go and I'll pull it shut behind me, honestly I will," I spoke loudly, sheepskin is thick.

He started to laugh now.

"Come on out, there's nothing to worry about."

"There is, you've called the police." I said.

"It's ok, I can call them back and say it's a mistake." He opened the door a bit wider and I heard him put something down on the floor. Through the gap at the bottom of the coat it looked like a feather duster.

"What were you going to do with that? Tickle me to death?" I started to laugh through my tears now seeing the funny side of the most ridiculous thing I had ever done in my life.

He laughed out loud now and so did I.

"Come on, you have to come out," he spoke softly and started to lift the coat off the hook.

I squinted like a mole in the daylight, and hung my head in shame.

"Well then, let's have a look at you," he said in a curious tone, half teasing but gentle as well.

"I'd rather you didn't," I said.

"You remind me of someone, humour me, please," he raised my chin with his index finger and I shut my eyes tight and held my breath. After an unbearable silence and weirdness I started to peep.

"I thought it was you, Stephanie Binks," he smiled and I found myself looking into the eyes of the man I had loved and lost years ago.

"Damien?" I asked quietly as I felt his arms tight around me and his face nestled into my hair. I laughed and cried at the same time and so did he.

Chapter 25

"Hadn't you better call your mother back?" Damien laughed.

I opted for a text instead, Damien had heard enough about my body hair really.

We drove in his car out on the same road out of town and we ended up in a beautiful pub with a roaring fire and a large glass of wine each. We talked about everything, greedily digging for information about the blanks in each other's lives we wanted to fill in. We laughed at some of our memories, and then cried together when Damien told me his dad had passed away only last year. We held hands and I noticed he wasn't wearing a wedding ring, but I was too scared to ask directly. He skirted around the issue of relationships and people in his life but nothing was said about a significant other and as the fire warmed by body, his presence warmed my heart.

He still looked like the person I knew, only older and if anything even more handsome with slight frown lines and a scattering of grey hair on his temples.

"Can I have my shoes back please?" We both laughed again as he handed me the fluffy boots. "I don't think these will suit me, never mind fit."

"I can't believe you were in that shoe shop at the same time as me and we didn't recognise each other!" I said pulling the boots on now and putting my shoes back in the box. "And then at the house, it's like fate that we were meant to meet up again isn't it?"

I looked up and saw that he was looking at me in a way that I'd rarely experienced first-hand. His expression was soft and his eyes were glistening, and if I didn't know better I'd say that he was feeling really emotional, overwhelmed even.

"Yes Steph, it's like we were meant to find each other again for sure."

I tilted my head to one side and questioned him, "Are you ok?"

"Yes, yes I'm fine. Just thinking about, you know… stuff. About you really… and how I thought I'd never see you again, how hard that was to try and get used to." He looked at me directly and took my hands in his, his face glowed gently in the fire light and my heart felt like it was going to explode right out of my chest. This was it! The moment when he says he can't be without me and we kiss…

"There is something I need to tell you Steph," he started and I tried to look demure and not excited out of my pants.

There was a sigh, then a pause, then another sigh.

"Well?" I encouraged him, trying to disguise my absolute glee.

He looked at me again. "It's just that I'm glad I found you." He pulled his hands away from mine and I quickly composed myself, tucked my hair behind my ears and said I needed to go to the ladies. I checked there was paper this time before I sat down on the cold plastic seat. Strange, it was like he wanted to say something but couldn't find the words. Maybe it was a man thing and he would come out with it in a few days' time when we'd had more time together, or maybe I'd had too much wine and I was picking it up wrong.

Either way it didn't matter, I had him back and that was the most amazing thing.

I went back to the table and phoned my dad to come and collect me, we made our way outside to wait in the car park. It was cold so we sat in Damien's car with the engine running whilst I kept looking in the rear view mirror for the parent mobile to arrive.

It was then that Damien reached out and stroked my cheek, he brushed my hair from my face and leaned in close.

"I never really got to finish kissing you Steph," I could feel his warm sweet breath on my neck and feel the heat from his palm as he gently pulled me towards him. I closed my eyes as our lips touched in the most exquisite and perfect kiss I'd ever known. It was slow and deep, gentle and passionate all in one and it made me feel alive and loved in a way I had never thought possible, until now.

Headlights illuminated the car park and I heard the familiar sound of Neil Diamond.

I pulled away slowly and reluctantly, rolling my eyes "Here he is, there's not many people like a bit of Crackling Rosie at full blast these days…"

Damien laughed with me. We'd swapped mobile numbers in the pub and he promised to call me really soon.

"Say hi to your folks for me," he said before I closed the car door.

I waved as I got in the front seat beside dad and even found myself singing along with Neil as I fastened my seat belt.

"Who was that love?" Dad asked.

"Remember my friend Damien, Dad? We used to do our homework together, they lived round the corner?" I said.

Dad looked quizzical. "Is that the family that left in a hurry? Clarke I think?"

"Yes that's them. Can you believe it we just bumped into each other, isn't that mad after all this time?" I said.

"I suppose so love. Where did you bump into him then?" Dad indicated to turn into their road.

"In a shoe shop," I stifled a giggle.

The house was warm and cosy and I could smell good things to eat when the front door opened. Mum was looking a bit flustered with her hair tied back and her apron on, the kitchen window was steamy and there were pans bubbling on the hob.

"It's beef darling, a proper dinner. I hope that's alright?" she shouted.

"Sounds great, Mum." I unzipped my boots and put on the slippers that mum had left out for me and went into the kitchen to see if I could help. I added the finishing touched to the table in the way of horseradish, mustard and salt and pepper, and filled the water jug. Mum started to mash and the sound of radio four rumbled in the background.

We small-talked over dinner and mum forced second helpings onto my plate, I asked if I could leave my fruit crumble to have after a bath. That would be fine and dad put the immersion heater on.

I didn't mention Damien. He felt like my secret, my perfect and fragile secret kiss. I didn't want anyone else's opinion or input to cloud the perfection. I felt like a moment in time had been frozen between only him and I, a perfect and intimate connection that made me feel like he owned my heart, and in truth I knew that he always had. It was now captured and etched in our memories and hearts and I wanted to be alone to relive every minute detail.

I ran the bath hot and deep and wallowed in the sweet smelling water, candle light flickered around the walls and the small tea light flames drew me back to the memory of the roaring fire from earlier in the day. I wondered if he was thinking about me. What was he going to say to me before he stopped himself I wondered? I knew he felt the same way as me, it radiated from him as he looked at me and that kiss… there was no way that that kiss was not as earth shattering for him as it was for me. I just knew it. Damien had started out as being Mr Interesting but I was certain now that he was Mr Right.

I dried myself off and towelled up my hair, mum had laid out cosy pyjamas for me and my old dressing gown was on the radiator warming up. I nearly jumped out of my skin when the text message came through, and immediately my heart started to pound. I opened the message envelope to see Damien Mobile and the text below read "Hi Steph, I know you said your train back is at 2:30, can we meet for lunch before you go?"

I squealed with excitement and quickly responded "Don't laugh if I turn up with one eyebrow."

And the reply came back asking me to go back to the same pub where we could have some lunch and that he would take me to the station afterwards.

That was the start of the wardrobe panic. Quite frankly I
hadn't planned on staging a seduction so the Asda v neck t
shirt and leggings that I'd packed were quickly discarded.
I told a fib and said to mum that I'd forgotten to pack for
the morning. She said I could have a look at her clothes if
I wanted to, or she could wash and tumble dry what I had
on. I guessed that the jeans could do with a wash, but that
the black bobbly jumper had seen better days.

Mum and I were about the same size which had always
been handy for us both, apart from my massive feet which
were almost the same size as my dad's. If I'd wanted
boots with steel toe caps I could have taken my pick. I
flicked through mum's hanging rail and found a soft grey
cashmere sweater and a co-ordinating scarf. The sweater
was gorgeous to touch, and I hoped that there would be
more touching and kissing tomorrow, a lot more! I hung
them on the back of my bedroom door and made my way
downstairs for my crumble and an episode of *Strictly* that
they had recorded.

The night seemed to pass slowly, I just couldn't settle
after the day's events. Images of The Haven and Damien
haunted me both separately and together, as I tossed and
turned and waited for sleep to come. The last time I
remembered looking at the clock the green glowing letters
read 1:37am and this must have been when I started to
drift. I dreamt of us as children, and as adults and
everything in between. There was even a moment when I
could see myself walking down the aisle to marry Jay, and
when I got to the bottom it was Damien who took my
hand from my father. I saw us having children and
growing old together, and laughing saying it's just like *On*

Golden Pond. And loving each other, in every moment living and breathing the love we felt. And of course making love, slowly and passionately just like the kiss we'd shared that afternoon.

I was sad to wake up the next morning, but had such a strong feeling that my dreams had shown me a glimpse into my future, the future that I had wanted for so long.

Stephanie's Journal - Lesson 10
Intuition, Signs & Signals

Part of being awake and growing on your spiritual path is becoming aware of the signs and signals that the universe gives you on your journey. If something comes on to your radar three times then it has some significance to you in your life right now. There is a part of you that is attracting this sign, based on what you are sending out there in your own energy field. This could be the universe bringing you something that you need to work on and release, or something new that you should try, or indeed somewhere that you need to go in order to link in to the web of possibility that is all around us – in order to meet that person you need to meet up with. So many of us dismiss signs and intuition because they are not logical, maybe it's time to let go of the logical and look for the magical!

"I'm not interested in your knowledge, I'm interested in your intuition – that's where genius resides."
Alvaro Castagnet

Chapter 26

It was about ten o'clock when mum started to hoover and
fluff cushions up because Hillary and her daughter Alicia
were coming over soon to do my "treatment". Mum was
irritated slightly as this had all been accelerated due to me
leaving a little earlier, and she laid some towels out on my
bed and tilted the venetian blinds "for modesty", and also
because she didn't like the window cleaner who was a bit
of a pervert and due today.

"Have you got decent underwear on darling?" she asked
me with a brand new pair of sensible white briefs in her
hand.

"Yes, Mum!" I said with indignation. "And anyway
she's not coming to look at my underwear!"

"I know, I just think you should make the effort. I've
seen some of those string things that girls your age wear
and they make my eyes water, I mean what's wrong with
proper knickers? It must be like having something in your
eye all day," she spoke as she walked up the stairs,
presumably to put her drawers in her drawers.

The doorbell rang as she was coming down the stairs
and she opened the front door wide and smiled, falsely if
you ask me.

"Come in, come in, how lovely to see you both. Yes
Stephanie's all ready, just go through…"

Alicia looked like a nice girl wearing a lot of makeup
with nail extensions and too dark a colour on her hair. She
also seemed a bit nervous and declined coffee or tea.

"Well you girls can go and get on upstairs and we can catch up over a cup of tea. Go on Steph, take Alicia up with you." Mum tilted her head in a pantomime jaunt.

I stood up and lead the way, it turned out that really you should have the wax pot heating slowly for ages before the client gets there but if we put it on a high setting the chips would melt quickly and it would all be good. I tried to make small talk, but there was nothing I knew about twitter or this year's big brother winner, so conversation was a bit difficult. Thankfully before long she was standing over the pot and stirring it with what looked like a lolly stick. It had melted down to the same colour and consistency of golden syrup, and smelt a bit like warm plastic.

Alicia asked me to take my jeans off and tie my hair back, in case any got caught when she did my top lip? Christ if she was that bad an aim I had better not bother. Sounds like my eyebrows were the least of my worries and I'd look like I had mange if she got it wrong.

"So erm, how many of these have you done so far Alicia?" I asked, feeling dreadfully exposed lying on a load of old towels in nothing but a pair of knickers and a t-shirt.

"Oh I haven't done any for real yet! Just seen it in the class that's all, but like my teacher says there is no substitute for real practice. That's why I am so excited that you agreed to let me come over!" she stirred again. "It's actually the maiden voyage for my wax pot!" And I had the awful feeling that the trip would be right up Shit Creek.

She leaned over my face and ran her finger between my top lip and nose.

"I can see what your mum means, but don't worry we'll have him off in no time."

"Him?" I was about to say, but instead "Jesus Christ!" came out quite viciously really, as molten wax dripped all the way up one cheek, across my lip and up one nostril.

"Shh!" she said and slapped some kind of cloth over my wound and smoothed it down onto my burning skin.

Then came pain that was far, far worse than anything I had ever felt in my life accompanied by a ripping off sound and Alicia stood above me looking proud, and showing me a cream cotton rectangle with a fine downy line of hair embedded in cooling wax and a tuft of nasal hair. I couldn't really see because my eyes were watering so much and she wasted no time in muttering,

"That wasn't so bad now was it?" whilst I took a sharp intake of breath as she began the same procedure on the left side of my pubic hair. I cried out in agony when she pulled and put my hands up to stop her doing the other side.

"Come on now, you can't go round lopsided!" she said and showed me something that resembled a dead rodent on the strip. "Look at that! You don't want the other side to be like that, do you?" she screwed up her face and shook her head.

"I honestly can't go through that again, I'll just use some removal cream or something and even it up." I pulled one of the towels over me and clamped my arms down on either side.

Access denied.

Alicia cocked her head to one side and seemed to be totally oblivious to my agony as she said "It's still ten pound."

It was in the bathroom that I saw the full extent of what she had done, and I waited there until I was confident that Mum had shown them out before I could face making an appearance.

"Stephanie, what the hell happened? I can't believe you did that, the poor girl! You could have at least let her get on and finish the job!" Mum was shouting from the bottom of the stairs.

"Well? Are you going to tell me? She's left the form for you to fill out so I've given her a good score for everything and you will just have to sign it."

I opened the door slowly, still in my knickers and tee shirt but with an obvious red slug shaped burn above my lip like one of those cheap, thin pork sausages before they are cooked. The left side of my privates looked like a half a gammon steak. Red raw.

"Bloody hell!" mum said and ran up the stairs. I winced when she touched my lip. "What have you done?"

"What have I done?" I said, laughing near to hysteria. "Me?"

"Well you must have put something on in there that's caused an allergy or something..." she said in disbelief.

"It was her mum, not me! The bloody wax was far too hot and I was the first one she had ever done!"

"No." Mum shook her head. "Her mother told me she was nearly qualified."

"She's just started Mum! I was the first one she's done, she told me!" I shook my head now and laughed more. "I was the guinea pig Mum, and look what she's done, I'm a mess."

"Oh God," she said and made her way downstairs, appearing moments later with a bag of frozen peas wrapped in a checked tea towel for "my parts" and a fish finger for my lip.

"Now just keep them on for a moment or two and it should help. I should have known after the eyebrow, I'm so sorry darling. The eyebrow must have been a first as well. First and bloody last then. I'll get you some savlon."

By the time I arrived at the pub to meet Damien the burn on my face was a faint pink stripe, but my jeans were chaffing dreadfully on my nether regions. This was so typical, the closest I get to a potential shag in nearly a year and I look like I have been engaging in some weird lop-sided pubic topiary.

Damien's car was in the car park when we arrived and I felt excitement well up in my stomach, making me a bit giddy. I flipped down the mirror on the visor and applied a bit more concealer over what looked now like a welt on my face, and some lip gloss.

"Thanks for the lift, Dad" I kissed his cheek and then smiled and wiped the makeup off with my thumb. "I love you."

"Love you too pet, let us know you are back safely."

Damien was at the bar drinking coffee when I walked in and his face illuminated when he saw me. He kissed my cheek and I breathed him in, I wanted the whole experience of him as soon as possible. I ordered coffee as well and we sat beside the fire again, chatting and looking at the menu but neither of us really hungry. There was

definitely chemistry between us, I could tell by the way
that he looked at me, and he held my hand as he was
talking. We finished one another's sentences and every
now and then I caught myself lost for words as I looked
into his eyes, knowing that he was my soul mate and he
always had been.

Maybe this was the reason that Jay and I didn't work
out, the silver lining in my life, or the pot of gold at the
end of the rainbow. I knew that the universe had answered
my prayers and that now things were going to be just
amazing for me.

"Steph, there's something I need to tell you." His
expression changed and he broke eye contact for a
moment. Here it comes! Yes, yes, yes! I do! I was
shouting in my head.

"It's not easy for me, so please forgive me if this comes
as a shock to you..." In my mind I could almost hear the
church bells ringing and see the confetti raining down on
us both as we smiled and kissed for the camera. I sat and
squeezed his hand, sensing that he was nervous and telling
myself that this was perfectly normal when you were
about to declare undying love for someone. I would make
it as easy as possible for him, so I smiled and waited.

"I'm getting married."

Granted, the only word I heard was married and before I
knew what was going on I threw my arms around his neck
and started to cry with joy.

"Yes, yes, you are!" I squeezed him tight and squinted
through shiny, happy tears. "You are getting married!"

"Well I didn't think you'd take it quite like this!" he said once I was back in my seat and he could breathe again, he seemed a little confused and perhaps even offended.

"What did you think I'd say?" I laughed and grabbed his hands again. "This is amazing, I can't wait to tell my parents!"

"Your parents?" he asked. "I mean they're nice people but they hardly know me now, I guess I could see if Joanna wouldn't mind them coming to the evening party..."

"Joanna?" I asked tentatively and in a much quieter tone.

"Yes Joanna, my fiancée. We've been together for a while now and she wants to tie the knot so we said, well...why not?" He looked concerned and I pulled my hands away, trying to compose myself against the avalanche of emotion that was about to bury me.

"Why not?" I repeated through a fake smile and breaking heart. "Why not indeed."

I excused myself to go to the ladies, where I cried solidly for five minutes and used up half a loo roll.

I didn't know how life could be so cruel. Everything I had learned and done so far could have never prepared me for this moment, I felt broken, shattered and nothing would be able to piece me back together. This was worse than the nightclub incident with Jay, why oh why did I keep setting myself up for this? Had I not learned by now that I wasn't destined for love?

I knew that I had to get to the train station and somehow face Damien one last time. I had to hold it together now and I closed my eyes and asked with all my reserves of strength that somehow the universe could help me say the right thing. I reapplied my make up and put on my poker face before I made my way back out into the bar area.

Damien was sitting in the same seat with his head in his hands. I walked up behind him and put my hand on his back, he looked up and leaned into me and for a moment I held him.

He sighed and I noticed that he'd bought a bottle of wine and there were two glasses on the table. He poured it out with a slow glug, glug and the logs cracked on the fire as we looked at each other. I broke the spell by raising my glass in a mock toast "to marriage". The glasses chinked together and we both took a big gulp.

"I hope you make a better job of it than me!" I joked.

"That wasn't your fault Steph," he said in a serious tone.

"Thanks but I was fifty percent of the package!" I tried to make light of the darkest and most awful moment.

"You know that's not true Steph, he was an arse and you deserve so much more."

He looked at me again, I turned away as my eyes welled up with tears. Why can't it be you? I kept saying to myself, please forget about Joanna and love me instead, please pick me.

"Steph, you're upset. I'm sorry if I led you on I didn't mean to, I would never, ever hurt you. I know I kissed you and I shouldn't have… I just needed to, I don't know why, it just felt right… please forgive me."

"There is nothing to forgive." I dabbed at the corner of one eye with the grey cashmere cuff and sniffed through my fake smile. "If you have found someone that you love that much then I am happy for you, really I am, I want you to be happy in your life with someone special…"

"Really?" he seemed surprised, disappointed and relieved all at once.

"Of course really!" I laughed superficially.

"Well, that's a relief I suppose." He seemed disappointed and relieved at the same time.

"Yes, for me too," I lied.

The atmosphere was unbearably tense now and I declined another drink, making the excuse that I'd have to be making a move soon to catch my train.

"I'll take you to the station." Damien stood up first and wrapped his scarf around his neck. His collar length hair was briefly wafted to one side and I noticed a faint scar behind his ear. I wondered if this had anything to do with the night of the fire and the first kiss, all of those years ago. Memories fade like scars but they don't disappear.

I said that I could get a taxi but was glad when he insisted that he would drive me, I felt like this could well be the last time I was with him and wanted every second to last forever. I noticed every tiny detail in an effort to etch the moment onto my heart, the way that the sun shone on his profile and the way that his hands gripped the steering wheel. I wanted to speak out and tell him that he was making a mistake, that he had made the wrong choice and that I would do anything to be with him. Maybe we could have an affair and he'd realise that he did love me and that we were meant for each other, and he'd leave Joanna after a few months…this was nonsense and wrong, the internal voice of desperation that was strangling every last objection from my rational mind. But the fact was that he was getting married and not to me.

To break the atmosphere Damien turned on the radio, and almost immediately changed stations as the beautiful sound of Barbara Streisand sang about being a woman in love and doing anything to get into your heart. The second present was no better with Whitney belting out I will always love you and the third nearly made me laugh at the irony when Roxette piped up that it must have been love, but it's over now. That's when the radio was switched off.

"How long until you tie the knot then?" I asked, bracing myself.

"Two weeks," Damien said and then glanced at me sideways for a reaction.

I deliberately looked out of the window so he could not see the shock or sadness written all over my face.

"That's really soon!" I tried to sound upbeat. "You must be really excited."

"I guess so, but you know weddings are girl's things really, Joanna is organising it. I am just going to turn up." He was guarded in his tone and I knew that he was trying to protect my feelings, but there was really no need I couldn't possibly feel any worse than I did.

"I guess so." I commented trying to sound interested but dying inside. "I hope she is your missing piece."

"Missing piece?" Damien asked.

"Yes, you know, your piece of the jigsaw. The piece that makes you complete, that makes the whole picture of your life come to life. The piece that helps it all make sense and fills in the gap. Your missing piece..." I was probably rambling, and my words were loaded with the feelings for him that were rushing through my emotions.

"...sometimes you don't even know it's missing until you

find someone special, and realise that they are a perfect fit."

"My missing piece..." Damien sounded wistful, then snapped back to reality. "You could say that."

He insisted on standing on the platform and although the sun shone brightly, it did nothing to take the chill out of the air or the pain from my heard.

As the barriers went down and the train chugged into sight in the distance Damien put his arms around me and held me tight. I pressed my face into his shoulder and swallowed back more tears, I could feel that he was doing the same and as I relaxed and tried to step back, he held me tighter.

"Take care Steph, promise me. Promise me you'll take care of yourself, you are precious." He raised my chin again with his hand and I closed my eyes. This time he kissed my cheek, and I could still feel it as I waved from the window, holding it together until the platform was out of sight.

Chapter 27

I felt like the days that followed were void of any joy or
happiness at all. I had marked on my calendar the date and
time that Damien was getting married, November 5th at
noon. I told Josie what was wrong when she commented
on my sheer lack of enthusiasm for life in general. I had
taken to wearing tracksuits and watching Golden Balls in
the afternoon. I was still fundraising to the best of my
ability, it's just that your ability isn't exactly sparkling
when you feel like life has kicked the shit out of you. I ate
more carbs than ever and would have gladly tried
corrugated cardboard if it had butter and jam spread
thickly on the top.

Life seemed to have lost its oomph for me in a big way,
and my well-meaning friends had noticed.

"Come on, it'll be fun!" said Hannah

"I don't want to, and any way I'm happy in my misery."
I didn't want to go out or get over it, I was happy to feel
every ounce of pain for the moment, it was a testimony to
how much I loved him.

"Stop being a martyr!" Hannah shouted down the phone.

But I couldn't be budged. I didn't want pizza or a movie,
I couldn't move on until after it was official. November
5th at noon, and once he was married to someone else I
knew that there was no chance he'd come back for me and
I would have to pull myself together. That meant three
more days of moping around in tracksuit bottoms.

There had been no contact from him, and I fought the
urge on an hourly basis to send a text or ring up about the

house. I wasn't ready to face it yet, I was in emotional rehab.

I awoke on the morning of the fifth and the sun was shining. I looked at the clock and sighed, it was nearly nine, only three hours to go. I wondered how he'd be feeling now, and what Joanna would be doing and what she looked like. I hugged my pillow in and pulled the duvet over my head. At ten o'clock I dragged myself out of bed and had a shower, I even washed my hair, which hadn't happened often in the past two weeks.

Wrapped in a towel I looked for something to wear, and realised that the mountain of dirty laundry in the corner of my room meant that my options were limited. I had a quick rake and found some leggings that passed the sniff test, they were a type of stretchy black velour that did me no favours but would be fine for another two hours of moping. The last resort t shirt was an eighties black on white number with Relax written on the front at a jaunty angle. I made tea, moped and made more tea. I combed my hair over my shoulders whilst it was still wet and let it dry naturally, it could kink up as much as it wanted today.

One hour to go now. The clock tick-tocked in the background as I flicked through television channels I wasn't watching, looking for a distraction.

It was half past eleven before long and I thought about them getting in to wedding cars, or maybe the bride wanted to be late and she's give it another ten minutes or so. I could imagine Damien in his suit and button hole, his best man fussing with his tie and cufflinks. I made more tea and looked out of the window at couples in the café. The tea cooled beside me and a thin skin formed on the top of the mug, wrinkly in the middle. I opened the window although it was cold, I wanted to hear the exact moment when the clock struck twelve. You could hear the chimes from the town hall from here. I heard the first chime and held my breath, the second and third followed on but I didn't register them.

I sucked the air into my lungs in short, sharp, punchy breaths and cried it out in a long and wailing sob that would have woken the dead. He'd gone and so had my chance of happiness, the pressure of the whole year seemed to pile up on me in that moment and I felt crushed by its enormity. I felt like I couldn't go on, it had all been too much and whatever Sue had predicted for me with regard to finding someone was bollocks. Or maybe I had found them and lost them, that was more like it.

I looked out of the window again, everyone seemed to have someone apart from me, and in a temper I turned and ripped off the pictures on my wall.

The collage of The Haven and Mr Right were torn in to tiny pieces and I shouted at the universe.

"There! It was never real! You tricked me!" My cheeks were fiery red as I threw handfuls of hopes and wishes from the top floor window, and they spiralled like multi-coloured confetti into the street below. "If there is someone out there for me I want to see him, in the flesh, not in a magazine! I want arms around me and someone in my bed, I need someone who loves me, someone I can love!" I didn't know who I was talking to and it didn't matter, I just wanted to vent my feelings.

I stood with my hands balled into fists looking out of the window, and through anger, frustration and tears said once more, "Please, send me my missing piece."

I sighed and looked down the road. There must have been a near miss as a car had swerved and a driver was shaking his fist and shouting something I couldn't make out. I was momentarily distracted from my own anguish as I saw someone running up the pavement, jostling shoppers and moving people out of the way. Another car horn blared as the lemming ran over the street without looking, crossing to the other side where he knocked a carrier bag out of a woman's hand, then quickly doubled back to pick it up and apologise, before he started to sprint down the street again.

I was intrigued by now, I had initially thought he had been caught shop lifting but there was no one chasing him, but he looked frantic. He was running sideways like a crab and looking at the numbers on the buildings as he passed them, and at one point tripped over his shoe lace and recovered in a half forward roll and kept going. He ran right under the window and then out of sight under the canopy of the shop next door, as I watched and smirked through my misery.

God knows what that was all about! There were people staring and pointing, shaking heads and talking about him. And then he came back, backwards. He double checked the number and when he saw the name plate said Prospect House he leapt the steps two at a time and knocked loudly. Then he made his way back down to street level and cupped his hands around his mouth.

I realised it was Damien just before he started to shout, "Stephanie, I know you're there, please come out!" I took a step backwards and hid behind the voile panel with my mouth agape and shaking my head, I must be hallucinating.

"Steph, please, I'm sorry!" then more knocking at the door.

What was he doing here? I didn't understand any of it, he was meant to be miles away saying "I do" to some bird called Joanna. It didn't make sense, I was busy getting over him and in order to do that he would have to go away! If I saw him I knew I would be right back to day one, which hadn't differed much for any of the days since I'd last seen him really, apart from what was on telly.

"Steph, please forgive me – I am a moron!"

"You said it!" someone shouted from the café.

I started to panic and sat on my bed telling myself to take deep breaths and just sit tight, he'll go away. Maybe he was having a breakdown, I knew I felt like I was. My fragile heart was beating so hard I felt like I was going to explode, I was crying again. I wanted to see him but I just couldn't set myself up for another journey into the dizzy heights of hope via, whoops the cavern of despair, and also you've lost your will to live.

"Steph! I'm not going until you come out! And if you aren't in, I'm not going until you get back!"

"How is she going to hear it if she's not there you moron?" from the café and more laughter.

And still he wasn't giving up.

"Steph, if you can hear me I want you to know that you are my missing piece…" he shouted. "It was always you and I thought that Joanna could fill your hole, oh God no, I don't mean your hole, Jesus Christ this isn't going well… I just mean that it's you – you are my missing piece, it's you Steph, I love you!"

I clutched both hands to my chest and gasped. I rushed to the sash window and opened it wide, I leaned out and shouted back, "Are you sure?" He looked up at me and I saw the truth in his face. He was wearing a charcoal grey suit with tails and an exquisite orchid in his button hole.

"I walked out on my wedding Steph, of course I'm sure," he shouted.

"You mean she dumped you for being a moron!" from the café.

"Would you kindly PISS OFF?" he shouted over the street and a woman covered her child's ears and scowled.

I felt like Juliet looking down at Romeo from the balcony, and as I made my way to the door in order to bound down the stairs and reunite with the love of my life, I remembered I was wearing velour leggings.

"I'm coming!" I shouted. "Just hold on!" and I started to fling clothes from one end of the room to the next. I opted for a pair of jeans and black jumper, and as I frantically dabbed on some foundation and mascara. I was brushing my teeth frantically and shouting, "Just two more minutes," in the direction of the open window when I heard a tapping on my door. Josie must have let him in through the front door! I looked out of the window to see if he was in the street, which he wasn't.

"Steph, it's me, please come out."

I got closer and leaned my head against the door, maybe he was doing the same on the other side.

"Damien, I'm scared," I said.

"Me, too," he answered.

"Really?"

"Yes really."

"But you walked out on your wedding day, why?" I had to know.

"Because you are my missing piece Steph, I love you and I can't let you go again," he said and sounded sincere.

"But what about Joanna?" I asked.

"We weren't right together Steph, I knew it deep down and so did she. Getting married just seemed like the next thing we should do, and we were doing it for all the wrong reasons. We were just going through the motions and when it came down to it we both knew it," he said.

"And any way she's off to the Caribbean with one of her friends later on today, I said she could change the booking details on the honeymoon, I knew I would be trying to find you," he sighed.

"Please let me in."

I turned the key in the lock and opened the door slowly, I couldn't maintain eye contact with him and hung my head a little. He pushed the door gently and made his way towards me, lifting me in an embrace and closing the door behind him. He lifted my chin with his hand and looked into my eyes.

"Look at me Stephanie, please," he asked, as I turned away and started to cry. He pulled me in tight and stroked my hair "I am so very, very sorry that I put you through that, please, please forgive me. I will never, ever leave you Steph, really. I love you so much." I cried in his arms until the tears wouldn't flow anymore, and then he held me at arm's length.

"Are you sure?" I mumbled into his morning suit.

"With all of my heart," he said. Then came the kiss I'd been dreaming about, and then there was no more talking for a long, long time.

Stephanie's Journal - Lesson 11
Self-Love & Loving Others

It's only right now that I realise what real love feels like. Love where you don't have to prove yourself or work for it, love that accepts you and lifts you up, love that understands you and flows easily into all parts of you, especially the scared parts that still think you might not be worth it. This is real love, without condition or expectation and without judgement. I know now through all that I have learned that this kind of love would never have been mine if I had not been on this incredible journey. I was never going to attract something so pure when I felt so soiled. The key to finding real love in my life was always in my own hand, but I had to unlock the door to loving myself first in order to have life draw this in for me and reflect it in my every moment. I love myself, and this has come back to me in the most perfect way imaginable.

"To love oneself is the beginning of a lifelong romance."
Oscar Wilde

Chapter 28

It's strange how relationships pattern you with expectation and experiences that you carry from one to the next. It's like each experience is integrated into who you are, becoming part of your makeup, good, bad or indifferent. When you meet someone new, it's like having an out of date sat nav, and using it to find your way through a busy city centre at rush hour. You end up finding dead ends and one way streets you never knew existed, you have to learn the territory all over again.

Everything was different with Damien, and for a while it felt strange. I mean this in a good way of course, but I also had to keep checking myself as some of my old ways of being together with someone occasionally tried to surface.

For example, Damien was totally transparent and trustworthy with money. It turned out that the estate agents he was working in was actually his and that he owned several properties in that local area that he rented out. He had bought the first two properties when the market was really low and they had shot up in value, so they had been mortgaged to release funds to use as deposits on others. He now had ten. He had formed a good relationship with the estate agency staff including the owner, and when it came for him to retire, Damien was offered the business. Property since then had had ups and downs, and it wasn't easy at the moment being in the middle of a global recession. Damien however had his own income from his rental portfolio to finance his needs, so there was a financial buffer in place for him.

I found this really difficult at first and kept offering to
pay for everything. Damien was great and laughed it off,
he conceded to allow me to get the odd lunch and bag of
grocery shopping but told me that in essence he wanted to
look after me. Now that's a mind flip when your
experience of being with someone bled you dry
emotionally and financially. But over time I learned to
receive and as the weeks passed I started to relax when the
bill came for dinner.

The other stark contrast was that Damien was always
where he said he was going to be. Now this might not
seem like a biggie to someone who has never been
betrayed, but believe me its astronomical. He left his
mobile phone lying around casually and when text
messages arrived and one day when he was in the shower
he shouted over to me to open the message and read it out.
I just couldn't do it, I felt wrong and intrusive and perhaps
there was a part of me that was terrified that it would be
from another woman. That day had to get out and dry off
to read it himself.

"What's up?" he asked.

"I just, I feel like I'm intruding if I look at your private
things…" I looked at my feet and felt the familiar wave of
past emotions pool around me and try to pull me under
again.

"Steph…" He put his arms around me and his skin felt
hot and damp. "There is nothing private here, we are
together, I love you and I will never hide anything from
you. I promise that. You have to let the past go, its keeping
you chained into emotions that you don't need now."

I swallowed the lump in my throat.

I knew he was right, he bent over and kissed me and I felt my heart start to thump in my ribcage. I kissed him back, pausing to open my eyes and stare into his, my hands cupping his face. The towel that he'd slung around his hips in a hurry worked its way loose and fell to the floor, and we both sniggered like teenagers. He pulled off my clothes and in moments we were back between the sheets we'd slept in, making love again. I felt like everything in my world was perfect.

When you are in love even the ordinary things feel extraordinary. I felt like I had stepped into a parallel universe where dreams can come true and everything can materialise that you want in your life. We walked hand in hand through autumn leaves in the park and stopped to feed the ducks, then sat on the wooden bench and talked about love and life and everything in between. I had never in my life felt connected and accepted at the same time, and I thanked God and the Universe with every breath that I had found this.

Our time together was never long enough. We filled it with movies, log fires, more talking and love making. Mornings came round all too quickly when I caught the train back home in order to keep going with the fundraising and searching for a place to relocate. I had asked Damien to contact the seller of The Haven and see if there was any chance for a rental with a view to buy later on, but the answer was a resounding no.

The property had been part of a deceased estate and the beneficiary lived in Australia. They wanted a sale now, and felt like the property needed to be vacant in order to secure this quickly when the right buyer came along. I still had a strong gut feeling that we were the right buyers, but you can't base an offer on instinct, I had to find the funds.

Josie wasn't optimistic and was going through a phase of clearing out cupboards and the attic, in order to make things easier in January. Her feelings that the project was finished were sending out that same signal to the universe, so footfall slowed right down. She spoke of retiring or finding a "real" job somewhere, and joked about having a "well deserved rest", but these statements were all loaded with the emotion of grief and loss, and she stuffed bedding into bin bags and donated toys back to the local charity shop. I kept affirming every day that the right place was coming our way and that we would be moving in January. My faith was waning too but if I had learned anything this year it was that you had to stay focussed on what you want, even when what you want seems impossible.

I went out to view the occasional property that would be open to a rental period with a view to buy, but none of them were quite right. Josie smiled at times at my optimism, and agreed that if anyone could find somewhere it would be me.

"I don't know how you are going to pull it off Steph, you'll need a miracle," she said.

"I know, that's what I have asked for Josie, it's ordered I just need to chase up delivery." I was determined to keep going until the end.

It was the second week in November already, Lizzie's birthday was on the sixteenth and she had a get together planned that we'd been invited to. This was the first time that Damien would meet any of my friends apart from

Josie, and Lizzie told me Hannah was coming along too with a plus one.

"Just a few fireworks in the back garden and some wine and nibbles" read the text. I knew that they would approve, they practically knew Damien's life story already from the excited phone calls and emails they'd had from me and they were so glad that I was happy.

I thought about Hannah having someone to bring and was intrigued to know what they would be like. She had never really spoken about her type before, and since I had known her there had been no significant other so I had no clue. Maybe they were in law like her and intelligent charming and serious, or maybe they were a bit of rough with a nose that looked like it had once been broken, an earring and tattoos. I knew for sure that they would have a big heart, and Hannah was a great judge of character.

I felt like it was a bit sad that Lizzie would be the odd one out, the only singleton.

When I told Damien this he looked coy and raised an eyebrow as he said, "Well I thought of that too."

"What do you mean?"

"Just that. It's a shame that it's her party and that she'll be on her own, but I might have a solution…" he smiled.

"Oh don't fix her up with anyone Damien that could go really tits up and ruin her night if they turn out to not get along!" I said.

"That's just it though, I'm sure they would." He left the comment hanging in mid-air so that I'd have to ask.

"What do you mean? Who is it?"

"I've got a friend called Matt that would be great for her," he said.

"Is he Italian, gay, married to someone else or a bastard?" I asked, ticking each point off on my fingers.

"None of the above," he smiled back. "I wouldn't set her up with a moron you know. I mean he's not as good a catch as me you understand... but I have heard women say he's like *Mark Darcy* whoever he is.... just call her and say it's plus two that you need."

"*Mark Darcy* eh? Maybe I'll keep him for myself..." I laughed and started a text to Lizzie, and a plus two it was.

When Damien and Matt came to collect me for the party I was like a version of the Michelin man with all of the layers I'd piled on. I started to regret looking like an overstuffed boiler jacket in a pom-pom hat when I saw how dishy Matt really was. The lighting wasn't good from the bus stop as I squeezed into the front seat, which was very low down, but I did see his handsome features and hear the most knicker-droppingly gorgeous voice as he introduced himself.

"Oh, hello. Nice to meet you." I held his gaze for a moment too long and there was a cough in the back seat.

Damien laughed, and I blushed. "Don't worry darling he has that effect on all the ladies," he said in a mock theatrical tone.

After a few minutes I started to feel unbearably hot. I unwrapped my scarf to start with and then took off my hat and gloves. I unzipped my coat down to the height of the seatbelt.

"Are you ok Steph?" Matt asked me.

"Oh yes, fine thanks just a bit hot you know. I've got five layers on, well four now."

"Bloody hell Steph, we're just going down the road not to Alaska you know!" Damien said from the back seat.

"I know, it's just I don't like getting cold and she said there would be fireworks. They aren't the same from indoors so I thought I'd get wrapped up," I said.

I pulled my arms out of my puffed up feather and down coat and left it in situ under my bum. It helped a bit but I could feel sweat beading on my brow still. I then pulled a knitted tank top over my head and dropped it beside my feet. Better again, but still too hot. My polo neck was next, which combined with the sweat wiped off much of my makeup. The two of them laughed and shook their heads as I said proudly,

"There, that's better. What?" I asked in all innocence.

I then realised that I had turned Matt's sports car into a mobile jumble sale and that I looked like the morning after the night before.

"Nothing Steph, nothing." Damien leant over and kissed my cheek. "You're perfect."

When we got there Lizzie was looking fabulous in a wrap-around dress in a deep plum colour and long black boots. I introduced her to Damien and he introduced her to Matt. There wasn't an immediate response from Lizzie, but moments later I saw her watching him as she poured drinks and made small talk.

"Steph, he's lovely!" she whispered to me.

"I'm so glad you like him, we were hoping you would…" I said.

"Not him, I mean Damien. Well I mean Matt is good looking, but you know how I am now, I'm very guarded. Is he gay or married to someone I know?" She laughed, and I did too. The healing between us had been done and it was great to have my friend back.

"No, Damien says not," I said.

"Well then, let's just see what happens then." Lizzie raised her glass and as hers clinked mine the doorbell rang.

I heard Hannah's familiar voice and remembered that she was bringing someone too, I made my way into the front room with Damien and Matt in order to let them get in.

Hannah's head peeked around the door and she said "Hi" to everyone.

"This is Matt, Hannah, Hannah, Matt. He's Damien's friend," I said.

"Nice to meet you Matt. I've got someone for you to meet too as it happens..." Hannah smiled and looked a little coy, then disappeared for a moment. We looked at each other and I shrugged my shoulders. Then she reappeared and walked into the room, holding hands with and declaring that she was pleased to introduce us to Sam.

Then she laughed out loud and Sam smiled at my stunned expression.

"I thought you'd be a bit spooked Steph, you are so lovely but so naïve!" Hannah turned to the beautiful woman standing next to her and kissed her full on the lips. "You had no idea did you?"

I felt my neck and face start to colour up like a turkey's as I stammered out, "Erm, well, er no I didn't have any, erm idea that you were, erm..."

"You can say it out loud you know Steph, lesbian." She laughed again as I started to choke on my wine. "It's fine you know. Did you never wonder why I never talked about men?"

I recovered from my coughing fit and said, "No, I never wondered, I just thought you were private."

"In her defence Hannah, you must be bloody private if she didn't know," chipped in Damien and everyone laughed this time.

"Yes I guess I am about my personal life," Hannah said and looked at Sam again, they smiled at each other the way that lovers do the world over and I felt their connection.

I was pleased for them and got them both a drink while I topped up my own glass and Matt helped Lizzie arrange the fireworks.

Party Selection Fireworks consisted of many of the old favourites I'd had in my parents back garden in childhood. Mount Vesuvius and Traffic Lights made an appearance. Matt had a bit of trouble gauging the fix on the fence post for the two Catherine wheels. One didn't spin at all and just farted out sparks in one direction, whist the other one spun right over the neighbour's fence onto the conservatory roof.

Lizzie loved her birthday cake that we'd arranged and joked about being twenty two this year as she blew out the handful of candles. Matt saved the day by opening the front door and wafting a copy of Cosmopolitan at the ceiling when the smoke alarm started. Eleven o'clock came quickly and Hannah and Sam hugged their goodbyes. Damien and I made our way out to the street and watched them walk hand in hand down the road, as the sky lit up purple, pink and green.

"They didn't go for the party selection box I'm guessing," I said above the overhead banging. "Guess not." Damien leaned in for a long slow kiss and I felt my back press against the side of Matt's car.

"This is perfect," I said.

"I know," he replied and kissed me again.

"I can't think of anything else that I want in my life, really. I mean this is how people must feel when they have everything they have ever wanted. It feels like that, like I've hit life's jackpot. I am so happy Damien, I love you so much."

I could feel tears welling up and one spilt down my cheek as I threw my arms around his neck and pulled him in closer.

"I love you so much too Steph, and I know what you mean. I've hit the jackpot too."

A shaft of light illuminated the street as the front door opened and Matt walked down the two steps at the front of the house. He turned and looked at Lizzie, paused and walked back up the steps to kiss her. "Happy Birthday" he said as he broke the embrace and Lizzie composed herself, tucking her hair behind her ears and smoothing down the front of her dress. She grinned at me as Matt opened the car.

"Thanks for coming, I'll call you, Steph!" and the door was closed with, I imagined, a smug and excited Lizzie standing in the hallway preening herself in the long mirror and thinking about how long she could leave it until she called Matt.

I smiled as we pulled away and thought about how everyone seemed to have someone now, now that I had someone.

"What are you thinking about?" Damien asked softly, we were both in the back seat this time.

"Just how mad things are, you know the law of attraction and all that." I snuggled into him.

"You really believe it?" he asked.

"Of course I do, it's what brought us together again after all this time." I sat up and clicked my neck one way then the other.

"Maybe there is something in it then, I guess there is loads out there that we don't know about or understand." Damien said. "Someone was going on the other day about 2012 and some doom and gloom about the end of the world, prophecies and stuff, but who knows?"

"I've heard about that," Matt said from the driver's seat, he turned down the radio a little. "People think it's going to happen next month."

"What?" I said.

"This big end of the world thing, it's going to be like the millennium bug if you ask me, a nonsense. But there are some people that really believe that this is it. It's all based on the end of the Mayan Calendar or something, the earth having a pole shift and all that." He indicated to pull in at Damien's house. "You should look on the web there's loads of stuff about it."

"Thanks for the lift Matt," Damien said as we got out onto the footpath.

"Yes, thanks so much," I reiterated.

"No problem, I really liked your friend, so let's hope she feels the same about me too," Matt said and I turned to walk towards the house with Damien.

"Steph…" Matt rolled down the passenger side window as he crept alongside us.

"Yeah?"

"It was great meeting you at last, and thanks for making my pal so happy," he said, smiling.

"The pleasure's mine," I replied and waved as he drove away into the night.

Chapter 29

Matt wasn't kidding when he said there was loads of
information online about 2012 and the end of the world. I
sat at the breakfast bar scrolling through web pages on
Damien's laptop, while he prepared supper and poured me
a glass of wine.

"Do you think this stuff is real?" I said.

"I don't know Steph. I vaguely remember seeing
something on the television about it a while ago and I
think that opinions were pretty much divided. There was
one camp that was full of the doom and gloomers and the
others were on about some kind of enlightenment and a
positive change for humanity," he spoke above the sound
of sizzling.

"That's mainly what it says here as well," I said. "So I
guess it depends on what you want to believe, there seems
to be a story that you could argue for both outcomes."

"Well, you believe in the law of attraction, you don't
want to be thinking that it's all going to go tits up now do
you?" he laughed, "Or that's that!"

I was engrossed still in the information I was reading,
this was amazing stuff all about planetary alignments,
earth energy grids and predictions from many years ago.

"It says that the winter solstice next month is the date
that will be the defining moment for us all, the twenty
first." Damien put a plate down next to me as I was
speaking, fish finger sandwiches with tomato ketchup. He
made his way into the front room, and I heard the sound of
the television. I shut down the laptop and joined him for a
moment, there was nothing on worth watching so he

turned down the volume. I finished my sandwich and stood up to go to bed, it was after midnight now.

"You coming up?" I asked and tousled his hair.

"Yeah, I'm knackered," he said.

He went to switch the television off and paused, Sky news were running a story to find the elusive *Euromillions* winner from earlier in the year that had not yet claimed their prize. The words 82 million were scrolling across the bottom of the screen and there was a countdown calendar on the wall. They were appealing for everyone to check bags, wallets, purses and draws in an effort to find the unwitting millionaire.

"No point in me checking, I never really put the lottery on." He switched off the set and the room went dark. "Like you said, it feels like we've won the jackpot now we've got each other."

I felt him reach for my hand and we made our way upstairs. We undressed and spooned into each other as I drifted off to sleep feeling so much in love and so blessed, yes I'd hit the jackpot for sure.

I woke before Damien, as the autumn light glinted through the gap in the curtains onto my face. I turned over and looked at the clock, it was just after nine. I loved mornings like this, bright and cold. I stretched and lay still. Damien was snoring lightly with his back toward me. The shaft of light highlighted all of the miniscule particles that were floating through the air, and lay in a stripe across his left shoulder and neck. I followed its path with my gaze and stopped just below his hair line. The skin here looked a different texture in the morning sun, and it was something I'd never noticed before. His dark hair was thick and he wore it a bit too long for my liking, but maybe it was to hide this birth mark or scar?

He stirred now and moved his legs, then stretched out his arms and rolled onto his back.

"Morning, beautiful," he said and slung his right arm around my waist, I naturally turned onto my left side and he drew me close.

"Good morning, yourself." I snuggled into him.

"What do you want to do today then? We could do some Christmas shopping, have lunch, maybe a movie?" He kissed the back of my neck.

"Or we could just stay here a while longer..."

"Can I ask you something?" I said softly.

"You can ask me anything, you know that." He nuzzled his face into my hair and squeezed me again.

"What's that behind your left ear? Is it a scar?" There was a slight pause before he answered me, and I hoped that I hadn't spoiled anything by prying.

"It's a skin graft." Damien threw back the covers and rolled onto his side, pointing at his left buttock. See how they took skin from here, and stitched it into my neck?" There was a patch that looked different in colour and texture to the rest. He pulled the covers back over us and threw his arm over me again.

"What happened?" I asked.

"It was that night in the woods remember? The night you ran down to the tracks?" he said.

"Really? You had surgery?" I was shocked as we had never really learned the extent of Damien's injuries form his parents, I suddenly felt even more guilty for leaving him to face the bullies on his own.

"Don't cry Steph, its fine," he said as his thumb wiped a tear from my cheek. "There was nothing anyone could have done, and if me getting a beating saved this beautiful face... then it was all worthwhile."

"But what about you?" I asked.

"I'm fine now, I had the skin graft in the burns unit, and the bruises healed. I've dealt with it all, and to be honest it's helped to make me who I am now," he said. "I had counselling and all that, which really helped me, I didn't do it all on my own."

"I feel awful about it all, I really do," I said and fought back more tears.

We had never really discussed that night until now and meeting Damien as he was now seemed to eclipse the version of him form years ago that had suffered so badly at the hands of Jessica Mason's gang. Jessica Mason. I had completely overlooked telling Damien that she was the person that was renting the house from me! How could I have possibly missed telling him that? It must have been a combination of being totally loved up and happy with him, and the workload and stress that I had going on with Prospect House. It honestly had slipped my mind entirely that this was the girl that had inflicted the scars on his body and his heart.

I was in a dilemma now, should I tell him that it's her or not? I mean why wouldn't I just say it? We didn't keep anything from each other so it would be easy to just come out with it, but the words were stuck in my throat. I sighed and thought about what I had been through in the last year, and before. I knew only too well how past experiences in your life could mould you into who you are today. There were days that I still struggled with my past, old thoughts and behaviours might come up unexpectedly and I had to be conscious of them, in order to stop them from sucking me back in. Forgiving Lizzie and Jay had been my greatest test, and I knew that I had cleared a lot of the feelings I had, but there was still resentment and anger there, diluted but still there. I hoped that time would be the great healer that people spoke of, and that there would come a time soon when I could look back over my history and not feel it quite so much. Hannah told me that it would come, but that it was all still so recent that I needed some chronological distance on it all.

"Do you ever get angry with them now?" I asked, wanting some kind of idea on how long it took to heal when you had been through so very much, and to see what his reaction would be.

"I don't get angry now, because I know that Jessica was in a bad place back then, and so were the people she was hanging out with. It doesn't excuse what they did, but it helps me to accept it, I've learned to look behind the behaviour and not judge them. I mean they must have had their own stuff going on to think it was ok to do what they did." Damien stretched.

"That's a wise thing to say," I said, and urged myself to just tell him! If the moment passed it would be even harder further down the line! It was the first time that it had come up, so it was the best possible time to just come out and say it.

"Not really wise, it's just part of the journey I've been on. I have learned that if I hang on to all of my old pain I

316

can't be happy in the moment." He sat up now and leaned over to look at the time.

"I do sometimes wonder what she's doing now..." he said wistfully. "If she's got kids or not, and if she managed to sort her own stuff out."

"She has," I said, and there was a pause.

"What? You know her? Now I mean?" He looked surprised and waited for me to start talking again.

"I do know her yes, but vaguely. I met her earlier on this year, about the time I moved here. She's got a little boy with autism and her husband left her. It was all a bit strange the way it happened really." I spoke about the furniture on *eBay* and the strange string of coincidences that led me to offering her the house that I once shared with Jay, and by the time I'd finished Damien was sitting on the edge of the bed shaking his head in disbelief.

"Wow. Isn't it amazing that she didn't mention the whole incident. Maybe she was too embarrassed about it? Who knows?" he said.

"You're not angry with me?" I asked.

"Angry?" he laughed "No way Steph, this is amazing. It's a chance to finally heal the past and let it go for good. Please tell me she is still there now?" He looked optimistic.

"Yes she is. And I have to go over within the next few weeks and do an inspection before I renew the tenancy agreement." I said and watched his face light up.

"Can I come too?" he asked.

"Of course," I answered.

Chapter 30

Damien dropped me back at Prospect House on Sunday night, everyone was sitting around the kitchen table when I got in and Jude had saved me some fruit crumble.

"How are you Steph? We never see you these days! You're either working your backside off or with lover boy!" she said as she poured piping hot custard over the golden crumbly topping.

"Working her arse off and shagging it off you mean!" Sheila butted in and everyone laughed as I turned scarlet.

"Well, what can I say – you are right on both counts!" and I laughed too.

Josie sat back in her seat and smiled at us all, partly satisfied but equally sad.

"This is probably the last time we'll all be together like this," she said, and I looked up at her. "I know it's difficult to leave places like this when you have stayed a while, it's like jumping out of a plane with a parachute on. No matter how much faith you have in that rip cord it still scares you shitless to jump." She took a breath and swept her gaze around us all in an anticlockwise direction, smiling at us each in turn. "But we have to, and if I could have it another way I would, but we have to go. I'm going to close things down here a couple of days before Christmas. I'm letting you all know so that you can make your plans to move on, and I will help you anyway that I can."

She turned to Asha and said, "Do you want to tell them?"

Asha smiled and said she would, she was animated when she spoke about finding somewhere for her and

Jamal that was near to her parents. It turned out that her husband had gone back to his native country last month and sold up the property and business that they had here in favour of starting a new life with a new lady friend in Pakistan. There was always the danger that he could return at some point, and the security in her new place would have to be up to standard, but it was a chance she felt she could take to be near her family again.

"I have missed them all so much," she said, "and Jamal has cousins that have never met him before, and my parents have only really seen him as a new-born. As long as we keep a really low profile we should be fine. I am getting some help to change our names by deed poll and I'm going to get my hair cut short and stop wearing traditional dress so that I fit in a bit more. And yes I am shitting myself, but I know it's what I have to do."

She looked at Josie now. "Thank you, for your safe space and for all of the help you have given me to move on, I couldn't have done it without you."

"You are welcome, and please keep in touch if you can." She squeezed Asha's hand.

"And you Steph? Any plans to move in with Damien?" All eyes were on me now and Josie smiled.

"Yes, I guess that would be the most natural thing to do when this is all done," I nodded.

"You can go anytime you know, Steph, I don't want you to feel like you have to keep flogging a dead horse with this place!" Josie said and heads nodded around the table. "What you have done for us all is great, but it's coming to an end now and unless we get a miracle, I think we're done."

319

There was silence now and a couple of looks of what seemed like defeat.

"Oh, right, well thanks for that," I said and looked around the table. "But I'm going to keep going until the very end if you guys don't mind. As it happens I have ordered a miracle, I just think that it's been delayed a bit," I laughed. "I've even found the perfect place for this project to move to, it's just a case of the finances coming together. So if you don't mind it's not over until the fat lady sings."

"I'm not singing," said Jude and everyone laughed again. "I for one will be making plans to go back home to my husband." There were mutterings and glances exchanged between us all. "Don't worry, I don't mean go back to him, I mean go back home to my husband. It has turned out that he's become really sick with cancer, in his bowels actually and it looks like the end is nigh. He's had the symptoms for years but he wouldn't go and get seen to, something about a finger up his backside and being embarrassed, and sadly by the time he went to the doctors it was really advanced. The bimbo has moved out because she couldn't deal with the colostomy bag, or the burn cream that is applied several times a day to the parts of him that had radiotherapy." There was no satisfaction in her tone, in fact she sounded sad but strangely detached. "The Macmillan nurse rang me a couple of days ago to say that he was asking to speak to me, and that's when we agreed I would go home."

"God, Jude, are you ok?" Sheila reached out her hand and put it on her arm.

"I am thanks. I think it's something I have to do to help me find my own peace of mind with all this. I really meant it when I made my marriage vows and even though so much has happened, I want to be with him for the end." We all understood what she meant, and offers of support and promises were made between us to help her though it in any way we could.

"I'm really going to miss you all," she said, echoing the emotion we all felt.

Josie turned to Sheila and asked, "Any plans for you yet?"

"I've got a sister that would help me out for a month or so, she lives near my old flat. I never went there before because she was shacked up with another bastard that thought it was ok to use her as a punch bag. He's gone now anyway, so I'll go there for a while and see what happens after that," she shrugged.

"What about you?" I asked Josie.

"Now you're asking…" she replied and shrugged herself. "I don't know exactly, I've thought about all kinds of options, getting a proper job, having something on a smaller scale like a day centre maybe, or hanging on for the miracle…." She smiled at me.

"Still not singing yet!" said Jude and we laughed again.

"I don't know what I'll do in all honesty, but I have a home and a husband so it's not as urgent for me. We have got a spare room if anyone doesn't get fixed up in time, please let me know." Her eyes filled with tears now and the reality of the situation was emotionally overcoming.

It only took moments for us to all be in tears, hugging each other and sharing wishes of good luck along with promises to stay in touch.

And that's how I remember it all starting to end. It felt sad and happy at the same time, doors opening and closing if you like. I doubted that I would ever have more genuine friends in my lifetime.

I know Lizzie and Hannah knew me well, but the women around this table were different. They had clawed their way through their situations and although the details of each story differed, there was solidarity here that could not be ignored. Since coming here we each know more of our own truth, and each other's. We created safe space to heal ourselves, and sometimes this healing took the form of a homemade meal, a haircut or a hug. We had all clung to the same piece of ship wreck here, and been buffeted about all over by life, but encouraged everyone to keep hold until calmer waters were on the horizon. This experience had helped to put me back together, and these women were all a part of that.

I went to bed that night feeling a mixture of emotions, recalling each story and also thinking of how far I had come. I called Damien to say goodnight, he was watching some late night television debate about 2012. "I'm just going to hold the intention that something amazing will happen on that day and that everything is fine." I yawned.

"Me too. It's already amazing anyway. I love you," he said.

Chapter 31

I awoke to the first covering of snow.

Soft, white feathery flakes swirled around the street below me as I watched out of the window and pulled my dressing gown round tighter. Christmas was coming, and hopefully so was my miracle. I had just over three weeks now to pull something amazing out of the bag, and although I had a nagging doubt I kept over riding it with positive thoughts and visualisations. It was a good thing that everyone had somewhere sorted out to move on to, from an energetic perspective that was keeping me out of the feeling of being desperate to move the project. I flicked on the radio while I pottered around with cups of tea and post it notes, scribbling anything else that I could possibly think of to save the day. Between the tunes there were snippets of conversation and then the news. I was in the shower by then and caught the end of the lottery appeal again, maybe if the lucky winner came forward they would want to donate a lump sum? Perhaps that was why I kept noticing the story in the media.

I laughed out loud and thought of how hard it was creating and extra fifty pounds never mind four hundred thousand. Still, it would be lovely to have anything that could help and I was not going to create any resistance by thinking less than completely positively.

"The money is easily available to move this project into The Haven" became my mantra for the next few days.

That weekend I had arranged to go and see Jessica about our agreement. Damien had stayed overnight with me on Friday for the first time, it was against the rules really but under the circumstances Jude and Sheila said it would be fine by them. Asha had left earlier in the week in a taxi, heading for somewhere in the midlands. So on Saturday morning at ten o'clock we were pulling on to the drive of the house that I used to live in.

Jessica's son was playing with a football in the front garden, I knocked on the door and by the time she answered, Damien and Max were having a kick about. I left them to it and took off my shoes and coat. Jessica made tea and I walked around the house, ticking boxes on a clip board. Most of what I saw was exactly as I had left it, and I surprised myself by having no real feelings of regret or sadness.

This was someone else's home now, not mine.

I could hear Damien shouting in the back garden now, and I looked out of the landing window to see that there was a makeshift goal out there against the fence. Max had scored and was running round with his jumper over his head.

I made my way downstairs and Jessica asked me if I wanted sugar. I didn't usually have any but asked for one. I was a bit tired, probably due to not eating this morning yet.

"Everything in order?" She asked, stirring, as the spoon clinked against the side of the mug.

"Yes, it's all great, Jessica. Perfect in fact." I sat at the familiar breakfast bar and passed over the inventory for her to countersign.

"Do you think it would be ok to stay then?" she asked.

"I'd love you to," I said and saw her breathe a sigh of relief.

"Thanks so much, we love it here." She looked out of the window at Max and Damien in the garden and smiled. "It hasn't been easy, but we're finally getting it together. Max has got some extra support at school now and it's really starting to show. His confidence and coping skills are getting much better."

I didn't know what to say about Damien, so I small talked for a while longer about the school and the neighbours, waiting for a break in the conversation. But how on earth was I going to bring the subject up? I excused myself to the bathroom and had a moment to think. When I came back into the kitchen I saw Jessica standing close to the window which was cracked open.

Max and Damien were sitting on the wrought iron bench beneath the window sill and Jessica could over hear what they were saying. She turned and looked at me and I saw tears on her face, as she gestured for me to come closer.

"I just don't know why they hated me so much," Max said, I could hear him sniffing back his own tears.

"They didn't hate you, they hate part of themselves," Damien said.

"Why did they keep taking it out on me?" Max asked.

"They didn't know that they hated themselves, it's complicated. I mean you are lucky because you have got a nice home and a mum that loves you and looks after you, apart from the bullies at school you feel alright about yourself don't you?" Damien waited for a response, then continued. "Maybe other kids haven't had the example or experience that you've had in your life. Maybe part of them is crushed because they don't feel loved or they have been hurt in the past, and they have buried that deep. So

325

deep that they don't know it's there, but every now and then that pain bubbles up and they lash out. The only way they know to make themselves feel better is by pulling other people down."

There was a pause and we heard the ball bounce a couple of times.

"So you mean that it's not their fault?" Max asked.

"I mean that some things have happened to them that have changed them, and they don't feel whole anymore. To feel whole again they feel like they have to take other people's confidence and self-worth," Damien said.

"Like stealing it back?" Max asked.

"Kind of, yes. Theirs was taken and then they take others to feel ok about themselves. But the thing is that they don't know this is going on." Damien said.

"So, they aren't doing it deliberately?" Max asked.

"They are doing it deliberately yes, we all have a choice about how we treat other people in every single moment. And they could choose not to be hurtful to others, of course. But the point is that now you know about what is behind it, you can look at it differently." Damien stood up and they started to kick the ball back and forth again.

"Like being more understanding?" Max asked.

"Yeah, that's part of it. Don't be pushed around by others, but it will give you the chance to see past their behaviour and not take it personally. It's not about you, it's their stuff," Damien said.

"So should I still tell the teacher?" Max asked "I mean, if it's not their fault."

"Yes you should tell, this is going to help them to take responsibility for what they are doing. And it will show them that you won't put up with it. And really Max, no matter what you have been through you always have a choice of how to treat people, and they hadn't learned that when they were mean to you."

Damien said as he tucked his hair behind his ear and gestured for Max to come closer.

I knew what was coming now and looked at Jessica for a second. Her hands here clasped together in a prayer like position, and her eyes were closed with tear tracks on her cheeks and lips pressed into something of a smile. I reached out and touched her and she looked at me and whispered,

"No one has ever reached Max like that, I can't tell you how much this means…what an amazing man he is…"

And then we saw through the long voiles that flickered in the breeze coming through the open window, Damien kneeling down so that Max could have a close look at his scar. Max outstretched his fingers and touched it lightly.

"Does it hurt?" we heard him say. I was fighting back tears now, I knew the irony in the situation and was waiting for the moment of realisation with Jessica.

"Not now," Damien answered.

Max stepped back and put his hand on Damien's chest. "What about your heart?" he said.

Jessica sobbed silently.

"I think that's healed now too," Damien said to him and opened his arms wide.

As Damien hugged Max tightly, I did the same for his mother who sobbed in to my shoulder until we heard the ball being passed around again.

"I was a bit of a bully at school you know," she said to me, whilst looking at the floor. "I guess it's coming back to me now."

"We all do things we aren't proud of," I said. "You need to forgive yourself."

"Maybe I do," she sighed. "I know I was mean to you about that jacket, and I'm sorry. I didn't realise it was you straight away. And you could still find it in your heart to be kind to me after all of that."

"I knew you were unhappy," I said.

"That's no excuse." Jessica filled the kettle back up.

"Not an excuse, but like Damien said, it's because you don't feel whole that you pull other people down," I said.

She turned around with her mouth wide open, and said quietly, "Damien?"

"Yes, that's Damien," I nodded.

"You mean the Damien that you hung out with at school?" she asked.

"Yes." I could see what was going through her mind as the gravity and irony of the overheard conversation crashed into her reality. She put both hands on the bench and hung her head in shame, shaking it from side to side and saying, "Oh my God," under her breath.

I walked over to her and put one hand between her shoulder blades, gently rubbing in a clockwise direction.

"It's ok Jessica, really it's ok. He's dealt with it and he's not angry with you now. You heard what he was saying to Max…"

"I just can't believe that he can be so forgiving," she said. "I mean, how can you get over something like that?"

The back door opened and Max stuck his head into the kitchen, "Mum I'm starving!" he announced and kicked off his trainers into the corner and made his way into the front room. We heard the sound of the television burst into life as Damien's silhouette appeared behind the glass panel, and he walked into the kitchen.

"Hi," he said to Jessica, and then looked at me. "All done?"

"Yes, we're all done." I looked from him to Jessica and back again. "Are you?"

He walked over to where Jessica was standing with her head in her hands and put both arms around her. He held her for a few moments and then said softly,

"It's ok Jess, really, it's all ok." He released his embrace and turned to me. "I'm done now."

Chapter 32

We didn't speak much in the car, the radio sang quietly in the background. When we came to the junction at the end of the street Damien put his hand on my knee said, "Thank you."

It was complete now, and all was well.

We drove past the places that I knew, the hairdressers, the chippy, the park and the corner shop. It seemed busier than usual, people were walking round in royal blue jackets with clip boards, stopping people and chatting. It was probably market research form someone I thought. Then I got a flash of the underside of a clipboard, a middle aged woman with brassy blonde hair and full makeup was talking to an old man that I recognised from around the doors. It said Lotto, and I guessed that they were promoting scratch cards or the like. I saw the old man laughing and digging in his pockets in the rear view mirror as we drove on.

"What do you make of the whole lottery thing?" I asked Damien.

"What do you mean?" he said, folding down his visor.

"I mean, if all of the law of attraction stuff is real, how does it work with lottery winners?" I asked.

"Well I guess that it's all about getting into alignment and letting it come in, from what I have read anyway... but I don't know how luck would figure in it, or destiny? If such things are real of course, according to the law of attraction they aren't," he looked thoughtful.

"I know, it's a puzzle isn't it? I mean Prospect House is such a great project and helps so many people that it deserves a big cash injection to keep going, but no matter how much I align to it or wish for it, it's just not happening," I sighed.

"I dunno Steph, maybe you're resisting it for some reason," he suggested.

"I don't feel like I am," I said.

"But didn't you once say to me that everything you order is out there for you, it's held in a kind of virtual bank account that only you have the pin number for?" he said. "If that's true, then it's there waiting for you to claim it or draw it in or whatever. You just need to find a way to do that."

I looked out of the window at the cars and houses passing us by.

"I guess I do," I said. "But quickly, there's not long left now."

I suggested after a couple of miles that we drop in on Lizzie, I hadn't seen much of her since her birthday. When we pulled up I was surprised to see the curtains closed and hoped Lizzie wasn't ill. I rang the doorbell and stepped back, using my right hand to shield my eyes from the bright winter sun I looked up at her bedroom window. I rang the bell again and waited. I reached into my pocket and found my mobile. Just then I heard footsteps on the stairs and the door unlocking.

"Oh, hello!" I said as Damien laughed at my embarrassment.

"Hi Steph, sorry about that we were, erm busy…" Matt stammered whist standing in his boxer shorts with Lizzie's trademark red lipstick on his neck and face.

"Just erm, tell her to call me soon," I said pulling Damien's arm and making my way back to the car.

He was giving Matt the thumbs-up and Matt was smiling back and waving.

"Well I guess they are getting on well then," Damien said as he started the car.

"I guess they are," I smiled.

Chapter 33

December came along with more snow, and Damien asked me to move in with him. I had to admit that it was getting lonely in Prospect House and there had been a couple of nights when I had been alone there, and I didn't like it. I wasn't scared or anything and I knew that Josie would be in every morning with the radio and the kettle on, but the nights that Damien couldn't stay were always long and unsettled.

It made sense in all ways, including the fact that I'd be closer to mum and dad for Christmas. I told Josie that I was going to keep working on finding us somewhere, and that I would keep in touch with her by phone and email. The regular donations that had been set up on monthly direct debit would be allowed to accrue in the bank account until we had a new place to go, and with me gone there would be no utility bills to pay for December so some savings could be made.

Josie was teary on the day that I left, and so was I. Damien loaded up the car and we said our goodbyes, she thanked me for all that I had done and said that the council was coming to take the furniture away later in the week.

"There's no need for it now, and it means that when the strip out starts in January, it won't be in the way." Her words were interspersed with deep sighs. "I'm probably going to have a last look around myself and then lock up."

"Do you want us to wait for you?" I asked.

"No thanks, this is something I want to do alone. Me and this old girl started out together" she patted the wall in the

hallway the way you would pat an old friend on the
shoulder, "I need to say goodbye to her properly."

I nodded my head in a gesture of understanding and
hugged her again.

"I'll be in touch," I said as Damien opened the front
door and picked up the last box.

"Merry Christmas, Steph, and a Happy New Year," Josie
said.

"Same to you," I replied.

Mum and dad were surprisingly good about me moving
in with Damien, I suppose in their eyes it was a whole lot
better than where I had come from. They had always liked
Damien, and Mum liked him even more when she learned
that the estate agents belonged to him and he wasn't a
humble employee.

Damien's house was beautiful to say the least. It was a
rambling Victorian terrace, over three floors that had been
lovingly restored to its former glory. High ceilings, deep
skirting boards, original architrave and stripped floor
boards all added up to the wow factor, and the oversized
mirrors and chandeliers finished the look.

I pottered around through the day when he was at work,
but no matter how hard I tried I couldn't relax into being
here and I still felt like guest. It must have been evident to
Damien as he suggested that we have a house-warming
party for me.

"What about the twentieth of December? We can ask
Lizzie and Matt and Hannah and Sam… that way we can
all get legless together and if the world does end overnight
we'll not know a thing about it!"

He laughed, every time anyone had mentioned the
winter solstice I had started affirming that something
amazing was going to happen for me on that day and all
was well. I was determined not to get sucked in to the fear,
and it's not like I could anyway when mum had busy with
Christmas preparations.

I agreed to the house-warming party, maybe it was just
what I needed to feel like I belonged here with Damien.

The second week of December was full of Christmas
shopping, writing out cards and putting up the tree, a real
one of course. I did feel a bit guilty for not doing any
work, but convinced myself that I was allowed some time
off for Christmas, and anyway the fastest way to bring in
what you have asked for is to be in a happy place,
according to many of the spiritual sources I'd read or
heard. I kept the details for The Haven folded up in the
back of my purse and every couple of days I opened up
the now dog eared sheet of paper and held it to my chest,
asking for this to be resolved.

I found that I was sleeping more than usual, and I noted
how easy it would be to get into the routine of having an
afternoon nap. It was on wind down, eventually
everything was good, just as Sue had said and I didn't
need to live on adrenalin anymore. I had someone who
loved me and wanted to look after me, a beautiful home
and a secure income with Damien's properties.

I watched back episodes of cookery programs in
preparation for the party on the twentieth, and by the
nineteenth I was all sorted and ready to hit Marks and
Spencer with my shopping list. I felt inspired to have a go

at making my own holly wreath for the door, and spice pouches to drop into the Shiraz to make mulled wine.

I waltzed around the shop singing along to the Christmas Carols and ticking off double cream, vanilla pods and olives. Things were good.

I rounded the corner and scanned the shelves for something for tonight and wondered if we could eat out instead. It was dark outside and I was probably too tired to cook by the time I got home and put all of the shopping away. I text messaged Damien and he said to stop by his office and we'd go from there. The taxi driver unloaded the bags straight into Damien's boot, it was freezing now so nothing would spoil.

We walked into the town and stopped at an Italian Restaurant that had recently opened and had good reviews. The delicious waft of garlic and olive oil drifted into the seating area as we sipped our drinks and waited for a table.

"What are you going to get?" I asked Damien, as I scanned the menu and looked over his shoulder at the specials on the blackboard.

"Maybe lasagne…what about you?" he said as the waiter came over with a pad and pen.

"Same," I said.

Damien laughed. He knew I couldn't bear to order anything new or different in case I didn't like it. I always went through the same silly scenario whenever we wanted a take away, of looking through the menu, dithering, and then going for exactly the same choice every time. It all stemmed from the fact that once I'd branched out and tried King Prawn Dopoiaza, burning both my mouth and

my arse beyond belief. 'Stick with what you know' was
my motto now, and the most culinary excitement I'd
ventured towards since then, was when Heinz put the hint
of Basil in the tomato soup.

We were led to a lovely table, tucked away beside the
window and the waiter lit the tea light in the middle.

"You know I've been thinking about The Haven,"
Damien said.

"What about it?" I asked him, curious.

"Well I've been trying to find a way to get it for you."
He reached for a napkin and then slipped his hand into his
inside pocket and pulled out a pen. He drew seven boxes
in a row and then two figures underneath each box.

"What's that?" I asked "Snow White's piggy banks?"

"No Steph, these are my piggy banks," Damien said and
turned the napkin round to face me.

"This figure is what is currently owed on the mortgage,
and this second figure is the profit made every month. I've
been trying to find a way to access this figure…" He
pointed at the first line, "without influencing this one too
much." He pointed the pen at the second row.

"I don't understand," I shook my head.

"If I can draw out enough money from the equity in
these properties, and still retain a good monthly income
from them for us to live on…I could buy The Haven and
your project could rent it back from me." He looked at me
for confirmation.

"You'd do that for me?" I asked, shaking my head.

"I know how much it means to you, and how many
people you could help. It just depends on getting the
deposit together and then your project being able to pay

rent that would cover the mortgage payments. As much as I love you and I want it for you, I can't do it if it's not viable, but I am trying to find a way." He reached over and took my hands in his. "You keep saying something monumental and amazing will happen on the twenty first of December, maybe that's it."

"Wow," I said. "I can't believe you'd do that for me, and the project."

"I've told you Steph, what's mine is yours. I just need to make sure that I don't put us in a precarious position financially. So I need you to have a really good look at the income you have generated and then come to me with a projection."

"Damien, that would be amazing, thank you for even thinking about it, no matter what comes of it I am so grateful that you would even think about it." I smiled at Damien and the universe for bringing me a step closer to what I had asked for, maybe Jude would have to sing after all.

Just then there was a smashing sound from the bar, the waiter was cursing in Italian at the tray of drinks he'd spilt. He switched to English and yelled over to a fair haired, pretty girl "Mandy, go and get pretty boy and tell him to clear this up, he's unblocking the gents."

"Charming," said Damien in a sarcastic tone. "I hope he doesn't go into the kitchen after the bogs!"

A tall man in jeans and some kind of workers overall appeared with rolled up sleeves and a plunger in his hand. He shook his head and left for a moment, coming back with a dust pan and brush. The waiter made his way over

to our table and folded the bill onto a plain white plate
with a handful of complimentary mint imperials.

The man behind the bar stood up and the glass splinters
chinked as he emptied the dustpan in to the bin.

"All done" he said in our general direction.

"Well don't hang around then, get back on washing up,"
the waiter said to him as he walked over and rang in the
money we'd tucked under the bill.

It was then that I looked up and thought that he was
being a bit harsh on the man, he was probably working for
cash in hand and was clearly given the worst and most
demeaning jobs going. When my eyes locked with Jay's I
caught my breath. He looked dishevelled and tired, down
and out really.

"What's up?" said Damien.

"It's Jay, that guy behind the bar," I spoke quietly and
tried not to stare.

"Who? Dog's Body?" Damien turned around but Jay
had gone, the door to the kitchen swung closed behind
him.

"Yeah, it was him," I said.

"I feel a bit sorry for him" Damien shook his head "But
then again, you attract what you are."

"Yes you absolutely do," I agreed, and although I felt
sad for Jay, I also felt that what I had just witnessed was
his own retribution.

Chapter 34

The following day I awoke with money on my mind. Other people's money that is, and if it would be enough to get what we needed and wanted. I pulled out the paper files and opened up excel on my laptop. It didn't take long to see that the most that realistically could be allocated to rent would be in the region of eight hundred pounds a month. This left enough to pay for gas and electricity, poll tax, water rates, television licence and insurance. There would literally be nothing left after this, but at least the basics would be covered, I rang Damien's mobile and started to excitedly ramble.

"Hold on, hold on Steph…back up a bit," he said, I could hear him scribbling figures done as I reeled them off. "Ok, ok let me have a look at this and I'll ring you back."

I made my way into the kitchen and put the radio on, before long I was elbow deep in pastry for my home made goats cheese and caramelised onion tartlets (thanks Delia) and the gammon was in the oven. I was just sitting down for a well-deserved cup of tea and sneaky *Gok Wan* when the phone rang.

"Hello Darling, it's your mother."

"Hi Mum, how are you?" I pressed pause on the woman with the oversized bust in the all in one body shaper.

"Oh, we're fine thanks. Just wondering how things are?" this sounded a bit loaded to say the least.

"Fine thanks, why?" I asked and there was a slight pause on the other end of the line before she burst in to nonsense about the neighbours and the last turkey in the high street.

"So I'll tell dad everything is ok and you're happy then," she asked.

"Yes Mum, are you making trifle?" I asked.

"Trifle?"

"I just thought you might have been at the cooking sherry," I said.

She laughed somewhere between theatrically and hysterically and said her goodbyes, hanging up quickly.

What on earth was all that about? I had no idea at all. I knew from experience that analysis of my mother's occasional bizarre behaviour was pointless, so I sipped my tea and went back to what I really should be wearing this season.

By the time six o'clock came I was the hostess with the mostess. The spare rooms were all ready with clean bedding and guest towels, bunches of holly and ivy adorned the dining table, and the two fires were roaring. I'd opened the wine to let it breathe and taken the gammon out of the oven to rest. I had time for a quick shower and change before my guests arrived, and as I dabbed on concealer and lip gloss.

Damien came through the door first, with a beautiful bouquet of flowers for me.

"What are they for?" I asked him, grinning from ear to ear.

"I don't need a reason to buy you flowers," he said, and my heart sang with the life I was now living.

"And they are also something of an apology..." he said as I looked at him and waited for an explanation, I started to panic, maybe he'd had a one night stand and shattered our chances of being together? I could get over it in time, I knew I could if it was just a one off I could go on and be strong, we all make mistakes…I braced myself for the sound of his voice again.

"Steph…" he said.

"It's ok, really it's fine, I know that people mess up and I can live with it. Really it's good that you have come clean because most men wouldn't…" I turned my head so that he couldn't see me crying, and began to make my way into the kitchen to find a vase to distract myself. I had to pull it together before everyone got here.

"Steph…what do you mean? No, No!" he ran after me and caught my arm, spinning me round to see the makeup running down my face. "There's no one else! That's not what I meant!"

"What?"

"There's no one else, that's not why I've bought you flowers… come here," then his big arms were around me and he rocked me gently. "That's not what flowers mean now Steph, and they never, ever will."

It turned out that the apology was actually about The Haven, and although I was sad at the news that we'd need more rental income to make the project work, I was relieved that that's all the news was.

I pulled myself together and made up my face again, chose some background music and poured myself some wine. I took a large gulp and it tasted different, maybe it had been corked. Damien checked and said not, but I went on to white for the evening instead.

We were laughing together about my mother's strange phone call when the doorbell rang, and Lizzie and Matt stood on the step with a bottle and an overnight bag.

Hannah and Sam arrived shortly afterwards, they had brought a poinsettia and some after eight mints.

The music played and the wine and conversation flowed, as I served up the starters and we all made our way to the dining room.

It felt really good to be with everyone, and Damien had been right, it did feel like home now. The main course was a success and the homemade vanilla ice cream was divine, especially with after eight mints spiked all over the top.

Damien insisted that I sat with my feet up as he loaded up the dishwasher, and made coffee. The conversation turned to couples and how we'd all found each other in strange circumstances, Lizzie and uninvited Matt at her firework party, Hannah and Sam through a mix up on a train and Damien and I through breaking and entering.

"What's going to happen to the house then?" Hannah asked, once she had caught her breath after laughing for ages about me hiding under a sheepskin coat.

"I don't know really, we were trying to find a way of pulling it off but it looks like it could be slipping away. I won't give up though, not until I absolutely have to," I said, stirring my coffee.

"It's such a shame," Sam said genuinely and turned to Hannah. "Can the demolition not be contested or at least delayed?"

"Sadly not," Hannah replied and shook her head.

"What time is it?" asked Lizzie.

"Nearly the end of the world," laughed Matt and kissed her.

"Enough with your 2012 drama, you can't watch the television this month without someone going on about prophecies and star charts." Lizzie laughed too.

"Well we've got ten minutes to go until it all happens according to the doom and gloomers." Matt raised an eyebrow. "Wouldn't you rather be doing something else? I mean I'm not guaranteeing anything but you know there's always scope for a big bang in my book…"

"Don't you ever think about anything else?" Lizzie squirmed out of his arms as everyone laughed along with them.

"Do you think it's all real Steph?" Hannah asked.

"I don't know what to think, some people think it's already happened back in October 2011 and some say that it's happening now, and what exactly is happening anyway? There's so much information out there I just keep getting my pole shifts mixed up with my periodic table," I laughed.

"I know what you mean. But there is something in it I think, there has to be or how would all of those ancient civilisations have been able to map time and stars the way they did? It's fascinating, whatever happens," Hannah said and squeezed Sam's hand.

There was a gentle clinking together of glasses from down the hallway and Damien appeared with champagne flutes and a bottle of bubbly.

"Where have you been hiding that?" I asked.

"In the car, it's bloody freezing out there!" he said as he twisted the bottle and braced himself for the pop.

He half-filled all six and then went round again when the bubbles had settled.

The clock chimed midnight just as he raised his glass high.

"Well, we're all still alive...that's a start." He scanned the room and continued, "I want to propose a toast to Steph's new home. She has been going round for weeks now saying that she feels like something monumentally brilliant is going to happen today, and I hope that this is it. I love you Steph and I want you to be here with me, in our home."

"Steph's new home" rang out and glasses clinked together over the table. I felt Damien's arms around me and heard him whisper, "I love you so much."

He reached into the drawer of the sideboard and pulled out an A4 white envelope, sealed with no writing on to define the contents.

"And this is for you." He passed it to me.

I held it tight and went into bewildered mode "What is it?" I said, and there were several answers of "open it and you'll see!"

I carefully peeled back the sticky side and pulled out the document within. I looked at Damien and shrugged my shoulders.

"I don't understand," I said.

Hannah was grinning from ear to ear, and I suspected that she'd had some involvement.

"Steph, it's the title deed for this house. Its half yours now, you just need to sign it in front of me and we can get it registered." Hannah turned the first page and showed me our joint names along the bottom of the second sheet of paper.

"It's your house now as well as your home," Damien said. "I want you to feel that you belong here, with me."

If there was ever a perfect moment in my life, this was it, and as we kissed and my friends cheered, I could hear fireworks going off in the background, others celebrating the coming of the golden age that we'd heard so much about.

Damien cleared his throat and turned to me again.

"There's something else I need to tell you…don't freak out but I've told a little white lie," he said.

Nothing could spoil this moment, and I knew from earlier on in the evening that this was probably something relatively trivial, or maybe he was joking about something to see my reaction.

"When you told me that you had a crazy conversation this afternoon with your mother I acted as if I'd had no idea," he smiled.

"What do you mean?" I wagged a finger at him playfully.

"I did know all about it because I was there when she called you." He made his face into a mock sheepish expression.

"What are you lot scheming? Were you hiding Christmas presents on top of the wardrobe?" I sniggered "And was my mother drinking?"

"No, and no actually. I went to see your father…" Damien's thumb was in his belt loop and his hand casually pushed into his jeans pocket.

"About the title deed?" I asked.

"No Steph, about this." That's when the small leather box came out of his pocket and into my hand, as he opened it and diamonds blinked against the red velvet lining he fell to one knee and I heard gasps all around the room and a stifled sob.

"Marry me Stephanie, you are my missing piece and I never, ever want to lose you again." He looked at me with devotion, sincerity and love and as the word "yes" passed my lips he was back on his feet twirling me around and everyone was clapping.

Chapter 35

I don't know what time we all got to bed eventually but it was late, and I woke up with a headache and a raging thirst. I crept to the bathroom and drank some water, brushed my teeth and had a pee. It was light outside, so that meant it was after eight o'clock, and when I looked out of the bathroom window it had been snowing quite heavily. There were footprints from next door's cat on our decking.

I looked down at my left hand and wriggled my ring finger, the diamonds cast tiny rainbows around the room and I closed my eyes for a second.

"Thank you," I said.

I made my way downstairs quietly, it was too early to ring Mum and Dad to tell them about the ring, which they had probably seen anyway, so I turned up the heating and put the kettle on. I opened the fridge and realised there was no milk, we must have finished it all last night. There was the empty semi skimmed bottle amongst the carnage of wine bottles and left over food.

The corner shop would be open by now, was it ok to go there in pyjamas? I'm sure they either wouldn't notice or wouldn't say, so I pulled on my fleecy boots and woolly hat, then reached for my coat. It wasn't there, I had hung it up in the wardrobe where Lizzie and Matt were sleeping. The only jacket was a denim one that I hadn't worn for months, but I was literally only going to the corner so it would be fine if I fastened it up and walked fast to keep warm.

The pocket made a jingling sound when I put it on, the sound of lose change which made things even easier as I wouldn't have to find my purse. I might even have enough for a magazine.

I opened the door quietly, things echoed around this big house, and I used my key from the outside to close the door. Then I was off, in a crazy half canter through a calf high snow drift in pyjamas and a woolly hat, fetching milk and magazines. I passed a dog walker and said a cheery "good morning"; I drew a blank there, as she kept her head down and scuttled off, so I just kept going. I had to wait at the junction for a van to pass, which of course contained two hunky workmen, the passenger looked over the top of their newspaper and winked at me. He wound down the window and shouted,

"Did he kick you out of bed love, he's a fool!"

I blushed and trotted around the back of the van, they tooted the horn and momentarily distracted me as my right foot landed in a small walnut whip of a dog turd. It wasn't frozen either, no wonder that bloody woman had looked so shifty; come to think of it she had no poop bag. The van pulled away and I looked around before I started to drag my foot behind me through the snow leaving an obvious brown trail of poo. The postman walked past and sniggered.

"Muck for Luck!" he said and kept going.

Why did people say that? There was nothing lucky about standing in shit, for god's sake. But I couldn't get angry when I approached the shop and saw the state of my reflection in the window, I looked like I'd got myself dressed out of the lost property box, in the dark with no

mirrors. And I was dragging my right foot along the
pavement like a polio survivor. I was still laughing to
myself when I opened the door. Mr Small (call me Colin)
was behind the counter in front of the portable gas fire
with a cuppa.

"Morning Stephanie" he said and looked me up and
down. "Everything alright?"

"Oh yes thanks, it's just we've got people staying and
I've run out of milk. I thought if I was quick I could get it
before they got up. And the thing is that they are sleeping
in the wardrobe room, well that's what we call it. Anyway
I can't get in for my clothes, or my coat for that matter." I
cast my eyes over the bottom shelf and saw that every
headline was either about the 2012 time bomb or the
elusive _Euromillions_ winner that couldn't be found.

"Oh I see," Colin said. He'd been really nice to me since
I'd been living here, I'd found out all about his wife
passing away three years ago and his daughter expecting a
baby any day soon.

"How's Natalie?" I asked, opening the fridge for a two
pint of semi-skimmed.

"Oh nothing yet, she's a bit fed up now but they won't
do anything until she's two weeks over due. That's a week
and a half to go." He rang in the milk and the magazine
and I eyed up the chocolate in the fixture.

"I'd better see how much I've got…" I started to pat my
pockets to find out which one had the money in and then
dug deep into the left hand one. I pulled out a tissue, one
piece of gum, a pink piece of folded up paper along with
approximately three pounds and sixty seven pence, at a
glance. I started to count the money up for certain and

thought about how a chocolate bar would help my hangover head, as Colin's eyes lit up.

"That's not a lottery ticket is it Stephanie?" He asked.

"Where?" I asked wondering if I should get a can of pop instead, not diet, I wanted fully loaded with sugar and caffeine. I walked over to the fridge as he took the small piece of folded up pink paper and smoothed it out on the counter.

"You know they've been telling people to check these, have you not seen it on the television?" he said excitedly.

"Yes I've seen it, but I bought that one ages ago, and I'd totally forgotten about it. It'll be no good now, I bought it in the summer." I reached out to take it back but he was insistent.

"The winning ticket was bought in the summer! That's why they are appealing for people to check now! Have you not seen them canvassing on the streets with clip boards?" He was starting to look like he was going to explode with excitement.

"I think I did once, a while ago, near where I used to live," I said. I was holding the can of pop now and could almost taste it, I wished he'd hurry up and let me pay.

"Near where you used to live?" Colin's voice was getting louder and he was becoming more animated. "Near where you bought this ticket?"

"Well, I guess so. I bought it on a whim at the corner shop at the end of the road." I spoke slowly, my mouth was dry and my head was hurting. Pop, milk, mag, and bed thanks.

"Stephanie, they only canvass outside of the shops that have sold the winning ticket! They can tell from their computers who sold it and they go there at the eleventh hour to find the winners. You know what that means don't you?" He was actually shaking. "It could be a biggie. They only look for winners that are entitled to one hundred thousand pounds or more!"

I paused for a moment, and took off my woolly hat, the combination of Colin's excitement and the gas fire on three bars was making me feel faint.

"Colin, is it ok if I open my drink please, I feel a bit funny," I said, unfastening my coat.

"Yes, yes of course, go on," he said without looking at me, he was pressing buttons on the lottery station and it was bleeping back at him.

I took three big gulps and felt better for it, while Colin tried to feed my ticket into the machine and check my lucky winner status. A wave of nausea passed over me and I wished that he would hurry up. It was the smell of my boot wafting upwards as the fire heated eau de furry turd up nicely.

I drained the can and looked up into the face of someone that may as well of found the elixir of life.

Colin looked like he was about to have a stroke, or maybe he was having one. His breath was short and his face was red, that bloody heater was on far too high, and he looked totally zoned out.

Maybe I should shout upstairs and see if Natalie was in the flat, perhaps he had one of those pump things for angina.

"Colin?" I said.

"COLIN?" and again.

352

This broke the spell for a moment and he calmly walked over to the door and spun around the open sign so that it now said closed. He dropped the latch. All kinds of scenarios ran through my mind in that moment, including kneeing him in the bollocks and running like mad on my shitty boot back home.

He walked towards me and looked me in the eye.

"St-St-Stephanie…" he stammered.

"Colin I just want to go home with the milk if that's ok," I squirmed.

"That's fine love, f-f-f-fine……but you have to keep really tight hold of this t t ticket…" he passed me the pink slip.

"Did I win anything?" I looked at him and tried to read his expression which at the moment registered as bewilderment in my mental directory.

He took hold of my shoulders and started to cry.

"You've won, the, j-j-j-jackpot Stephanie, the b-b-big one. Sorry I st-st-stammer when I'm up a h-h-height!" he was spitting a bit in my face and I wiped it with one hand. "S-s-s-sorry" he said.

"What jackpot? It was ages ago when I bought this, I've missed the boat Colin, it's a mistake!" I said and took a step back from his spittle.

He took me by the hand and led me around to the machine to see for myself.

Someone tried the door and we both jumped, and then laughed and laughed and laughed, until I was crying too.

"Oh my God Colin," I screamed and snatched the ticket. I ran and slipped all of the way back up the road to the house and was shaking so much I couldn't get my key in

the lock. Then when I eventually opened the door and
stepped into the vestibule I dropped the keys on the tiled
floor and the sound echoed up and down stairs in the
sleepy silence.

I stood still and bit hard on my fist to stop myself
screaming with excitement.

Damien appeared at the top of the stairs and looked
down at me.

"Jesus Christ, Steph, what's happened to you?" he said
in a stage whisper "And what's that bloody smell?"

"Come down here, quickly!" I whispered back.

"Are you crying? And what the hell are you wearing?"
he said as he got closer he could see that I was looking
odd to say the least.

"Come and sit down," I said, jumping in the air several
times.

"You're like a bloody box of frogs, what's happened? I
want you to be excited about being engaged but bloody
hell!" He sat in his boxer shorts and bed head in the front
room and I fiddled with the television remote. I had to
open the curtains a crack to be able to see what I was
doing and Damien shielded his eyes and squinted.

The news came on to the screen and the sound blared, I
jumped and turned it down quickly.

'And now for today's top story, the *Euromillions* lottery
winner who only has until midnight tonight to claim their
prize...'

"What's your point, we know about this Steph it's been
on for ages now." He stood up, probably to put the kettle
on.

"No wait," I said and grabbed his arm.

'The ticket was sold in the summer in this corner shop…' the newsreader said as pictures of my old street scrolled across the screen and the people in clipboards stopped people to ask them if they played the lottery. 'Canvassers have been trying to locate the winner but to no avail…'

"I don't get it Steph, what's it got to do with us? Are you going to tell me you feel like a lottery winner again?" he laughed. "I get it, I know you do," he kissed my forehead.

"Even better than that…" I squealed as the winning numbers and lucky stars scrolled across the bottom of the screen along with the date on the ticket. "Look."

I handed him the pink slip of paper and waited while he registered the enormity of what was happening here. They all matched up with the numbers on the screen and one by one we checked them, then checked them again, then again and then the jackpot figure flashed up.

'It's amazing that there was only one winner on this *Euromillions* triple rollover, and if that lucky person can put their hands on the ticket between now and midnight they can claim their astonishing prize of eighty two million pounds – get looking in your drawers, pockets, purses and under your mattress…it could be you!'

I turned down the volume as the adverts took over, and we sat and looked at each other.

"Do you think it's really the winning ticket?" Damien said.

"Colin put it in the machine in the shop and it said that it was!" I squeaked.

"Maybe we should ring them up or something?" Damien turned the ticket over "There's a claim line number on the back." He picked up the phone and dialled the number "Don't get too excited Steph, sometimes machines make mistakes…wait until you've spoken to them… hello, hello yes my girlfriend, erm fiancé wants to speak to someone in the claims department please." He passed me the phone and I ran around the room with it before I could speak.

"Hi, yes I'm Stephanie and I think I might have won a prize…" the nice lady then asked me what the date was on the ticket, the actual numbers on the ticket and a serial number too.

"No way… NO WAY!!!!" I screamed out loud and threw myself on top of Damien. "It's the winning ticket, it's the winning ticket, oh my god Damien, we are millionaires!" The call disconnected in all of the excitement and I had to ring her back to make arrangements to get the ticket to them quickly. They said that I should sign the back and keep it in a really safe place, someone was on the way to our address imminently. She also said that it was often really tempting to tell everyone you knew, but that sometimes it was best to keep it to ourselves at first.

We sat and looked at each other, was this really happening?

"Steph, you don't get it do you? We've been walking around saying that we feel like we have won the lottery, we've said it over and over and we've drawn it to us! And you have kept saying that something monumental is going to happen today, and this is it!" Damien kissed me all over my face and started dancing around the room.

"What are we going to do with it all?" I asked.

"I know, there's so much, we could never spend it all ourselves," Damien said, pacing around now.

"The woman on the phone said we might want to keep it secret for now. I don't know how on earth we'll do that! I feel like I am going to explode!" I said.

"Wait a minute Steph, maybe she's right…it's been all over the news remember, maybe we need to play it cool for now, if we can that is. OH MY GOD!" He scooped me up in his arms and twirled me round.

"Stop, stop I feel sick!" I said and sat down on the sofa.

"We need to get changed then and sorted out…you'll have to sneak into the wardrobe room and get some stuff, I can't go in case they are doing things…" Damien pulled me up by my arm.

"Go on, just get me some jeans and a jumper, socks and pants. I'll jump in the shower."

I stood up and he said, "Remember, don't say anything!"

Chapter 36

It was confirmed later that day that I was the jackpot winner and the ticket was taken to keep safe. We wouldn't have the funds until after Christmas, and it was excruciating to keep it secret. Luckily everyone thought our strange behaviour was excitement about getting married. Damien's mother had gone off on a cruise, and we were invited to my parent's house for Christmas day.

"I've been thinking," I said to Damien on Christmas Eve, "we need to make a list."

"It's a bit late now Steph, Santa's elves have already packed up the sleigh!" He linked arms with me as we walked along the high street in the snow. The magnificent Christmas tress was all lit up and the *Salvation Army* were rattling tins and singing their hearts out. Damien threw in a hand full of loose change with a "Merry Christmas" and I said,

"That's what I mean. Surely you have been going over and over who we can help?"

"Of course I have, and I totally agree, it's an obscene amount. Far more than we will ever need Steph, we absolutely should use it to do some good for others." He went into the stationery shop and bought a notepad and pen and we made our way to a cafe on the corner.

"OK let's see how much we need first, and then how much we've got to play with." He started to note down numbers and % that I didn't understand, and I went to the counter to order tea and cake.

"Right. If we pay off the mortgages on my properties altogether that will give us an income of about £3,500 per

month, but there will be tax to pay and also upkeep etc.
That will cost about £157,000. Then we will want to pay
for the house we are in, or move?" He looked at me and I
shrugged.

"I like it here," I said.

"Me too. So that's about 65k then. So we'd be in a
position then with minimal outgoings and a good income.
Then we'd need a buffer in the bank of about 2 million,
maybe 3 to be realistic and guard against inflation, interest
rate rises, the property market crashing and all that..." I
tried to keep up.

"So was does that mean in real life?" I asked.

"It means that based on what you won, you'd have about
78ish to give away and we'd still be sitting pretty." He
underlined the figure twice.

"That's a whole lot of money," I said. "And a whole lot
of help for people."

"I know it sounds crazy Steph, but you are sure you
want to give it away?" Damien asked and poured more
tea.

"I just feel like I finally get it. I mean, we will have
more than enough for us and we'll never, ever want for
anything at all with three million in the bank and the
properties paid for......and I know now that I can draw
more in if I want it or need it. You said it yourself, it's
what I've been focussing on and aligning with and that's
why its here." I looked up and he was smiling.

"You're so right you know, and I have always loved that
show *The Secret Millionaire.*" He reached for my hand.
"As long as it feels right to you, that's all."

"If I keep hold of it all I won't be in the flow anymore and it would be through fear. I've had enough fear in my past and I don't want to create any now."

"Well let's start the list then!" he said and tore off a sheet of paper for himself, and passed me the notebook and pen.

We sat all afternoon in the café writing down names and ideas, and talking about people we knew and loved. We were clear that we weren't trying to rescue or fix people, or disempower them and that in some cases it would be more appropriate to give a gift instead of money. We had also chosen projects and charities that we felt were really worthwhile to donate to, and these ranged from local playgroups and spiritual arts centres, to *Cancer Research* and lots in between.

Damien phoned the client that was selling The Haven and offered the full asking price, which was of course accepted straight away, and solicitors were instructed.

"But when are we going to tell people?" I asked "If we tell a few, the news will spread like wildfire and then it won't be a surprise."

"What we need is everyone together in the same place and we can do a kind of announcement!" Damien said.

"But how will we get them all together?" I said. "They would all be suspicious!"

Damien tapped the pen against his teeth and looked out of the window, the staff were clearing tables and making it obvious that they were wanting to close and get home, well it was Christmas Eve after all.

"I've got it!" Damien smiled. "Let's see how fast we can organise a wedding!"

"You are a genius!" I said, pulling on my coat and scarf and folding my list into my pocket.

Chapter 37

Christmas Day was magical, I slept until about ten o'clock and Damien brought me breakfast in bed. We opened our gifts to each other and packed overnight bags for Mum and Dad's. We called into the corner shop on the way, it was always open on Christmas day for a couple of hours in the morning for people that needed tin foil, gravy granules and the like. We hung around until it was empty and Damien reiterated to Colin that no one was to know yet about the lottery win yet, and that he was on the list for a little something when the cheque cleared if he could keep his word.

Colin said that of course that would be fine and please forgive him if he was distracted but that Natalie had been in labour all last night and he was literally just waiting for the call. "What a day to be born, I mean you could call him Jesus if you had a boy!" he said flustering around.

"I'm sure he'd appreciate that in the school yard," said Damien, but Colin didn't hear, he was turning off lights and fastening his coat.

"I'm going to go down to the hospital and just wait there I think, I can't stand it here on my own," he said as he bustled us out towards the car.

The day went well at Mum and Dad's, they marvelled over the engagement ring when we first arrived and then bickered a bit over the roast potatoes. We were all sitting in the front room waiting for the Queen's Speech when Mum asked about wedding plans.

"Well we thought we'd have something quite small really, close friends and family only," I said.

"Intimate," said Damien.

"Yes, sounds lovely. Have you got any dates in mind?" Mum asked.

"Erm, well the sooner the better really…..I can't wait to be married to your beautiful daughter and I don't see any reason to wait." Damien kissed my cheek and Mum smiled her approval.

"Maybe in January?" he continued, and I smiled and nodded, trying not to burst out laughing as Mum got completely the wrong end of the stick.

"Well that will give you a year darling, a whole year to plan what you want and in that time your hair will grow a bit more and you can go back on a diet." She took a slurp of her sherry.

"No Mum, January, as in next month," I said sniggering, and the sherry fountain sprayed out of her mouth and right up the wall, accompanied with coughing and spluttering sound effects.

This woke my father up who had been dosing in his chair, he sat up straight with his party hat at a jaunty angle and said, "Have I missed it?"

"They're on about getting married next month!" mother shrieked. "I've never heard such a thing!"

"Well what is there to organise really, Mum? All we need is a dress and a suit, 2 rings and a reception. That's it," I said, laughing at her getting more and more het up.

"What about other people darling? Invitations and things? People will want to get prepared. I mean I know you lot do everything on *Facebook* or text messages but you have to give the older generation a chance here! Some things have to be done properly!" she poured more sherry into her glass and glugged half straight away.

"It will be fine, I promise you. I have staff that will help to get it all organised and all I want is for you and Steph to go shopping together and get pampered ready for the big day. It will all come together so please don't worry about a thing," Damien said, laughing too at her reaction.

"Well, I just don't know where you are coming from I really don't." She shook her head and tut tutted. "But it's your business anyway."

There was a pause and Dad started to snore lightly.

"Wouldn't have happened in my day!" Mum said under her breath and turned up the volume a bit for the National Anthem.

Damien was true to his word and as soon as the guest list was finalised he took care of printing and sending all invitations. Wedding banns were read in church, even though I was divorced the vicar was quite liberal. Flowers were ordered and photographers booked, and we spent several evenings eating out deciding on caterers and menu. As well as this the owner of The Haven had agreed to exchange contracts early, in order to give us access for renovating the property.

New Year's Eve came and we cuddled on the sofa with a takeaway. I wasn't even bothered about having a drink, and by the time midnight came we were creating our own in bed. As I lay in the afterglow listening to Damien's heartbeat I thought about how different this was compared to last year.

Chapter 38

The days flew by and I worked on pulling together the final list of gifts and surprises for our friends and family, by the middle of January I was almost sorted. I was waiting for delivery of two new cars and confirmation of a round the world trip, and mostly everything else was in place.

Damien had someone project managing the renovation at The Haven, so all we had to do was choose which kitchen, carpets and paint and it was all done for us. The contractors promised that the project would be completed by the big day. We told people that we were renting the house for the event from a friend of Damien's, to keep costs down and make sure that it didn't feel too formal.

The demolition had begun at Prospect House, and I'd had contact from Josie to say that she had taken a holiday in the Canary Islands with her husband. She couldn't bear to see the place being ripped down, I imagined that it would feel like part of her was being ripped to pieces too after all of the love and care that she'd poured in to the place. She said that they were overdue some quality time together, and that the British weather was getting her down. They returned from their trip two days before the wedding, and would love to come along.

I went shopping with Mum for a wedding dress and found just what I wanted in a gorgeous boutique just out of town. I was surprised when the proprietor said that I needed it altering around the waist and bust slightly, as it was a size sixteen. But she said that it had been imported and sometimes the sizes were a bit iffy. She fixed me up with shoes and a tiara, and when mum saw me in the changing room she sniffed and dabbed her eyes with a tissue.

"Darling it's perfect," she said fluffing out the ivory lace train. "He is a very lucky young man."

We went for a posh lunch and mum ordered wine with hers, I had water, hoping that it would contribute to wedding slenderness and also wine made me feel a bit sickly these days. It was probably since the house warming party, when I had a bit too much, but I was usually alright after a few. Maybe I had an intolerance or something? I'd read about that and seen it on day time television. You could get skin prick tests like the celebrities.

With only seven days to go it was all coming together. The cars had been delivered and were in the garage at The Haven tied up in great big bows. The cheques had all been raised and were enclosed into beautiful cards that we had written personal messages in for each recipient. Most of the building work was done and the decorators were in now, we just needed to think about staging all of the furniture and making up the beds. Some of what we had ordered was self-assembly, so the handyman that Damien used for his property portfolio was on standby for the delivery.

I had never felt so happy or so tired in my whole life!

We had booked a honeymoon to take the day after the wedding, and I couldn't wait to put my feet up at last and have Damien all to myself for two weeks. I picked up my dress with three days to go and took it to my parent's house, I declined my mother's offer of her neighbour's daughter doing my hair and make-up "as a gift" and reminded her about the waxing. I would have probably ended up looking like a drag queen with a complimentary orange spray tan. Lizzie was going to help me on the morning of the wedding, we'd had a practice run at the makeup counter and felt confident.

The day before the wedding I was all packed up and ready to go to my parents overnight, it was the first time we'd slowed down since Christmas, and as the case was lifted into the car, I cried. I don't know where it came from or why, but emotion flooded through me, and my smile cracked as the tears rolled down my face.

"Hey, hey, come on…" Damien said and his arms enclosed me in a safe and loving embrace. "What's this all about?"

"I really don't know…I just feel so overwhelmed…" he held me close and let me release the mixed up feelings that were appearing for me, creating an emotional cocktail that had knocked me off my feet. My sobbing began to subside and he wiped the tears from my face.

"I've got a surprise for you," he said. "But you'll have to get into the car!"

We laughed and he hugged me again, he kissed the top of my head and opened the passenger door for me. "Your chariot awaits madam!"

I had been so busy with the wedding plans and the surprise gifts and donations that I hadn't been to The Haven since the works began. Damien swung onto the drive and I held my breath. The brass name plate was polished now, and glinted in the sun, and the trees that lined the driveway had been tidied up and all of the leaves of autumn had been swept away.

The majestic front door had been painted a glossy black, and a gold door knocker had been hung just above eye level. Two bay trees stood at either side of the door, they had been tied with thick white ribbons that gently danced in the cold breeze. Damien turned the key in the lock and I stepped onto a highly polished floor. The staircase swept round to one side and the glass chandelier gently scattered light and rainbows on the walls.

"It's perfect," I whispered.

Oversized vases of flowers adorned each of the rooms downstairs, all in a wintry theme, and the huge dining table was pushed back against the wall and set up like a bar with all kinds of alcohol and glasses form one end to the other. New carpets were springy and deep underfoot, and the reclaimed fire places were draped in garlands and long white ribbon. Candelabras were placed in each corner, and extra seating was dotted around in clusters, each seat covered and again tied with a white ribbon.

"You like it?" he asked, a cautious note to his tone.

"I love it, I absolutely love it! It's perfect, it's absolutely perfect! Thank you so much!" I held his face in my hands and kissed him full on the lips. "It is the most perfect place for our perfect day…and Josie is going to be beside herself that this place belongs to her!" I stood and twirled around, taking it all in, and gratitude emanated from every pore of me.

Damien put his arms around my waist and kissed my neck. "I'm glad I got you alone for a while Steph, I wanted to say something…" he said as he led me to the front room and sat beside me on the sofa.

"I know this has been a crazy whirlwind of a journey…" he began and held my hand in his, "and that it's all been a bit rushed maybe…." he took a deep breath, "but I want you to know that tomorrow means so much to me, you mean so much to me."

"I know Damien, and you to me."

"But I want you to know that when we are making vows to each other, for me, it's real."

"Me too."

"I don't want to own you, or control you Steph, all I want it to give us the chance to grow together in the love and tenderness that we share, and become the best of who we can be with the love and friendship we have. I promise you I will never leave you, I will never hurt you deliberately, and I will never take lightly those vows tomorrow. When I say them to you, please look deep into my eyes and know they are from my heart and soul. I have never loved anyone like this before, and I will be honoured to have you as my wife."

"You've set me off again!" I made light of the fact that I was crying now, and I shook my head as I looked at him.

"I feel exactly the same, you truly are my missing piece."

"And you are mine."

The light was changing now and the sky turned yellow and red, from the bedroom we could see the dark silhouettes of the trees against the bright backdrop. Damien turned and kissed me gently, then passionately, and I kissed him back with love and lust flowing through every part of my being. I hadn't realised what a turn on true romance actually was, I breathlessly unfastened his shirt and ran my fingers through his hair. I climaxed intensely and almost immediately when we rolled into the sheets and he climbed on top, and didn't stop trembling until the room was completely dark and we were entwined together in the afterglow.

"We'd better straighten the bed up!" I laughed and Damien tickled me in the ribs playfully.

"The next time we're together naked you'll be my wife!" he said as we giggled under the covers and swore that this would stay a secret between us.

I was teary again when Damien dropped me off at my parent's house, I didn't want to be away from him. It must have felt like an occasion because Dad had the takeaway menus out on the kitchen bench.

"Now I'm not having anything from that Tandoori Delight mind, I could do without trotting down the bloody aisle tomorrow," he said as Mum rolled her eyes. "And come to think of it last time I had the Cantonese Canter up the bloody stairs after their sweet and sour, so I'm not getting anything from that bloody Chinese Garden either. Might as well have cut out the middle man and put it straight down the bog. In fact I'm getting fish and chips and you two can please yourselves." He went upstairs for a 'sit down' with the paper.

"He's a bit nervous about his speech darling, and it's playing havoc with his bowels, you know what he's like."

We all had fish and chips to be in the safe side, and by the time the nine o'clock news started I was yawning.

"I'm off to bed," I said and Mum heated up the beanie sack in the microwave for my feet. I set the alarm for eight and wriggled into the single duvet that smelled of home.

Chapter 39

The next day was cold and bright with a dusting of snow and sparkling frost.

Lizzie arrived early, Matt had stayed overnight with Damien as part of his best man's duties. I was ushered into the shower so that my hair could be rolled up into fat curlers and I sat in my dressing gown with a mud pack on eating a bacon sandwich. After another cup of tea Lizzie painted my nails and mums, and after my face was mud free set about moisturising my pinkish skin and plucked out the odd stray hair from my eyebrows.

We laughed and sipped champagne and Lizzie said "breathe in!" whilst she fastened each tiny hook and eye. My makeup was glamorous but not over the top, and my tiara was woven perfectly into my hair, styled into soft waves.

We were all ready when the cars and flowers arrived, and dad linked my arm as we made our way to the shiny black Rolls Royce, complete with white ribbon. It wasn't a long drive to church and before we got out of the car dad turned to me and said,

"You alright love?"

"Yes thanks dad, I'm fine," I answered. "A bit nervous, but fine."

"You look really beautiful Steph, I'm so proud of you," he said and smiled at me, as the driver came around and opened my door.

Damien didn't turn around to see me until I was two steps away from him, and when he did his expression made me melt. He was clearly so much in love, and so was I, that it felt like everything in our lives had come together to lead up to and create that perfect moment – right then and there.

I didn't see the faces of the guests, in my reality there was only the two us there. Luck may have played a part here but I knew in my heart that it was destiny that we were together, and I wanted to be his wife more than anything.

We made our vows and as Damien slipped the ring onto my finger he looked at me with his head slightly on one side and raised his eyebrows before he spoke. Yes, I remembered last night too, and I smiled coyly back at him.

Confetti rained down on us and cameras clicked as we kissed in the doorway of the church. Friends and family shouted their congratulations and we smiled and held hands, making our way to the car and then onto The Haven.

We kissed in the back seat and talked about how people were going to react to the surprise we had in store. We were first to arrive and offered champagne by one of the waitresses in the lobby. The guests started to arrive soon after, and were all complimentary about our choice of venue, and what a marvellous idea it was to have the reception in a big country house.

As we greeted everyone, I was getting more and more excited about the surprise and so was Damien. We opened the buffet and let people mingle, while we met at the bottom of the stairs and confessed that we were both fit to burst. After a while there was a ding, ding on a wine glass and dad started to unfold a piece of paper. Looking at

everyone over the top of reading glasses he spoke about
how proud him and Mum were, and how much they loved
me and wished us well. He revisited memories of my
childhood and recounted funny stories and milestones. He
was visibly relieved when he had finished and applause
rippled through the room.

Damien stood up next and a hush descended on
everyone, as he composed himself and through genuine
emotion spoke of how I was the missing piece in his life
and that his heart had always belonged to me. By the time
glasses were raised to the beautiful bride there was hardly
a dry eye in the house, and I had to use my napkin to
rescue my mascara.

Damien stayed on his feet and cleared his throat.

"Now ladies and gentlemen, we have something of
surprise for you all," he said and scanned the room to see
everyone's expression.

He took my hand and I stood up and took a deep breath.
I squeezed Damien's hand and squealed with excitement
as my heart raced and adrenalin coursed around my veins.
You could have heard a pin drop in the room, as Damien
and I looked at each other and laughed with nervous
anticipation.

"Steph would like to say something," he said and raised
his eyebrows whilst gesturing to the audience with one
hand. "Go on Steph."

I stood grinning for a moment longer and looked at
everyone as they waited for my voice. There were only
forty two people here, but they were the people that had
meant most to use in our lives, the family and true blue

friends that you loved and protected beyond reason, and for many, today was going to be life changing.

"We've had a secret for a few weeks and we didn't want to tell anyone until you were all together…" I started and Damien nodded in encouragement. "Some of you won't believe what I am going to tell you now, but please know that it is not a joke or wind up, it's all true and we're still coming to terms with it ourselves…"

The atmosphere was silent but loaded with anticipation as I took another deep breath and choked back emotion and tears of joy.

"We had some good luck at the end of last year you see, some really, really good luck and we already felt totally blessed that we'd found each other again, but this…" I gulped, "…this was something really amazing."

I could feel Damien's arm around my waist and I looked up at him. He thumbed away a tear from my cheek and kissed my forehead. "May I continue?" he asked softly, and I nodded.

"Many of you will have been aware that there was a national campaign running at the end of the year to find the winner of the triple rollover lottery jackpot, it was all over the press…" There were rumblings and murmurings of conversation now and a couple of people sat up straighter in their seats. "And as you may recall there was one winner, and that winner did not want any publicity…"

I looked up and saw Hannah looking like she was about to explode with excitement and her head shaking in disbelief at the same time. I nodded in her direction and he let out a yelp and covered her mouth.

375

"Well ladies and gentlemen, here she is!" Damien's
voice rang out into the room and I heard my mother
asking the people on either side of her what was going on.
Then there were shouts of "Really? Really? It was you?"
then clapping and cheering broke out and I felt Hannah's
arms hugging me tight while she shouted,

"Oh my God Steph, oh my God!"

It took a while for people to get back into their seats, and
as they all looked our way in total bewilderment I called
them to order with the ching of my spoon on the
champagne flute.

"And the reason that we waited until today to tell you all
is that we wanted everyone that we loved and cared for to
share this with us. I bet every one of you has a mental list
of who you would include in your good fortune if you
ever did get a huge sum of money…well look around you
now, because every person that you see here today is on
our list!"

Heads turned from side to side and laughter broke out
spontaneously in one corner of the room, and some crying
too. I couldn't hold back my tears any longer and I
searched for Josie and Lizzie, Hannah and Sue to see their
reactions. Sheila and Jude were sitting quite close to me
with their mouths agape and Asha was frantically clapping
like a wind-up toy.

Mum and Dad were shrugging shoulders and telling my
aunt and uncle that they had no idea and that it had to be a
mistake, surely not our Stephanie, I might have not
checked the number properly etc.

"So if you can all make sure that you are in the seat that
you were originally allocated…" one or two people

swapped around "and feel underneath the table directly in front of you, there will be an envelope with your name on it." I said. There was a sound of tape coming off the underside of the tables amongst the high pitched chatter.

"We want you to know that we have given to each of you what we feel will help you and serve you at this time in your lives. For some of you it will be a cash amount and for others an actual gift, and in three cases I think there's both. But please know that our intention was to do the best that we could for you, from our hearts." Damien echoed this sentiment and then added that there was a hand written card inside each envelope from both of us, a personal message to each person, of love and gratitude for being here today and a part of our lives.

"Don't you want to open them?" he laughed and there followed a frenzy of envelope ripping, screaming, hysterical laugher and two cousins running out into the garage clutching key fobs to new cars.

I have to say that the feeling of giving to others was as good as the feeling that I had back in Colin's shop when I initially realised that I had won. Mum and Dad were among the first to congratulate us and thank us for the cheque we'd given them, through tears of happiness and pride my mum spoke that she loved me and that I was a bugger for keeping it a secret. Hannah and Sam were delighted with their round the world holiday and spending monies, and Lizzie and Matt said that they might join them – after all they could afford it with the cheque we'd written them. Jude, Asha and Sheila had all been gifted enough money to secure their futures no matter where they chose to live and with whom. Their money in each case was ring fenced legally so that in the event of marriage or divorce it would still be theirs and would never go into the matrimonial asset pot to be split. There was also a separate trust fund for Jamal that would ensure that university fees would be covered if he chose to go.

More champagne was brought out and the waitress circulated as people talked about the amazing day and what they were going to do with themselves now they had more choices in their lives.

Josie made her way up to me and found it really hard to speak through her tears. With her voice cracking in places and pausing to take a breath every now and then she eventually expressed how much the donation we had given to The Prospect House Project meant to her.

"Steph, this will help so many women in need, you have saved lives and families by doing this, you really, really have. Thank you so very much for entrusting me with this, I will be such a good custodian of this money."

I hugged her in tight and said, "I know you will Josie, I know you will."

"Now I can find somewhere to relocate and keep going" She said "Maybe Damien could help me find somewhere perfect."

She looked around the room and then back to me.

"Wasn't there something else in your envelope Josie?" I smiled coyly.

"Oh yes there was, it was a key, I wasn't sure if we all got one so I put it in my purse." She said.

"No, you were the only one," I said "Let's go and get it and I'll show you what it's for."

Her hands were trembling as she opened the clasp of her brown leather purse, and in amongst the loose change was a shiny silver key. It took Josie a moment to fish it out and then she followed me into the lobby.

"I'm glad you like it here Josie," I said and turned to her, holding both of her hands.

"I do Steph, it's a lovely place, the perfect place for a day like this…" and as our feet crunched in the gravel I closed the heavy wooden door behind me and turned to Josie.

"Let us in then!"

She looked confused.

"Let us into your house."

There was head shaking and more confused expressions, which suddenly morphed into the kind of hysterical joy you see screaming out of a child on Christmas morning.

"Mine? Mine? Oh my God Mine? Steph, really? Mine?" She turned the key and pushed the door open, the noise of the party drifted towards us. Then she shut it again, and opened it again and laughed again.

"We thought that if you owned the property there would never be any fear of eviction or demolition again, and that the project makes enough monthly income to pay you a nominal rent. So you'll be the landlord and manage the finances accordingly. And then when you retire, you can either move in here yourself, sell it, rent it out or pass it on."

"I just can't believe it Steph, I am amazed, it doesn't feel real."

"You deserve it Josie, after all that you have done for others this is the universe paying you back and saying thank you."

We went back inside and I looked for Sue. Someone said she was upstairs, we had suggested that she stayed overnight and I'd put he in the front bedroom with the en-suite.

I knocked on the door quietly and waited for her to say "come in".

"Steph!" he said and walked towards me, embracing me in a heartfelt hug and kissing my cheek.

"Hi Sue, I just wanted to see you away from all of the craziness and say a massive thank you for how you have helped me." I sat down on the chair in the corner of the room and sighed "When I look back at the year I've had you weren't kidding when you said it would all change!"

Sue laughed, "It's been quite a journey for you, and never a dull moment either. You've come such a long way and it's all coming full circle for you now. You've learned and lived each lesson along the way Steph. Yes you have transformed your life, but you have done it all from within, step by step and built the life of your dreams."

She smiled and said thank you for her "fee", as promised I had settled up my account and paid her what I felt was fair for the work she had put in with me. It just so happens that when you've got eighty two million in the bank you can afford to pay very generously.

"What you did for me is worth every penny Sue, really. I don't know where I would have been without your support and guidance."

"That's very gracious of you Steph, and thank you," she said.

"I just don't know what I am going to do with myself now! I mean when we get back from our honey moon. It's not like I have to work but I feel like I want to do something, I guess it will unfold." I could hear the band tuning up downstairs ready to take us into the evening.

"Well maybe I can help you with that a little..." Sue said with a wry smile.

"Ah yes! I bet you know what's what!" I said and leaned in closer to her. "What do you see coming up for me?" I said in a mock spooky voice.

"Well then... did you follow the initial instructions of writing everything down? Each lesson I mean?"

"Yes, in a journal, it's all there."

"Good. All twelve lessons and your insights in the right order for each month that passed?"

"Yes, just as you said this time last year."

"Good. Because that is your next task. To take these twelve lessons, universal principles of transformation and get them all type faced, aligned and edited up into the book that is going to help millions of people around the world."

"My book?"

"Yes Steph, your book, with your lessons, insights and wisdom. With spaces for people to write down their thoughts and feelings about each lesson, and the relevance in their life at that time. Like a workbook people can follow a process and start their own transformation, based on what you have lived and learned."

"I hadn't thought of that," I said.

"I know you hadn't. And you are going to be travelling around telling people about how they can use these universal principles to change their lives, heal themselves and relationships and generally get unstuck. The world needs this now, the time is here for massive change."

"And I can be part of that?" I asked.

"You are part of it already," she answered.

"Wow! Who would have thought that I could go through all that I have and come out of the other end with something so amazing?" I said. "I'll start as soon as we get back from honeymoon."

"You will use all that you have learned to attract a publisher easily and quickly, within about three months I feel, but your promotion and travelling will have to wait for about eighteen months."

"I can't wait that long, you said yourself it's got to get out there, the time is now!" I said with gusto.

"I'm afraid you're going to have to wait," Sue said and smiled at me. "You have no idea do you?"

The band started to swing into action downstairs with their version of *Baby Love*.

"No idea about what?" I asked and shrugged my shoulders.

"Steph... you're pregnant!" she said as my jaw dropped and I threw my arms around her.

Stephanie's Journal - Lesson 12
Release Resistance

Being in the flow of life means surrendering your fears
and resistance. It also means that you have to allowing
what you have asked for to come into your experience.
It's being who you really are and allowing yourself to
express this in your life. It's when all of the dots join up
on the individual moments in order to create what you
have wanted, and it only comes to you once you have
learned the way that the universal laws work to support
this. The way that your life turns out is no accident, it's
a combination of living consciously, learning life's
lessons and flowing with the universal energy source
that is everywhere. Every one of us has the opportunity
to do this for ourselves and to take responsibility for
our own life. The last twelve months of my life have
been my greatest challenge and my greatest gift.

"We must be willing to let go of the life we have planned,
so as to have the life that is waiting for us."
Joseph Campbell.

Summary of the Twelve Lessons

Lesson 1 – Be open to change and possibility
Lesson 2 – Self-sabotage
Lesson 3 – You attract what you are
Lesson 4 – Release what does not serve you
Lesson 5 – You are a creator
Lesson 6 – The Law of Karma
Lesson 7 – The Law of Reflection
Lesson 8 – Compassion and forgiveness
Lesson 9 – You can't fix other people
Lesson 10 – Intuition, signs and signals
Lesson 11 – Self-love and loving others
Lesson 12 – Release resistance & allow the flow

Visit Kate's website: www.kate-spencer.com

Acknowledgements

I have love and gratitude for so many people in my life that help me and support me, so that I can get my message out there to the world.

My husband Darren who has always encouraged me to be who I am. You are the foundation that allows me to build the dream for us all. My parents, Pam & Graham Thom. I never doubt for a moment that you are proud of me and love me wholeheartedly, even though I am adopted. It's a joke, right?

My daughter Amy and my niece Anna. The two most precious souls that light up my life in so many ways. You are loved beyond measure.

And my sister Emma, this book was written for you. You know why, and that is enough.

I am blessed to have good friends that I can rely on to be honest, prop me up and help me out when life throws me a curve ball. Jane Turner, Sheena Waters, Anna Pereira, Anne Strojny, Claire Mitchell, Emma Holmes, Jennie Harrison, Michelle Emerson, Margery Gledson, Amanda Fletcher, Sara Douglas, Carrie Craig Gilby, Lydia Boylan, Kerry Hodgson, Jill Newton and Rachel Noble. And last but by no means least, Nicola Oliver, who asked me one night to run around the block in my pyjamas and post the first three chapters of the Twelve Lessons manuscript through her letterbox.

The rest as they say is history.

Also available:

Twelve Lessons Later

By Kate Spencer

Chapter 1

"You're blooming!" said Sue as she threw her arms around me.

I hugged her momentarily before she stepped back and held both my hands at arm's length, fixing her gaze on my enormous bump.

"Blooming big you mean!" I puffed, getting my breath back from the stairs.

We both laughed and Sue led the way to the small and familiar room. The traffic noise wafted through the window, along with a slight breeze that I was grateful for, and the floral curtains brushed against the windowsill.

We small talked for a while, filling in some of life's blanks, until the conversation naturally turned to what the future may hold. Sue pulled up a chair opposite me, reaching for her well-worn cards.

"I won't say parenting is easy, Steph, but it's worth every second."

"I can't wait. But I do wish I could jump straight to the umbilical cord being cut," I said.

"It's natural for you to feel a little nervous the first time." Sue shuffled the cards as she spoke and I slipped my pumps off under the table, airing my feet and ankles.

"I just can't stop myself from watching those programmes on the television about childbirth. It's ridiculous when I know about Law of Attraction! I should be focussed on everything going smoothly instead of panicking along with the rest of them and stuffing in even more biscuits." I shook my head.

"As long as you remember that they choose the dramatic births that will pull in viewing figures, and in real life it's hardly ever like that," said Sue, still shuffling. "Have you started nesting yet? I had a friend that felt compelled to have such a clear out that her poor husband came home from work and had hardly any clothes left!"

"Crikey, I don't think Damien would be impressed with that!"

"Neither was Barry," laughed Sue and handed me the deck.

"Just focus on receiving what is right for you right now," Sue said and sat back in her chair. "And no, I'm not telling you if it's a girl or a boy!"

I closed my eyes and shuffled for a moment or two, remembering how anxious I was the first time I'd sat in this seat. So much had changed since then, and it was all going to change again any day now. The baby started to turn inside of me, new life that I would be bringing into the world. I placed a hand on my bump and smiled to myself. Not long now. Sue had entered *The Zone* as I was shuffling, and when I placed the cards on the table her eyelids fluttered.

"The first thing I get through for you is that you need to do all you can to stop being afraid."

I kept quiet as she drew a breath and exhaled slowly, fighting back the urge to giggle, which was better that the urge I had last time to shit myself or run.

"Afraid that is of things going wrong. Not during childbirth, although you are worried about that and every first-time mum is, but things going wrong in general. It seems that a part of you feels that this life you are living is too good to be true, that you maybe don't entirely deserve it, and that it could be taken away from you in any moment." She opened her eyes and stared right at me. "I call it The Push Away, others would say resistance."

I didn't know if I should speak or not, so I nodded.

"This happens when you ask for something from the universe and it's either manifesting in your experience or just about to, and the human part of you starts to go into fear."

"So you block it?" I asked.

"Yes. The fear creates an opposite vibration to the one that you were sending out, the one that has drawn the experience in," said Sue.

"But I love the life I have now," I said and shrugged my shoulders slightly.

"Yes, but there are aspects of it that you are fearful of losing. Remember that the universe responds to how you are *feeling*, it's the emotions and the feelings that set up the vibration and frequency that attract in a match."

"I'm not sure I get it," I said and shook my head.

"I know you love your life and you are grateful Steph, and that's all good. Don't go into fear of losing it, there is no reason why this is not the way things are now."

"Ah, ok. That's a relief."

"See?" said Sue. "You feel relief when I confirm that because it calms the part of you down that is in fear."

"Ah, right," I said as the penny dropped.

"And so it is," Sue replied and dealt six cards face-down in front of me. She turned the first card and the image was one of a large old book and a quill writing the word *Lessons* across an open page. "I thought this one would come up for you," she said.

"This card has two messages for you, Stephanie. The first one is that there is going to be a lesson coming up for you soon..."

"I figured."

"BUT the lesson in your case is about knowing when a lesson is happening. You are at a point on your journey now where you need to be able to recognize the difference between random life events and lessons." Sue raised her eyebrows and waited for my confirmation.

"So how do you know?" I asked.

"Well, how can I put this... lessons feel different. They are often uncomfortable for a start, and there is often some kind of challenge or struggle involved."

"I thought I'd been through all of this, Sue. Can't I just have the good stuff now?" I said, somewhat deflated.

"Lessons are inevitable I'm afraid, as long as we are human. And when you are on a path of growth and enlightenment the universe keeps sending them to help you on your way."

"I don't think I can take anymore after the last twelve."

"But the gift in the lesson is always worth the lesson itself, that's the point of going through them," Sue reassured me. "Just look at the gifts you received last time."

I thought for a moment and felt my baby move again, right on cue. "Yes, of course you're right," I sighed. "I couldn't have the life I live now if I hadn't been through the learning."

"Exactly. So don't fear what's coming up, just know that you are now at the stage where you need to be able to recognize your own lessons as they appear in your life. You need to be able to step back from them and know that they hold the key to your growth and evolution, and that you're being sent what you need in any given moment."

"Even if it's really tough?"

"Those are the lessons that will accelerate you like nothing else. The bigger the lesson, the bigger the gift."

"Ok, I'll try to remember that when it's hitting the fan."

"That's why it is so important that you know it's a lesson coming up, you need to be able to detach yourself and not get sucked into any drama that is playing out around you. Look at the experience from a higher-self perspective and see past the behaviour and the human moments that we all love to whip up with our ego. You are more evolved than that now."

"I'll do my best," I said in a less-than-confident tone.

"It's going to take a while to master this one, and the rest actually," said Sue and continued quickly before I could object. "But don't worry about that, you need to have an overall intention that everything is happening perfectly, Stephanie, that it's all unfolding the way that it should be."

"So you mean these cards aren't for the next six months?" I asked.

"No, not this reading. There is no timeline here. It's about you learning what you need to at the right time for you, and that will vary depending on what you have going on in your life in that moment."

"So lesson one is about lessons, right?" I checked before I reached into my bag for a notebook and pen.

"Yes, but it's actually lesson thirteen," Sue corrected me.

"Ah yes! I've learned twelve so far." I opened the notebook at a clean page and started to write.

"You have, but you need to be mindful as well that lessons can come back again." Sue sat back in her chair and I looked up.

"You mean if you don't learn them?" I asked.

"Yes, if you don't learn them or work with them in your life then you can find that they come back up, and sometimes it's tricky to see them. Usually because the human side of us and our ego thinks that we have done this before and learned what we need to, so we become closed to learning anything else."

"Lesson One – Be Open to Possibility."

"Correct. And lessons sometimes have different layers to them Stephanie, different facets or aspects if you like."

"This is getting really complicated." I absent-mindedly tapped the pen on my teeth.

"It can be, but remember that you get what you believe, so thinking that it's going to be complicated will only make it so."

"You Are a Creator – Lesson Five."

"Yes, now see what just happened there?" Sue asked but continued before I could answer. "You are seeing the different lessons that are playing out at given times and how they overlap with each other to create a whole fabric of learning."

"Ok, I think I'm starting to understand," I said.

"You will, at the perfect time." Sue said as she reached for the second card.

"Be Present," she said.

"That doesn't sound so bad," I said scribbling it down.

"Well it's something that a lot of people struggle with Steph, it's actually quite a skill."

"How so?" I asked "I mean how hard can it be to show up and be present?"

"It's not just about showing up, it's about being really present in the now time, in *that* moment and all of you being there to experience it," Sue said.

"Like being fully in the moment?" I asked.

"Yes, and making sure that you are not allowing your mind or your consciousness to wander back into the past, into worry and old situations, and equally not spending time in the future, worrying about what may or may not happen or always wanting things to be ok one day."

"Ah right, I think I get it," I said "So wherever you are, make sure that you are there altogether and not distracted."

"Yes, but it's more than that. Have you had that experience where you are speaking to someone and you know that they are not really hearing what you are saying? I mean they might be listening but they are not *hearing.*"

I thought for a moment and recalled a conversation I'd had with Damien just before we left home, about dropping me off here and then picking me up again after his meeting, and how he'd spoken in all of the right places, but I knew his mind was on the agenda with the recruitment agency he had an appointment with.

"Yes, I get it now. And you've told me a bit about that before, about the present moment being where your power is and that it's important for attracting in what you want in your life."

"That's right, you need to be present when you work with Law of Attraction in order to create the frequency in the now time of what you want to draw into your experience. It's no good sending a message to the universe that says it's going to be ok in the future, or you will never experience the good stuff in the now." Sue looked at me and I confirmed my understanding with a nod as she turned the next card.

"Discernment," she said as I looked at the picture in her hand, showing someone waving to someone else. "This card is about discernment and being selective in relationships, and knowing that sometimes people move in and out of our lives for good reason."

"Is that the whole reason, season, lifetime thing?" I asked.

"Yes, in a nutshell I suppose it is. But it's also about being selective in the first place about who you allow into your energy, and about being ok about letting things drift when they need to." She continued, "And that is sometimes not so easy, when it involves friends or even family members."

"Oh?" I commented.

"When feelings and expectations are involved it's sometimes hard to detach, even though it is in your best interests. The thing to remember is that the more you evolve and heal and grow, the less resonance you might have with people that are not on that path. This can lead to you feeling that you don't have much in common anymore, or interactions can become uncomfortable."

As I scribbled in my notebook, Sue continued.

"Heal Yourself," she said as the next card showed a picture of a beautiful woman sitting peacefully and surrounded by a golden glow. "This card shows that you still have work to do to heal your old wounds."

Jay crossed my mind and I surprised myself with a shudder and a flashback to being on my knees in front of him in a nightclub toilet - my lowest point for sure.

Sue sensed this and reassured me "You have come such a long way Steph, in a really short time, and you should be really proud of yourself."

I suddenly felt teary, I had been on quite a journey for sure and maybe I didn't give myself the credit I ought to for getting this far. "I know you're right Sue. I still have moments where I don't feel worthy of Damien and I know it's a hangover from my past. It just sneaks up on me every now and then and I'm back there feeling needy and desperate and not good enough."

Sue passed me a tissue and I dabbed at my cheeks, not
knowing why I had suddenly felt so overwhelmed, and putting it down to pregnancy hormones.

"This stuff can take a long time to heal Stephanie, and some
people never do. Some people live their whole lives playing
small and not feeling good enough because of something that
has scarred them and made them feel unworthy." Her tone
was compassionate and I felt her hand reach out for mine.

"You can do this, Steph," she said and I raised my chin. As
my eyes met hers I felt that she could see into the depths of
my soul.

"That means such a lot coming from you," I whispered.

"I believe in you." Sue smiled and I smiled back weakly.
"Now you need to work on believing in yourself and healing
those old wounds. Because as long as they are with you,
Steph, they are active in your vibration and your energy
field."

"And good old Law of Attraction will deliver me a version
of what I am sending out there?"

"Exactly."

"There is no way I want to go through any of that again," I
said shaking my head. "I'm going to work on that for sure."
Sue smiled and although she didn't say it, I knew she felt
proud of me for starting to bring it all together.

"Drama Queen," she said as the next card showed a theatrical set with someone in an over-the-top costume, in front of
an audience. "Don't be dragged into the drama of what is
playing out in human or earthly terms if you can help it. Step
back, take a breath and look at the situation from a more
evolved perspective. That goes for your own drama or someone else's, because other people's dramas can suck you in."

"I know people like that!" I commented as my mother entered my mind, and Sue turned over the next card which
would represent lesson eighteen.

Sue laughed as she explained the meaning of the next card
which showed a picture of someone dragging a heavy load up
a hill and the description said Burden.

"I like to call this one The Shit Cart." I laughed too and
wondered what on earth she could mean. "This card is about
you dragging someone else's shit cart. Honestly, there is just
no other way to put it, really, Steph!"

"Well you certainly don't need to explain that in detail, I
definitely get the idea!"

"I'm glad you do, sometimes when it comes out it's for
someone all serious and I'm dying to laugh! Anyway it's got
two meanings really, and I like to think of it this way. Everyone has a cart that they drag up the hill called life, and as we
go through our stuff we tend to fill it up with all kinds of stuff
that we are not ready to get rid of or process, and it slows
down our progress hugely…"

"With all of the shit that we can't resolve?" I asked and
laughed.

"Yes!" Sue snorted. "Exactly that!"

"So it's a bit like Lesson Four, Old Stuff Keeps You
Stuck?"

"Yes, because whatever is in that cart is also in your vibration and you will attract more in, or a version of that stuff
in…"

"More shit?" I asked and we both knew that we had lost all
chance of this being serious as we laughed and laughed.

Sue eventually composed herself and took a breath. "When
this card comes up in a reading it's about you sorting out your

own stuff, releasing what you don't need, healing your wounds and cleaning up your vibration but it's also about other people as well…"

"Other people's shit cart?" I asked in a mock serious tone and we both collapsed in giggles again.

"Yes actually, other people's burdens are not for you to carry. When you take on other people's stuff and try to re-solve it for them, you are actually being unkind to them and yourself."

"Unkind?" I asked, surely it was selfless to help people with their shit?

"Yes. Think of it this way, everyone comes here to earth as a soul with their own stuff to experience and learn whilst they are here in human form. So that means that everyone has unique lessons that they are going through in their life in order to evolve, and if someone steps in and shortcuts this lesson, or stops you from learning it, then it's not learned and experienced for you."

"So it comes back?" I asked.

"Yes, often it will, or an aspect of it will come back, or maybe that person will just stay stuck in their own stuff and be disempowered because they don't know how to move forward themselves," Sue said.

"But is it not mean to see someone struggle and not help them, though? I mean that's not exactly spiritual?" I asked.

"You are right, Steph, and there is a very subtle difference here. When this lesson comes up for you it's important to know that you can support someone and give them guidance and signposting, but always do this in a way that you feel will empower them and help them to sort out their own stuff. It's the difference between buying a man a fish and showing him how to make a net, see?"

"I think so. It's a bit like lesson nine, You Can't Fix Other People."

"A little like that, yes. That's also about allowing people to take responsibility for themselves, without you judging the outcome or taking any ownership of what they do or don't do… knowing that it's their stuff really. This lesson is more about you not taking other people's stuff on and sorting it out for them."

"Ok, so what do you mean by signposting?" I asked.

"Showing them the way to be able to sort it out for themselves. This could be giving them good advice, connecting them with a service they need or a professional person, buying them a book you know will help, or making suggestions and being supportive. You can do all of those things without actually getting involved in their stuff and doing it for them."

"Right, and dragging their shit around." I laughed again.

"Exactly!" laughed Sue "We all need to sort our own shit cart out and let other people sort theirs."

"And I need to get Jay out of mine," I said.

"You do, and once you have you will feel so much lighter and life will flow better for you, Steph. But don't beat yourself up, it's a journey and it is going to happen when the time is right. Big stuff is never easy to move on from, and that goes for us all. This lesson will go hand in glove for you with healing those old wounds."

"You're right," I sighed, knowing that even when the healing was done there would likely be battle scars that would always be a weak spot. "I have to go easy on myself."

"Yes, because if you start to beat yourself up about it then you will create more resistance. Remember Lesson Eight, Compassion and Forgiveness. You need to apply this to yourself as well as others." Sue smiled and concluded the reading by saying, "We all do the best we can, Steph."

"And when we know better we do better," I added. "And hopefully I know better now."

Sue returned the cards to the deck and folded them back into the silk patterned scarf I knew kept them safe.

"Thank you. That's plenty to be going on with," I said and closed the notebook. "How long will it take me to get through them?"

"That's unwritten as yet," said Sue. "It depends on different factors, it could be months or it could even be years."

"Years?"

"Well maybe a couple. You've got to get through them so that you can include them in your book."

"Oh yes, the book," I said tentatively, although it sounded like a great idea in principle I had no idea where the time to write it was going to come from, especially with more lessons and a baby due any day.

"How long is it going to take me to write a book and get it published?" I sighed. "Are you sure it's me that's meant to be sharing them?"

"All I get through is that it's going to happen at the perfect time Steph, and that being impatient will delay things."

"That's a lesson in itself right there."

"Maybe there are things that have to happen before you get lined up with the right people?"

"Like what?"

"That's for you to find out!" laughed Sue. "Remember, this next chapter is all about you recognizing the lessons and going through them yourself. It's about you being more empowered and applying what you have learned so far."

"I might not like flying solo!" I objected.

"You won't be, but the message is loud and clear from your guides, the universe or whomever you believe in. This is time for you to be more tuned into your own journey. I'll be your safety net and if anything doesn't make sense or you find yourself in a pickle you can come back, but this next step is for you to take."

I sighed and patted my bump. "Next time I see you I might not be alone."

"I'm sure you won't be," said Sue and I heard a car honking from the street below.

"That might be Damien," I said, using the edge of the table to heave myself up before looking at my watch.

"Good luck, Steph. It's all going to be fine with the birth so you don't need to worry," Sue hugged me tight.

"Really?" I asked.

"Really," she said. "It's going to happen perfectly, although at the time it might not be *your* version of perfect, just know that it's all fine. And before you leave I'm being asked to tell you that no matter what anyone else says it *is* going to be fine. You have to remember that everyone has had a different experience and they don't necessarily know about the way energy works, so they go into the situation in fear and expecting the worst."

"And then they draw it in?" I asked.

"Yes, but you know better so you can do better. Get aligned with the experience that you want and don't let other unconscious people knock you off your perch. It really is going to be fine, I promise you."

"Thank you Sue, I have been worried," I admitted.

"I know you have, love, that's why this is coming through for you." Sue squeezed my hand and then allowed her palm to float above my bump for a second.

"Can't wait to be here, this little soul is really excited about coming to earth." She smiled and closed her eyes. "You've been chosen and so has Damien, just like all babies choose their parents... but this little one is going to be different to others, in ways that you will find out when they get here. They had to come to someone *awake* they are saying, because they will need to be raised consciously." She paused and took a deep breath. "And you need to go home and pack your hospital bag, they'll be here sooner than you think... and no they won't say whether they are a girl or a boy!" Sue snapped back to reality as the car horn sounded again.

"I should go," I said. "I'll let you know when the baby comes, and I'll pack my bag this afternoon."

"Yes, I would if I were you," said Sue as I stuffed my notebook into my handbag and turned to waddle towards the door.

Chapter 2

"Well?" Damien asked as I opened the car door.

"Not that much really. More lessons and knowing when lessons come up really." I pulled out as much seatbelt as I could to get over my bump.

"But nothing bad though?" he asked distractedly as he indicated to get back into the traffic flow.

"No, nothing bad. But apparently I do need to pack my hospital bag soon. Baby is going to come earlier than expected."

"We've got four weeks yet!" He waved to the bus driver that had flashed him out.

"Not according to Sue, and she's never been wrong yet."

"Well you'd better get packing after this midwife thing then."

"I will, maybe after a lie down, I'm so tired. Sue said that the birth was all going to go well by the way and that I shouldn't worry."

"And she's never been wrong yet." Damien reached over and patted my bump.

"You can never get a space round here."

"Just pull in and drop me off, it's fine," I said, reaching over to unfasten my seatbelt.

"Are you sure?"

"Of course I'm sure, it's only going to be ten minutes on panting, pushing and gas and air."

Damien indicated left and kissed my cheek when the car came to a stop. "OK then, I'll get parked down the road, ring me when you are done and I'll come back up."

"Just have a coffee at the café on Bridge Street while I'm going through the gory details."

"Thank God for that, do you need a push to get out?" he sniggered.

"I'll get you back for that! I'll have you know I am blooming."

"I agree, blooming big."

The automatic door swooshed open for me and warm air mixed with piped music wafted in my direction. I approached the reception desk and checked in for the midwife, she tapped my details on the keyboard and told me to take a seat.

The waiting room was standard magnolia, with a rack full of leaflets ranging from athlete's foot to dementia and everything in between. I reached for a magazine and started thumbing through it, wondering how on earth celebrities managed to look so groomed and slim during pregnancy? I felt like a house end and with only a few weeks to go, the fear that I was going to have to push this baby out was looming. No matter how many times I heard it was the most natural process in the world, the only comment that stuck was Asha telling me it's like shitting a melon.

Stop thinking that! I said to myself. *It's all going to happen perfectly, it IS happening perfectly.*

"Is it your first?" a stranger spoke.

"Oh, erm yes... and you?"

"Not likely she's been round the block more times than you've had hot dinners!" a woman snorted next to her.

"Shut it, Sylvia, or we'll talk about why you're here!" she retorted.

"I was only joking, there's no need for that," Sylvia mumbled.

403

"And there's no need for you to be here if you'd used that cream and kept yourself to yourself," the first lady stage whispered and her friend glared.

She turned back to me. "Anyway love, is that your birth plan?"

I had an envelope folder on my knee containing all of the forms that I'd filled out since my first appointment. Damien and I had gone over the birth plan last night and I'd tucked it into the front, ready to discuss.

"Yes, today's the day to go through it all before the big push!" I laughed nervously and thought about the melon again.

"Water birth is it?" she asked and her friend sniggered.

I had no idea what could be funny about that. "Yes actually, how did you know?"

"It's the in thing now, everyone seems to want a water birth for their first one, along with the mood music, reflexology and nothing else but gas and air..."

"I must be so predictable, that's exactly what I've written down." I felt a bit embarrassed and really wanted my name to be called. These two might be from the school of hard knocks but I wasn't. I wanted it to be a wonderful experience and so did Damien. They could mind their own business. Sue had told me to ignore other people's opinions, and that advice couldn't have been more timely or relevant right now.

"Well pet, it usually starts all hearts and flowers and before you know it it's backside over elbow, and your legs up in stirrups while you're shouting at him for getting you into this mess." They both cackled at their hilarious comment, and I gulped.

"They still have stirrups?" I asked in a quiet voice.

"Don't worry. If they aren't quick enough to get you tied in they'll just get a couple of doctors to hold your legs and look up your flue while you push," said Sylvia, and her friend agreed.

"There's no dignity in having a baby."

"You're right, Denise."

"I mean look at that girl up your street, what was her name again...? We used to call her Shrek, no one knew how on earth she'd fallen pregnant..." Sylvia was on a roll now and the room seemed to be getting hotter.

"Or who he was," Denise chipped in to fill in the blanks.

"She had a rough time of it mind, what with the escalator and all that, and once they'd managed to stop it they still couldn't get that smocky dress pulled out of the teeth so they had to rip it, and by then there was a crowd."

"Well what do you expect? No one goes on like that shouting and wailing when their waters break. If she hadn't been so dramatic and leaned over the side she wouldn't have got tangled up." Sylvia shook her head at the ridiculousness.

"Still, it's not right having to walk the length of the shopping centre with your backside hanging out of maternity knickers just because there was no wheelchair... and it's not like things looked up much." Denise let the statement hang in the air for a few moments as her and Sylvia exchanged a knowing look.

"What happened?" I asked quietly.

"Well, she'd been going on about a water birth," Denise continued.

"You could say she nearly got one," Sylvia said.

"More like 'over the water birth' really."

"The traffic was gridlocked because of the football and the roadworks. They couldn't get her to hospital in time, so she had him in the ambulance."

"On the city bypass, on the bridge over the river."

I could feel myself getting a little dizzy, the air felt thick and hot and stale and I clutched my birth plan tighter. "Really?" I asked wide-eyed and worried.

"And they had nothing to give her for the pain, which must have been awful. Quite honestly that kid's got the biggest head I've ever seen..." As Sylvia spoke I started to fan myself with the folder and unfastened the top button of my linen maternity shirt.

"Twenty-eight stiches she needed and that cognitive behavioural therapy for the trauma. I heard she's got a claim in."

"What the hell for?" asked Denise.

Sylvia lowered her voice, which was ironic since there was only the three of us there. "Well, she must have, you know *followed through* shall we say and apparently the ambulance driver opened the back door and chucked it out! White van man and his pals behind started honking the horn and cheering her on when he saw her flat on her back with her legs in the air, and nothing left to the imagination.....apparently that's post-traumatic stress nowadays... and she can't get over it."

"*She* can't get over it, poor bloke if you ask me he should be claiming against her," Denise said as I felt myself digging my nails into my palms.

She looked at me and registered my horror. Her tone changed and became far more upbeat as she patted my knee. "Don't look scared love, things like that don't happen very

often. Usually it's all straightforward. Having a baby is the
most natural thing in the world."

An uncomfortable silence descended apart from generic
panpipe music in the background. I tried to relax and focus on
my breathing, reflecting on what Sue had said about being
present and not going back over old stuff or forwards into
fear. I was allowing other people to drag me into an energy
that I didn't want, and I needed to bring myself back to the
present moment and get aligned with the outcome that I
wanted once more.

I was abruptly brought back to reality, as in an effort to
change the subject Sylvia asked,

"Have you got your bag packed yet, love?"

Signs & Serendipity.

"I'm doing that this afternoon," I mumbled. I really didn't
want to talk to them anymore and I fiddled with my sleeve
trying to see my watch. How much bloody longer was this
going to take? I seriously might have to go and stand outside
and get some air. The receptionist could shout out of the door
when my turn arrived. I could be present on the road side a
whole lot easier than in here. I just wanted to talk about my
fabulous birth plan with my lovely midwife and get back to
Damien, who probably thought I had eloped by now. This had
to be a lesson coming up. It certainly ticked the box labelled
extremely uncomfortable. I tried to sit back and breathe, to
work out what the universe was trying to show me, but all I
could think of was 'avoid idiots.'

"Well, you want to hurry up, how many weeks are you
now?" Denise just wouldn't let it go.

"Thirty-two."

"Well, don't forget to pack some food. Not for him for you, you look like you like your food," Sylvia chipped in.

"Right," I said through my teeth and forced smile.

"You'll need some calories if you're in labour for a couple of days, love. I mean I've always been lucky. It's like shelling peas and they said this time I'll have to call the ambulance as soon as I get a twinge, but some people are at it for days." Denise really should approach the charm school for a refund.

"Slow labour they call it."

Shut up Sylvia ran through my head as I tried desperately to remember what had Sue said about discernment. I could feel myself starting to choke back tears, my mood had been all over the place this last two weeks and it took nothing to set me off. I'd been fine when I left Sue, and she had promised everything would be ok, so I just needed to believe that.

I took a deep breath and said, "Well, it'll probably all be straightforward," hoping that was an end to the conversation.

"That's what they all say, then the pain starts and you've got no idea what's going to happen next."

Seriously Sylvia could you piss off?

"They don't feed you once you're in there, in case you need an emergency caesarean. You'll be Hank Marvin if you've been struggling on for 72 hours, nil by mouth," she said trying to be helpful.

A welcome break in the conversation opened and I sighed, shifting position in the chair to see if I could relieve the dull ache in my back. I closed my eyes and tried to relax into the plinky plonky piano that was tinkling quietly through the speakers now.

"It's no wonder they used to eat the afterbirth." The voice cut through the momentary peace like a rat up a spout.

I couldn't help the vomit suddenly rising in my throat, or the accompanying retching sound.

Also available:

Twelve Lessons

The Journal

By Kate Spencer

Not just a self-help book, and not just an inspirational diary.

Both.

Because you are living a spiritual life in real life.

Because you need space to write your everyday stuff, and factor in retrogrades and manifesting with the moon.

Because you need to know how to use the Twelve   Lessons principles to create positive change in a real-life way.

Because you need to be organized (with a sprinkling of woo-woo).

A modern day spiritual manifesto, journal and diary all in one ~ infused with love, inspiration, support and encouragement to help you to create your best year yet.

Lightning Source UK Ltd.
Milton Keynes UK
UKOW02f0616200317
297047UK00004B/306/P